I0728837

THE MALACHITE QUEST

ALSO BY AERIN APELTUN

<u>THE CURSED WEAPONS TRILOGY</u>
The Amethyst Talisman
The Malachite Quest
The Opal King

<u>CRYSTAL BLOODS SERIES</u>
Crystal Bloods

THE MALACHITE QUEST

THE CURSED WEAPONS: BOOK 2

AERIN APELTUN

Elsewhen Press

The Malachite Quest
This updated edition published in Great Britain by Elsewhen Press, 2026
An imprint of Alnpete Limited

Copyright © Aerin Apeltun, 2024, 2025. All rights reserved
The right of Aerin Apeltun to be identified as the author of this work has been asserted in accordance with sections 77 and 78 of the Copyright, Designs and Patents Act 1988. No part of this publication may be reproduced, scanned, stored in a retrieval system or transmitted in any form, or by any means (electronic, mechanical, telepathic, magical, or otherwise) without the prior written permission of the copyright owner. No part of this book may be used or reproduced in any manner for the purpose of training artificial intelligence technologies or systems. In accordance with Article 4(3) of the Digital Single Market Directive 2019/790, Elsewhen Press expressly reserves this work from the text and data mining exception.
Map © Aerin Apeltun 2023

This book was originally published by SmashBear Publishing, 2024.
This is a new updated edition.
Elsewhen Press, PO Box 757, Dartford, Kent DA2 7TQ
www.elsewhen.press

British Library Cataloguing in Publication Data.
A catalogue record for this book is available from the British Library.
ISBN 978-1-917507-24-0 Print edition
ISBN 978-1-917507-34-9 eBook edition

Condition of Sale
This book is sold subject to the condition that it shall not, by way of trade or otherwise, be lent, re-sold, hired out or otherwise circulated in any form of binding or cover other than that in which it is published and without a similar condition including this condition being imposed on the subsequent purchaser.

This book is copyright under the Berne Convention.
Elsewhen Press & Planet-Clock Design are trademarks of Alnpete Limited

Designed and formatted by Elsewhen Press

As part of our environmental awareness approach, in a bid to reduce paper and ink usage, the print edition of this book has minimal margins and leading, and the body of the text is typeset in Adobe Garamond Pro that typically requires 27% less ink than Times New Roman. We use Print on Demand to reduce wastage and unnecessary transportation and storage.

This book is a work of fiction. All names, characters, places, and events are either a product of the author's fertile imagination or are used fictitiously. Any resemblance to actual events, places or people (living or dead; High, Middle, or Low Blood) is purely coincidental.

*To "Earwig", for his poetry,
and his unique style of storytelling…*

CONTENTS

THE BLOOD RULE DECREE OF AERBA

1. There will be three Blood Classes - High Bloods, Middle Bloods, and Low Bloods
2. The High Bloods will consist of the Royal family and extended relations
3. The Middle Bloods will include other Nobles, high status citizens and Priests
4. The Low Bloods will include all other citizens
5. Sexual Relationships outside of Marriage are strictly forbidden
6. All Sexual and Romantic Relationships, including Marriage, between Blood Classes is strictly forbidden in order to keep the Blood Classes pure
7. Entering into Marriage or Relationships with citizens of other Lands of the same Blood Class will be permitted but are greatly discouraged and Royal Approval will be required
8. Entering into Marriage or Relationships with citizens of other Lands of a different Blood Class is strictly forbidden
9. Entering into Marriage or Relationships with members of the same sex whether in the same or different Blood Class are strictly forbidden whether Aerban or from another Land
10. All Citizens names will be taken from the Father's Family Line/Land
11. All Citizens Blood Classes will be taken from the Mother's Blood Class
12. Citizens born out of Wedlock will automatically be Low Bloods and their parents Demoted
13. The King has the power to Demote a Citizen from their birth Blood Class as he sees fit
14. The King has the power to enforce the Execution or Imprisonment or Demotion of any Citizen found to be disregarding any element of the Blood Rule Decree at his discretion

As laid out by King Cinquefoil in the year 3929. Rules 7, 12 and 13 amended by King Finule the First in the year 5643

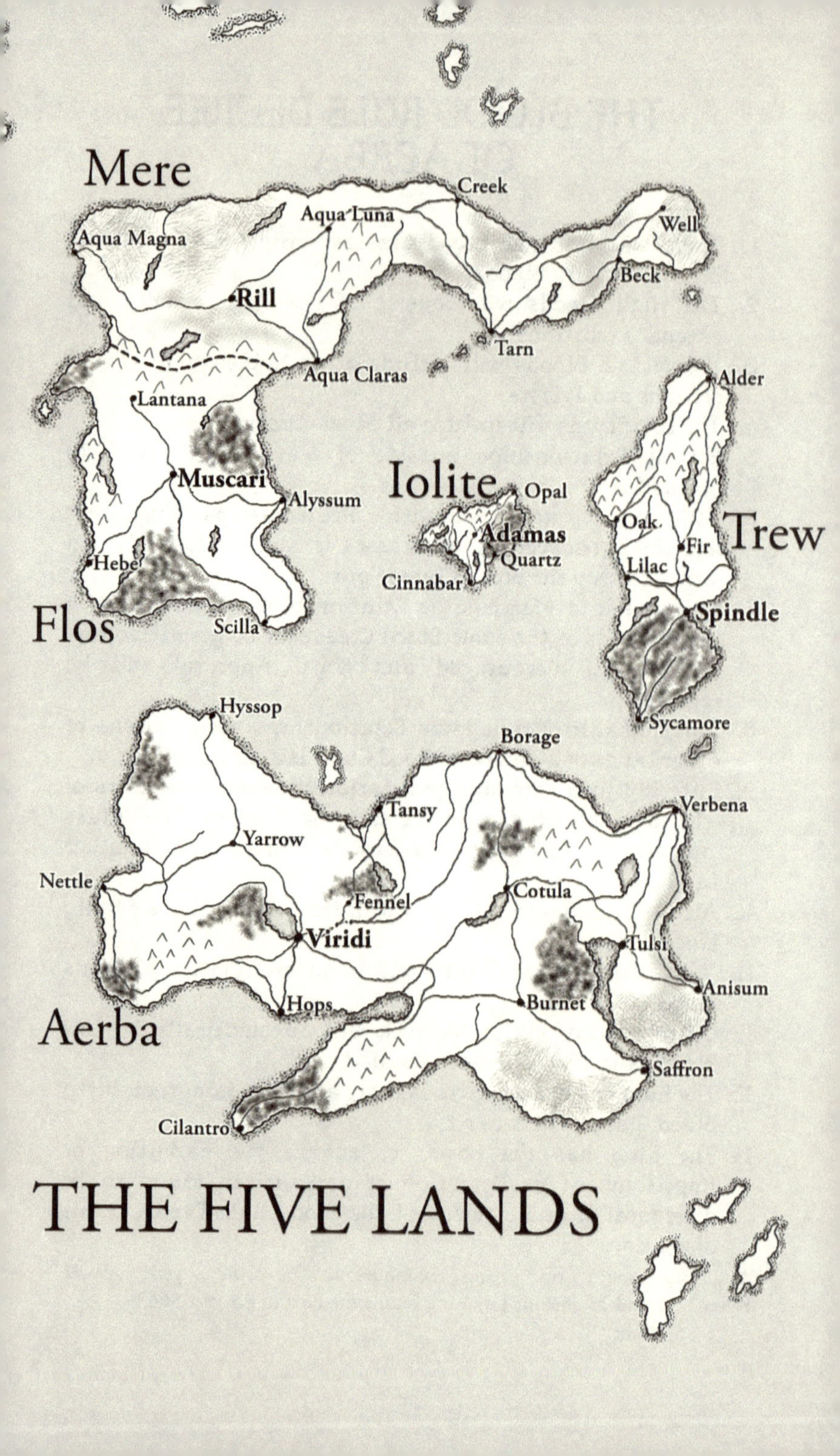

Mere
Creek
Aqua Luna
Well
Aqua Magna
Beck
Rill
Tarn
Aqua Claras
Alder
Lantana
Iolite
Opal
Oak.
Trew
Muscari
Adamas
Fir
Alyssum
Quartz
Lilac
Hebe
Cinnabar
Spindle
Flos
Scilla
Sycamore
Hyssop
Borage
Verbena
Tansy
Yarrow
Nettle
Fennel
Cotula
Viridi
Tulsi
Hops
Anisum
Burnet
Aerba
Saffron
Cilantro
THE FIVE LANDS

CHAPTER ONE

I opened a door into a small storeroom at the front of the creaking ship where sunlight entered from two portholes, cutting through the darkness. Little motes of dust played in the golden light. I stepped in. Prince Valerian of Aerba followed me into the room and closed the door behind us. He smiled at me, his straight, long maroon hair tied up in a traditional high Aerban ponytail that swished gently with the rocking of the ship. His pupils dilated as he reached out and moved a copper curl behind my ear.

'What was it about me you noticed first, Samphire?' he asked, brushing his lips gently against mine, making my heart race.

I grinned as I tilted my head up to look at him. He was three or four inches taller than me, and the most handsome young man I knew. 'Other than the fact you were holding your knife at my throat, you mean?'

He winced. 'Sorry about that.'

'It was your gorgeous amber eyes,' I said, 'and the way you rub the back of your neck when you're embarrassed or anxious.'

'I do? Oh.' He started to move his hand up to his neck but thought better of it, a flush appearing high on his cheeks. 'I see what you mean.' He placed his hands firmly on my waist.

'What about me?'

'Your amethyst eyes captivated me, and your smile, and then your kindness sealed my doom,' he said as he gently ran a finger over my lips.

'Doom?' I asked indignantly.

'You enchanted me,' he said, brushing his warm lips against mine again, making me melt inside. 'You fascinated me. I'd never met anyone like you before. Until you, I hadn't looked at a girl, but you stirred up these feelings I never knew existed. Each day I fall in love with you a little bit more.'

I draped my arms over his shoulders, a hint of sandalwood swirling around us from his body. 'I like the sound of that. You're my first and only love, Rian. You crept into my heart, and before I knew it, you'd made a home there.' I shifted his hair from his face. 'Do you believe in true love?'

'I do, because I see it every time I look into your eyes,' he said, his love for me written across his face, flowing through his body as he held me to him.

'So do I. Now, please will you kiss me?'

He smiled his lopsided smile. 'If you want.'

'I want,' I said, delicately licking my lips. 'Besides, I thought we were here to–'

'We are,' he said, his rich voice suddenly husky. His eyes darkened further, and he leant towards me, tilting his head slightly as our lips met. He tasted of the honey tea he'd just drunk. 'I wish we'd found this room sooner,' he said, taking hold of my hand that wore his gold ring – my wedding ring – with engraved vines of Thyme twisting between little sparkling diamonds.

'We had, but it was locked until now,' I said. 'Someone's kindly opened it up for us.'

He gazed at me. 'I know I said I wanted our first time to be unhurried and special, and I'd hoped for a more suitable place and time, but I don't think I can wait any longer.'

'It will be special,' I said pressing my finger to his lips, then undoing his burgundy coat with its gold hem, pulling it off as he did the same to mine. 'And anyway, it's far more comfortable than a hammock, and I can't wait any longer, either.'

Grain sacks filled the room; a little hard, but not too uncomfortable for what we had planned. The ship rocked gently, the sound of the waves drifting into the little room as the prow cut through the water like a blade.

'I love you, Phire. I love you with my body and soul,' he said. A kind of want, a hunger, had appeared in Rian's eyes, something I hadn't seen before, and it sent shivers of excitement down my spine. He leant towards me, his lips meeting mine in a kiss of such exquisite tenderness that my knees buckled and I fell backwards, taking him with me, landing on the sacks, not even pausing for breath. His mouth was sweet and hot, his tongue gentle. Ever since I'd met him, he'd made me feel things I'd never felt before; rich, glorious things.

'I love you too, Rian,' I said, holding him close, a silken knot forming in my stomach.

We'd been waiting for this moment for so long, ever since we'd first realised our feelings for each other in the days when I'd been cursed, doomed to die as my life drained from me. Then, we'd been falsely imprisoned by his brother, King Chervil, and Rian had been sentenced to death for their father's assassination. All Chervil's lies. Rian's world had fallen apart in such a short space of time he was still coming to terms with things even now.

Rian slid his hand down my side. I could feel his fingers trembling slightly, and a little shiver of warmth ran through me.

We'd escaped the Aerban capital, Viridi, with Rian's friends, and had set sail for a new life all together. During that dark time in the dungeons, Rian and I had exchanged vows. Not technically a legal marriage ceremony, perhaps, but the best we could do in the circumstances, and to us more binding than anything formal. Until now, though, we'd never had the chance to be together, alone, long enough to…

Rian's hand slid around my back, pulling me closer. 'I want you, wife. I want you now.'

A firestorm swelled inside me at his words. I kissed the rose-beige skin of his neck, tracing a small path of kisses up towards his ear lobe. He uttered a strange little gasp that made me pause and smile. I'd spent my eighteenth birthday on our travels; Rian's twentieth had been spent at sea only the previous week. I peppered his ear with kisses, feeling his body tense as he held me. He moved back a little and I made a grab for his shirt, my hands shaking slightly, pulling it up towards his head.

'Rian! Phire! Where are you?' Tarragon's deep, husky voice cut through our tryst like a knife.

'Dammit,' Rian said, his shoulders slumping as I let go of his shirt. 'I don't believe it. We finally find somewhere suitable on this old tub to be alone together for more than five minutes and Tarragon decides to come looking for us.'

I sighed.

'We'd better see what he wants,' I said, rather annoyed with Rian's cousin for spoiling our first time before it had even properly begun. 'And it had better be good. Anyway, we don't want him barging in when we're, you know…'

Rian grinned mischievously, then stood up, sighed, and tucked his shirt in, picking up his burgundy coat from the floor and dusting it off. I sat up and picked up my purple coat as the door opened.

'Rian? Oh, here you are,' Tarragon said, his golden-brown eyes narrowing, and a frown creeping across his rose-beige face.

Although two years older than the prince, the cousins had grown up together and always been close.

'Oh, bugger, sorry,' Tarragon said as his cheeks turned a beautiful strawberry colour while we put our coats back on and I stood up. He cleared his throat. 'Captain Hyssop thought you should know there's an Aerban Navy Patrol Ship shadowing us, has been for about twenty minutes now. He's suggesting we head into Flosian waters immediately.'

'We didn't want to head that close to Flos until the last minute,' Rian said, 'but I guess under the circumstances he's probably right. I'll go and see him.' He turned a moment, pausing to give me a little kiss with his soft, intoxicating velvet lips before leaving the room, giving Tarragon a small scowl for good measure as he left.

I followed him out the door, Tarragon elbowing me as I left the room. 'Getting up to no good, Phire?' he asked, adjusting his sun-bleached brown hair in its messy ponytail. He was around Rian's six foot in height, lithe and very strong, and I was very fond of him – despite his interruption.

'Chance would be a fine thing, but we have exchanged vows, Tarragon, and under the Blood Rules it's at least kind of allowed as far as I know; you and Willow, on the other hand, don't have that excuse at the moment,' I said primly.

Tarragon winced.

I smirked and followed Rian up the wooden steps and out onto the deck. I straightened my white-bordered purple coat at the top of the stairs. Although we all had our Aerban clothes, and the others still wore their hair in the style of their homeland, they had long since discarded the gold-embroidered black silk headbands identifying them as King's Warriors. That life lay in the past.

As I stepped out on deck, Anise grinned at me, his violet-blue eyes sparkling in his beautiful, unblemished rose-beige face. A year older than me, we'd become close friends and I valued his counsel. He winked at me as he smoothed his straight black hair over his shoulder. I wouldn't mind all the knowing looks if Rian and I actually had something to be embarrassed about, but the fact we hadn't rankled slightly, and I now feared we'd missed our chance on this trip; we were due to arrive in the Flosian port town of Scilla tomorrow morning.

Willow came over to me, coughing gently, her asthma better at sea. Her black hair, made frizzier than normal by the sea air, moved in the breeze as the sun shone on her light sienna skin. The same age as Anise, she was an expert lock picker and a good fighter. A little shorter than me, she had an infectious smile that always lifted my spirits, and she'd become a good friend during our travels.

'Well, how was it? And more to the point, how was *he*?' she asked softly.

'Are the Nightshade's spies aboard, shadowing our every move?' I asked, irritated, looking around to make my point. 'It's none of your business.'

'Bobbins.'

'Anyway, we didn't get the chance. Your boyfriend interrupted us.'

She giggled, her deep brown eyes sparkling in the sunlight. 'The forward storeroom? Tarragon and I found it a week ago. That's when I first picked the lock. I must've forgotten to lock it up again last night.'

I sighed. 'You could've told us about it earlier,' I said, annoyed at the revelation and our missed opportunities as I walked over to the bow.

As I moved, the purple crystal sword and shield, now the *Once-Cursed Weapons of Aerba*, joined me. Their straps magically appeared on my back, securing themselves around my chest as the three-foot sword materialised in its scabbard, and the wedge-shaped shield with its slight cut-outs on either side at the top settled into place. The gold and silver sword hilt caught the sun, as did the shield's golden enarmes. As the weapons were no longer cursed we'd given them new names, suggested by Rian: Deorwine for the sword, and Glædwine for the shield. Both were old Aerban words, meaning 'Dearfriend' and 'Brightfriend'.

Willow swore. 'I'll never get used to that,' she said. 'I'm surprised you have.'

'I haven't had much choice,' I said ruefully, glancing over my shoulder at the amethyst weapons glistening on my back. 'But they can be useful.' I took a deep breath of salty air.

'Weren't you taking a risk with Rian?' she asked, standing beside me and looking out over the waves.

'What?' I frowned, turning to her.

She leant towards me. 'You don't want any little Rians,' she said in a low voice.

'You're a fine one to talk,' I said. 'The amount of times you and Tarragon have disappeared off together since I've known you.' Willow's face flushed. 'Anyway, I dare say what Anise gave me from his Herb Chest was the same as what he gives you.'

Willow's face flushed even more. 'I didn't know you'd spoken to Anise.'

'He seems to have a quantity of Silphion powder in his Chest,' I said, driving the point home. 'All for you?'

'Maybe. Better safe than sorry.'

'Exactly. Anyway, we didn't need it, we've got Tarragon.'

Willow grinned. 'I'll have a word with him about being more subtle.'

I raised my arm to shield my eyes from the sun. Despite the warmth, I'd tried to keep my arms covered during this trip.

Otherwise, my pale skin liked to burn. On the horizon, a ship with the green sails of the Aerban Navy shadowed our path. 'Is that them?'

Willow nodded. 'They've been there, stalking us, for almost half an hour.'

Captain Hyssop started barking orders. 'Loose t'gallants! We'll try and outrun her!' The sailors ran around the deck and climbed the rigging, obeying his commands.

'Do you think they'll try and board us?' Willow asked, watching the Aerban ship.

'They've got to catch us first,' I said, the salty air whipping my copper hair into my eyes. I quickly tied it back up in the Aerban style, watching the distant green sails billowing in the wind. The ship lurched as we hit a big wave, and we both grabbed for the rail.

'I'm going to need more of Anise's herbal sea sickness tea before too long,' Willow muttered.

'You've been much better on this trip.'

'Only because Anise keeps plying me with his tea.'

'We're lucky to have him,' Tarragon said, joining us. 'Not sure where we'd be without him.'

'Seems Chervil is keeping a watch on us,' Anise said, his voice smooth like butter, as he came over with Sage. The two young men held hands, something they'd never have dared do back in Aerba.

I smiled at the two of them. 'Looks that way, doesn't it?'

'He won't be stupid enough to try and take us here, not when we're so close to Flosian waters,' Sage said, squinting at the ship, but his brown eyes had a fleck of worry in them as the breeze caught his straight, dark brown hair and tugged at his burgundy and black-edged coat.

A year older than Rian, Sage was also his cousin. His single silver earring in the shape of a sprig of thyme jingled as it dangled from his right ear. A similar height to me, he looked immaculate, as always, just like Anise, and the scent of violets and lemons swirled around him.

'Hmm.' Willow didn't look convinced.

'Aerba isn't going to risk all-out war with Flos.'

'I thought war was imminent anyway,' I murmured.

Anise gave me a pained look. 'The last thing we need is a war in the Five Lands.'

'If the Fire Opal hadn't been taken, then Aerba wouldn't even be considering war with Flos,' Sage said, his rose-beige face crinkling as he frowned.

'But we still don't know Flos stole it,' I said.

'That's why we're going there,' Rian said, coming over with Captain Hyssop. He stood beside me, slipping his arm around my shoulders. 'To find out whether they have it or not.'

'And to search for Mal,' I said softly. My brother, Malachite, had been imprisoned by my stepmother, Juniper, Mistress of the Island of Iolite, and Leader of the Iolite Coterie of Assassins. I knew he was alive, but I didn't know where, and I had to rescue him. My quest for Malachite consumed me.

Rian glanced at me, his amber eyes full of sympathy and hope. 'We'll find him. We'll find them both.'

I nodded. 'I know we will.'

'If we don't lose them, we'll head into Flosian waters,' Hyssop said, his green eyes staring out over the churning waves at the other ship. 'We'll escape them one way or another, but a little subterfuge might be useful. Oregano! Change the ensign flag to the Flos one.' A stocky, bald sailor nodded and made his way across the deck. 'Anyone comin' up on us will think we're a Flosian ship.'

Rian nodded. 'I get the feeling you've done this before.'

Hyssop grinned back. 'It pays to be prepared,' he said, heading back down the ship.

By nightfall, the Aerban ship had been lost to sight. Hyssop had succeeded in outrunning them, but even so he kept a watch all night.

As we edged ever closer to Scilla, a cold dread started to seep into my bones. Finding the Fire Opal was important, but finding Mal even more so, at least to me. Although, Hyssop's revelation that the Opal was a Magical Artefact that could be used in the hands of an Elemental Angle Spinner, if they still existed, had made it imperative we get hold of it as soon as possible. Where Juniper might have imprisoned Mal, if not in Iolite, I didn't know. My friend, the assassin Onyx, said my brother was still alive, as he was too important for Juniper to kill. I just hoped he was right, and that someone in Flos knew where Mal was. I'd fled the Coterie and couldn't go back to find out more.

I stood on deck the following morning as the Flosian coast slid past, the sea crashing into the cliffs as seagulls and guillemots spiralled above the coastline, their plaintive cries echoing my mood. The port town of Scilla wasn't far away now. I raised the spyglass I'd borrowed from Hyssop to my eye.

For a moment, the sunlight glinting on the waves blinded me. Then the walled harbour revealed itself. The docks thronged with merchant vessels and a number of naval vessels. Were they readying for war already?

The cream limestone buildings of the town had thatched roofs, and they huddled like sheep on the side of a steep hill that led down to the water. The place heaved with people moving up and down towards the ships. I looked closer. The roads down to the port were full of the vivid blue suede tunics of the Flosian military, interspersed with the white tunics of the town guards. I lowered the spyglass. Our Aerban clothes would stand out immediately. They'd arrest us before we'd even stepped foot on dry land.

I turned, heading across the deck to the cabin. The wooden door creaked open and I entered the main communal area where the others sat talking.

'We've got a problem,' I said.

Rian turned towards me from where he'd been studying a map with Sage. 'What is it?'

'The whole town is rammed with soldiers and town guards.'

He winced. 'Damn. I guess we should've expected that.'

'We'll never get off the ship,' I said. 'We'll have to come up with another plan.'

CHAPTER TWO

'Everything's fine, Phire,' Anise said from his seat in the corner, sitting in a relaxed fashion.

'I fail to see how,' I said, grabbing the wall as the ship caught a rogue wave, sending us lurching to the left.

He grinned. 'I have these.' He pointed to where some packages now lay strewn across the floor, courtesy of the rolling ship.

Sage narrowed his eyes. 'Are they what I think they are?'

Anise nodded. 'The Iolitian clothes we used when we visited the island.'

'How did you get hold of them?' Rian asked, picking one up.

'Brought them with us, just in case.'

'You think of everything, don't you?' Sage asked.

'I try.'

A little smile crossed my face. 'Perfect. The Flosians won't take any notice of us if they think we're Iolitian Middle Bloods. We should be able to move around quite freely.'

'We'll have to change our hair,' Willow said, screwing her nose up as she sipped on the herbal tea Anise had made her for her sea sickness.

'Better that than be imprisoned,' Tarragon said, sorting through the packages before handing them out. 'Let's get changed. Willow and I will use the storeroom.'

'I bet you will,' I muttered, giving them a little scowl as the two left the room. Rian glanced at me and gave me a wry smile.

'You and Rian change first, we'll be back in a minute,' Sage said to us, and he and Anise left, closing the door behind them.

I opened the two packages Tarragon had given us, frowning as I took in the black tunics, light mail shirts, cotton undershirts and black suede britches of Iolitian Middle Bloods. I sighed.

'I thought this was all behind me,' I said, trying to suppress a shudder. 'I never thought I'd wear clothes like this again.'

Rian slipped an arm around my waist. 'It's behind you – they're disguises, not your true clothes now. Remember that.'

I twisted around to look at him. 'And what are our true clothes now? I'm not sure they're Aerban, either.'

He frowned, a pained look in his eyes. 'I know. I don't have an answer now, but one day we'll find a home again, for all of us.'

'I hope so,' I said with a sigh.

He bent forward and kissed my nose. 'You'll see.'

'Hmm.' He let go of me and I slipped off my purple coat.

As we changed, I noticed Rian tucking my Amethyst Talisman, one of the ancient Magical Artefacts, into his tunic, and smiled. He'd worn it since we'd made our vows to each other, and it had since saved my life, breaking the Curse that had come upon me when I'd taken up the Cursed Weapons. It was my wedding gift to him, as his gold and diamond Thyme ring had been to me.

Rian adjusted his hair, letting it fall loose from his traditional high Aerban ponytail. He ran his fingers through it as it fell about his face. My heart did a little skip as I gazed at him. Reaching towards him, I shifted it from his amber eyes.

'Don't tie it back, I like it loose,' I said, my hand lingering on his warm cheek.

'Don't all Iolitian men wear it in a low ponytail?' he asked, his cheeks flushing slightly at my touch.

'Most, but not all. You wouldn't look out of place in Iolite with it loose like this.'

'Then if you like it, I like it,' he said with a smile that could melt a glacier. He took my hand into his and kissed my palm, sending little shocks though my skin. 'Leave yours down, too. I think you look lovely like that.'

Blood rushed to my face. 'I do? I always think it looks a bit messy, out of control.'

'Not at all. I mean, it may look a little wild, untameable, but then that's you.'

'I'm wild and untameable, am I?' I raised an eyebrow. Was that a compliment or an insult?

He reached out, slipping a curl behind my ear. 'I mean, it's like you in that it's independent and free.' Compliment, then. 'It suits you.'

'Well, it is Iolitian, so it'll be fine. As long as it doesn't keep flicking into my eyes, I'll keep it like this, then.'

He smiled and nodded, and we finished dressing. I attached my Malachite War Fan to my belt, the one my brother had given me for my sixteenth birthday, but didn't bother with the Cursed Weapons. They'd sort themselves out.

The thought of Mal made my nose tingle, bringing tears to my eyes for a moment, and resolve to my heart. I would find him.

We made our way out on deck. Tarragon and Willow were already there, and Sage and Anise soon joined us, all now with low ponytails and in Iolitian clothes. Tarragon gave Rian a strange look as he inspected his cousin's hair.

'Not tying it back?' Tarragon asked.

'Thought I'd wear it like this for a while,' Rian said. 'See what it's like. I have it on good authority that it's still Iolitian.'

'True. Maybe I should try it, too.'

'You keep yours tied back,' Willow said.

'Why?'

'Because you'll only get irritated if it keeps flying across your face. I know you.'

'You're probably right, y'know, it'll only annoy me.'

I looked out across the water at the rapidly approaching harbour.

'Anise, why the mail shirts?' Willow asked. 'We didn't have them last time.'

'This time it's different,' Anise said. 'Flos doesn't want Aerbans here. We need to be prepared.'

'Will our weapons be all right?' Sage asked. 'I mean, they're not, strictly speaking, Iolitian.'

'You could have picked them up anywhere,' I said. 'One sword is usual in Iolite, rather than your two Aerban ones, but not compulsory. It's the clothes and hair that's most important, no one will take a second look at our weapons.' I glanced at the purple crystal sword and shield on my back. *I hope.* 'My cousin, Jasmine, has a farm just north of Scilla. We'll go and see her, see if she has any news that could help us.'

'She's a Middle Blood?' Anise asked.

'No, a High-Middle.'

'A what?' Willow asked. 'Bobbins. You made that up.'

'No, I didn't. They have five Blood Classes here – as well as the usual High, Middle and Low, they also have High-Middle and Middle-Low.'

'Really? They allow intermarrying between Blood Classes?' Sage frowned.

'Yes, except for High and Low Bloods – that's still illegal. The Blood Class is still dependent on the mother, though. Jasmine's mother was High, her father Middle, so she's a High-Middle.'

'Flos is a little more enlightened than Aerba,' Rian said, a little bitter tinge to his voice. 'But no Blood Classes would be even better.'

I glanced at him. I knew how much he hated the whole Blood Class system. As a Middle Blood of Iolite, I could never legally, as far as Aerba was concerned, be with a High Blood Aerban. Even having discovered my true ancestry was from High Aerban Blood, Rian's brother, King Chervil, would still have never let us be together because my High Blood great-great-grandmother had been Demoted for running off with a Flosian Prince. But none of that mattered to Rian. He just wanted me – whatever my Blood Class. Wherever I was from.

'I take it there are no mynogres in Flos?' Sage asked, his brown eyes narrowing. 'I don't want to run into them again.'

'Not as far as I know,' I said. 'There may be tree dryads in some of the forests, but not mynogres.'

'Tree dryads?'

'You know, the nature spirits that are said to be connected to the trees in some forests. They're supposed to look like beautiful young girls.'

'We don't have them in Aerba,' Rian said.

'We don't in Iolite, either, but they're certainly talked about in Flos.'

'Are they friendly?' Sage asked.

I shrugged. 'As far as I know they are. I've never heard of them being referred to as malevolent.'

'Then tree dryads I can cope with. Just no more mynogres.'

The ship jerked as we hit a big wave outside the harbour walls. A wall of water curved over the bow of the ship, heading towards us. Rian made a grab for me, but before I could duck out of the way, Tarragon raised his arm in a futile attempt to ward off the water. The wave skewed and landed back in the water, missing us entirely.

Rian's eyes went wide in amazement.

'That was lucky,' Tarragon said with a grin, peering over the side of the ship.

I narrowed my eyes, looking at him suspiciously, but he just grinned back, totally oblivious to what he might have just done – at least, what it *looked* like he might have just done. But how could he have done that? Stopped a wave in mid-flight? Unless he was a Water Spinner? *Don't be daft.*

No one else had noticed anything off. Well, maybe Rian looked a little unsure. He glanced at me, raising an eyebrow; I shrugged back. It was probably me imagining things. Perhaps a gust of wind had caught the wave and turned it away from the deck. I looked back towards the harbour. We'd sailed past the walls now and had nearly reached the docks.

'We'd better get our packs,' Rian said, turning towards the cabin. 'We'll buy horses as soon as we get into the town.'

'I wouldn't mind stopping at the market,' Sage said, his nose twitching.

'For supplies?' Tarragon asked.

'Hyssop's given us enough for a few days, and if we stop at Jasmine's, she'll be able to make sure we have what we need,' I said.

'No, I want to visit their perfume stalls,' Sage said, looking straight ahead.

'You want to do what?' Tarragon choked on the water he'd just sipped from his waterskin.

'You heard me.'

'What do you want with perfume?'

'Never you mind,' Sage said, glancing at Anise whose face had a healthy pink hue.

Tarragon shook his head.

'I like a nice rose perfume, myself,' I said.

Rian grinned at me, leaning towards my ear. 'So do I,' he murmured softly. 'Maybe I'll buy you some.'

'You're impossible,' I whispered back.

'I try.'

My face warmed.

'Flos makes the best perfumes in the Five Lands,' Sage said, unperturbed by the rest of us.

'They make the only perfumes in the Five Lands,' Willow said.

'The soil here is extremely good for flowers. That's why they grow so many,' I said as the sailors shouted to each other and set about bringing us dockside.

'I wonder if they started growing the flowers, then named the land, or if it was the other way around,' Anise said.

I shrugged. 'Don't know.'

We gathered our packs and met Captain Hyssop at the now-lowered gangplank.

'Well, take care of yourselves,' Hyssop said, shaking our hands each in turn. 'I hope we meet again one day.'

'You've been a good friend, Captain, we won't forget it,' Rian said.

'I'm sure you won't, Prince Valerian, and I won't be forgettin' you in a hurry, either. Perhaps next time we'll meet in happier circumstances?'

'Let's hope so. Stay safe.'

We made our way down onto the dock. Two soldiers in blue suede tunics covered in little metal studs looked at us, then carried on.

'Iolitians,' one muttered. 'Probably assassins. Leave them alone.'

The other nodded, giving us a wide berth.

'Perhaps your former profession will come in useful after all,' Tarragon said softly from beside me, a sparkle in his eyes.

'Maybe it will,' I said. I was still acutely aware of the inch-high tattoo of a flaming circle with an "I" in its centre that sat on my right wrist covering my little cluster of freckles, even if it was still hidden by the sandalwood-smelling leather wrist strap Rian had given me so long ago. The Coterie saw it as a proud mark of honour. I saw it as one of shame. A brand I'd like to be rid of.

We walked up the steep hill, weaving our way through the noisy townsfolk as they rushed down to the docks and back up into the town, steering clear of the soldiers and the white studded tunics of the Town Guard, forging on towards the market. Salt and fish filled the air, and as we got closer to the merchants, the scent of flowers joined in. It all contributed to a strange, confusing combination of smells that gave me a headache. Willow started coughing. While Sage, Anise, and Rian went off in search of perfume, we found a horse trader and purchased six reasonable-looking beasts, tacked them up, and loaded our packs onto the saddles.

'I'm hungry,' Tarragon said. 'I'm going to find something to eat.'

'You and your stomach!' Willow shouted after him, shaking her head. 'He's always hungry.'

'He's a big, strong young man. He needs his food, especially if you keep wearing him out,' I said, smirking.

'Very funny.'

The sun shone directly above us as Sage and Anise returned with Rian, who looked quite pleased with himself. He walked over to me.

'For you,' he said, producing a small pink glass bottle from his pocket. 'So you can always smell of roses.'

I took it from him, smiling as I opened it. I sniffed. It was such a delightful, light scent, it almost took my breath away. I dabbed a little on and slipped the closed bottle into my pocket.

'Thank you,' I said, leaning towards him and kissing his cheek. I noticed him inhale. 'You like it?'

He smiled at me, his eyes lighting with desire. 'I do, very much. Damn, Sage may be right about perfume.'

Tarragon returned a moment later, walking along with a big grin on his face, his hands full of pies.

'I thought we could all do with something to eat,' he said, handing them out.

'Meat pie?' Sage asked, sniffing at it. 'Great idea.'

We quickly ate the warm, juicy meat pies – although I noted a lack of herbs – then mounted up and rode towards the town gates. The cream limestone of the buildings reflected the sunlight, making the streets bright and warm.

'They take security seriously,' Willow said, eyeing the big wooden gates and high limestone wall running around the town all the way to the docks.

'You never know if any Aerbans might come visiting,' I said with a grin.

Willow grinned back. 'True.'

I glanced back down the street. Exiting an inn, and heading in the direction of the docks, were two men. Two men that sent shivers down my spine. Sunstone, with his spiky white hair, and Hematite, his straggly blond hair catching the breeze. They were great brutes, thick-necked and with muscles of iron, incredibly strong, not to mention masters with the sword. They rarely ventured away from Iolite, usually remaining in the Crimson Castle, acting as Juniper's personal bodyguard. When they did leave the island, it was on her express instructions. Why they'd be in Flos eluded me, but we needed to keep away from them.

'Let's go, quickly,' I said to Rian.

He glanced at me. 'Problem?'

'Assassins.'

'Tarragon, let's move,' Rian said, urging his horse into a trot as we left the gates, and then into a gallop, leading the way. The others exchanged a few confused looks but followed him without question.

We rode on for a league before slowing our mounts. I kept looking behind, but they obviously hadn't seen us, and weren't following. I breathed a sigh of relief, and quickly explained to the others who they were.

'Juniper's bodyguards?' Tarragon asked.

I nodded. 'Although, they're sometimes sent out on commissions or to bring someone back to see Juniper.'

'They wouldn't be after us, would they?' Willow asked, nervously looking over her shoulder.

I shook my head. 'No one knows we're even here. Those two are sent out on commission when Juniper wants to make a statement to someone, or wants to make absolutely sure an important and well-paid commission is completed. One that needs brute strength – she'd have no reason to send them after us. I think it was just coincidence they were here. After all, they were heading for the docks, not inland. I think we're quite safe from them, especially if we keep going.'

'But doesn't Juniper know where your cousins live?' Sage asked. 'Maybe she sent the assassins to see if your relations had heard from you.'

'Unlikely,' I said. 'Juniper wouldn't send those two on that sort of mission, and anyway, Jasmine and Erica are under the protection of the Royal Family. She'd open a whole can of worms if she went after them. She wouldn't dare.'

We cantered out into the open countryside, following the paved road northwards past fields full of narcissus, tuberose, and lavender that danced in the onshore breeze. The colours of the flowers mingled with the green of the grasslands and the sparkling azure sea, still visible in the distance. The colourful landscape lay peppered with little white beehives, their residents buzzing busily from flower to flower on important missions, and little huts housing the flower farmers' perfume distilleries.

'What does Juniper do with the people she gets Sunstone and Hematite to return to Iolite?' Rian asked as he rode beside me.

I glanced at him. 'Sure you want to know?'

He nodded. 'I want to know everything about your former life. I'm not just your soulmate, but your best friend, too. I want to share these things with you, help bear your burdens, if that's what they are?'

They were burdens, all right. I took a deep breath and gazed out over the beauty of the flowery landscape. 'Those two are often sent out when Juniper wants someone to see Serpentine.'

'"See Serpentine"? You're dancing around the truth.'

'You're very perceptive.'

'Not perceptive, I just know you, that's all, and you're sugar coating it.'

I sighed. 'All right. When Juniper wants them to be punished, or to die a particularly lingering, horrifically painful death, and she doesn't want them assassinated quickly, she has them brought back to Serpentine.'

'Her executioner?'

'Executioner, torturer – he's both.'

'He's really that bad?'

'He's evil.' I swallowed. 'Not long after Father died – so, a number of years ago – Juniper took me and Mal down into his chamber. The "torture" chamber, Mal called it. And he was right. It was full of...' I took a breath. 'Bloodied knives, axes, saws, chains, ropes, and on the floor… The blood was thick in places, despite the drains he'd had installed. The smell was – I can't even begin to describe it. Juniper wanted to impress on us what would happen if we disobeyed her. We've never run so quickly from anywhere.'

Rian looked at me, pain and sympathy in his eyes. 'And the threat of Serpentine and his torture chamber has been hanging over your heads ever since?'

I nodded. 'Mal and I knew if we didn't do what she wanted, we could end up there, or Beryl would, which of course at the time scared us witless. We didn't want Beryl harmed, and neither of us wanted to end up in there, either. Who knows what he'd have done to us. I just hope Mal never got taken there. Anyway, we were so scared that we had no choice but to do what Juniper wanted.'

Rian reached out and took my hand, squeezing it. 'You never have to worry about that place again – and neither will Mal, once we find him.'

'I know.' I squeezed his hand in return, looking at his pale face. He truly understood the misery of what we'd endured, what we'd faced on a daily basis, and I loved him all the more for it.

A gust of wind brought the strong smell of lavender blasting around us. Behind us, Willow coughed.

'You all right?' Tarragon asked.

She nodded. 'I'm fine.'

Rian let go of my hand and smiled.

Wanting to change the subject, I called ahead to Sage. 'Did you find what you wanted in town?'

He nodded, slowing his horse so he rode beside me, his eyes alight. 'Exactly. It's a perfume with violet, rose, and tuberose – quite exquisite.'

'I don't really know much about tuberose, other than they're those flowers over there,' I said, pointing at a field of waving, half-closed white flowers.

'It's quite powerful; creamy and earthy. The flowers bloom at night. It's extremely expensive, partly because it's so exotic, sensual, and can even—'

'Phire doesn't need all the details,' Anise said. 'I'm sure she gets the general idea.'

I smiled. Yes, I did. And it appeared Sage may have converted Rian.

'When will we reach Jasmine's?' Rian asked.

'By late afternoon,' I said. 'We'll be there well before dark.'

'Good,' Willow said, coughing. 'I'm all right, but all these flowers are making my chest tight.'

'I'll give you something for that when we stop,' Anise said.

Willow nodded gratefully and coughed again.

We rode on through the afternoon, and as the sun painted the blue sky with brush strokes of pink and gold, we crested a hill and gazed down on Jasmine's farm. It lay below us, a vast quantity of fields full of flowers, animals, and cereal crops covering the land as far as the eye could see, and at its centre a vast, sprawling house of creamy limestone with two floors. Its thatched roof sat neat with ornate straw birds along the ridges adding to its opulence. I gazed out over the flower fields interspersed with areas of white wooden bee hives where the inhabitants buzzed from flower field to flower field, pollinating the plants. Honey and beeswax were big businesses in Flos – they used candles here rather than pitch torches.

'I thought you said your cousin had a farm,' Tarragon said, raising an eyebrow as he turned towards me in his saddle.

I frowned. 'What do you think that is down there? A small holding?'

'It's more like a royal estate with a country house villa at its centre than a farm.'

I shrugged. 'It's still a farm. No one asked how big it was. I didn't think its size was relevant.'

Tarragon shook his head as Rian shot me a grin.

'Your idea of "farm" and Tarragon's are obviously different,' Willow said, laughing.

We rode down to the farm past fields where Low Bloods toiled in the afternoon warmth, their heads down as they wiped perspiration from their brows. We continued on up to the house and into the side stable yard, which sat empty. Everyone must have still been out in the fields.

'Amethyst? Amethyst!' A young woman in her late twenties ran into the stable yard, her shoulder-length blonde hair swinging about her face, her blue eyes wide in shock. 'We thought you were dead!'

CHAPTER THREE

I shook my head, slipping down from my horse. 'Not yet, Jasmine, despite various attempts,' I said, giving her a big hug.

'That was the last report from Aerba, that their Cursed Weapons had killed you – not that we get many reports, now, what with the war,' Jasmine said, glancing at the others.

'War?' Rian dismounted and joined me. 'Has it begun?'

Jasmine's blue eyes narrowed. 'Who's this?'

'Prince Valeri—'

Jasmine clamped her hand around my mouth. 'Shh! Didn't you hear me? We're at war with Aerba, or as good as. Why have you brought him here?' Jasmine hissed, her pale skin blanching further. 'You could kill us all.'

'I didn't know Flos *was* at war with Aerba, yet,' I protested.

'Well, technically, we're not quite, but it won't be long before we are, the way things are going. King Chervil seems intent on it. Look, it's really dangerous in Flos for any Aerbans now.' She eyed the others. 'I take it they're not Iolitians, either?'

I shook my head.

Jasmine sighed. 'You keep dangerous company, Amethyst. Look, I'll find you somewhere to sleep, but I daren't have you in the house. Soldiers have started to patrol, particularly along the coast and near to it. They stop regularly at the larger houses to inspect them. In fact, Major Larkspur is having dinner with us tonight, and the last thing we want is for him to find you all here. I'm sorry, but you'll have to sleep in a barn, I'm afraid. Not what you're used to, Your Royal Highness, I know, but it's too dangerous for everyone if you stay in the house.'

'That's fine,' Rian said, nodding. 'We quite understand. A barn will be a welcome change to the hammocks we've had since fleeing Aerba.'

'Fleeing?'

'Chervil was going to execute me, until Amethyst rescued me from the scaffold.'

Tarragon coughed.

'With a little help from my cousins, Anise and Willow,' Rian said, indicating the others.

'We've all left Aerba,' I said. 'If any of us go back, they'll kill us.'

'You don't want to have to convince the soldiers of that, though,' Jasmine said, looking at the empty stable yard. 'I don't think they'd be in the mood to believe you. Come on, I'll take you to a barn in the lavender fields. It's not used at this time of year, so you'll be left alone and quite safe.'

I nodded. 'Thank you, Jasmine,' I said, squeezing her hand.

'Yes, well, it's the best I can do,' she said, nodding and leading the way out of the stable yard.

This wasn't the welcome I'd expected. Although, if war really was imminent, I didn't blame her for her reaction.

Jasmine led us out into the fields as the sun set, away from the house and any curious workers. After a ten-minute walk, we reached a large, well-kept hay barn, nestled in amongst the lavender fields near a little stream. Quite picturesque. Inside were bales of hay that could be made into quite comfortable bedding for the night, with more up on a platform above, reachable by ladder.

'I suggest you sleep up there,' she said, looking up. 'The horses can be tied up at the back of the barn where there's some food for them. There are buckets there, too, so you can fetch water from the stream.' She turned to look at me. 'I'm sorry things are like this. I'd much rather have you at the house and entertain you all properly, but it's too dangerous for you and us.'

'We understand, really,' I said.

'I'll send Hyacinth down with some food once it's dark. You shouldn't need a fire; the nights have been quite warm lately.' She let out a little sigh. 'I'm sorry, Amethyst. I'll come and see you tomorrow morning. We can catch up then, once the Major and his men are long gone.'

I nodded. She gave me a quick hug and hurriedly left the barn.

'Is she always like that?' Tarragon asked, watching her head back to the house.

'No,' I said, shaking my head. 'I've never seen her like that before. She's really spooked by us being here. Things must be worse than we thought. All the talk of war must be more serious than we'd realised.'

'This isn't right,' Rian said, shaking his head, his shoulders sagging under some invisible weight.

Tarragon glanced at his cousin, who now wore an uncomfortable look on his face. The thought of his brother starting a war with Flos sat heavily on Rian. This wasn't what he wanted for his homeland. Or Flos.

We made the horses comfortable and arranged beds for ourselves up on the raised platform, as Jasmine had suggested. As it got dark, I stood by the door, nervously watching for Hyacinth, but who knew what time he'd get away and be able to bring us some food. The others remained above me, talking in low voices. The snap of a twig made the hairs on the back of my neck stand to attention. In one fluid movement, I grabbed my War Fan from my belt, flicked it open, and stood ready to fight. The gemstones sparkled, the malachite leaves of the Fan glowed in the evening light, and the blades on the Fan shone in the light of the moon that filled the lower portion of the barn.

'Still got that damn Fan of yours, I see, Amethyst.'

I sighed with relief. 'Of course, Hyacinth. You know I don't go anywhere without it,' I said, retracting the blades and returning it to my belt.

'It's good to see you,' Hyacinth said, coming into the barn with a crate. He put it down and gave me a hug. His shoulder-length blond hair and blue eyes were very like his wife's. 'I wish the circumstances were different, though – or, rather, that your friends hailed from somewhere other than Aerba. Then you could've stayed in the house and we'd have looked after you properly.'

'We hadn't realised things had got so bad since we left Aerba.'

'The whole of Flos is on a war footing, has been since King Finule blamed us for the loss of the Fire Opal. Things have got a lot worse, though, since Chervil took over as King. I think we'll be at war by the end of the month, maybe sooner. We just don't know.'

'But if Flos didn't take the Fire Opal, who did?' Rian asked as he joined us.

'Prince Valerian?'

'I'm not a prince anymore,' Rian said awkwardly. 'I've left that life for good.'

Hyacinth nodded. 'Well, I don't know the answer to your question, I'm afraid. But whoever did must have known the hornet's nest they'd stir up when they stole it.' He crouched down to the crate. 'Here, there's food, drink, a flint, and a few candles, but do be careful – hay burns, as you know, Amethyst.'

I fluttered my eyelashes innocently at him. 'I don't know what you're talking about, Hyacinth.'

'Yes, you do. Just keep them up the top and the barn doors shut. That way, the light won't be seen from outside. And stay in the barn, I don't know when Major Larkspur will leave. We don't want him finding an Aerban Prince on the farm, even if he is an *ex-*Aerban Prince.'

'Thank you, Hyacinth.'

He nodded. 'I'll leave some food outside for you tomorrow at first light. Jasmine will come and see you in the morning as soon as she can get away.' He reached over, pulling the barn doors closed as he left. 'Goodnight.'

I lit one of the candles and looked at the contents of the crate. 'Let's get this up to the others and eat.'

'What did he mean about the hay?' Rian asked curiously.

I screwed my nose up. 'I had a little accident last time I was here, that's all.'

'Accident?' he asked, raising an eyebrow.

I sighed. I was going to have to tell him, even though the memory made me cringe with embarrassment.

'It was late summer. Mal and I were helping with the harvest and I happened to knock over a candle and set light to a haystack. I wasn't looking at what I was doing, too busy joking with everyone. We only just got it out before it set light to a whole field of them. Mal said…' I swallowed. Mentioning Mal made my nose tingle and my eyes well up. 'He…he said…'

Rian slipped his arm around me. 'Tell me later,' he said, kissing my head.

I nodded, fighting back the urge to burst into tears. 'Let's get this up to the others.'

We carried the crate up to the platform, emptied the contents, and tucked into a meal of warm meat and vegetable stew before settling down to sleep. Rian put his blankets over mine and we lay together, enjoying each other's warmth.

'You were hoping for something different from your cousin?' he asked in a soft voice so as not to disturb the others.

I nodded. 'I didn't think coming to the farm would be such a problem for her – not like this, anyway. It hadn't occurred to me I'd be putting her and Hyacinth in any danger.'

'We.'

'What?'

'*We're* putting her in danger, not just you.'

'I know, but—'

'This isn't your fault, Phire.'

'I suppose not, it just feels like it is.'

'It's Father and Chervil's fault for accusing Flos, and the fault of whoever actually stole the Fire Opal in the first place,' he said, pulling me towards him, engulfing me in the sandalwood coming from his body. I drank it in, relishing the calming fragrance that warmed my core, rather wishing we were alone in this hay barn, not surrounded by the others. Free to do what we wanted. What we'd wanted for some time.

'I don't want Jasmine and Hyacinth in any trouble,' I said.

'They won't get into trouble – it'll be fine.'

'I hope so.'

The sun rose early along with me. I'd slept fitfully, pretty sure I'd kept Rian awake, though he denied it. He sat beside me, pulling his boots on as I chewed on a nail. Something had been bothering me for ages, I'd just not got around to speaking to him about it.

'How did you track me, back in Aerba, after I left the palace?' I asked.

He turned to look at me and grinned. 'Your horse's shoes. They had a strange design carved into them.'

'But how did you know it was me you were following?'

'They were the only set of hoof prints outside the palace walls different to everything else. Plus, they were near the west side entrance where a horse had obviously been waiting for a while, churning the earth up next to an ancient rose bush in an area by an old well. You'd also snagged your black tunic on the rose bush there and left a bit of material behind; Iolitian material. We were able to track your horse's prints after that.'

I frowned, shook my head. 'I didn't get a horse until I was outside the city, and I wasn't wearing my black tunic, I had an Aerban Middle Blood's beige coat on. And I went in the back entrance, not the west entrance.'

'You sure?' he asked, his forehead furrowing.

'I know which way I got into the palace,' I said, giving him a long look. 'And it wasn't the west entrance, and I had no horse. I think someone wanted you to follow me – they deliberately set me up to get caught.'

'Get us to deal with their problem for them, before you got back to Flint?' he asked, raising an eyebrow.

'Hmm.'

Rian shook his head. 'And I very nearly did,' he said ruefully, rubbing the back of his neck and looking away.

'But you didn't,' I said, squeezing his hand. 'And I'll always be grateful for the fact you believed me.'

His eyes clouded. 'I don't know I exactly believed *everything* you were saying at the beginning – not as such. It was more that something didn't add up, and your denial made me even more suspicious.'

'I could've been lying.'

'You could have,' he said, nodding. 'But you'll never get your eyes to lie. They betray you every time,' he said, kissing my nose. 'I knew right from the beginning you were telling the truth about Angelica, even if I didn't understand exactly what was going on.'

'Guess I'll have to work on the eyes, then,' I said with a grin.

'Don't you dare, I love you the way you are,' he said, smiling. 'I'm just going to check everything's okay outside.'

Willow moved over to talk to me as Rian made his way down to the barn door. He carefully opened it and peered out, sunlight flooding into the barn, then disappeared out the door to walk around the barn and check all was well.

'I'm just glad we're not at sea,' Willow said, brushing her hair. 'Being on land is so much better.'

I giggled. 'No seasickness.'

'Exactly. I mean, being at sea is kind of refreshing. But when you're throwing up every other minute, it gets rather tiresome.'

'I can imagine.'

'Did you see Hyacinth?' Rian asked, coming back in with a bowl. That was quick.

'No,' Sage said from below us.

'He must have left this while I was around the back of the barn – it's fruit of some sort.'

'I was hoping for a little more than fruit,' Tarragon said, groaning from where he still lay in the hay behind Willow.

'Be glad you're getting anything at all,' Anise said from where he sat below us with Sage.

I left the upper platform and made my way down to the barn floor as Rian pulled the door closed again. He turned towards me, holding a bowl of bright, ruby-red berries, and popped one into his mouth.

'These are amazing. They taste of lemons,' he said, taking another.

In amongst the berries sat a blood-red bead.

Hell's teeth.

A chill rolled through me.

'Want one?' he asked, passing them towards me.

I lunged towards him, swiping them from his hand. The berries and the small red bead scattered across the floor with a clatter.

'Spit it out, spit it out!' I screamed at him.

His amber eyes widened as he bent over, spitting the berry and its juices onto the floor.

'Whatever's the matter?' he asked. 'They're just berries. Hyacinth left them for us.'

'You don't know that,' I said as a tidal wave of panic rushed at me, my heart stuttering and my hands clammy as I grabbed hold of him.

'But Hyacinth said he—'

'How many have you eaten?' I asked, trying to keep my voice level, trying not to burst into tears of terror.

'What?'

'How many berries have you eaten, Valerian?'

His eyes narrowed. 'You never call me that.'

'Just answer the damn question!'

'Two or three? I'm not sure. I picked a few up,' he said, giving me a "what's wrong with you, have you just gone mad, girl?" look.

I stopped breathing for a moment. 'They're Flosian Mandragora Berries,' I said.

'So what?' he asked, a bewildered look on his face. 'They're delicious. I wonder why we never had these back in Aerba.'

'You ate one?' Anise asked, rushing over, his face white.

'I ate a few – they were nice and lemony. What's the problem?' Rian asked, annoyance in his voice.

'They're poisonous,' I said. 'Deadly poisonous.'

'They can't be. Why, by the Herbs, would Hyacinth leave us poisonous food?'

I glanced at the little red bead on the floor. 'He didn't.'

CHAPTER FOUR

Fear clutched at my heart as I stared at the carnelian bead nestled amongst the berries on the floor. How had the Coterie assassin found us? I'd skin him alive for this. I glanced at a pale-faced Rian. I'd failed my husband. I'd vowed to be his shield. Instead, I'd let him down, maybe fatally.

'Poisonous?' Rian asked, less sure of himself now. 'Exactly how poisonous?'

I glanced at Anise. He looked back at me before turning to Rian.

'Fatal,' Anise said.

Rian's rose-beige face drained of all colour as his eyes narrowed. 'Exactly how fatal?'

Anise flinched.

'Oh, damn,' Rian murmured, rubbing the back of his neck.

'But how many did you eat?' Sage asked, running up. 'I mean, surely it has to be a reasonable number? A few won't hurt, will they?'

'One is enough to kill, Sage,' Anise said quietly.

'Really?' Sage blanched.

'And he ate more than that.'

'What about an antidote? There must be an antidote. Can we get hold of the herbs? Anise? Can we?' Rian asked, his face etched with fear. 'Anise?' he almost begged.

'There is no antidote,' I said, taking Rian's hand, holding back tears for his sake. 'That's why the Coterie use them – they're mistaken for other things. You only need the unsuspecting victim to consume a single berry rather than a whole meal of something, or a full glass. People don't suspect until—until it's too late.'

Of all the poisons available to the Coterie, this was by far the cruellest, resulting in a horrifically painful and lingering death. I knew what awaited Rian – I thanked the Stars that he didn't. Nausea gripped me. A cold sweat broke out on my forehead. I was helpless.

'The room's spinning,' Rian said, grabbing my shoulder to stay upright.

'We need to get him to lie down,' Anise said. 'This isn't going to be pretty.'

'We'll never get him back up there,' Tarragon said, indicating the platform as he hurried over with Willow.

'Bring him over here,' Willow said, quickly arranging some hay into a makeshift bed on the ground floor, away from the door and the horses.

Tarragon and I steered Rian over to the corner of the barn, helping him to lie down. His once-pale skin had become flushed, his breathing erratic and fast. How much was fear, and how much the poison, I didn't know. I held his hand, feeling his heartbeat become increasingly uneven.

'Am I going to die?' Rian asked, looking up at me, his pupils dilated.

'Of course not,' I lied. 'We'll think of something.' We *had* to think of something. I refused to lose him to Carnelian and poison.

'If I am, I want you to know I love you and it's only ever been you and I wouldn't change a thing, wife,' he said, his voice quavering as he gripped my hand, his eyes unfocussed.

'Same here. I love you with all my heart, husband,' I said, tears welling in my eyes as I struggled to maintain my composure.

'You look all blurry,' he said.

'I won't let you die,' I said, refusing to accept the inevitable outcome of the poison that I knew all too well from my training with the Coterie. I glanced at Anise. 'It's come on so fast,' I murmured. 'I didn't realise it could do that.'

'The riper the berries the faster the effects, particularly if he's had several,' Anise said. 'But even so...' He hesitated, turned away from Rian, then spoke in a low voice only Tarragon and I could hear. 'You know what's going to happen, right?' he asked softly. 'Over the next couple of days or so?'

I nodded. Dizziness, flushed skin, blurred vision – they were happening already – then stomach cramps, fast heart rate, very erratic breathing, hallucinations, and before the end, spasms, and finally...

Knowing my husband was going to suffer terribly for the next few days, then die in agony, filled me with rage and helplessness. There wasn't a damn thing I could do about it, and it drove me mad.

Anger welled in my veins. Anger at Carnelian. Anger at the Coterie. Anger at Beryl and Juniper. If Rian died, and that was an almost definite outcome, I'd suspend my no killing rule and go straight to Iolite and kill them all. I swore it. I clenched my fist, my mouth dry, my heart breaking.

'I'll speak to Jasmine, see if Flos has any antidote we don't know about,' I said, letting go of Rian's hand.

'Don't leave me,' Rian said, his dilated eyes looking through me as he reached out for me, begging me to stay beside him. 'Please don't leave me.'

The fear in his voice tore at my heart. 'I won't,' I said, leaning towards him and kissing his forehead, taking his hand again. How could I go now, when he so desperately needed me?

'I'll go and speak to Jasmine,' Anise said. 'It's possible she might know something that can help us.'

'No, I'll go. I don't look as Aerban as you. Less likely to attract attention,' Willow said, moving towards the door. 'I won't be long.'

'But she said to stay inside,' Sage said, doubt filling his voice. 'We don't want to be caught by soldiers.'

'I think we're past worrying about that, don't you?'

Sage nodded slowly.

Anise carefully gathered up the berries as Willow left, collecting them into a little pouch along with the red bead. I wondered where Carnelian was, but I suspected he was long gone. He wouldn't hang around to see his handiwork take effect. He didn't need to. He knew what would happen, what torment he'd left in his wake.

When I did find him, Serpentine's amusements would be nothing compared to what I would wreak on him. He'd wish he'd never been born. Vengeance burnt in my core. He wouldn't escape my wrath, and neither would Beryl or Juniper – not if Rian died.

'Anise might be able to do something to help him,' Tarragon said, resting a hand on my shoulder as Anise rummaged through his Herb Chest with his tongue out as he concentrated. 'He is quite a genius when it comes to herbal remedies, y'know.'

I did know. But not this time, though. I knew that well enough, and so did Anise. A little worm of hopelessness wriggled about in my chest. He might ease Rian's suffering, but I didn't see how he could ever cure him. It was impossible. There was no hope.

Before long, Willow returned with Jasmine. She rushed in, her face pale and drawn as she crouched beside the stricken prince.

I turned towards her. 'Are there any Flosian remedies for the berries?' I asked, more in hope than anything.

'I'm sorry, Amethyst, but we don't know of any,' Jasmine said. 'The only people I know of that ever survived Flosian Mandragora Berries' poison were... It doesn't matter now. It was only a myth, anyway, and so long ago. There's nothing that can be done to save him.'

Anise glanced at Jasmine, a strange look in his eyes, but he remained silent, turning back to his Herb Chest.

'There's really nothing we can do?' I pressed. 'Nothing at all?'

Jasmine shook her head. 'Just keep him as comfortable as you can, and maybe—' She hesitated a moment, lowering her voice. 'Ease his passing.'

I gasped, my mind baulking at her suggestion. Help Rian die? *Never.* It went against everything I believed in. I couldn't be a party to that.

I shook my head. 'No,' I said emphatically.

'I don't think you realise how bad it's going to get, Amethyst,' my cousin said, bowing her head. 'It will be suffering in the extreme. Worse than any method of torture you can think of.' Having lived in the Crimson Castle with Serpentine and my stepmother, I could imagine quite a few. 'He'll beg for death before the end.'

For a moment, I thought I might vomit.

'We're not going to kill him,' I said in a quiet voice so Rian wouldn't hear, my teeth clenched.

'Do you want him to suffer?' she asked. 'Do you want to make him endure the very worst of agonies?'

'Of course not, he's my... we're... he's...' I couldn't finish, the words stuck in my throat, tears welling in my eyes. My heart raced and my hands began to tremble.

'Oh, I see – oh, Amethyst, I'm so sorry, I didn't realise. But if you love him, you may have to let him go.'

I froze.

I'd heard that before, and in the end hadn't complied. And I wouldn't this time. My heart stuttered. I couldn't. I couldn't kill him. I loved him.

'I have some herbs that will help sedate him, see him through some of it,' Anise said, holding his Jade Amulet in one hand, his forehead furrowed. 'I have something I found in the Chamber of Earth that might help, too. I'll finish preparing them.'

'You can stay as long as you need,' Jasmine said, resting her hand on my shoulder. 'Larkspur's gone and won't be back for a couple of weeks now. I'll get you that food I promised. Perhaps Willow can come with me to collect it?' She started to turn away, Willow following her, then glanced back at Rian. 'I'm truly sorry, Amethyst. You've already suffered enough loss.' She bowed her head and left the barn.

Her words echoed in my head. I'd lost my mother and my father, my brother languished in a prison somewhere, my sister had betrayed me, and now I was losing Rian, my husband. My chest tightened, and for a moment the walls of the barn felt as if they were forcing their way in on me as my breathing became difficult and my palms clammy. I took a few deep breaths. I couldn't collapse in a blubbering heap now. Rian needed me to stay strong for him. I could fall apart later. Fall apart when…

'How are you doing?' Tarragon asked, sitting on the other side of Rian.

'You w-won't stay still, you keep moving,' Rian said, his voice quavering as he spoke. 'Like you're on a ship a-and I'm not.'

'Some would say you've been at the Pine Wine again.'

'I hate that s-stuff. I don't drink.'

'You remember the first time you drank it by accident, courtesy of your sister?' Tarragon asked.

'Couldn't s-see straight for a week,' Rian said, a smile playing at the corner of his lips, but not quite filling them. 'R-rather like now. Angelica told me it was currant cordial.'

'Except it wasn't. She gave you a whole glass full.'

'I didn't realise.'

'No reason why you should, seeing as she drank the same amount you did. I think she and Chervil had a bet to see which one of them could trick you into drinking it.'

I shook my head. 'At least my siblings didn't spend their time trying to trick me into things.'

'Toying with Rian was all they had to amuse themselves, until he got wise to them. Well, until we *all* got wise to them,' Tarragon said, shaking his head. 'It took us a while, but once we had, they never managed it again.'

'I wanted to believe them,' Rian said. 'They were my brother and sister.'

Tarragon grunted. 'In blood only. Not in any other way.'

'Isn't that the truth,' Rian muttered.

'I always thought Angelica was falsely implicated in these things,' Sage said from where he sat on a sack of feed by the barn wall, tugging at his earring. His face was etched with fear and hopelessness, rather like the look behind Tarragon's eyes. They both knew it was only a matter of time before they lost their cousin.

'Unfortunately not,' Tarragon said.

'I know that now.'

Rian let out a little half laugh. 'I learnt my lesson with the wine, though. I-I've never touched a drop since, and I never will again. I absolutely hate all a-alcohol. Saliivia, too.'

'Here, drink this, Rian,' Anise said, coming over with a cup full of dark green liquid.

'Not wine?' Rian asked as I helped prop him up into a seated position.

'No, medicine.'

'What's it t-taste of?' Rian asked, squinting at it suspiciously.

'Medicine. Now drink it up, all of it,' Anise said, helping Rian take hold of it and guiding it to his mouth with one hand, the other betraying his anxiety as he held his Amulet.

'It's f-foul,' Rian spluttered. 'What is it, week-old dish water?'

'I wouldn't know, I've never tasted week-old dish water. Now finish it. All.'

Rian made a face, but did as instructed, then lay back down.

'Good,' Anise said. 'That'll help you relax.'

Rian sighed. 'I should never have eaten those d-damn berries.'

'You didn't know. How could you?' I said brokenly, stroking his hair.

'You d-did.'

'I saw the bead first, and only then realised what they were,' I said, bowing my head, wishing I'd seen it sooner.

'Bead?' Tarragon looked at me.

'A carnelian bead.'

'Carnelian, the assassin?' Tarragon asked, his eyes wide. 'Bugger me.'

'He doesn't give up, does he?' Rian said, wincing.

'I thought his commission to kill you had been stopped or I'd have been more careful,' I said. 'I'm so sorry, I let my guard down and I shouldn't have.'

'This isn't your f-fault,' he said, reaching up and gently touching my cheek. 'You can't be responsible for everything.'

Watch me. I took his hand. 'If I'd known—'

'Rian could still have eaten the berries even if you had,' Anise said. 'You can't control everything we do, Phire.'

He was right. I couldn't. But it didn't make me feel any better.

'I'll go and check outside, make sure he's not still around,' Sage said, getting up. Staying here watching his cousin die wasn't something Sage looked comfortable with. In fact, from the expression on his face, he found the whole thing very hard to handle.

'He'll be long gone,' I said.

'Still, doesn't hurt to make sure,' Sage said, flinching as he glanced at Rian.

'I'll come, too. Maybe I can do something with the lavender,' Anise said. 'I might be able to improvise something to help.'

Tarragon looked at me, his eyes full of pain. Who knew what he saw in my amethyst eyes as Sage and Anise reached the door, but it was deeper than even he was feeling. Rian suddenly uttered a cry of pain so heart-wrenching I gasped involuntarily as he doubled up, clutching at his stomach, gritting his teeth. My chest tightened at his torment.

'Anise! Get back here,' Tarragon yelled.

Anise came running back, Sage right behind him, and crouched beside Rian as the prince writhed in agony, his breaths coming fast as he groaned with the pain. I still held one of his hands, now so uncharacteristically cold and clammy.

'Is that the drink you gave him?' Tarragon asked. 'What was in it?'

'No,' Anise said. 'It's the poison progressing.'

'But you said "days", not hours or minutes.'

I glanced at Anise, who shook his head. What the hell was going on? And why, by the Stars, was it so quick?

'This is all happening too fast,' Anise muttered. 'I don't understand it. This is all progressing too rapidly. It shouldn't be like this.'

Rian cried out again as his stomach cramped and his muscles tensed all over, his grip on my hand becoming painful, but I didn't let go. I sat there for what felt like hours, holding his hand, enduring the cramping pains with him. By the time Willow returned with a basket of food, Rian's face had a greyish cast to it, his cheeks hollow. Cold sweat plastered his hair to his face and neck, and his eyes darted about, oblivious to all he saw.

Willow almost dropped the basket when she saw him. 'How? What...' She put the basket down, her eyes wide with horror, her hands going to her mouth.

Tarragon moved over to her and slid an arm around her shoulders. 'It's all right,' he said. 'He's still with us.'

'B-but so... I mean, he's...'

I looked at Rian's dear face. The stomach cramps had mercifully stopped, but his heart pounded as if he were on some impossibly long sprint. How his body could take much more, I didn't know. He had already endured so much suffering. His life hung by a thread, and at the moment, I couldn't be sure if he was conscious or not.

'There's food, not that anyone will want any,' Willow said in a quiet voice. 'What can we do, Anise?'

Anise shook his head. 'Nothing. I've done all I can. There's nothing else we can do. I'm sorry, Phire.'

My head ached with fear and frustration. My heart twisted inside me. I wanted to run – I couldn't bear to see Rian like this – but I wouldn't desert him, not when he needed me most. We were all helpless in the face of Carnelian's trap. I muttered all kinds of oaths silently in my head as I cursed the Coterie and started imagining all sorts of ways to kill Carnelian. Slowly.

For a while Rian lay quiet. He drifted in and out of consciousness, fitfully sleeping, if you could call it that. The others nibbled at Jasmine's food, but I had no stomach for it. I sat holding Rian's hand, stroking his hair, my heart slowly shattering as my head pounded. I whispered to him, spoke of my love for him, how he'd changed my life, saved me. How much he heard, if any, I couldn't be sure, but I continued all the same in the dim hope that perhaps he could hear some of it, or, if not the words, the reassuring sound of my voice at the very least.

By late afternoon, Rian's skin had started turning blue. His haggard face spoke of the pain he endured, but his grip on my hand remained firm, as if I somehow anchored him to the world. The little diamonds on my ring of Thyme sparkled in the light as I held his hand. My wedding ring. Rian's ring.

His eyes snapped open. 'Father? Why are you doing this to me? Don't you love me? Is it because I remind you of Mother?' His face contorted, and although he looked at me, I knew he was seeing nothing of me or the barn.

I glanced at Anise, who shook his head sorrowfully.

'I'm here, Rian, it's all right,' I said, stroking his hair. 'I'm with you.'

'You've always hated me,' Rian said, his eyes far away. 'Angelica and Chervil have always hated me, too.'

I swallowed. 'You're here with me, Rian, you're safe from them. Please, my love, fight it, fight it if you can.'

'I won't let you kill her, Chervil! I love Samphire. Leave her alone!' Rian's free hand came flying at me before I had time to duck. His fist connected with my cheek, and I fell backwards.

Tarragon and Anise ran over to us, grabbing Rian's flailing arms, trying to calm him down. I rolled into a sitting position, nursing my face.

'Are you all right?' Willow asked, racing over with Sage. She looked at my cheek. 'You're going to have a big bruise.'

It felt like it. My cheek throbbed harder than my head hurt.

'Doesn't matter,' I said, turning back to Rian. He'd stopped struggling and lay peacefully again.

'It won't be long now,' Anise said quietly, looking sadly at the prince, his eyes glistening.

Willow made a strange little sobbing sound as Tarragon took a sharp breath.

'Are you sure?' Tarragon asked, his face grim and grief-stricken.

Anise nodded.

'Maybe... maybe we should leave Phire with Rian for a little bit, give them some time alone,' Sage said, his head bowed.

Anise nodded. 'We'll be just outside if you want us, Phire,' he said, leading the others out.

Tarragon glanced back before shutting the door behind them.

I sat beside Rian, taking hold of his hand again. I leant forward and kissed his lips. They were like ice. Never before had I felt him this cold. He was always warm, if not hot. Always. I moved back, swallowing hard, a wave of fear spreading over me. I was losing him. I sat holding his hand for a while, stroking his maroon hair, hoping in some way I gave him comfort.

'Please don't leave me,' I murmured. 'Not now we're together. Fight this, Rian, fight it so we can be together, like I fought the Curse. I want to be with you. I need you, Valerian. I love you.'

Suddenly his face contorted. He gasped in agony. His eyes snapped open. Spasms wracked his whole body as the poison filled his veins. His muscles tensed and released, tensed and released. He cried out. His cry spoke of such torment I wondered if Jasmine had been right. I should ease his passing.

CHAPTER FIVE

'Anise!' I yelled.

Rian's torture continued.

Should I do something? Should I…

My gaze shifted to my War Fan dangling at my hip. I could slit his throat so he'd be dead in seconds. I'd been taught exactly how to do it. How to kill quickly and efficiently. I could relieve his pain. Release him from his living hell. But could I really kill him? Kill the man I loved with the Fan my beloved brother had given me?

Rian's body spasmed again and he cried out, his grip on my hand drawing blood where his nails cut into my skin.

But I still couldn't do it. Despite his torment, I couldn't do it. I didn't have the courage to free him.

He relaxed.

'Ph-Phire? Are you still there?' Rian's voice came out thin and raspy.

'Yes, yes, I'm here,' I said, moving his hair from his face, a tear escaping my eye. I shifted position, resting his head in my lap, and held him in my arms – while I still could.

'Don't g-go.'

'Never.'

'Everything's so d-dark. Everything hurts.'

'I know, my love,' I said. I bent forwards and gave his icy lips a kiss. He didn't respond. Had he even known I'd kissed him?

'I w-want your amethyst,' he said, blindly searching for the Talisman with his free hand.

'It's here,' I said, drawing it from his tunic. I had this strange feeling it was alive as I touched it, and I placed it in his hand, mine clasped around his.

He sighed, his breathing laboured.

As I held his hand around the Talisman, his skin began to warm. More than warm. His hand became hot. Suddenly his whole body raged with a fever higher and hotter than anything I'd ever encountered before. Sweat beaded on his forehead as his temperature rose and rose. This wasn't right. It shouldn't be like this. I didn't recognise this as a symptom of the poisoning at all.

'Anise!' I called again. But he didn't come.

Rian's body became impossibly hot to the point where I could barely touch his skin, but I doggedly held onto him, refusing to let go even as his skin began to burn mine.

His body stiffened. He gasped. Then his whole body shuddered.

'Rian?' Fear spiralled in me.

He gasped again. Moaned as if in such torturous pain he could take no more. My eyes filled with tears. I should have done what Jasmine had said. Shown mercy. Not forced him to endure this – this torment, suffering. This misery.

He went limp in my arms.

'Rian? Rian!' No response. I shivered. I leant to kiss his lips, but they were so impossibly hot they burnt mine, and I swiftly drew back. Had he gone? Slipped away? A sharp ache filled my chest, splitting my soul in two.

Carnelian would die.

Beryl would die.

Juniper would die.

Anyone who got in my way would die. Then I'd climb to the top of the highest tower in the Crimson Castle and throw myself off. I had nothing without Rian. Even thoughts of Mal couldn't quell my anger and my utter despair.

I squeezed my eyes shut, trying unsuccessfully to keep the tears in, and Rian's lifeless body out, as if I could somehow change the course of events, bring him back. But I couldn't. My body shook, my heart lurched in my chest, and the headache thundered in my skull.

Don't die, come back to me. The thoughts swirled chaotically in my mind as I held onto his limp form. *I'm sorry I failed you. I vowed to be your shield, but I've let you down. I'm so sorry. Don't go. Stay with me.*

A sudden, brilliant white flash made me start. I opened my eyes. Had I imagined it? With the stress of Rian's passing I was seeing things – or maybe madness was taking hold of me. A wave of exhaustion washed into me and my body shook.

'Samphire?'

I gasped. Startled, I let go of Rian's hand. I looked down at him. His face, although etched with fatigue, had a rosy colour to it now. His eyes sparkled like amber diamonds as he gazed back at me, for a moment not quite focussing, then clearing.

'I'm here with you,' I said, my voice strained as I kissed his hot, salty forehead, a tear slowly running down my cheek. 'I'm right here.'

He let go of the Talisman and reached up towards my face, his hand still hot to the touch from the strange, brief fever. 'You saved me.'

'No, I didn't, I—are you feeling all right?' I asked, stunned. One minute I thought him dead, the next he was talking to me quite coherently.

'I've never felt so tired, and everything aches, but I'm still alive,' he said, struggling to sit up.

'You need to rest,' I said, trying to stop him.

'I can rest sitting up,' he insisted.

'I—I thought I'd lost you,' I said, the tears coming now. Drained both physically and emotionally by what had happened, I fought to remain calm, my hands trembling slightly. 'I thought—'

He wiped the tears away, pulling me towards him. 'I'm fine,' he said, hugging me. 'Anise must have got it wrong.'

Anise had got pretty much everything right, other than the speed at which the poison had taken hold – and the fever, and Rian's apparent recovery.

'Do you remember any of it?' I asked.

'Not really,' he said, his forehead furrowed. 'Not much after the room spinning and lying down. Maybe the odd bit, like you remember a dream.'

I nodded. Probably for the best. 'I can't believe Carnelian was able to track us,' I said, shaking my head. 'From now on, I'll kill anyone who tries to lay a finger on you.'

He smiled. 'Don't go down the path you've avoided for so long, even for me.'

'I'd do anything for you,' I said, looking at him, staring into his amber eyes, into his soul.

'I know, and that's what scares me,' he said, a little furrow appearing on his forehead again. 'Don't be Lady Merciless, please, even for me. Be my Samphire.'

I lowered my head and nodded. Best not to mention the murderous thoughts I'd had when he lay writhing on the floor such a short time ago. 'I'll be your Samphire, just don't expect me to stand back and let someone hurt you if I can stop them, though.'

'Of course not.' He smiled. 'Kiss me,' he said, leaning towards me. His lips were warm but not as hot as they had been, and I wondered what, by the Stars, had just happened.

The barn door opened slowly.

'Phire is he—has he...' Tarragon's voice trailed off as he stood frozen to the spot, looking at us in shock. He had a knack for interrupting us.

'He's fine, thank you for asking,' Rian said, his voice strong and unwavering once more, back to the voice that could melt glaciers.

Anise pushed past a wide-eyed Tarragon. 'But how?' he asked, running over. 'I mean, you should be dead.'

'I thought he was,' I murmured with a sniff.

Rian looked at me, a cloud passing behind his eyes. 'I'm fine,' he said, squeezing my hand to reinforce his point.

'Ow!' A sudden pain shot through my hand. He'd pressed on the bloody wounds from his nails.

He inspected my hand as the others rushed in. He looked up at my face, only now noticing the bruise coming out on my cheek. Frowning, he reached out and turned my head so he could get a better look.

'What happened to you? You look like you've been in a fight,' he said, gingerly moving a curl from my bruise. 'Who was it? Was it Carnelian?'

'She was in a fight with you,' Tarragon said, his eyes still wide in disbelief, his voice trembling slightly.

'What?' Rian looked sharply at him.

'You've been thrashing about a bit,' Tarragon said.

'It wasn't deliberate,' I said. 'It's fine. I'm fine.'

'I'm sorry,' Rian said, his face mortified.

'Forget it.'

'Anise might have something for the bruising.'

'I think we're more interested in you, at the moment, than me,' I said.

Anise looked Rian over, then turned to me. 'What happened?'

'He had these spasms, then a sudden fever, then he woke up,' I said.

Anise's tongue slipped out between his lips as he thought, a little frown furrowing his forehead. 'I suggest you get comfortable and get some sleep, Rian,' he said finally.

'You need it, if the dark bags under your eyes are anything to go by,' Sage said, trying to pull a smile despite the confusion registering on his face.

'Thanks,' Rian said, giving Sage a long look. 'But what I'd really like is something to eat and drink.'

'Well, just a little,' Anise said, nodding. 'I'll heat some of the stew Jasmine sent us. You've been through a lot today; you could probably do with a little something.'

'Haven't we all,' Tarragon murmured as Willow stepped towards him, ducking under his arm and wrapping her arms around his waist.

'How are you going to heat it?' Sage asked.

'Jasmine said there was a little fire pit out the back. The workers use it in the winter when they're out this way,' Willow said.

Anise and Sage went and heated the stew, while I made Rian more comfortable, and Willow and Tarragon found some water for him.

Once Sage and Anise returned, we all ate some stew, then settled down to sleep, an early night upmost in our minds after the stressful day.

'Should we set a watch?' Tarragon asked.

I shook my head. 'Carnelian will be long gone. It's standard Coterie procedure. Kill your mark and go, or leave your poison and let it do its work,' I said, trying to suppress a shudder. 'He won't think he needs to stay, and anyway, he'll know we're looking out for him now, so he won't dare try anything again so soon. He's probably halfway back to Iolite by now.'

'I might need a little help getting up there,' Rian said, looking up at the platform.

'You're staying right where you are,' I said. 'I don't want you falling off the ladder on your way up.'

'But—'

'I'll stay down here with you, don't worry,' I said as a little satisfied smile crept across Rian's tired face. I brought our bedding down and lay next to Rian, watching him as he went to sleep, my hand resting on his torso sensing his now-regular heartbeat. The Talisman lay on his chest, almost seeming to glow in the dim light. I lay next to him, exhausted, but not daring to go to sleep, terrified that if I did, when I woke up this would all be a wonderful, mad dream, and his limp body really would be lifeless beside me.

I listened as everyone drifted off to sleep, then kept watch over Rian as the night drew on, slowly but surely heading once more towards day. My hand never left his chest. The rise and fall of his ribcage as he slept gave me comfort, his steady breathing a relief after the previous day. When the others finally climbed down from the platform the next morning, Rian still lay sound asleep. Sage went out the back of the barn with Willow to cook some breakfast.

'I'll stay with him for a bit,' Tarragon offered. 'You go out and stretch your legs.'

I nodded and left the barn, aware of Anise following in my wake.

'Did you sleep at all?' he asked.

I shook my head as we walked. 'No, I didn't dare.'

'Then you should try to a little later,' he said. 'You won't do him any good if you're ill, too.'

'I don't understand what happened, why he survived,' I said, rubbing my forehead.

'Exactly what happened after we left?'

'He started having these horrific spasms over his whole body, writhing in pain, then all of a sudden he had this raging fever. He was burning hotter than I've ever known anyone to, even Mal when he had Morbilli Rash, and that was a fearsome fever.'

'Morbilli's quite often fatal. Your brother was lucky.'

'I spent days mopping his brow, keeping him cool until the fever broke.'

'But Rian?'

I stopped walking. 'He burnt like fire for a few minutes – he was so hot I could barely touch him – then he went limp. I thought he'd—' I hesitated at the memory— 'gone, but then he suddenly started talking to me as if nothing was wrong. You never mentioned anything about a fever, and I don't remember it from my training.'

Anise cocked his head, frowning. 'And he recovered after this brief, extreme fever?'

I nodded.

'Curious. It's almost as if... no, that's daft,' Anise said, smoothing his hair over his shoulder, his face creased.

'What's daft?' I asked.

'Well, I have heard of a few who survived the berries, but that was long ago. No one has survived them in recent times.'

'And do we know why they survived?'

Anise shifted uncomfortably. 'Well, there were rumours. Hearsay.'

'Rumours?'

'Hey, you two, come and eat – I've cooked the eggs and bacon Jasmine left yesterday,' Sage said, coming around the corner of the barn with Willow. They each carried three plates of steaming-hot food.

'Should we wake Rian?' I asked Anise as we walked back.

'He probably needs food as much as sleep, so I think we should,' Anise said, nodding. 'He can go back to sleep after. We won't be moving on for several days. He'll have to convalesce for a while.'

We went back into the barn and I gently woke Rian. Once he'd properly woken up, he devoured the plate of food, as well as half of mine. I took it to be a good sign. After a minor protest, we managed to encourage him to go back to sleep, Anise taking a turn to watch over him.

'You need some rest,' Anise said to me. 'Go and have a nap.'
I nodded.
Jasmine peered into the barn.
'Soon,' I said, standing up and going over to her.
'How is he?' she asked.
'He's going to be fine.'
Jasmine frowned at me and took my hand, leading me outside into the sunlight. 'He should be dead, Amethyst. No one ever survives Flosian Mandragora Berries. This isn't right, unless…'
'Anise said a few did,' I said.
Jasmine looked uncomfortable. 'And did he tell you when and why they recovered?'
I shook my head. 'We never got that far.'
She shivered.
'Tell me, then,' I said, anxious to know.
'The few that recovered – it was hundreds of years ago,' she said, gazing out over the gently shifting fields of lavender that looked like a giant purple sea, waves moving slowly across it. 'They were all High Bloods, and they all had Magic running through their veins.'

CHAPTER SIX

'What?' I asked, a chill creeping through my bones.

'They were all Fire Angle Spinners. They literally burnt the poison from their blood – the only way to be free of the poison and survive it.'

'But that's a myth, there's no such thing as Mag—' I stopped short. I sounded like Sage, and I knew it wasn't true; Deorwine and Glædwine were evidence of Magic. I swallowed. 'Tell me more.'

Jasmine sighed. 'Hundreds of years ago, High Bloods practised Magic as Elemental Angle Spinners.'

I nodded.

'The Blood Decree wasn't introduced to control the people and to keep each rank pure for the nobility and the common people in their place, as King Yarrow said, but to keep the Magical Bloodlines pure, to stop Magic from being diluted and wiped out. The Blood Rules were there because those in charge feared the loss of their Elemental Magic.'

'Are you saying High Bloods still have Magic? That Rian has Fire Magic?' I looked at Jasmine, my eyes wide, my mind spiralling at the notion. Could it be true?

'It's the only way I can see he survived the poison. There's no other explanation. Although, even in the past, the ones that survived only ate a single berry, not several, so I can't fully explain his recovery, even if he has Fire Magic.'

Rian, a Fire Angle Spinner? Could Jasmine be right?

I shook my head. 'It seems so unlikely that Elemental Angle Spinners still exist.'

'Oh, I don't know,' Jasmine said. 'Makes perfect sense to me, especially after what's happened. Listen, you must stay for the next few days. Rian will need time to recover from the effects of the berries. I'll keep the food coming to you, and I'll make sure you have enough supplies when you leave, too.'

'Thank you, Jasmine. You've been wonderful.'

She shrugged. 'Anything for my little cousin.'

'Can I ask – do you know anything about Mal? Have you heard anything about where he might be imprisoned?'

She shook her head. 'I'd heard he wasn't dead, unlike the first reports, but I don't know where he is.' She scratched her nose. 'It's possible our cousin, Erica, may know. She still lives in the capital, in the palace compound. She's a minor royal, but she has connections with various information networks across the Five Lands. I suggest you go and see her, but for the Flowers' sake, be careful with your Aerban friends. Give them Iolitian names while they're in Flos. The way things are at the moment, if they're caught in the capital, they'll be executed – and you, too, for being with them.'

'Thank you,' I said nodding. She headed back to the house and I went into the barn.

I walked over to Anise and Rian.

'I'll stay with him,' I said. Anise nodded and got up. I lay down next to Rian, curling up in the hay beside him.

A warm arm slipped across my waist. Rian pulled me to him, until I rested against him. He made a contented little sound, his body relaxing. I couldn't help the little smile that broke out across my face. I wasn't sure if he was awake or doing it in his sleep, but whichever it was, I loved him for it.

After a couple of days' rest, Rian was getting a little fractious. The bags under his eyes had gone, but despite his protestations, it remained obvious he still didn't have his stamina back and needed to convalesce a little longer. Personally, I welcomed the forced rest. The chance to recover a little from the recent traumas. Rian didn't. He insisted on getting exercise, so Tarragon and Willow took him for a short walk in the lavender fields around the barn. I would have gone, too, but the lavender irritated my nose if I got too close. I didn't want to spend the rest of the day sneezing, my eyes streaming with tears, so I stayed behind and sat outside the barn with Anise.

'Why didn't you mention Magic burning off the poison when Rian was ill?' I asked him as I gazed out over the lavender fields. Rian paused in his walk and turned towards me, giving me a wave. I waved back.

Anise frowned. 'Because I didn't know for sure if the old tales were true, and even if they were, I didn't know if Rian had any Magic – if it was still in the Royal Line. And he'd eaten several berries, too, which only made his poisoning worse. But it seems the tales were true after all.'

'What did he say when you told him?'

'I didn't.'

I turned to Anise. 'Why not?'

Anise shrugged. 'He's got enough to worry about at the moment without that, too. I didn't think he needed the extra burden at present.'

'What do you mean?' I asked.

'Recovery was known in the distant past, but even then it was incredibly rare, and only in cases where a single berry had been eaten, and only amongst the most powerful High Blood Spinners.' He paused. 'Phire, you ought to know, those that did survive, there was always a side effect,' he said, looking uncomfortable.

'Side effect? He looks all right to me,' I said, gazing at Rian who appeared even more robust today than he had yesterday.

'All the men who ever recovered couldn't... when they first got better, they weren't able to... they...'

'What is it, Anise?'

He coughed delicately. 'There's no easy way of saying this, Phire. He won't be able to, you know...'

'Know what?'

Anise sighed. 'Be intimate with you,' he said, his face as red as the Mandragora Berries.

Hell's teeth. He might as well have kicked me in the stomach.

'At least for a while. It's only temporary, but I don't know how long for – it was said that for some men it was only a year or so, others decades.'

'Oh.' I spent a moment taking in his words. I swallowed. 'So he knows?' I asked, looking out across the flowers.

Anise nodded. 'I felt it only right to tell him. I mean, the effects of the poison will eventually leave his system – but it could take many years. I just don't know how long it'll be.'

I nodded. 'Thank you for telling me.'

'I thought you should know.'

'How did he take it when you told him?' I asked, my eyes tearing.

'Quite stoically, actually. Far better than I'd feared, but I'm not sure it's fully sunk in yet. It might take him a while.'

My heart sank, his words a stone weight. The thought of not being properly intimate with Rian for many years filled me with sorrow; but if it filled me with sorrow, how did it make him feel? It didn't change my feelings for him one bit; if anything, it made him more precious.

'You can tell him about the Fire Magic when he's had a chance to recover properly,' Anise said. 'One thing at a time, eh?'

I looked out over the lavender. Rian, Tarragon, and Willow were making their way back. 'Yes, one thing at a time,' I said, recomposing myself.

'I'll go and help Sage with the meal,' Anise said, getting up and walking around the back of the barn.

'Nice walk?' I asked as the wanderers returned.

'Lovely,' Willow said, slipping her hand into Tarragon's. Tarragon looked at their joined hands and frowned, but didn't let go of her.

'You having a nice chat with Anise?' Tarragon asked.

I glanced at Rian. He frowned, his face strained, then looked out over the fields rubbing the back of his neck.

'Just talking about the healing properties of lavender,' I lied. 'He and Sage are preparing the meal at the fire pit.'

'We'd better go and check on them – I don't want Sage burning anything again,' Tarragon said.

'Bobbins,' Willow said. 'He didn't burn anything last time. It was just well cooked.' She shook her head as she followed Tarragon around the back of the barn.

Rian looked at me, took my hand, and led me into the barn. 'We need to talk,' he said, ushering me up to the platform where we'd taken up sleeping again. We sat on the hay beds in silence for a moment, Rian catching his breath after the climb. 'Anise – he's told you? About me? About what I can't do?'

I nodded, my heart lurching as I saw the pain and distress in his eyes.

'I'll let you go, renounce our marriage, not that it was a proper legal one anyway,' he said, his voice wavering slightly.

'Oh, no, you don't,' I said. 'You're not getting out of our marriage now, not because of this. It's proper to me. We pledged ourselves to each other, made vows, and we meant it.'

'I know, but that was then, and things have changed significantly now.'

'Don't you dare try being all honourable and noble with me, Valerian. I love you.' My voice had an edge of steel to it. Having got him, I had no intention of letting him escape me now on a technicality. 'Besides, it's only temporary.'

'But it could be decades before I can be a proper husband to you,' he said, rubbing the back of his neck and looking away. 'By the Herbs, until then, we can't—'

I put my finger to his lips. 'Hush, it doesn't matter.'

'Of course it matters,' he said defensively, taking my hand.

'What I mean is there are plenty of other ways to, you know—' I raised an eyebrow suggestively— 'in the meantime.'

'Have you been talking to Tarragon?' he asked.

'Not yet, no. Give me time and I will. It may not be decades, it might just be a year or two.'

'I'd hoped to have a family with you one day in the future.'

Blood rushed to my face. 'And in the future we still will, we'll just have to be patient.'

A rosy blush appeared high on his cheekbones. 'Maybe we should've taken our chances in the hammocks after all.'

I couldn't help but laugh. 'Really? That would probably have ended in disaster for both of us.'

He looked up, a wan smile on his face. 'But—'

'No buts. I'm sticking with you, whatever life, or the Coterie, throws at us, Valerian, so you should just get used to it.'

He nodded, smiling. 'I don't deserve you,' he said.

'True,' I said, pulling him towards me and kissing him soundly.

'I love you, and I'll love you even more if you stop calling me Valerian.'

'And I will once you stop this daft talk.'

He smiled. 'All right.'

'Now, you need to take a rest after your walk.'

'I'm fed up with resting,' he said with a pout. 'I'll go mad if this carries on much longer.'

'Tough. You need to be strong again when we travel on, and you got out of breath just climbing up here.'

He winced. 'I thought you hadn't noticed.'

'Well, I did. So do as you're told.'

'Yes, Samphire.' He grinned, kissing me on the nose with his hot lips. 'Whatever you say.'

'Did I ever tell you you're impossible?'

He shrugged. 'Can't remember. I've been ill.'

'Hmm.'

One afternoon I sat outside the barn in the sun while Rian slept. The others were walking in the fields close by. I got out my father's book on Elemental Angle Spinners and Artefacts. Since it had dried out from the various soakings it had experienced, I'd been able to prise a few more pages apart. I started to read.

"Each Artefact has an Element associated with it, which can increase the power of an Angle Spinner with that Element without tiring them. For example, Rose Quartz is a Water Artefact and will enhance a Water Spinner's power, Aquamarine an Air Artefact that will increase an Air Spinner's power, Jade an Earth Artefact, and Amethyst a Fire Artefact. These increased powers enable great feats of endurance and strength

without causing fatigue in the Spinner. Without Artefacts, a Spinner can tire quickly if they use their power for great deeds or for an extended length of time, but eventually that Artefact's ability to enhance the Spinner's Elemental power will wane until it becomes just a gemstone."

I closed the book, my heart racing. Amethyst, a Fire Artefact that enhanced a Fire Spinner's power? Could that be another reason that Rian had had the strength to recover from Carnelian's attempt on his life? Rian had clutched my Amethyst Talisman in his hand when he'd had that fever – had he survived because of its additional power? I didn't know, but it certainly posed a few answers to the many questions.

Rian had pretty much regained his full strength when we got ready to leave a couple of days later. He still tired sooner than normal, but he was a world away from the first few days after his poisoning. I, on the other hand, was exhausted – I wasn't sleeping well, mainly because I always had half an eye open at night in case Rian got ill again, but also, when I did sleep, I now had nightmares. Nightmares of Rian. He'd be lying in the straw, writhing in agony, crying out in such pain I'd wake with palpitations, my body covered in sweat. Thankfully, Rian didn't wake and notice.

Jasmine and Hyacinth came to see us off as we gathered our packs and horses together.

'Take care, Amethyst,' she said. 'Things are even worse with Aerba now than when you arrived, so make sure you all appear as Iolitian as possible.'

'We will.'

'And remember, out on the plains, *"Keep your fire burning like day—"*

'"*—to keep the Dire Wolves at bay*", yes, I know.' I nodded.

'Thank you for everything,' Rian said. 'Especially the supplies.'

'You're welcome. Just look after her.' Jasmine nodded at me.

'She looks after me, but I'll do my best,' Rian said with a grin.

'Stay away from the west, if you can – there are droughts and crop failures towards the west coast,' Hyacinth said.

'I thought it was the east coast that was affected,' Anise said, his forehead furrowed.

Hyacinth shook his head. 'That's in Aerba and Trew. Here, it's the west coast.'

'We'll head straight for Muscari and Erica, so we should be fine,' I said, giving them both a hug before mounting my horse.

'It's ironic, really, because western Mere has apparently been hit by heavy rains,' Jasmine said.

'But it's all desert up there,' Tarragon said, adjusting his horse's reins.

'All the same, be careful,' Hyacinth said.

'We will.' I smiled, and we rode away through the fields of sheep and colourful flowers.

'I really like your cousin, Amethyst,' Tarragon said, glancing sideways at me.

'Call me that again and I'll put my War Fan to use.'

'And she's very good with it,' Sage said. 'I've seen her – more than once.'

Tarragon swallowed. 'Sorry, Phire.'

'Jasmine can get away with it, but no one else can,' I said, keen to put the assassin, Amethyst, into a box and out of my life forever. I glanced at Rian, whose raised eyebrow made me rethink. 'Except for you, in certain circumstances.'

Rian grinned smugly.

I shook my head. *Men.*

'What was that about Dire Wolves?' Willow asked. 'I thought they were myth, not real.'

'There are rumours about Dire Wolves roaming the grasslands between Scilla and Muscari City,' I said. 'Sometimes people with animals are attacked by wild beasts, but it's rare and probably only ordinary wolves, not anything mythical.'

'How big are Dire Wolves?'

'About the size of a small horse, apparently, but I've never seen one. I've always kept my campfire burning all night, just as Jasmine said.'

We joined the main road north to Flos' capital city, Muscari, passing vast fields of jewel-bright flowers with heady scents, small distillery huts, as well as fields of crops, and sheep and cows, nodding to the merchants and other travellers as we went. Willow coughed a little, but Anise had already plied her with an asthma remedy. Luckily there were few soldiers, and those we did see were travelling at speed, southwards.

'Doesn't look good, does it?' Tarragon said after a group of blue tunic-clad soldiers rode past us at a gallop.

Rian shook his head. 'No, it doesn't, and I fear for the common people of Aerba. If I was in charge...'

'If you were in charge this would never have happened,' Sage said, a sour note to his voice as he gazed at the dust cloud the mounted men had left in their wake.

Rian sighed. 'Well, I'm not.'

'Of course, having a Flosian by your side would have helped, too,' Tarragon smirked.

I raised an eyebrow. 'Is that how you think of me now? Flosian?'

He shrugged. 'Don't know, really. You're a bit Iolitian, bit Flosian – even a bit Aerban, I suppose.'

'She's Samphire, and it doesn't matter where she's from,' Anise said, smiling at me. 'We love her just the way she is.'

'Yes, we do,' Rian said, giving me a little look that warmed my heart.

I peered back at him through my lashes. I had to pinch myself from time to time, a little bit of me convinced this was all some sort of dream and I'd wake to find him dead in my arms. But I didn't.

In many ways, I was still coming to terms with my new friends. Back at Iolite's Crimson Castle, I hadn't had many friends, only Mal, and – I thought – my sister, Beryl (I'd been very wrong there), and Onyx. Other than that, no one, even though I was the Master of Iolite's daughter. At times it had been lonely. Very lonely. I certainly hadn't experienced the kind of love, acceptance, and friendship I had now. Friendship I'd move mountains to keep. I'd move whole islands for Rian.

After a long day in the saddle, we stopped at a village inn at the edge of a woodland, taking three rooms. No sooner had we stopped than the clouds opened and a rainstorm descended on the village. Thank the Stars we'd made it here before the rain had started or we would've been soaked.

As we dropped our packs in our room I glanced at Rian. His face looked pale and drawn – maybe we should have made him rest another day or two, but it had been hard enough to convince him to rest for as long as we had. We ate our evening meal, and I left the others drinking while I took Rian up to our room.

'I'm fine,' he said, closing the door behind us. 'We can spend a little more time downstairs.'

'No, we can't, and it's not as if you're going to drink goblets of Flosian wine like the others, anyway,' I said firmly. 'And neither am I, for that matter. You need your rest after today. Now, get into bed.'

'Is that an offer?' He raised an eyebrow and grinned, before he remembered. His shoulders sagged and my heart tore.

'Come here,' I said, stepping over to him and giving him a hug. 'You're just tired. It's been a long day and you're still getting over your illness.'

He buried his face in my hair, and as I held him, I suddenly realised his whole body was shaking.

CHAPTER SEVEN

'Rian?' I pulled back, my heart skipping a beat, taking his face in my hands, brushing his maroon hair from his wet eyes. 'What is it?'

'I'm sorry.' He tried to turn away, his eyes full of tears, one stray one escaping and falling down his cheek. 'I'm just feeling sorry for myself.'

'Don't,' I said, kissing the salty tear away. 'Don't ever be sorry. A few days ago, I thought I was going to lose you forever, but by some miracle you're still here with me. I wouldn't change anything.'

He looked at me, his amber eyes swimming in tears. 'Really?'

'Really. I want you. Nothing else matters.' I kissed another salty tear away, then took hold of his shaking hands.

'I thought, at one point – no, more than one point – I thought I was going to die.'

'You said you didn't remember anything much.'

'I lied.' He looked at the floor and then back at me. 'I remember most of it, the stomach cramps, the dizziness, the hallucinations, and the pain – and those last spasms when I thought that was it, I was about to die and I'd never see you again. Darkness beckoned, and all I wanted was to hold your Talisman you gave me, hold your hand, and know you were there with me at the end.'

A tear rolled down my own cheek. 'I wasn't going to leave you, not when you needed me most.'

A little smile crept across his lips. 'Then there was this heat, this fire inside me, and I knew I would live,' he said, his tired face frowning slightly. 'You kissed me. You saved me.'

'As much as I'd like to claim responsibility for saving you with a kiss, I don't think I did.'

'But your kisses gave me hope, gave me love.'

'You remember the others? I didn't think you would.'

'I'd remember you kissing me if I was dead.' A little lopsided grin appeared on his face.

I sighed. 'I don't think that's possible,' I said, then paused. 'You know, at the end, for a moment, I did think you were dead.'

He smiled at me. 'Your faith pulled me through.'

I swallowed. It almost hadn't, and the guilt of what I'd almost done hit me.

'What is it?' he asked, frowning.

'N-nothing.'

'Tell me.'

'Jasmine said you'd get so bad that it might—' I hesitated. 'It might be better to ease your passing.'

Rian raised an eyebrow.

'A-and I almost did,' I said, studying the floor.

He slipped his hand under my chin and raised my face towards him. 'Out of love.'

I nodded, the tears flowing again at the memory. 'I couldn't bear to see you suffering such pain, such torment.'

He pulled me to him and held me close, his warm, strong arms around me. 'I come from good stock, Phire. I'm strong. I handled it.'

'Just.' *Because of your Magic and the Artefact.*

'Like I said, your faith in me, in you, pulled us both through. And we'll be stronger for it.'

I nodded. 'You don't blame me? For having those thoughts?'

He shook his head. 'In your place, I'd have thought the same things if I'd seen you in that sort of pain.' He staggered slightly.

'Come on, you need to rest,' I said, unbuckling his twin swords from his back.

'Perhaps you're right.'

We took our outer clothes off, leaving our undergarments on – I didn't trust the bed linen enough to take everything off – and got into bed. We lay in each other's arms, holding each other tight to reassure ourselves we weren't dreaming the other into existence.

'I'm sorry. I vowed to defend you, be your shield, but I failed,' I said, tears stinging my eyes.

'What? You helped heal me,' Rian said, propping himself up on one shoulder and turning my face towards him.

'But I should've realised Carnelian would still come after us, not let us go.'

'How? You had no more idea this was going to happen than any of the rest of us. This isn't your fault, don't you dare start thinking it was.'

'I...'

'You *are* my shield. You defend me every day and I love you for it – as I try to protect you.'

'I know,' I murmured. But I'd so nearly failed.

'Now, let's both get to sleep,' he said, lying down.

I held on to his warm arms, clasping them tight, my head on his chest listening to his strong, steady heartbeat. He drifted off quickly. I, on the other hand, slept little. When I drifted off, my dreams showed Rian lying on a bed of straw, his face twisted in pain as spasms wracked his body. On one occasion, I awoke with hot tears in my eyes. I glanced at him in the shaft of moonlight creeping into our room from the window and hugged him tighter, reassuring myself of his presence. He shifted slightly but remained sound asleep. I'd so nearly lost him, and I now cherished him more than ever. I'd never take him for granted again.

For the next couple of days, we rode on as woodland gradually gave way to grassland. With no more inns until much nearer Muscari, we had to camp. As it got warmer, we reduced our pace for the horses' sake. Riding on the next day, we passed a small group of wagons, the men whipping the horses on at speed.

'What's wrong with them?' Tarragon asked.

'Maybe they heard you were coming,' Sage said, straight-faced.

Tarragon glowered at his cousin.

'Something's not right,' I said, watching them rumble away across the plains.

We urged our horses on. The sun was high above us. I wiped the perspiration from my brow. My horse snorted as it flicked its ears, trying to waft away an errant fly. Out over the plains, birds dived towards insects singing in the lush grasses, catching them like Mal caught colds, before swooping away. The thought of my brother brought me up short. Every day we searched, he languished longer in a prison somewhere, and if it was anything like the prison at the Aerban palace, it wouldn't be pleasant. I feared for him like I'd never feared for him before, even when he'd been sent out on difficult missions.

Rian glanced at me, a little frown forming on his face as if he'd read my mind. I gave him a little smile.

Another group of wagons came towards us, goats tied behind, moving quickly along the dusty road. As they drew level, Tarragon called out to them.

'Hello, friend, what news?'

'Go back,' said a large, bald-headed man driving one of the wagons. Sweat dripped down his plump face, and he dabbed at it with a yellowed handkerchief.

'What's the problem?' Rian asked.

'Dire Wolves out on the plains. They're taking our livestock and horses at night. We even heard they took two men last week. Turn around now, if you value your lives. There are no settlements for another two days. You're riding into hell,' he said, urging his tired-looking horses on.

I looked at Rian. He chewed his lip, eyes troubled.

'We've come this far; we need to keep going,' he said finally.

I nodded in agreement. We had no choice if we wanted to get to Muscari as soon as possible.

'Are you sure?' Sage asked, watching the wagons disappear in a cloud of dust.

'The alternative is heading back south to Scilla,' I said, 'then going up the coast road, or trying to get passage on a ship north to Alyssum, and then ride west to Muscari, all while pretending to be Iolitian. Not to mention it'll add up to three weeks to our journey time.'

'Three weeks we don't have,' Rian said. 'We'll keep going. Muscari is only three days away.'

'We just need to keep the campfire burning at night.'

'We can set a watch,' Tarragon said. 'Take it in turns to keep the fire well alight.'

Willow and Anise nodded; Sage didn't look so sure.

We camped in the open centre of a small thicket with enough brush to burn until morning. Despite Rian's protests, I made him rest and not take a watch. He wasn't happy, and let me know it, at length, but I remained unmoved. We endured a brief shower overnight, the thicket giving enough protection to keep the fire going. But the next day, we set off under clear blue skies, the insects and birds out again in force. Not to mention flies, which quickly became irritating.

'What are those birds doing?' Willow asked. 'They seem to be flying around in circles. Are they ill or lost?'

A little chill swept through me as I watched them, and a little fear. They circled around in the sky, their wings spread, keen eyes looking at something below them. Their sharp cries rushed across the swaying grasses.

'It's not far ahead. We can take a look,' Tarragon said.

'We may not want to,' I murmured, staring at the sky.

As we drew closer, I squinted at the birds, now more than small black shapes. Their wingspan must have been over five feet across, and their tails long and fanned. Golden feathers adorned the top of their wings, white underneath, and their legs a dark brown. They made a sound like mewling cats as they soared above us, circling what could only be carrion – and something large at that. I recognised them as Golden Flos Buzzards, and they didn't waste their time on small dead mammals. I shuddered.

'There's something over there,' Willow said, pointing a hundred yards off the road.

'Are you sure you want to take a look?' I asked, flinching at the prospect of what we might find.

'Might as well,' Tarragon said.

'You know those birds are Buzzards?'

'So?'

'There's going to be something big and dead over in that direction.'

'Let's take a look,' Rian said, urging his horse off the road and in the direction Willow had pointed.

I shook my head. As an assassin, I'd seen plenty of people in various states of death, whether stabbed, garrotted, poisoned, and with various amounts of blood and entrails, but if this was Dire Wolf work, then all of that may be nothing compared to what lay up ahead. I took a deep breath, wiped my sweaty palms on my britches, and reluctantly followed the others, my mouth drying out like the Mere deserts.

Sage's horse reared, and he barely stayed on. Anise and Willow's horses refused to move. Rian swore. In amongst the long grasses lay two horses, and the remains of a human. Man or woman? I couldn't tell because the body was so mangled and torn. Blood and guts from both human and beast intermingled on the ground, flesh torn from the bone, partially devoured.

'Bugger me,' Tarragon said, grimacing.

'I tried to warn you – Dire Wolves,' I said, swallowing hard as Willow slipped off her horse and vomited into a clump of long grass.

'Let's keep going,' Rian said, his face pale. 'We need to find somewhere with enough kindling and wood for the fire tonight.'

I scanned the countryside. That wouldn't be easy. Although the grasslands stood interspersed with little copses of trees, they were few and far between, and this part of the plains we were crossing had one solitary tree off to the west. Riding at night, though, would only attract attention. We had to find somewhere to stop.

'Come on,' I said as Willow remounted her horse. I led the way back to the road, and we cantered on across the grasslands, the day drawing perilously close to evening before we found a small copse of trees for our camp. We rode into the centre and dismounted.

'We need to get a fire going now,' I said. 'And a good-sized one at that.'

Tarragon tended to the horses as the rest of us collected as much dead wood as we could find, and Anise set about lighting the fire using his tinder box. In minutes we had a roaring campfire going. Sage cooked the meal and we all ate, although after witnessing what we had earlier in the day, not with quite as much enthusiasm as usual.

'I'll take a watch tonight,' Rian said as we ate. 'You're going to need my help, too.'

'You're not strong enough yet. You need your sleep,' I said.

Anise nodded.

'Rubbish, I'm absolutely fine now,' Rian said, a little scowl passing across his face. 'I'll take my turn like everyone else.'

I sighed. 'All right, have it your own way.'

The sun kissed the horizon as I got up from the fire to have a quick check over the plains before we settled down to sleep. The dead bodies had thrown everyone, and my assassin training made me more aware of our surroundings than ever. And of possible danger.

'See anything?' Rian asked, coming to stand beside me, looking out over the flat landscape.

'Not at the moment,' I said, staring out at the grass.

'Are you always on the lookout for danger?'

'Most of the time, except for when I missed those berries. I let my guard down then, and I can't afford to do it again'

'You can't spot every danger.'

'I can try, though.'

'You worry too much.'

'I know.'

A little voice at the edge of my mind clamoured to be heard. I held it at bay, wondering if I should heed it. I gave in.

'You're a Fire Angle Spinner – you know that, don't you?' I asked, still looking out at the grasslands that turned inky blue in shadow as the last remnants of light faded from the golden sky. The moon had risen, and little brilliant white stars began to twinkle in the velvet night sky.

Rian stood silent for a moment before letting out a long breath. 'I was beginning to wonder.'

'Jasmine and Anise both said it was the only possible way you could've survived the poison.'

'There was no other way?' he asked, looking at me. 'No other way at all to survive it?'

I shook my head. 'No.'

He ran his fingers through his hair, distracting me for a moment as my heart lurched against my ribcage and my blood surged molten in my veins.

'But why hasn't it shown itself before?' he asked, his forehead furrowed. 'I mean, I don't understand why it's here, now, so suddenly.'

'Maybe it's been there all along and you haven't noticed it – it's not as though you were looking for it,' I said, that same niggling voice shouting at me from the corners of my mind. *It'd always been there.* 'Do you remember in Fennel, when I had the children, and we were about to jump between the buildings?' Rian nodded. 'Just before we jumped, the flames died down so we could cross. I think that was you.'

'What?'

'Tell me, do you remember what you were thinking?'

'Only that the flames were too big, and you and the children would be burnt if you tried to cross as it was. I suppose I was wishing they'd die down a bit.' His eyes widened. 'And they did.' He chewed his lip. 'You know, when Chervil tricked me into taking that Saliivia, I was really ill. I had a brief high fever then, too.'

'Anise said the high dose you had could kill – perhaps you unwittingly burnt it from your blood, like you did the poison.'

He nodded slowly. 'I guess that could explain why I survived.'

'Then there's the fact you're hot.'

He turned and grinned impishly at me. 'Why, thank you.'

I flushed. 'No, not like that. Well, actually, you are, but that's not the point.' He continued to grin at me, amused by my flustered state. 'Would you stop that? I'm trying to be serious. What I mean is your skin, your lips, your mouth – you're always warm, or hot, never cold. Even after being shipwrecked, when I was freezing cold, you were warm.'

He frowned. 'Now you mention it, you're right. I rarely ever feel cold.'

'And after almost drowning in the sea at Iolite, when we were escaping the Coterie,' I said, remembering the feel of his skin under my hands when I'd touched his bare chest. 'You should've been cold like me, but you weren't. Your Magic Angle has been there some time, you just never knew, and from looking at Father's book, I think my Talisman enhances your power when you hold it and use your Magic. It's a Fire Artefact.'

'It is?'

'Apparently Amethyst enhances a Fire Spinner's power, so that could be another reason you beat the poison. You were holding it at the time.'

He nodded slowly. 'I asked for it, didn't I?'

'You remember?'

'Yes. Perhaps on some level, I knew. Somehow instinctively realised the Talisman would help me.'

'Maybe.'

'You know, it's odd, but sometimes it almost feels as if it's alive when I hold it. There are times I could swear I can see it glowing gently, too.'

'Hmm. I've noticed that recently as well. I never saw or felt it before you touched it. Perhaps your power has something to do with it. And, if you're a Spinner, it's likely Tarragon, Sage, and Anise all are, too.'

'And you?' he asked, looking at me.

I shook my head. 'I'm Middle Blood, like Willow.'

'But you're not – we know that now. You should be a High Blood. Perhaps you have a Magic Angle, too.'

'Well, if I do, I haven't a clue what it is.'

'Maybe we should keep an eye out in case the others do have Magic,' he said, rubbing his head thoughtfully. 'Just in case.'

'Not a bad idea,' I said with a nod.

He turned towards me. 'But for now, I want to attend to something else.'

'What?' I frowned at his determined, yet loving, voice.

'Kiss me. You haven't kissed me properly since we left Jasmine's and I'm feeling neglected.'

I rolled my eyes skyward. 'Neglected?' I asked, a smile forming on my lips.

'All right, not really, but I still want a kiss,' he said, his voice hoarse with anticipation. 'So kiss me, please.'

'I suppose you did ask nicely,' I said, leaning towards him, tilting my head a little and closing my eyes. Our lips met as he slipped a hand around my shoulders and pulled me closer, the other resting on my waist. I relished the sweet smell of sandalwood as it engulfed me, and I ran my fingers slowly into his hair as we banged noses. I opened my eyes; he was looking at me.

He moved back a fraction. 'You're almost as keen as me,' he murmured, his mouth a hair's breadth from mine, his eyes golden pools in the moonlight.

'Keener,' I whispered back, capturing his mouth with mine and kissing him again with enthusiasm, tasting his hot mouth with my tongue. His forehead furrowed for a moment, and this time he closed his eyes.

A bloodcurdling sound ripped through my nightmares. My eyes snapped open. Darkness closed in around me; the moon was covered by clouds. I glanced at the campfire. Nothing but embers. I turned to Rian – he'd fallen asleep beside me sometime during his watch. I'd told him he wasn't strong enough yet. If only he'd listened.

'Up! Everyone up!' I yelled, scrambling out of my blankets, Deorwine immediately in my hand.

Rian sat up. 'Oh, no! I'm sorry, I must have fallen asleep.'

'Don't worry about that now, just get your swords ready. Can someone get that fire going again?'

'My tinder box is in my bag,' Anise said, fumbling around in the dark. 'I'll never find it in the pitch black.'

'You'd better try,' Sage said as another howl tore at the air, closer this time.

'Where are they?' Willow asked from behind me.

'I'm not sure,' Tarragon said, his voice strained.

'Dammit, I can't find my swords,' Rian said, groping around in the darkness. 'This'll have to do.'

A guttural snarl to my left had the hairs standing up on the back of my neck, my heart pounding and my mouth dry as the desert. I held Deorwine in my cold, clammy hand, facing the great beast. The clouds drifted away from the moon. In front of me stood a waking nightmare. The size of a small horse, the Dire Wolf stood staring at me with its threatening golden eyes, a growl coming from low in its throat as its huge fangs dripped with saliva and rotten flesh. I swallowed. The wolf rivalled the mynogres in size and ferocity. As another four wolves appeared from out of the trees behind it, my heart fell.

'What do we do?' Willow asked shrilly.

'Kill them,' I said.

'We don't stand a chance – they'll have us on the ground, tearing our throats out in no time,' Sage said, his voice ice.

'Then you can try running, but I don't recommend it.'

The lead wolf howled, an ear-splitting sound that flew through our little camp, making me want to press my hands to my ears.

Instead, I readied Deorwine, wondering where I'd put Glædwine – obviously not far enough away for it to come to me, but not close enough to find in the darkness.

The wolf pounced toward me.

'No!' Rian yelled.

He lunged in front of me, a flaming branch in his hand.

CHAPTER EIGHT

Rian beat the yelping wolf back, the blazing orange-red flames swirling around the end of the branch, flickering brightly. 'Stay back!'

I'd wondered what he'd picked up in the dark instead of his swords.

The other wolves looked less sure now as Rian waved the flaming branch at them, forcing them to stop in their tracks. Snarling, they made little scurries towards him. The branch flamed brighter, driving them back. The Dire Wolves' nerves broke, and they disappeared at a run into the trees and out across the plains.

Rian stood in front of me, his body heaving as he breathed, exhaustion singing from his tense muscles. I stepped over to him and gently placed a hand on his shoulder.

'No question now, eh?' I asked.

He turned towards me, his eyes full of relief and a little fear. 'No. I don't think so.'

'What happened?' Tarragon asked, his eyes wild. 'How did you set light to that without Anise's tinder box?'

Rian looked towards him. 'I'm a Fire Angle Spinner.'

'Really?' Sage asked, eyes wide.

Anise smiled and nodded.

'You knew?' Sage asked his boyfriend.

'I had a sneaking suspicion he might be,' Anise said, looking a little smug.

'If you can light fires, get ours going again,' Tarragon said, sweat glistening on his brow in the light of Rian's torch.

Rian nodded and set the branch into the glowing embers of the fire as we gathered more wood and placed it with the branch. In minutes we had a raging campfire blazing away once more.

'If we keep that going now they won't bother us again tonight,' I said, throwing another branch on for good measure.

Rian sat down, looking mortified. 'I almost got us killed because I went to sleep. You were right, Phire, I'm still not back to full strength yet. I should have listened.'

'You and your Magic saved us,' I said, slipping my arms around his shoulders. 'I think you can be excused, but from now on, you pay a bit more attention to me and rest when I tell you to.'

He nodded, and yawned. 'Sorry, everyone.'

'Bobbins, forget that,' Willow said, looking excited. 'I want to hear about your Fire Magic. When did you know? How did it first happen? Tell us everything.'

'There's not much to tell, really,' Rian said. 'I didn't know I had any Fire Magic until after I'd been poisoned.'

Tarragon frowned. 'What do you mean?'

'The Fire Magic burnt away the poison in his blood,' Anise said. 'If it hadn't, well...' He waved his hands expansively and I shuddered.

'I wouldn't be here,' Rian said, his face grim. 'Anise and Jasmine first suggested that's what happened to Phire. She was the one that mentioned it to me, but I think, deep down, I already knew.'

'So you knew?' Tarragon asked, looking at Anise.

Anise shrugged. 'I guessed. A few things weren't adding up when he was ill – or, rather, they were.'

'So how did you do it?' Willow asked, stifling a little cough. 'How did you clear the poison?'

Rian shrugged. 'I really don't know.'

'Probably a natural self-defence reaction,' Anise said. 'Your body did it automatically, you didn't need to consciously do a thing.'

'I'm glad it did.'

'And that's the only other time you've used it?' Sage asked. 'Other than just now?'

'I think I may have done other things before and not realised it. This was the first time I did it on purpose. I couldn't find my swords in the dark, only the branch, and I knew we needed fire, so I focused on it, kind of willed it to set light, and it did.'

'Amazing,' Tarragon said, grinning.

'But why you?' Sage asked. 'I mean, why doesn't anyone else have this Magic? I thought it had died out, other than Phire's weapons, of course.'

'And her Talisman,' Anise said.

'Maybe that helped you, too,' Willow said. 'You know, when you were ill.'

'It's a Fire Artefact,' I said. 'It's quite possible a combination of its power and Rian's Fire Magic saved him from the poison.'

Rian pulled my Amethyst Talisman out from his tunic. It sparkled in the firelight as it swung on the silver chain in its little swirling silver wirework cage, sending purple flashes across our campsite.

'You were holding it?' Tarragon asked. 'When you were sick?'

Rian nodded.

'Perhaps you subconsciously knew you needed it,' Anise said. 'Used its power to clear the poison.'

'Maybe,' Rian murmured, slipping the Talisman back under his tunic.

'Should we try and get some more rest?' Tarragon asked, a strange look flickering in his eyes.

Sage looked at the sky. 'Not sure it's worth it. It'll be light soon. Why don't we eat something and start at first light?'

Rian nodded. 'Good idea. Let's get as far away from here as we can.'

We did as Sage suggested and set off as the dawn sky grew silver then gold, then blue. Our little group chatted as we rode, except for Tarragon. He stayed at the back, a permanent frown on his face, which I couldn't decipher. What *was* bothering him? That evening, having finally left the grasslands behind, we passed fields of flowers, distilleries, and crops, reaching the first settlement we'd seen in days. We took rooms at a small inn, and headed for the taproom. Tarragon left out the back door.

'I'll catch you up,' I said to Rian, who wearily followed the others to order our evening meal.

Tarragon stood in the stable yard leaning against a wall, scratching his chin.

'What's the matter with you?' I asked, coming to stand beside him.

'Why would something be the matter?' he asked, scratching his chin again.

'You've been quiet all day and spent the whole time looking worried, or frowning, so I'd say something's bothering you.'

He glanced at me, his golden-brown eyes troubled. 'Phire, it's… well, it's that, y'know, if Rian has a Magic Angle then, well, maybe, as his cousin, do you think…?'

'That you have a Magic Angle, too?' I asked.

He nodded, forehead furrowed.

I nibbled on a fingernail for a moment before replying. 'Magic was supposed to run in the High Blood Line, so, if Rian has the ability, I imagine it's possible for you to have it, too,' I said. 'And Sage, and Anise.'

He sighed. 'That's what I've been thinking,' he said. 'During my time at the Iolite University, I studied history, as you know. Centuries ago, High Bloods did have Elemental Magic. The thought of it still being there, in our blood, is rather scary. I mean, what if I have a Magic Angle and use it by accident? Hurt someone?' His eyes clouded.

I patted his shoulder. 'I don't think it works quite like that. Every time Rian's used his it's been a conscious decision, even if he hasn't actually realised it at the time, and rather than hurt anyone, he's saved us. It's not happened spontaneously, without reason.'

'Hmm. It's all right for you and Willow, you don't have to worry.'

'As Rian reminded me, I'm actually a High Blood, too.'

'Of course, sorry.'

'Doesn't matter. I can't say I've ever noticed anything, so maybe I don't have an Angle.'

He stretched his neck, releasing his tense muscles. 'I guess we'll see, and so will Sage and Anise.'

I nodded. 'Just keep an eye out for anything odd.'

He grinned at me. 'Maybe I'm an Air Angle Spinner – that would be really useful next time we go to sea. I could get us where we're going at top speed and Willow would love me more than ever because she'd have less time to be seasick.'

'She loves you at the moment,' I said, giving him a grin and elbowing him gently. 'I don't think you need to be an Air Spinner to improve her opinion of you.'

'She does, doesn't she? And I love her, too. I just wish it could be official.' He sighed.

'We're not in Aerba now.'

'No, that's true,' he said, turning to look at me. 'What about you and Rian? Sorry about the storeroom on the ship, I didn't realise what you were up to. If I had, I'd never have interrupted you. So, have you had the chance since?' he asked, raising an eyebrow suggestively. 'Has he finally...?'

My heart lurched. Should I tell him? Should I tell him to speak to Rian? Neither idea seemed entirely appropriate. 'Mind your own business,' I said primly, flicking my hair over my shoulder.

He laughed. 'I'll find out all the details from him later,' he said, buffing his fingernails on his tunic.

'I'd rather you didn't,' I murmured. The last thing I wanted was Rian being upset by Tarragon's questioning, and Tarragon would needle him for all the gory details, of which there were none.

Tarragon frowned. 'Whyever not? We've always told each other everything. We're not going to stop now,' he said, grinning mischievously. 'I thought he might like a few tips – it would be in your best interests, as well as his.'

I chewed my nails again. 'Talk to Anise, then decide if you want to speak to Rian.'

'What?'

'Promise me.'

'All right, but I don't see why.'

'Just talk to Anise first, and if not for my sake, do it for Rian's, then you'll understand,' I said, before heading back into the inn, leaving Tarragon suitably confused.

That night Rian decided to settle down to sleep early, much to my surprise. I'd been expecting another fight, but instead I didn't have to try to persuade him at all.

'Are you feeling all right?' I asked, reaching out to touch his forehead. No fever – good.

'I'm tired,' he said as I removed my outer clothing and joined him in the bed, scrambling under the grey-looking covers.

'Is that all? Are you sure?'

He nodded. 'I just want to be with you, hold you, know I'm not alone. After the poison, at the darkest moment, I was scared of being alone, of being without you.'

'But I was there, I was never going to leave you.'

'I know, but I feared it more than anything, more than dying. And now, I can't get those images out of my head, and if I do manage to, and I want to show you how much you mean to me, how much I need you, want you, I can't.'

I reached out and stroked his hair. 'You don't need to show me anything, I know you love me.'

'I – I'm finding it hard to come to terms with what's happened to me.'

'It's going to take time, my love. You aren't going to get over this in a few days. But you've got me, and if there's anything I can do to help you, all you have to do is ask.'

'I know,' he said, his eyes misty. 'I just want you to let me hold you. That's why I wanted an early night. To be alone with you.'

I slipped my arms around him as he pulled me close. 'Then hold me, and I'll hold you, too.' I snuggled into him as sandalwood caressed us. Thank the Stars I'd told Tarragon not to speak to Rian. It would be rubbing salt in a new wound, and in the long run it would only upset them both. 'You're showing me right now, *and* when you protected me from the Dire Wolves, just like you vowed to. You don't need to do anything more,' I said.

I had to pretend that it didn't bother me, but a part of me grieved for our loss, even if it was temporary. I lay content and secure in his arms, but I also knew having him with me meant more than anything. If he'd died at the farm, if Carnelian had succeeded, after killing the assassin, Beryl, and Juniper, I'd have had nothing left to live for. Overall, the poison's side effect was a small price to pay for Rian's life.

'Yes, but—'

'Stop right there. We'll get through this together. Hold me, try to get to sleep. You need your strength.'

'Hmm,' he murmured, resting his head against mine as he slowly dozed off.

I slept fitfully. My dreams were full of poison and Rian writhing in agony. I kept waking, hot and sticky, my hair plastered to my forehead, my heart racing. Each time I held him tighter, seeking reassurance. This wasn't the first night to unfold like this, and I knew it wouldn't be the last.

The next day, the city of Muscari rose out of the multi-coloured, perfumed, flower-filled fields that covered the countryside here. We were all relieved to be off the grassland plains and away from the Dire Wolves. Willow's cough returned once we were amongst the flowers, and Anise handed her one of his remedies to help her. Eventually we reached the city, and rode up to the gates, the great cream limestone walls putting those of Scilla to shame. They towered above us as we joined the queue into the city, where the embroidered silver rose flags of Flos fluttered high above us on their emerald green backgrounds from every available flagpole.

'Jasmine suggested giving you Iolitian names while we were in Flos, to be on the safe side,' I said. 'We don't want them carting you off to the prison because you're Aerban.'

Rian nodded. 'Might be an idea.'

'So, what names are you going to give us?' asked Willow. 'You're the expert in Iolitian names.'

'Any suggestions?'

I'd thought about this earlier. 'Willow can be Sapphire.'

She grinned at me. 'I like that.'

'Tarragon can be Tourmaline,' I said as he nodded. 'Sage, what about Spinel?'

'Sounds good,' Sage said.

'Me?' asked Anise.

'Agate?' I suggested.

He nodded.

'And me?' Rian asked.

I frowned, pondering a name beginning with R, but couldn't come up with anything suitable. What about V?

'How about Viridine?' I asked.

He grinned. 'I quite like that. What is it?'

'It's a green mineral.'

Rian nodded.

'Now, don't forget them,' I said.

'You think we'll get in?' Tarragon asked softly.

'I hope so,' Rian said.

'Hey, you, stop!' A city guard, spear in hand, held his hand up in front of Sage and Anise, stopping them dead. 'Who are you? You look Aerban.'

'Excuse me, sir,' I said, yanking my horse towards the guard. 'We're all together; we're from Iolite.'

The guard's eyes narrowed. 'Can you prove it?'

I swallowed. I'd hoped to never have to show this again. I pulled Rian's leather wrist strap down and away from the tattoo on my wrist. The black Coterie tattoo of the flaming circle and letter "I" identifying me as an Iolitian assassin sat proudly on my pale skin, daring the guard to make a wrong move.

The guard took a step back. 'You have business here?' he asked hesitantly.

I shook my head. 'Just passing through,' I said. 'We don't want any trouble, only a bed for the night and we'll be on our way. Our business is north of the city.'

'Then be sure you leave tomorrow,' he said, waving us all into the city, a look of distaste on his face.

I nodded. 'Thank you, sir.' We rode up the busy street.

'That was close,' Rian said from beside me.

'Too close,' I said, my heart thudding after the encounter.

'They usually let assassins into cities like that?' Sage asked, frowning.

'If they know what's good for them, or we may decide to do a free killing. Them.'

Rian glanced at me. 'It happens often?'

'More often than you might think. If challenged, it can actually help us gain entry because people are scared of us, but generally we try to keep a low profile. Unless forced, of course.'

'You ever had any trouble?' Sage asked.

I shook my head. 'But I always made sure I was with a crowd of people so I couldn't be singled out.'

'Wise,' Anise murmured.

'I said that tattoo might come in useful.' Tarragon grinned at me.

Perhaps it had, but I still resented it.

We followed the street towards the city square where a great market thronged with people. Whatever you wanted to buy could be found here: food, clothes, medicines, tools, flowers, and perfumes. The smell of food mingled with flower perfumes, the noise of the citizens filling the air. We paused at a couple of food stalls as we moved through the crowds to replenish our supplies before continuing on.

'Where exactly is your cousin, Erica?' Rian asked.

'She and her husband, Gladiolus, live inside the palace compound, over there,' I said pointing across the square.

'Well, before we meet them I'd like to visit the flower market area,' Anise said. 'They may have some useful blooms I can dry for my Herb Chest.'

We all dismounted, following Anise into the rows of flower market stalls all brimming with strongly-scented blooms of white, yellow, blue, and red. He and Sage left their horses with us as Willow and Rian looked at the flower stall nearest to us. Anise started inspecting all the different flowers; he was in his element.

The thought stopped me in my tracks. Was he, though? Was Earth his Element? With all his expertise with herbs and medicines, maybe it had been staring me in the face all this time. Did he know?

'Phire, I spoke to Anise,' Tarragon said quietly from beside me, scratching his chin. 'I mean Agate.'

'Oh,' I said, looking away from Anise. 'And?'

His expression deepened with sorrow. 'I'm so sorry. I had no idea, and I won't say anything to R—Viridine. Agate thinks it's best not to at the moment. He thinks he's still struggling with it all.'

I nodded. 'He's right, he is.'

'I'm even sorrier I interrupted the two of you now,' he said, bowing his head, his expression contrite. 'It might have been your only chance, and I ruined it for you both.'

'You didn't know this was going to happen any more than we did,' I said, resting a hand on his arm. 'If we'd known, we'd have done things differently, too.'

'Do you think, at some point, he may find talking about it helps? I want to do what I can for him.'

I chewed my lip for a moment. 'Maybe, in time, but for now I think it's still too raw. Give it a couple of weeks, then maybe you could try and speak to him if he doesn't come to you first – I know how you two share things. Wait a bit, see how he reacts then.'

Tarragon nodded as Rian and Willow returned.

Rian had a white rose in his hand. 'For you,' he said, holding it out to me, his cheeks pink.

I took it from him and sniffed it, delighting in its delicate fragrance. 'It's beautiful.'

'Like you.'

'Why don't you talk to me like that?' Willow asked Tarragon.

'I do, I just don't do it loudly in public,' Tarragon pouted.

'True.'

I gazed at the rose, then out over the market place as Anise and Sage came back. A figure walked, or rather limped, between the stalls, head down, cloak hood up but long black hair poking out from it. A figure I thought I recognised, but it couldn't be. He was dead, wasn't he? I squinted, trying to see more clearly. The man's muscles strained the seams of his ill-fitting clothes as his hood slipped. He quickly raised it again, the sun sparking off a golden ring, but not before I'd seen his features clearly, seen his piercing green eyes; eyes that made me shudder.

I gasped. For a split second I saw the hideously-scarred face of Sorrel, Sage's older brother.

CHAPTER NINE

How could Sorrel still be alive?

Sage's brother was good friends with Chervil, and had happily worked for the new King of Aerba. Sorrel had tried to kill me, amongst other things. Thankfully, he'd failed. I'd fought him off a couple of times, but Rian had finally seen to it that he left me alone. We'd last seen Sorrel struggling in the poisoned Viridi moat. We'd all assumed he'd died from the toxic effects of the acid-like water, or drowned, but we were obviously wrong. Very wrong. He was alive and wearing what looked like a Nightshade ring. Had Sorrel joined the infamous Aerban spy network since we'd last seen him?

I took a step back straight into Rian.

'Ow!' he said, grabbing my shoulders to stop me from knocking him over.

'Sorry,' I said, twisting around. 'I've just seen Sorrel.'

'What?' Sage blanched. 'You can't have.'

'Isn't he dead, though?' Tarragon asked, scanning the market place for his cousin.

Anise peered into the crowd. 'Not if – if someone healed him.'

'Even you couldn't have done that with herbs, and certainly not in a few short weeks,' Sage said with a frown.

'He could if Magic was involved,' I said, the thought making me squirm.

'Exactly.' Anise nodded. 'Earth Magic could enhance the medicine and produce rapid healing.'

'You think Chervil has an Earth Angle Spinner?' Tarragon asked, aghast. 'One making medicines and remedies?'

I shrugged.

'It's not impossible, Tarragon,' Anise said. 'We have a Fire Spinner with us; who's to say Chervil doesn't have an Earth Spinner?'

Rian smiled nervously at the mention of his Magic Angle. He had yet to come to terms with his new abilities.

'But why is he even in Muscari?' Willow asked. 'What could he possibly want here when Aerba is basically at war with Flos?'

'Probably stirring up trouble,' Sage said sourly. 'Like usual.'

'Possibly… Sage, did he used to wear a gold ring?' I asked.

'No, he never liked jewellery,' Sage said, his hand going

unconsciously to his earring. 'Used to make rude jibes at me for mine. Why do you ask?'

'Because he had one on,' I said. 'I think it was—'

'A Nightshade ring?' Rian cut in, a startled look in his eyes.

'Exactly.'

Sage shook his head in disgust. 'Finally sold his soul to the devil, then.'

'Wouldn't put it past him, y'know,' Tarragon said. 'He's probably here to cause trouble or to spy.'

'Or both.'

'Come on, let's get to the palace,' I said. 'We don't want him spotting us.'

I led the way through the market and out towards the palace. We passed the Temple of Flowers where people jostled, trying to get into the painted limestone building, the strong scent of flowers seeping out its door, making my nose tickle. I never went in if I could help it, because it made me sneeze and my eyes run. The great building's bright, almost gaudy colours broke up the monotony of the cream city as we continued our journey.

The walls around the palace compound were almost as high and thick as those around the city. We reached the palace gate, the guards looking smart in their pale blue uniforms, swords at their waists and spears in hand.

'Let me do the talking,' I said as we approached them.

Rian nodded and the others hung back slightly.

'What is your business here?' a burly-looking man asked in a particularly unfriendly voice, his spear at the ready.

I dismounted, indicating for the others to do the same. 'We're here to—'

'Lady Amethyst? Is that you?' came a voice from my right.

I shuddered internally at the use of my Iolitian name and turned to find a grey-haired man, his emerald green silk tunic shining in the sun, striding through the palace gardens towards the gate.

I bowed, gesturing for the others to do the same. 'Prince Monkshood, how wonderful to see you.'

The guards looked questioningly at Monkshood.

'I can vouch for Lady Amethyst, she's a cousin to Lord Gladiolus and Lady Erica,' Monkshood said. 'I've known her since she was small.'

The guards nodded and backed away.

'May I introduce my friends, Your Highness,' I said, gesturing to the others. 'Viridine.'

Rian bowed.

'Lady Sapphire,' I said, 'and Tourmaline.'

I noted Willow giving Tarragon a quick elbow; he'd forgotten his Iolitian name already.

'Agate and Spinel,' I finished as Anise and Sage also bowed.

Monkshood nodded. 'I'm pleased to meet you. Does Lady Erica know you're coming?'

I shook my head. 'I'm afraid it was all rather last minute. Hopefully it'll be a nice surprise.' I smiled.

'I'll take you to her,' he said. 'You! Lads, take the horses to the stables.' He gestured to three boys tending an adjacent flower bed.

We grabbed our packs and the boys took the horses away as we followed Monkshood. We made our way through the lush and verdant palace gardens surrounding the buildings. Jewel-coloured flowers bobbed their heads in the breeze as their scents wafted around us. Fountains gurgled between silver birches, poplars, and even Flosian Pear Trees with their fruit weighing down their boughs, waiting to ripen in the sun. Small gravel pathways cut between well-manicured lawns and towards low cream stone buildings as the main paved path led up towards the palace proper, its pale limestone carved with flowers, gold leaf highlights accentuating the reliefs.

'He knows about you?' Rian asked softly.

'Being an assassin?' I asked. 'By the Stars, no. If he did, he'd have me executed on the spot. I was sent to kill his son a couple of years ago, but Mal must have got there first. If he knew...' I shuddered.

'Do Jasmine and Erica know?'

'No, not even Jasmine and Erica.'

'More secrets,' Rian said.

'More lies.'

We crossed the gardens and entered an archway into a little courtyard area. Monkshood entered the building, returning quickly with a woman in her late thirties dressed in a pale green silk gown, embroidered with gold and silver thread flowers, that fell to her ankles.

'Amethyst?' she asked, her blue eyes wide, her blonde hair swaying as she moved her head.

'Erica,' I said, moving over to her and giving her a hug.

'Whatever are you doing in Muscari?' she asked, looking towards my friends.

'I'll leave you now,' Monkshood said, walking away.

'I need your help,' I said, waiting until Monkshood was out of earshot to speak. 'It's Mal.'

Erica's porcelain skin blanched. 'Come in.'

'You know something?'

'Come in,' she said, ushering me inside with the others. She took us through the entrance hall and into a large, opulent sitting room with soft, silken seats, and windows that looked out on the gardens, a little fountain giggling just outside. We left our packs by the door as a servant came in and put down a tray with empty glasses, water, Flosian wine and fruit cakes on a highly-polished mahogany table.

'Thank you, Tulip,' Erica said. 'I was about to have some afternoon refreshments with Gladiolus and a few of his men, but he just sent a message to say he's tied up with the King and they won't be joining me now. Looks like we can still make use of it, though.'

Tulip started to pour the wine into the glasses and pass it out. Rian respectfully declined, instead settling for the water, as did I. Erica gestured for everyone to sit down. I perched on a sofa next to Rian.

'These are my friends, Lady Sapphire, Viridine, Tourmaline, Agate, and Spinel,' I said as Tulip left the room. I slipped Deorwine and Glædwine from my back.

'Are they what I think they are?' Erica asked, still standing, her eyes narrowing. 'The Cursed Aerban Weapons?'

'They're not cursed anymore,' I said defensively.

'Leave them outside in the courtyard somewhere. I don't want them here in the house.'

'I can't. They come to me on their own if I move too far away.'

'I thought you said they weren't cursed now?'

'They're not, but they're still Magical. They spontaneously appear on my back if I go too far away from them. Although not cursed, we're still bound together, somehow.'

'It's rather disconcerting the first time you see them appear on her back from nowhere, Lady Erica,' Rian said. 'May I suggest she leaves them out in the corridor? You don't want an unnecessary fright.'

Erica looked at him.

'Viridine is my…' If I said "husband" Erica might just faint, but boyfriend didn't seem the right word either.

'Soulmate,' Rian finished, standing up and taking Erica's hand and kissing it.

'Soulmate? But I've never heard of you before,' Erica said as I put the weapons out in the corridor. 'Amethyst has mentioned a friend called Onyx.'

A little flicker of annoyance crossed Rian's face as he sat down again.

'That's because we've met since I last saw you – it has been two years,' I said.

'Four.'

I frowned as I sat down on the sofa. 'Has it really been that long?'

'Since Juniper last let you out to see us? Yes.'

'She didn't let me out this time.'

'No, you escaped, or so I've heard. I know what's been going on.'

I flinched. 'All of it?'

'All of it. And I know it wasn't your fault.'

'You're very well informed,' Rian said, raising an eyebrow.

'It's the only way around here. If I didn't keep up with things, they'd let me fester while the men did the work,' Erica said. 'So, I have my own network to keep me informed of things, Prince Valerian.'

Rian's eyes widened.

I gasped. 'You know that, too?'

'Don't look so surprised, Amethyst. I know who they all are, even in their Iolitian clothes and those ridiculous low ponytails. And I know you two are together.'

'And will you…'

'Don't be ridiculous,' Erica said, sitting down. 'We may be virtually at war with Aerba, but I know that's Finule and Chervil's doing, nothing to do with Prince Valerian.'

'I'm not a prince anymore,' Rian said stiffly.

'I heard that, too.'

'I am trying to track down what really happened to the Fire Opal, though. Do you know anything?' Rian asked.

'I know Amethyst didn't take it, but one of the Coterie did – when they killed Princess Angelica,' Erica said.

Mal took it? Surely not? Why would he do something like that?

'Are you sure?' I asked, stunned. Assassins weren't normally called upon to steal.

'Someone paid to have it stolen, but I don't know who. What I do know is it isn't in Flos or Mere.'

'Iolite?'

She shook her head.

'Then we go to Trew,' Rian said, looking at Tarragon, who nodded.

'And Mal, what do you know about him?' I asked. 'I was told Flos may know where he is.'

Erica sighed. 'I've heard whispers. Juniper somehow persuaded a less-than-reputable member of the Flosian Royal Family to assist in his abduction, and she's now imprisoned him.'

I frowned. Something about all this didn't sit right. Just how had Mal been able to kill Angelica and then get to Flos where he was abducted, in time for Flint to know, so he could then lie to me about Mal's death when I met him at Tansy? Surely there hadn't been time for all of that to happen?

'And drugged him,' Erica continued.

What?

'Drugged him?' Anise asked.

'To keep him tractable, so he won't cause her any trouble and try to escape, because let's face it, if he got half a chance he would. He's a good lad like that. He'd have made an excellent Master of Iolite. Anyway, she's apparently got something special planned for him, and probably you, too, Amethyst. You must stay on your guard.'

'But where is he? Is he in Flos? I have to find him,' I said as Rian's hand slipped into mine.

'No, he's not here, but your stepmother has great connections in Mere,' Erica said. 'They have numerous islands. I suggest you go to the capital, to Rill. Go to the East Quarter, to a man named Calder. He has contacts at the palace that I've found useful over the years, and he also spies for Flos. Speak to him.'

I nodded. So Mal was still alive, imprisoned somewhere with the help of Flos, and maybe Mere, too? I'd only been to Mere a couple of times. Juniper tended to send Onyx when we had a commission there because he fitted in perfectly, whereas my pale skin stood out against the burnt sienna skin of the Mereans, and my copper hair looked nothing like their black. Willow, with her Merean heritage and brown eyes, would fit right in, just like Onyx. The rest of us wouldn't.

A knock at Erica's apartment door broke the silence that had descended.

'Excuse me,' she said, getting up and leaving the room.

'We'll find him,' Rian said quietly. 'Don't worry.'

I nodded.

Erica returned, a smile on her face. 'Word has got around that you're here, Amethyst. You've been invited to dine with the King.'

I groaned inwardly. This had only happened once before. I'd always had a dim view of High Bloods, at least until Rian, his cousins, and Anise. Although my extended Flosian family included Erica, a High Blood, I'd only ever visited her with Jasmine (because she'd insisted) and had always avoided any others, where possible. Even when I'd visited with Jasmine, I did my best to keep a low profile. Prince Monkshood had known Erica and Gladiolus forever, so I'd got to know him on my visits with Mal, but I'd had nothing to do with the rest of the Royal Family. The one meal I'd had with King Narcissus happened only because Jasmine and Hyacinth were there, and then it took place under duress. Narcissus hadn't improved my views on High Bloods – totally out of touch with his people, pompous and arrogant.

'All of us?' I asked hopefully. I didn't want to do this alone.

She shook her head. 'No, and it's probably for the best – they may be recognised. Didn't King Narcissus visit Aerba a number of years ago?'

Rian nodded. 'When things were less fractious.'

'It's too dangerous for any of you to go, but you'll have to now you've been invited, Amethyst.'

Hell's teeth.

'But I've nothing to wear,' I said. Perhaps I could get out of it after all. It would be tedious and brain-numbing.

'I've got something you can borrow.' Erica smiled. 'You don't need to worry, we're a similar size.'

Oh, good. 'Thank you,' I mumbled.

Later that evening, I found myself being poured into a floor-length purple silk gown with laces at the back. Its low-cut neckline showed more than I'd like, the silver flower embroidery sparkling in the candles scattered around Erica's apartment. My hair, longer than the Flosian women's, had been piled high on my head, a look I found almost as uncomfortable as the dress. I couldn't wait to get the garment off and free my hair. And as for the painful, toe-pinching shoes…

Rian walked into our room as Erica's maid left. His eyes widened and his pupils dilated in the candlelight as his breath suddenly hitched.

'You—you look beautiful,' he said, coming over to me. He moved a curl from my face, his fingers lingering on my cheek as his other hand moved to rest on my waist.

'This dress is so tight I feel as if I might burst out of it at any moment,' I complained. 'I hate corsets like this.'

'Maybe you do, but you look stunning in it,' he said, leaning forward to kiss me. 'I rather wish you were staying here so I could look at you all evening.'

I smiled, unable to remain grumpy in the face of such adoration. 'So do I.'

'Amethyst, time to go,' Erica called from the corridor.

I sighed. 'I'd better go. But I'll be back as soon as I can,' I said, leaving the room. 'Rest while I'm gone.'

'Yes, Amethyst.' Rian grinned.

I made a face at him and left, joining Erica. As I reached the outer door to the apartments, she screamed. Deorwine and Glædwine's straps secured themselves around my chest.

'Can't you stay behind, just this once?' I asked them, but they stayed put. However, silver embroidery matching the pattern on my dress gradually appeared along the straps, making them quite ornate and beautiful. I raised an eyebrow in surprise. At least the purple crystal matched well with my dress. Maybe I could leave them outside the banqueting room somewhere.

'I now see what you mean,' Erica said, her voice quivering. 'Are you sure they're not cursed?'

'No, not cursed, merely persistent.'

We walked across the torch-lit gardens and into the palace. A little alcove stood near the door to the reception chamber, and I quickly removed the Weapons and hid them up in a corner, hoping I wouldn't move too far away from them during the evening.

'Will they stay there?' Erica asked dubiously.

'I hope so,' I said. 'I'll just have to stay up this end of the room.'

She nodded and led the way past two guards and into the chamber.

I'd obviously been invited to some previously-arranged banquet, rather than dinner, from the number of guests in the room. At least I wouldn't have to speak to the King personally, but other than Erica and Gladiolus, I knew no one, and every single person in the room was a High Blood. Although my previous dislike had been laid to rest, I still shuddered at the thought of having to indulge in polite conversation with them all.

'Amethyst, how lovely to see you,' Gladiolus said as I entered the palace chamber with Erica, taking my hand and kissing it. 'I'm sorry I wasn't able to welcome you sooner.'

'It's good to see you, Gladiolus,' I said. 'I hope you've been well?'

'Tolerable,' he said with a smile. 'If we'd known you were coming we'd have prepared for your visit.'

'It was a little last minute, I'm afraid.'

A servant came around, handing out glasses of Flosian wine. I took one, more to be sociable than because I had any intention of drinking it.

'Gladiolus, Poppy wants to speak with us,' Erica said. 'We'll be back in a minute, Amethyst.'

I nodded as they walked to the other side of the great chamber, preferring to linger near the door, lest the Weapons decide to make an entrance of their own. Only now did I take in the huge, ornate candelabra with its flaming candles, and the intricately woven tapestries of flowers covering the walls. A world away from the austere Crimson Castle that had once been my home.

I stood alone, wishing I had Rian beside me. With such a large number of guests, the room quickly became hot. I took my malachite War Fan in my spare hand and opened it, gently wafting cooler air in front of my face. The green stone contrasted rather nicely with my dress.

Vast, deep emerald drapes hung behind me where a doorway led out onto a balcony. I moved towards the opening where a cooling breeze swept in. Voices drifted towards me from outside, and I couldn't help but overhear.

'You're sure they're here? At the palace?'

I recognised Prince Monkshood's voice.

'I saw them myself. They're staying in your Lady Erica's apartments.'

A shiver worked its way down my spine. I knew that voice, too.

Sorrel.

CHAPTER TEN

'You took a risk coming here, being Aerban,' Monkshood said to Sorrell as I surreptitiously backed towards the balcony, doing my best to remain hidden by the drapes.

My heart thudded as I eavesdropped.

'It's part of our pact, isn't it?' Sorrel asked. 'Me coming to Muscari to keep you informed? I help you ingratiate yourself to King Narcissus and the Council, and then, when he's unfortunately killed, you step in and take control. We all get what we want.'

'And the Lands reunite? But with me in charge in Flos, like was promised when you first approached me?'

'Under Chervil's guidance, of course – that's what the Nightshade and Chervil have promised you, isn't it?'

'Yes, it is. They'll honour it, won't they?' Monkshood's voice had an element of concern in it.

'Don't worry. As long as you keep your end of the bargain, Prince Monkshood, they'll keep theirs.'

How could Chervil be doing this? Manipulating Flos into virtual surrender?

Sorrel coughed. 'Chervil doesn't want all-out war with Flos, even over something as precious as the Fire Opal. It's in nobody's best interests.'

'But we didn't take it, Sorrel. We don't know where it is.'

'*We* know that, Your Highness, but the people don't have to,' Sorrel sneered. 'Flos' capitulation will be all the more real for them thinking that, though. Chervil will have Aerba's honour restored and will rule both lands, reunited once more, with your assistance in Flos.'

The bastards. They'd deceive the people of Flos and Aerba without a second thought. I couldn't believe it.

'Very good. And you'll deal with…'

'We'll make sure the King dies at the appropriate moment, and in the appropriate manner.'

'Assassins?' Monkshood hissed as my heart froze.

'Just let the Nightshade deal with this. It's not for you to worry about, but be ready to move when the time comes, understand?'

'Yes. You're sure all these young people are Aerban? I don't want to cause tensions with Iolite – after all, Amethyst introduced them to me with Iolitian names, and Lady Amethyst is most definitely an Iolitian. I've known her since she was little.'

'She may have introduced them as Iolitian, but I've known the five of them all my life, Monkshood. Of course it's Valerian and the others.'

'Does Lady Erica know about them? Being Aerban?'

My heart skipped a beat.

'I don't think so. They were introduced to her with Iolitian names, too, or so her servant told me. I don't believe she knows anything about this at all. Amethyst has pulled the wool over her eyes, too – like she has yours.'

'What do you mean?'

'She's an assassin.'

I stifled a gasp. Almost stopped breathing.

'Amethyst?' Monkshood's voice hardened.

'One of the Iolitian Coterie's finest, the Lady Merciless.' Sorrel almost seemed to purr as he spoke.

I resisted the urge to go out and hit him.

'Then it will be good to take her, too,' Monkshood said, his voice like granite. 'The Coterie killed my son – some petty squabble with a young nobleman. I dealt with him, but the Coterie still needs to answer for their misdeeds.'

'Then arresting and executing Lady Merciless should satisfy your need for vengeance.'

'It will help.' The prince hesitated as I drew in a long breath. 'Erica knows about Amethyst and her involvement in the Coterie?'

'No, not that I've been able to find out. She's totally oblivious to her relative's dirty secret.'

I swallowed. Good.

'I'm glad. Erica has always been loyal to Flos, and I don't want her involved in any of this,' Monkshood said. 'I'll send the guards to arrest them all now.'

I stepped back, my mouth dry and my breathing shallow. How could this be happening here? A Flosian Prince in league with the Aerban King and the Nightshade? I really couldn't believe it.

'No,' Sorrel said. 'Wait twenty minutes until the banquet starts. That way, no one will hear anything – including Amethyst. Then she won't be able to stop them from being arrested.'

'You may be right,' Monkshood said. 'I'll go and arrange it now.' He paused. 'And Amethyst? Do I disclose her assassin background?'

'Do you need to? She's brought an Aerban Prince into your midst. What would you normally do to someone who did that in these circumstances?'

'Arrest her as a traitor, and execute her.'

'Then that'll be enough. The Coterie may come in useful later, whatever your opinion of them, so let's not drag them into this now. Arrest her as soon as the banquet's ended. Let her enjoy her last meal, though,' he said, a cruel laugh drifting into the chamber. 'Then she can join the others for a few last hours before you execute them all.'

I very nearly ran out to attack Sorrel, but restrained myself. It would help no one. I needed to get away and warn the others immediately. We had to leave. I backed into the drapes, holding my War Fan over my face as Monkshood entered the room, striding across it away from me. I glanced back to the balcony, but Sorrel had gone. My heart thudded in my chest, hitting my ribcage uncomfortably. I clenched my fist around the stem of my wine glass. We had to move, now. I quietly made my way towards the door, weaving my way through the other guests and leaving my wine glass on a side table as I went. I glanced back. On the far side of the room, Erica and Gladiolus were talking to someone.

'Are you all right, Miss?'

I turned to see a formally-dressed guard in a light blue uniform frowning at me from his position at the door.

'Yes, I just forgot my handkerchief. I'll be back in a moment,' I said, smiling as sweetly as I could, and then I left the palace.

I ran through the gardens, holding my skirts up so I didn't trip, the Weapons joining me, keeping to the shadows, desperate to get back to Rian and the others. I burst into the apartment, dashing into the sitting room. Anise and Sage sat lounging on the soft seats, drinking wine.

'What's the matter, Phire?' Anise asked, standing up, eyes wide.

'Sorrel's here; he's told Monkshood about us – they're coming to get us in a few minutes,' I said, managing to get the information out between gasps of air after my run.

'Where is he?' Sage asked, his teeth clenched. '*I'll* kill him this time.'

'Not now,' Anise said, resting his hand on his boyfriend's shoulder. 'We need to get away.'

Sage nodded reluctantly. 'I'll get the horses, meet you at the edge of the garden; you get our things,' he said to Anise.

Anise nodded.

I moved along the corridor to Willow and Tarragon's room. The noises coming from inside made me pause, reminding me of the inn in Borage so long ago. But I didn't have time for niceties. I did them the courtesy of knocking loudly. No reply. I turned the door handle. Idiots. They'd left it unlocked. I opened the door. Tarragon moaned. Thank the Stars they were both totally under the covers on their bed. As I stepped in, Tarragon's red face appeared from under the silk sheets.

'By the Herbs, Phire, do you mind? We're a little busy—'

'Get up. Sorrel's here; he's betrayed us. The guards are coming for us in a few minutes,' I said, cutting Tarragon short. 'Hurry!'

He nodded and I left the room, closing the door behind me. I took a deep breath. That could've been a whole lot worse. I rushed down to the room Rian and I were sharing. I opened the door.

Hesitated.

He lay sound asleep, his bare chest rising and falling as he slept on his back, lower half covered by the white silken sheets. For an insane moment all I could think of was how I wanted to stay here, drink him in, how I wanted to see *all* of him. I swallowed. There was no time for thoughts like that now. I ran over to him, keen to wake him as gently as possible. I kissed him.

A little smile spread across his face. 'Phire? You back already?' he asked sleepily.

'Wake up, Rian, we've got to go,' I said. 'Sorrel told Monkshood we're here.'

His eyes snapped open. 'What?' he asked, immediately alert, frowning at my slightly dishevelled appearance and flushed face.

'The prince is sending guards to arrest us in minutes.'

Rian sat up, scrambling free of the covers with only his undergarments on. 'I'll get dressed.'

We quickly gathered our things together.

'Are you changing?' he asked, glancing at me as he finished dressing.

'No time,' I said. 'We need to leave now.'

We moved out into the corridor with our packs as Tarragon and a bedraggled-looking Willow joined us.

'Sage has the horses,' Anise said from the door.

'Then let's go,' Rian said.

We ventured out into the dark gardens, night-blooming flowers filling the air with their sweet perfumes. The fountains continued to burble as we moved quickly through the shadows, across lawns, and towards Sage and the horses, keeping off the crunchy shingle paths where possible to reduce noise.

'There are guards patrolling over there,' Sage said in a low voice, indicating closer to the palace. 'We'll have to be careful.'

Rian nodded. 'Mount up,' he said as he climbed into his saddle.

'I'm going to need help,' I said, my gown hindering my efforts to mount my horse.

Rian started to dismount.

'It's all right, I'll help you,' Anise said, giving me a leg up into my saddle.

A ripping sound made me wince. If I ever got Erica her dress back, it would be with some mended seams. We rode for the palace gates, the two guards that stood looking outwards taking little notice of us as we left the compound.

'That was lucky,' Tarragon said, glancing back. 'They're more interested in keeping people out than in.'

'Getting out of the city's going to be harder,' I said. 'The City Gates are closed at night.'

'Then we'll have to persuade them,' Rian said, his hand going to the hilt of one of his swords.

I nodded, although a quieter approach may be preferable; we'd have to see. We rode through the streets towards the closest gate, the East Gate, passing inns where patrons sang and laughed raucously. The smell of beer, wine, and food permeated the air outside them. Dodging a couple of inebriated men who were busy dancing with each other, we reached the street to the gate. We stayed in the shadows until we could see what lay ahead.

'There are only two of them,' I said, peering at the guards as they stood near a flaming brazier which cast flickering shadows across the pale stonework.

'But the gate's shut,' Willow pointed out. 'We can't just ride through them.'

'Those gates are on a pulley system, we only need to slice the rope and they'll open,' Anise said, eyes bright.

'But we'll still have to stop and tackle the guards,' Sage said. 'This isn't going to be easy.'

'Leave this to me,' I said, dismounting and handing my horse's reins to Anise. The rip in my skirts came up to my knee on one side. I grabbed the material, ripping it to my lower thigh, immediately regretting it as the cool night air caressed my skin, making me shiver. I unpinned my hair and mussed it up a little.

'What are you doing?' Rian hissed at me.

'Getting us out of here. Count to fifty, then ride down to the gate.'

'I hate it when you do this,' he said, his expression pained.

'You should be used to it by now,' Tarragon said as I ran down the centre of the street, making no attempt to hide myself.

'Help me, please,' I called to the guards, waving at them in a distressed manner.

They turned towards me, holding their spears at the ready, then relaxed.

'What is it, Miss?' the taller one asked me as I approached.

'There's a group of men after me,' I said, trying to sound as scared as possible. 'Please help me, they tried to kidnap me.' I indicated my torn dress. 'I barely got away,' I said with a sniff.

'We'll look after you, Miss,' the shorter one said.

Rian and the others started down the street, the sound of the horses' hooves echoing around the buildings.

'That's them,' I said, moving behind the guards.

They stood in front of me, readying their spears. In one swift movement, I grabbed my Fan and slammed the metal handle into the back of the neck of the shorter guard. He fell to the ground, unconscious.

'What the…' the tall one began.

I hit him across the face with the butt of my Fan before he realised the danger he was in, sending him careering into a wall. He slumped to the ground. I opened my Fan and pressed the button to release the blades. The polished silver cover of my Fan, embossed with the sun, moon, and stars, shone in the firelight from the brazier, the green malachite leaves almost glowing. The faceted stones of dusky rose, sky blue, and spring green set in the silver glittered like ice in the sun, the amethyst at its base sending sparks across the gates.

I quickly moved over to the pulley system holding the gates shut and slashed at the rope. The sound of rusty cogs and wheels split the quiet of the night like a knife as the gates crashed open. By now, Rian and the others were with me. Anise held my horse's reins out to me. Remounting would be difficult without help and I looked around, searching for something to stand on.

Rian reached out towards me. 'Come on,' he said. I grabbed his hand, his strong arm pulling me up behind him.

I flinched at the sound of another big tear in the material of my dress as I climbed up, my other leg feeling the cool night air, goose pimples breaking out on my skin. We rode through the gates and out into open countryside, cantering along the road. I held on to Rian, his warm body helping to keep at bay the cold night that threatened to seep into my bones because of my thin silk dress.

The grassland surrounding the city gradually broke up into little rocky hills and valleys that loomed out of the moonlit night. We rode all through the dark hours until the city lay far behind us and dawn neared. By then my eyes were tired and heavy, and my body ached. The sun rose and dawn sent her silvery fingers across the sky, eventually staining it pink and gold, and finally blue, as we rode.

'You think they'll send anyone after us?' Willow asked as we slowed, glancing warily back over her shoulder.

'Hard to tell,' Tarragon said. 'Depends how much they really want us, I suppose.'

'So what happened with Sorrel at the banquet, Phire?' Anise asked.

'And why's he in Flos?' Sage asked.

CHAPTER ELEVEN

I told them what had happened at the banquet, and the conversation I'd overheard.

'So, Sorrel's definitely working for the Nightshade,' Willow said, shaking her head.

'Who are going to assassinate King Narcissus so Prince Monkshood can take over as Chervil's pawn,' Sage said, disgust in his voice. 'That's appalling, not to mention sick.'

'But to reunite the Lands?' Tarragon asked. 'I don't think Aerba and Flos have ever been one land, only as part of the Five Lands, but never just the two of them.'

That's what worried me. I shrugged. 'I don't know what was meant, but that's what was said. Reuniting the Lands.'

Tarragon shuddered. 'But to pretend to go to war on the pretence of the Fire Opal having been stolen by Flos, it's unbelievable, especially when Chervil knows it isn't true.'

Rian sat quietly in front of me as I held his waist, his muscles taught.

'You all right?' I asked him softly, resting my chin on his shoulder.

'I can't believe my brother would do this,' he said, bowing his head, his whole body tense. 'Dammit, even Father would never've been so underhanded; threatened war because of a feigned slight, then got the Nightshade to assassinate King Narcissus so his puppet could take over. Chervil has always been ambitious, but this? Dragging our land, our people – *my* people – into a war like this? It sickens me to the core.'

I hugged him from behind. 'I'm so sorry.'

'At least you found out what was happening, what we're up against.'

'And saved our lives, coming to warn us,' Anise said from beside us.

Tarragon nodded. 'She saved all of us.'

I glanced at him. 'Sorry about last night,' I said, wincing. 'It was rather urgent, that's all.'

He grinned at me. 'No harm done, y'know.'

Willow's face turned red and she looked away.

I thought about Sorrel and Monkshood's conversation and frowned.

'Do the Nightshade go in for assassinations?' I asked. 'I thought they were more about spying, except for when they were trying to kill me, of course.'

'Usually it's spying and covert work, really, rather than killings,' Rian said. 'It does happen on rare occasions, or so I've heard, but not generally. Why?'

'I just wondered,' I said, a little worm of doubt wriggling in my chest. I feared that this might be more far-reaching than we'd thought.

'Someone's going to have to deal with Chervil, y'know,' Tarragon said, looking sideways at Rian. 'Probably permanently.'

Rian looked straight ahead, not answering his cousin. What exactly was running through my husband's mind?

We rode on for a while as the sun rose.

'I suggest we stop for a short time and rest the horses, then continue,' Rian said as we turned a corner in the road.

'This valley looks good,' Anise said, pointing off the trackway. 'There's a little stream, too, for the horses.'

We rode a short way up into the valley until we were hidden from the road before dismounting and tending to our horses. I looked at my torn dress. It now had two high splits in the fabric on either side of the skirt, up to well above my knees. Cold wasn't going to be the problem now; it would be the opposite. The exposed skin on my neck and chest would soon be burning in the sun, along with both my legs.

'I need to get changed,' I said, grabbing my pack. 'Rian, will you help me?'

He nodded and followed me up the little valley to an area behind some jagged grey rocks covered in moss and lichen that afforded us some privacy. I put my pack down and tried to undo the back of my dress, but I couldn't get hold of the laces. There was a reason High Blood ladies had maids.

I glanced at Rian. 'Can you undo these laces at the back?' I asked. 'I can't reach properly.'

'Of course,' he said, stepping over to me. I felt him hesitate a moment. He moved my hair and kissed my shoulder, sending sparks through me, before gently taking hold of the intricate lacing. As he loosened the dress, the feeling of being released from the bonds came as a tremendous relief. For the first time in hours I felt as if I could breathe again.

I took a deep breath, filling my lungs. 'That's so much better,' I said as I wriggled out of the silk dress, leaving my undergarments on. 'Thank you.'

'I thought you looked rather good in it,' he said, his back to me as he rubbed his neck. 'I mean, you look lovely anyway, but that dress really highlighted your waist and...'

'And?' I asked archly.

'Other areas.'

I pulled my clothes out of my pack. 'You don't have to turn away, you know.'

'I know,' he said, glancing at me for a moment with a big, appreciative smile before looking back down the valley. 'It's more I don't want anyone disturbing you while you change.'

'You mean Tarragon?' I asked, wrestling with my shirt.

'He has form in that area. Yes.'

'I think I rather evened the score last night,' I said, pulling my leggings on, trying unsuccessfully to suppress a giggle.

'Oh?' he asked, turning back to me. 'How did you do that?'

'He and Willow were, as he put it, "a little busy" when I went to warn them yesterday evening.' I grinned. 'Luckily for me, they were under the covers or it could've been quite nasty.'

Rian laughed. 'Serves him right for the times he's interrupted us.'

'I thought so, too,' I said smugly.

'Is that why you were saying sorry to him a little earlier?'

'Yes,' I said, gathering my things up. 'I thought it only right to apologise.'

'Do you think you'll ever wear that again?' he asked, looking at my dress as I stuffed it into my pack.

'I doubt it, it's torn to shreds. It probably needs remaking rather than mending. Why?'

'Just wondered,' he said, his eyes shining.

'I hope Erica and Gladiolus forgive me for running off like that and taking her dress, or rather, ruining it.'

'I'm sure once they find out what's been happening, they will.'

'It might depend on whose story they hear first, though,' I said. 'And it won't be mine, unfortunately. Maybe we can get this Calder in Rill to send her word about what's really going on, and about Monkshood.'

'She'll forgive you,' Rian said, taking my hand. 'She's your cousin.'

I smiled at him, and we walked back down the little valley to where the others had started eating bread and ham.

'If we're going to Rill, we'll need to start riding north soon,' I said, sitting down and chewing on a piece of bread Anise had passed me. 'Either that or head for the coast at Alyssum and take a boat north to Aqua Claras and then travel to Rill that way.'

'Bobbins. More ships.' Willow screwed her nose up at the prospect.

'I think you know which way Willow and I would prefer,' Tarragon said, taking another bite of bread and ham.

'Will it make much difference, timewise?' Rian asked.

I pondered for a moment. 'It'll probably be quicker over land, maybe take ten days or so. The question is do we have enough provisions to last that long? There aren't any towns going north. There's the odd settlement and farm, but we'll not come across any inns or markets until we reach Rill.'

'We're fine for provisions,' Anise said. 'I made sure we stocked up in Muscari market.'

Rian nodded. 'Then we go north across land,' he said. 'Avoid another sea journey for now.'

'We'll travel east along the Alyssum Road until the countryside turns to moorland,' I said. 'Then we can travel north unhindered by rocky valleys and ravines blocking our path.'

'It's a good thing you know the land around here.'

'Isn't it?' I grinned. 'Once we've left this road and go north, we'll reach a forest, and I know there's a lake and river up there. Beyond the forest are mountains that act as the border with Mere, but after that I don't know, other than we continue north through desert to Rill. I've travelled extensively in Flos, but not Mere. All I know of that is from Onyx and maps, not first-hand, except for right by the coast.'

'It'll do,' Rian said, doing his best to reassure me.

'What I'd like is a rest,' Tarragon said.

'You had a rest at Jasmine's Farm,' Sage said.

'Yes, but that was ages ago.'

'Only just over a week,' Willow said.

'It feels like forever.'

'Maybe we can rest a while in Rill,' Rian said. 'But our top priority now is finding Phire's brother. Every minute in Juniper's hands…'

'Will be torture,' I finished, an unwelcome shiver moving down my spine. At least Juniper had intended to have Flint kill me after Princess Angelica's assassination. Mal's fate of imprisonment by the Coterie Leader didn't bear thinking about. I had to save him if I possibly could. No one else would free him, and the pressure weighed on me. My greatest fear that wriggled inside me was that he'd suffer more because I'd escaped her clutches. An arm slipped around my shoulders. I looked at Rian through watery eyes.

'We'll find him, and soon,' he said.

I nodded.

We travelled through broken countryside as the morning wore on. I rode on my horse once more, although I think Rian would've been happy with me staying with him, but this meant the horses would all stay fresher.

'It would be good if we could find somewhere to camp with water for the horses tonight,' Sage said during the afternoon.

'It might also be an idea to stop a little early,' Anise said. 'We got no sleep last night at all.'

'Good idea,' Rian said with a nod.

'There's some water about half a league ahead,' Tarragon said absently as he gazed into the distance.

'There is?' Willow asked, raising an eyebrow.

'A waterfall, pool, and a stream. The stream will be fine for the horses.'

'And you know all this how?'

'I...' Tarragon started. He looked at us as he realised what he'd said. 'Um, I don't know how I know, I just do.'

Willow shook her head.

How could he know where the nearest water was? Unless...

As the sun headed for the horizon, we found a quiet valley with a small stream meandering down it. We rode a way up into it until a curve in it shielded us from the road. A little further up, a waterfall cascaded cheerily into a deep, crystal clear pool before weaving down the valley in a sparkling ribbon, exactly as Tarragon had described.

'Have you been here before?' Rian asked, his eyes narrowing with suspicion as he looked at his cousin.

'No,' Tarragon said, his face turning pink. 'It must have been a lucky guess.'

'A guess?'

Tarragon nodded. 'It happens.'

'Quite so specifically?' Rian asked, raising an eyebrow.

'Leave it, Rian,' Tarragon said, annoyed at the questioning, but I caught the look of confusion, and even fear, behind his eyes.

He knew.

Or, he had a sneaking suspicion, just as I had.

We made camp, and then I headed for the pool for a quick wash. I discarded my clothes and swam out into the refreshing, if slightly cold, water. I glanced back at the shore where I'd left Deorwine and Glædwine propped up against a rock.

'Don't you dare,' I said, glowering at the purple crystal sword and shield. 'If you try and join me I'll likely drown, and you'll go down with me. So don't even think about it.'

Once I'd satisfied myself they weren't going to try and drown me, I swam up and down to keep warm. I ducked under the water, coming back up, trying to clear my eyes, standing shoulder deep.

Rian stood by the side of the pool, watching. How long had he been there?

'You look like you're enjoying that,' he said. 'May I join you?'

'But you don't swim,' I said.

'It doesn't look too deep. Anyway, you can teach me.'

Before I'd even answered, he'd slipped his clothes off, only my gently glowing Amethyst Talisman left around his neck, and jumped in. Not that I minded, although until now we'd never seen each other totally naked, and a shiver went through me as my heart raced. I'd been expecting this, looking forward to it, but until now it'd never happened, for one reason or another. Even when we got changed into our Iolitian clothes we'd still had our undergarments on, and at night on Hyssop's ship we'd slept in hammocks below decks with the rest of the crew, no room to ourselves, and I wasn't getting undressed down there for all the men to see. Camping with the others also made it awkward, and with the state of the bedding in the inns we'd visited, I wasn't getting naked. Erica's might have been a different matter, but Sorrel put paid to that.

Rian waded over to me, smiling.

Now, when maybe I should have been embarrassed, I wasn't, but I did start to tremble a little. He wasn't ashamed, either. Quite the opposite, in fact. As he approached, the cold water around me began to warm. He suddenly ducked under the surface, coming back up, hair dripping, water cascading off his toned muscles.

'Are you doing that?' I asked, enjoying the warmth.

'Doing what?' He frowned, wiping the water from his eyes.

'Making the cold water warm.'

He shrugged, moving closer. 'I thought it was a bit cold and it'd be nice if it was warmer, then it was.'

'So it *is* you.'

He smiled again. 'Must be.'

We stood shoulder deep in the water, less than three feet apart, looking at each other.

'Can I kiss you, wife?' he asked, his eyes sparkling in the light reflected off the water.

'You don't normally ask now,' I said, frowning.

'Yes, but this time it feels different somehow,' he said, taking my trembling hand and interlacing his fingers with mine.

'Why?'

His pupils dilated as he looked into my eyes. 'You're not wearing anything,' he said, his breath hitching as he rubbed the back of his neck with his free hand, droplets of water sparkling in the last of the sunlight as they fell back into the pool. 'And neither am I.'

'So?'

'It just doesn't seem right to kiss you when you're naked without asking permission—' His voice caught. 'At least, the first ti—'

'Come here, husband,' I said, stepping forward and closing the distance between us.

He leant towards me, but I pulled him in for the kiss, capturing his mouth with mine, the water getting hotter around us as our bodies touched. His arms slid around my back as he held me close, shaking slightly, and I slipped one arm around his warm, broad shoulders as I caressed his wet hair with my other hand. A little silken knot formed in my stomach. His hot body rested against mine; there were definite advantages to being married to a Fire Spinner. He was always warm. A little over two weeks ago, I couldn't have imagined this happening. I'd thought I was losing him forever, but here he was in my arms, and for a moment I felt lost in a dream.

'Rian! Phire! Stew's ready!' Tarragon shouted from the camp.

Rian rested his forehead on mine. 'He better not come looking for us.'

I giggled. 'Coming!' I shouted back to Tarragon. 'Now, hopefully, he won't.'

Rian smiled. He brought a still-shaking hand up to my face, caressing it as his other rested at my waist, and kissed me again, long, ardent and deep.

'We better get out. Did you bring any towels?' he asked finally.

'I brought mine, didn't you bring yours?'

'This was a little spur of the moment.'

'Good thing I was prepared,' I said smugly. 'Come on.'

We made our way to the edge of the pool and climbed out. I grabbed my towel and dried quickly, then held it out towards him, suddenly realising he'd been watching my every move. His cheeks were flushed as he looked at me, at *all* of me, his irises just amber rims. He smiled such a tender smile I felt my heart swelling in my chest as I took in all of him.

'You're beautiful,' he murmured, his voice a little hoarse, desire written all over his face.

'You're not too bad yourself,' I said, appreciating his lean, muscular male body. I wanted to do so much more than kiss him. I wanted to…

'We'd better dress or Tarragon will be down here looking for us,' Rian said reluctantly, making a face that set me giggling.

I handed the towel over and turned away.

'Then again…' His hands landed on my hips, firmly bringing me to a stop before I could move any further. Then he leant towards me and tenderly kissed the side of my neck.

'Hmm, that's nice,' I murmured, tilting my head back.

'For me, too,' he said, slowly spinning me around towards him. He looked deep into my eyes and smiled, his own sparkling in the light. He pulled me gently to him, his warm hands going around my waist, holding me close against his hot, wet body as we kissed, lingering, before finally letting me go. 'I'm sorry, I couldn't resist, and as much as I'd really like to stay here with you like this for the rest of the evening, we ought to dress before Tarragon comes looking for us.'

'You're right, he'll be here any moment,' I said as I gazed breathlessly at Rian, my heart thumping away.

Rian smiled again, and took the towel from around his neck where he'd placed it and started rubbing it over his arms to dry off. We got dressed and headed back to our little camp, hand in hand.

CHAPTER TWELVE

'I've told you, there are no Dire Wolves around this part of Flos.'

Tarragon, however, didn't appear to be convinced by my words. The worried look in his golden-brown eyes remained as he put two more logs on the evening campfire. His taut muscles only helped to make the atmosphere more uncomfortable.

'I think we should set a watch, just in case, and keep the fire burning,' he said, finding another log.

Rian rolled his eyes to the night sky. 'We're perfectly safe here; it was only out on the plains south of Muscari.'

'Even so…'

'I thought you wanted to rest,' Sage said.

'Not if I'm going to get eaten by a Dire Wolf,' Tarragon said grumpily. 'I'd rather be tired than dead.'

'You're not going to be eaten by anything,' I said. 'I've been this way before, many times, and not had any problem. As long as we make sure the fire's going well before we go to sleep, it'll all be fine.'

Rian sighed. 'If you really want, we'll set a watch, but I think it's a waste of time.'

'Good,' Tarragon said, ignoring our reservations. 'Willow can go first, I'll go last.'

'I will?' she asked. 'You're the one who wants to stay awake, not me. I'm quite happy. I trust Phire.'

Tarragon looked a little hesitant. 'So do I, but just in case – better to be safe than sorry, don't you think?'

'All right,' she said, screwing her face up and offering him a little scowl. 'If you insist.'

'We'll take second and third,' Anise said, nodding to Sage, who didn't look overly pleased, either.

'We'll take the next two, then,' Rian said, sighing.

'I'll do it, you still need your rest,' I said.

'I'm getting stronger all the time. I'm basically back to normal.'

'Then let's keep it that way, shall we?'

Rian uttered a few choice oaths as we made our way to our bedding and snuggled under the blankets. He slipped an arm around me, holding me close.

'I will do the watch with you,' he murmured in my ear. 'I insist.'

Don't bet on it.

My nightmares of Rian writhing in agony had receded somewhat, and I slept well until Anise woke me several hours later. Rian lay beside me in a deep sleep. I slid gently from his arms and out from the blankets. He'd been holding me in a bid to wake up when I moved, but he'd failed, and I tucked the blankets in around him. I looked at his face in the firelight. He looked more boy than man as the orange-red light flickered across his face. Even more adorable. My heart surged with love for this remarkable young man, and I smiled. I took my place next to the fire as Anise went to sleep, feeding it with a few branches to keep it going.

Everything had been a whirlwind since leaving Iolite on my commission to kill Princess Angelica. There had really been no chance to take stock, to rest, and let everything sink in. The only chance had been our sojourn at Jasmine's, but I'd been so caught up in Rian's poisoning and his recovery that it hadn't felt like a rest or break of any sort. As Rian's strength improved, I found I slept less and fatigue began to get the better of me, but I had to continue for Mal's sake. Every moment I rested, he suffered. Tears filled my eyes for a moment as I thought of him, what he might be going through. I wiped my eyes and put another branch on Tarragon's fire.

I glanced at Rian. Still fast asleep. Good. He needed his rest, whatever he said. He'd been so close to death, and all because of Carnelian, Beryl and Juniper.

The murderous thoughts I'd had when Rian lay ill came flooding back, even though he'd said he didn't want me to be Lady Merciless. In all honesty, neither did I, but the Coterie had to pay for their crimes in some way, even if it wasn't with their lives. I couldn't let this go so easily. I chewed my lip as I sat thinking. After my watch, I silently woke Tarragon. He nodded, and I returned to Rian, snuggling back under the blankets.

Cold metal rested at my throat.

I opened my eyes. The silver light of dawn stained the sky above.

'So, you're an assassin, Amethyst?' Prince Monkshood stood holding his swordpoint to my throat.

Hell's teeth.

My pulse raced as I glanced around. Tarragon lay on the ground near me, a soldier holding a sword at his chest. He swallowed and looked apologetically at me. He'd fallen asleep – despite his pleas for a watch because of Dire Wolves, he'd nodded off. I could sense Rian's rigid body behind me. The others all lay with soldiers around them holding them to the ground with their weapons.

'And you're working with the Nightshade,' I said, keeping my voice level.

Monkshood's eyes widened. He quickly composed himself.

'I don't know what you're talking about,' he said. 'But then, you're an Iolitian assassin, a member of the Coterie, so I should expect nothing less from you, Lady Merciless.'

By the Stars, that name would haunt me forever.

'And you've brought Aerbans into the heart of Flos,' he continued. 'We're on the verge of war with Aerba, and yet you bring the enemy right into our palace.'

'We weren't there to harm anyone,' Rian said. 'We're not working with Chervil – unlike you.'

'Silence!' The soldier standing over Rian pushed his sword further towards Rian's throat.

I gritted my teeth, clenching a fist.

'I always thought you were a friend, Amethyst, not an enemy,' Monkshood said. 'Get up.'

He moved his sword from my neck far enough to let me move, and I got to my feet. I glanced at the Weapons, but they were right beside me. Too close. I looked at Rian. His face was strained as he gazed back at me.

'Get up, all of you,' Monkshood said. They all did as he said, scrambling free of their blankets. 'Take any weapons they have on them.'

A soldier took a knife from Sage, who scowled at the soldier for good measure.

'You're all going back to Muscari to answer for your crimes,' Monkshood said. 'One of you bring those crystal weapons with you – I understand they're cursed, and we don't want them giving this assassin any sort of advantage.' He turned to me. 'We've always welcomed you in Muscari, and yet you spent your life deceiving us all, even Erica.'

'I've never done anything to her or you, or Flos,' I said.

'You are part of the organisation that murdered my son, and now you will pay for that crime.'

'She had nothing to do with it,' Rian said, trying to take a step forward, but a soldier restrained him.

It was true – although I had been sent to kill him. It was just another occasion when Mal had got there first, thankfully.

'Whether she did kill my son or not is irrelevant,' Monkshood said. 'She's guilty of other murders.'

'I've never killed anyone,' I said.

'That's not what I heard.'

'Because you heard it from my lying brother,' Sage said, jaw set.

'Your brother?'

'Sorrel.'

Monkshood shook his head. 'Don't know what you're talking about. My information has come from Flosian spies.'

'Liar,' I said.

Monkshood rubbed his chin. 'You know, we don't need to take them all back, just her,' he said, looking around. 'You might as well kill them here as at the palace. It'll save time, and we won't need to bury their bodies. We can leave them for the animals to pick their bones clean.'

Willow gasped.

Monkshood turned his attention away from me for a split second.

'Like hell you will.' I slammed backwards into Monkshood.

The Flosian Prince yelled. Stumbled and fell. I rammed my elbow into the face of the soldier beside me, standing next to Rian. The others took their chance.

Rian launched himself into the soldier behind him as Tarragon punched the soldier next to him. Anise ducked under the sword of the soldier behind him, and brought his knee up into the man's stomach. Willow twisted around and hit her soldier in the face, thrusting her lower palm upwards and into his nose – there was an awful crunch as the cartilage and bone broke, followed by blood as he cried out in pain, his eyes tearing. Sage, meanwhile, smashed his fist into his soldier's stomach and again into his jaw, flooring him.

I turned around, only to find Monkshood back on his feet, his arm around my waist and sword resting across my throat in a split second.

'Stop! All of you!' he ordered.

My mouth suddenly dried and my heart clamoured in my chest, beating uncomfortably fast as I grabbed at the arm holding the sword, but he was strong, and there was no way I was prising it away from my neck. I took a breath, trying to steady my nerves.

'Let her go,' Rian said.

'So, what is she to you, Prince Valerian? Your whore?'

'My wife.'

I felt Monkshood tense.

'And you will let her go,' Rian said, his voice like granite.

Monkshood hesitated. 'No. I will take at least one of you back to the palace. King Narcissus will be most grateful.' He looked around at his soldiers who were in various states of semi-consciousness and unconsciousness. 'I will leave with her, and you can all go. Just leave Flos and never come back. But I *am* taking the assassin with me.'

I couldn't do anything. With Monkshood's blade so close to my throat, I had no wiggle room. His arm was crushing my middle and even making it hard to breathe. The Weapons would be of no use even if they did come to me. I'd never get hold of them from my back. I was in a pickle and no mistake.

'No, you will let her go.' A flame appeared in Rian's hand. It burnt brightly, a brilliant red with golds and oranges, his amber eyes flickering with the same intensity.

'By the Flowers, what is that?' Monkshood let go of me. 'Witchcraft!' he hissed as I darted away from him.

'No,' Rian said. 'Not witchcraft. Fire Spinner.'

Monkshood blanched and ran. He disappeared around the rocks and down the valley, and the sound of horse's hooves echoed around the ravine walls as he galloped off.

The flame in Rian's hand died and vanished.

I swallowed and looked at him in awe. 'Thank you,' I whispered before flinging my arms around his neck and burying my face in his sandalwood hair.

He wrapped his arms around me. 'You're welcome, wife,' he said, kissing the side of my head and holding me for a moment as my pulse and breathing steadied. 'Anything for you.'

Tarragon shifted his feet. 'I'm sorry about—'

'No time for that now, Tarragon,' Rian said as I stepped back. 'Let's get out of here.'

Tarragon nodded contritely. We gathered our things, checking the soldiers wouldn't cause us any further problems – Sage hit one just to make sure. Anise put out the fire in such a way as to make it smokeless as we tacked up our horses, and then mounted up.

'We'll go this way,' Rian said, leading us up the valley away from the road.

We trotted past the pool and waterfall, and even though we hurried anxiously along, Rian had time to flash me a grin. We may never come back to this place again, but it would always hold a special place in *our* hearts, and be a cherished memory for us both.

We rode up out of the valley, onto rolling purple, heather-clad moorland, and broke our horses into a gallop, not looking back.

'I'm so sorry,' Tarragon said once we were well onto the moors above the valley. 'I must have nodded off.'

'And after you made such a fuss about setting a watch,' Sage said. 'If there had been Dire Wolves, we'd all have been dead, no thanks to you.'

'Like I said, I'm sorry.'

'It's done now, forget it,' Rian said.

'I'll stay up with him another time,' Willow said. 'We'll do our watches together, that way one of us will be able to keep the other awake.'

'Perhaps we should do all our watches in pairs,' Anise said. 'It makes more sense.'

I nodded.

The moorland stretched out around us and we ate on the move, not daring to stop as we cantered across the scrubby ground. The sun sailed across the sky, little puffy white clouds periodically casting little shadows across the heather.

'You should have woken me,' Rian said later when we stopped to camp in a little hollow in the moors. He gave me a little scowl. On this occasion I didn't care; it had been for his own good. 'I'll be taking my turn with you tonight. In fact, we'll take first watch. That way you can't sneak off and leave me sleeping, and neither of us will drop off.'

'I don't sneak,' I said, knowing today I was fighting a losing battle. Although, to be fair, I was surprised I'd managed to outwit him last night. I could see now, taking first watch, I stood no chance.

'You're an assassin, of course you sneak.' Tarragon grinned as he helped Anise start the cooking fire. Why they hadn't asked Rian, I didn't know. Although I wasn't sure anyone, including Rian, was used to the whole idea of Magic Angles yet, even if he had used his Fire Magic to save me. That had been more of a last resort situation.

'Ex-assassin,' I said primly.

'But the training comes in handy, doesn't it?'

'I suppose.'

I sat up with Rian for the first watch, but the night proved uneventful, and at first light we were back in the saddle, heading north towards the Great Flosian Forest – at least, that's what Mal had always called it. I wasn't sure it had an actual name.

The sun beat down on our heads as we travelled, and we removed our chainmail shirts, perspiration on our brows. The mail shirts were a hindrance, if you asked me. The Coterie mainly avoided wearing them as they restricted movement and sometimes jingled and clinked, giving you away at an inopportune moment. Onyx sometimes wore one, but I remained unconvinced that they were necessary. To me, it was all about speed. I regarded mail as a nuisance.

We saw no one all day as we rode across the scrubby moorland and through little valleys, splashing through streams and sending water droplets into the air that caught the sun like dazzling stars. Wild moor ponies grazed peacefully in the distance as Burgundy Grouse and Flosian Moor Pipits called around us, the smaller birds swooping low over the heather, keen to find insects for food. We paused, allowing the horses to drink in a stream, before continuing on. In the distance, a great green wall rose in front of us: the forest.

'It's huge,' Willow said, looking at the trees spreading from horizon to horizon.

'It looks rather foreboding to me,' Sage muttered.

'I think it's beautiful,' Anise said, a slightly dreamy note to his voice.

I glanced at him, wondering, considering his love for herbs – in fact, for nature in general – whether he might be an Earth Spinner.

'You would think like that,' Sage said. 'Anything to do with plants and you're off in the clouds.'

Anise shrugged. 'So? What about you and your perfumes?'

'Entirely different,' Sage said, looking away. 'And you promised you wouldn't mention that in public.'

'But they already know.'

I caught Tarragon grinning at Rian.

We rode towards the trees, the afternoon sun making the leaves of the oak forest a golden-green in the light. The branches waved gently in the breeze, almost looking as if they were beckoning us into their green embrace. Anise was right, they were beautiful. Urging our horses into the forest, we followed an animal track meandering through the trees, still heading north. The sandy path wove through the forest, ferns and blue wild flowers on either side of us

'I don't think we should light a fire while we're in the forest,' Anise said suddenly, looking around. 'I don't think they'd like it.'

'Who wouldn't like what?' Tarragon asked, peering between the trees. I couldn't see anything out of the ordinary, either.

'The oaks.'

Sage groaned. 'Are you serious? Cold rations for the next, how long, Phire?'

'Couple of days,' I said. 'If we make good time.'

'*Two days* because the oaks wouldn't like us building a fire so we can have a hot meal?' Sage looked to the leaf-canopied sky.

'You're joking, aren't you?' Willow asked, frowning.

'No,' Anise said with such steel in his voice we all looked at him in surprise. It was so out of character for him to be like this.

'I'm sure we can survive on cold rations if it means that much to you,' Rian said, a confused look behind his eyes.

'It does.'

I looked at Rian, who shrugged at me. I couldn't understand why Anise was reacting the way he was, but he was adamant about it, so, rather than have a long, drawn-out argument, we all kept quiet, exchanging puzzled glances. I'd certainly never seen him like this before.

I gazed into the trees, some almost sixty feet high, their broad green leaves stretching above us in a green veil. Below, ferns and grasses swayed gently, and the sound of distant animals drifted through the trees. Evidence of rabbits from their droppings, and acorns gnawed apart by squirrels, littered the ground. Birds I couldn't name called amongst the distant boughs. We moved steadily along until reaching a grassy glade as the forest became gloomy, the sun setting away to the west. We dismounted and made camp.

'How are we going to see if we don't have a fire?' Sage asked sourly.

'Moonlight,' Anise said.

'That'll be romantic, but not a great deal of use if it gets cloudy.'

'Guess we'll have to get to bed early – ow, what was that for?' Tarragon asked.

'You know what it was for,' Willow said.

'At least we won't need to set a watch in here,' Sage muttered.

Rian had been very quiet during all of this, and after our moonlit supper we settled down to sleep under our blankets.

'What's the matter?' I asked him quietly.

He lay on his back, one hand under his head, looking up at the velvet sky with its pinpricks of starlight shining benevolently down on us.

'I don't know, I just don't feel entirely comfortable in the forest,' he said. 'Like the trees don't want me here.'

I tried not to laugh. 'What do you mean? I don't think the trees have actual opinions.'

'Even so…'

'It's probably more that you can't see very far – it makes me a bit nervous.'

'Your assassin training?'

'Probably. Try and get to sleep. I'm sure the forest is quite happy to have you in it.'

'Hmm, maybe.'

I smiled. Where he'd got such a notion from, I didn't know.

Dawn had only recently broken when I awoke. Birds sang and insects chirped as the forest came alive. Hushed voices came from my left, into the trees. I looked around our camp – Anise had gone. Odd. I scrambled out of our covers carefully, so as not to wake Rian, and crouched low as I gazed out into the forest. A fine mist swirled between the trees at ground level. About twenty yards away I could see Anise, talking – but to who?

I went to investigate, moving silently amongst the trees and the undergrowth, the smell of wild flowers and loamy soil around me. Deorwine and Glædwine soon decided I'd got far enough away from them and joined me as I sneaked along. Maybe Rian had been right, after all – I did sneak. As I got closer, I stopped dead.

Anise appeared to be talking to two ghosts. Two green ghosts.

CHAPTER THIRTEEN

Whatever these spirits were, more were joining them from the trees, as if they emerged from the great trunks themselves. I rubbed my eyes. No, I wasn't dreaming, and I wasn't imagining it. As I ventured closer, I realised the ghosts were actually pretty young girls, their skin a pale green with the texture of bark. They fluttered their eyelashes at Anise, their rich brown eyes sparkling in the dawn light. Their deep emerald hair, intertwined with leaves of gold, glistened. They wore simple dresses of deep green moss with bronze leaf embellishments, and on their heads sat crowns of leaves in green, gold, and bronze.

Were these the dryads I'd heard of? The tree spirits? Whatever they were, I could see straight through them, and it sent a shiver down my spine. I could see ferns and trees through their bodies as if they were just wisps. I rubbed my eyes again. Was I still dreaming after all? I'd always imagined dryads to be substantial creatures, not ghost-like in appearance. One of them pointed towards me. I stopped, embarrassed at my intrusion, but Anise beckoned me over.

'It's all right, they're friendly,' Anise said with a smile. 'They're the dryads of the oak trees that grow here in the forest.'

'They are?' I asked, coming over cautiously, Deorwine poised on my back – not that you could kill a ghost. Could you?

'Interesting. I didn't think you'd be able to see them.'

'I can't, really. They look like ghosts. Is that what you're seeing?'

Anise frowned at me. 'No, Phire, they're as solid as you or me.'

'Er, no they're not. At least to me they're not. I can see straight through them.'

'To you, Earth Spinner, we are real, but to all other humans in your party we cannot be seen, except for this one,' the dryad closest to Anise said in a lilting voice. She had an oak gall resting in the curls of her hair.

'Why's that?' Anise asked.

'Because your Magic Angle makes you special.'

It seemed my suspicions had been confirmed; Anise was indeed an Earth Angle Spinner.

'There are so few Spinners these days, it is a privilege to meet you,' another dryad with brighter green hair said.

'What're your names?' I asked.

'We don't have names, we are our trees. As long as they live, so do we, but we have no names.'

'Oh, sorry.' I hoped I hadn't upset them. I didn't know what dryad etiquette was.

'You have one with you that we fear,' an older dryad said, her dress shifting as she moved. 'We do not want him here, he is danger. He must leave.'

I frowned. Rian. Had he picked up on the dryads' displeasure at him being in the forest?

'He means you no harm,' I said. 'He will be very respectful of you and your forest.'

'Fire is death to us. Fire Angle Spinners are death to us,' she hissed. 'He cannot be allowed in our forest. He must go. He is danger. He is death.'

'Not this one,' Anise said. 'He won't hurt you, you have my word. Prince Valerian is my friend. I'll vouch for him. He'd never do anything to hurt any of you.'

The dryads looked at each other, then moved away, talking quietly amongst themselves for a few moments. They nodded and shook their heads, then returned.

'If the Earth Spinner gives his word no harm will come to us, we will offer you safe passage through our ancient glades,' the first one said. 'If the Fire Prince tries to hurt our trees, there will be immediate punishment – death.'

I glanced sideways at Anise.

'We understand, and thank you,' Anise said, nodding.

'Who are you talking to?' Sage asked, coming through the trees.

'Dryads,' Anise said with a grin.

Sage started to laugh then thought better of it. 'Seriously?'

'Yes,' I said. 'I can see them too, sort of.'

Sage narrowed his eyes, trying to decide if we were making fun of him or not. 'All right, I'll believe you. But if I find out you're pulling my leg, I'll be quite upset with you, Anise.'

'I can see them because I'm an Earth Spinner,' Anise said smugly.

'You are?' Sage asked. He rubbed his forehead. 'Makes sense, really – you and your herbs, and plants, and what not.' He looked at me. 'What's your excuse?'

I didn't have one. 'Well—'

'They're going to give us safe passage through the forest,' Anise said. 'They'll show us the quickest way through.'

'If you ready yourselves, we'll guide you now,' the first dryad said.

'Thank you,' Anise said with a nod.

We hurried back to camp where Rian and the others had started to wake up. I knelt down beside him on the grassy ground. I would have to be very tactful.

'I know why you don't like the forest,' I said. 'And you were right, it – they – don't want you here.'

'Who doesn't?' Rian asked, wiping the sleep from his eyes.

'The oak dryads,' I said.

'Where?' Willow asked, looking around. 'Where are they? I've always wanted to see a dryad. Have they gone already?'

'Unfortunately, you can't see them,' Anise said. 'Only I can see them, and Phire.'

'It's because Anise is an Earth Spinner. And they're not keen on you because you're a Fire Spinner,' I said to Rian.

'I said I felt the forest didn't want me here,' Rian said, a little wide-eyed, his muscles tensing. 'Please tell them I won't set anything alight. I don't want to hurt them. Really, I don't.'

'It's all right,' I said, placing a steadying hand on his shoulder. 'They know. Anise gave them his word you wouldn't start any fires.'

'Good,' Rian said, relaxing a little. 'I won't. So, why can you see them? Are you an Earth Spinner, too?'

'I don't know why I can see them, but I'm no Earth Spinner. Anise is the one with green fingers. I'd wondered for a while, actually.'

Anise bowed his head. 'So had I, truth be told. I thought that was what was going on with me.'

'Why didn't you say anything?' Sage asked. 'You could have mentioned it to me, you know.'

'I thought you might think I was going mad. I guess I didn't want to say anything until I was sure, and now I am.'

Tarragon scratched his chin. 'The way you are with herbs and flowers – we should've guessed earlier.'

'He's a genius with herbs,' Sage said, a big smile on his face as he gave Anise a kiss. 'And he's all mine.'

Anise's eyes widened in shock. Sage didn't usually indulge in public displays of affection. They both turned red as they looked at each other, then at us.

'Sorry,' Sage muttered.

'Don't be,' Rian said. 'You're not at the Aerban Court now, you're alone with us. You can do what you want.'

'Within reason,' I murmured, glancing mischievously at Tarragon, who turned pink.

'Thanks,' Sage said.

Anise grinned.

I started gathering our things up before Rian got any ideas. We headed off through the trees, Anise in the lead as he chatted with the dryads. At least I could see them. To everyone else it must have looked like he was going mad, having some strange one-sided conversation with himself. I rode behind Rian, watching a number of dryads that followed him closely, scrutinising his every move. One walked particularly close beside his horse.

'I still don't feel comfortable about this,' he said, gazing into the trees.

'Don't worry, Fire Prince, neither do we,' the dryad beside him said, glowering at him.

'He won't do anything,' I said, attempting to reassure the creature. 'He won't hurt you or your trees.'

'What?' Rian asked, frowning at me. 'Were you talking to me?'

'I was talking to the dryad walking next to you.'

'What? Where? Tell her I'm really not going to set light to the trees or the forest or anything,' he said, squinting as if that would help him see her. 'I want the dryads to know that.'

'Hmm.' The dryad shook her hair, a little sprinkle of leaves scattering about her. 'I suppose he seems honest. Does he belong to anyone?'

'Belong?' I asked. 'What do you mean?'

'Does he have a mate? He's quite sweet, I suppose, for a human male. His hair's the colour of autumn leaves. I'm beginning to think I rather like that about him.'

By the Stars. 'He belongs to me,' I said quickly, before she could get any other ideas, although bearing in mind he couldn't see her, I wasn't sure how that would work. 'He's mine.'

Rian looked at me quizzically, a little grin playing on his lips.

'Look after him, then,' the dryad said. 'He appears genuine enough, and he's very handsome – for a human.'

I smiled. 'He is, isn't he?'

'You're sure you want to keep him?'

'Most definitely.' I nodded.

'What's she saying?' Rian asked, frowning.

'She's remarking on your good looks,' I said. 'And your hair being the colour of autumn leaves.'

Rian turned the colour of a strawberry. 'Don't be daft, I'm not good-looking,' he said, turning away. 'I'm too tall and awkward.'

'Rubbish,' I said. 'You're very handsome, and she agrees.'

The dryad nodded, another little shower of leaves swirling

around her. 'For a human,' she said again, wanting to make her point.

Rian huffed and glanced at me, then turned away again, but I noticed a pleased little smile spreading across his face.

The dryads spent the day guiding us through the forest. We ate only cold rations, but that wasn't really a great hardship. As the day drew to a close, they showed us to a large grassy clearing where we could sleep. We camped, once again eating a cold meal out of respect for the trees.

'How long do you live?' I asked later in the evening, as Anise and I sat chatting with the dryads.

'As long as our trees,' the dryad who had been shadowing Rian all day replied. 'That can be hundreds of your years.'

'And what do you spend your days doing? I mean, what do you do, exactly, other than look after your trees?'

'We guard the forest, nurture the animals, and tend to all of the trees.'

'Do any dryads ever leave?' Anise asked.

Another, younger, dryad laughed. 'We can't leave the forest because of our trees, but why would we want to? Everything we need is all around us. We don't want to leave. What a strange question.'

'It's a beautiful place,' Anise said. 'I can see why you wouldn't want to leave it.'

The dryad smiled. 'You don't want to stay here, do you? You seem to understand us so well, being an Earth Spinner. We could build you a house out of the dead limbs of our trees and you could stay with us forever, living in the forest.'

Anise glanced at Sage, then shook his head. 'Thank you, but no, I don't think I can. That's not to say I'm not tempted, but I couldn't leave him, however much I wanted to live amongst your trees.'

'Oh, well,' she said, getting up, the other dryads following her lead. 'We'll leave you to sleep. You humans need it, for some reason.'

'Can I ask you, why is it I can see you?' I asked. 'I'm not an Earth Spinner.'

'No, you're not,' she said. She looked at me quite seriously. 'Don't you know what you are yet?'

I shook my head. 'No. Can you tell me?'

She laughed, a little silvery laugh like a breeze high up in the trees. 'You're so funny, you humans. How can you not know what you are?'

'No one's ever told me,' I said, a little irritated now.

'Come, sisters, we must let the humans rest,' the elder dryad called from across the clearing.

The young dryad ran off, laughing with her sisters.

'That's annoying,' I said, pulling a blade of grass from the ground. I suddenly realised what I'd done. I looked around furtively, quickly putting it back, trying to hide it in amongst the rest of the grass. I didn't know how the dryads would feel about me pulling up pieces of their forest because I happened to be cross with them.

'What is?' Rian asked, coming to sit beside me.

'If I have a Magic Angle, I think that dryad might know what it is, but she's not telling me. Although, having said that, she could be teasing me. I don't think I have a Magic Angle at all. I just happen to be able to see the dryads.'

Rian slipped an arm around my shoulder. 'I'm sure you have a Magic Angle.'

'But if I do, what is it?'

'Well, you're not Earth, we know that,' Anise said, smoothing his hair over his shoulder.

'Or Fire, or they'd stay away from you like they do me,' Rian said, making a face.

'So that leaves Water or Air,' I said.

'Or Quintessence,' Anise said, looking up.

'I don't think so.'

'Why not?'

'Father's book spoke about Quintessence, and the Quintessence Angle Spinners all came out with their Magic when they were quite young. I've never had anything like that happen to me.'

Rian shrugged. 'Water or Air, then? It must be one of them.'

'I'm still not convinced I have a Magic Angle.' I pouted. I was slowly becoming surrounded by Elemental Angle Spinners. At this rate, it would only be me and Willow without an Angle, and I was beginning to feel a little inadequate.

'You can see the dryads; you have a Magic Angle,' Rian insisted, giving my hand a reassuring squeeze. 'You'll find out what it is. Don't worry.'

But what was it? Maybe I'd never know.

CHAPTER FOURTEEN

'They want to introduce us to the Queen of the Forest,' Anise said the next morning after we'd eaten another cold breakfast.

'Really? Why?' Sage asked, looking around.

'They like us, and she wants to meet us, that's why.'

'Even me?' Rian asked, looking a little unsure. 'I'll stay away if she prefers – I don't want the Dryad Queen to worry about me setting fire to anything.'

'It's fine, she wants to meet you, too,' Anise said.

'But we need to keep going,' I said dubiously. Delaying to meet the Dryad Queen when I wanted to get to Mal as soon as possible annoyed me somewhat.

'We don't want to offend them,' Anise said in a low voice. 'They assured me it wouldn't add much to our journey, and they have helped us. We'd never have made such good time through the forest without them, Phire.'

I nodded, agreeing reluctantly.

We mounted our horses, following the dryads through the trees that shifted gently in the morning breeze.

'They've taught me a lot about the trees and their properties,' Anise said from behind me. 'I think I might be able to come up with even more remedies now. They'll be so useful.'

'You've got a lot already,' Sage said sourly. 'Are you really sure you need any more?'

'I'm always open to new medicines. You know that, Sage,' Anise said. 'And you never know when they might come in handy.'

'True.'

The path we followed couldn't have meandered more if it tried. My mood darkened as we rode, our little "side adventure" and the slow, twisting track getting to me. I also had this strange sensation we were being watched, which, when you're surrounded by dryad ghosts and their trees, I suppose wasn't a great surprise. Even so, that and the fact the trees seemed to crowd in on me didn't help lift my spirits.

The dryads appeared to be a little more comfortable now with Rian being in their forest, and didn't keep such a close eye on him anymore. I noticed he'd started to relax a little, his muscles less strained today as he rode along than they had been yesterday. The dryads' trust made us all feel a little easier.

Rabbits scampered happily across our path, and squirrels

appeared to welcome the dryads as they passed through the trees, leaping from branch to branch with a kind of joy I'd never seen in an animal before. After a brief lunch, we continued. As the afternoon wore on, the birdsong around us grew to a crescendo as we moved through the forest. Constant background music, not a cacophony of sound but an overture of coherent tunes. A strange and wonderful melody. Anise's face was alight with excitement. Large bluebell-type flowers sat between the trees, almost the size of my head, as well as other large blooms.

Anise's eyes had almost come out on stalks as he gazed lovingly at them. 'Interesting. I've never seen anything like this before.'

Neither had I.

Then, in front of us, two large, old oaks, one on either side of the pathway, grew up and across, intertwining with each other in a large archway of branches and emerald leaves.

'Leave your horses,' the older dryad said, pointing to a grassy area beside the path.

We dismounted, leaving our horses tied to bushes with our packs. I squinted at the sky. Colour gradually drained from it as the afternoon headed towards evening. I sighed. We weren't leaving the forest today; the earliest would be tomorrow morning. It was a delay I feared Mal could ill afford, but I had no choice.

Entering through the oak archway, we found ourselves in a huge clearing. Oak trees dotted around the open space reached into the sky, arcing overhead, and provided a canopy of broad leaves that acted as a roof. The surrounding trees and thickets formed green mossy walls, and soft grasses made a beautiful carpet across the floor. Tables sat at the sides of the area, leaving an open space in the centre.

Dryads sat expectantly, gazing at the plates and bowls of berries, fruits, nuts, and seeds waiting to be eaten on the tables. Jugs of wine littered the moss-coloured tablecloths, and wine glasses shimmered in the last of the sun that skittered in through tiny holes in the leafy roof.

At the far side of the green chamber stood a wooden throne on a raised dais, and perching on the throne sat the Dryad Queen. She was taller than her sisters, and her green bark-like skin shone with a golden tinge. Her deep brown eyes and bright green hair complemented each other, and her gown of green moss was unlike anything I'd ever seen before. Little gold, bronze, and copper leaves peppered her hair and whole outfit, and every time she moved a little shower of bright green leaves appeared in a flurry like winter's first snows. She had an ethereal, almost ageless, beauty, and the way *all* the young men looked at her wasn't lost on me.

Rian glanced at me. 'I still prefer you,' he murmured in my ear as if reading my thoughts. 'You'll always be the most beautiful woman I know.'

'Glad to hear it,' I said.

He could be really quite romantic when he wanted. Sometimes I wished he'd do it a little more often.

I frowned. 'Wait a minute, you can see her?'

His brow furrowed. 'Er, yes, now you mention it. I can see all of them.'

Then I realised, so could I. The dryads were no longer ghosts to me, they were as solid as Rian or Anise. Magic wove itself through the glade, making the dryads visible to all of us, and strong Magic at that.

'This way.' The older dryad led us between the tables and seats, and to the Queen's dais. 'Sister Majesty, our visitors,' she said, curtseying, her dress rustling.

Willow and I curtseyed. I did the best I could with my crystal weapons on my back – the silver-threaded embroidery that had appeared on the straps before the Flosian Banquet was still inexplicably there – and the others bowed, too.

The Dryad Queen turned to us. 'You are all welcome here,' she said, her voice rich and silken with the faintest rustle of leaves in the wind. 'Even you, Fire Prince, you, too, are welcome to my home.'

'Thank you,' Rian said, a nervous edge to his voice as he bowed again. 'You're most generous, Your Majesty, although I'm not a prince any longer.'

She waved her hand, dismissing his comment. 'So, you're the ones,' she said, looking at us all, each in turn. 'Yes, I believe you'll do. You have a strength there. I am satisfied. This is good.'

I frowned, looking at the others then back at the Queen Dryad. 'I'm sorry, Your Majesty, but the ones who'll do what?'

'Come, come, you do not need to pretend. We know about you all, my dear. And we know what you are, in particular. How special you are, and what you are capable of. What all of you are capable of.'

I wished I did.

'You do?' I asked as butterflies fluttered unpleasantly in my stomach. What did they know? Did she mean about me being an assassin? That wouldn't cause them problems, would it? Rian's initial misgivings may have been valid after all.

'Our eastern borders burn with winds of sea salt, ailing our leaves and bark. To the north, the cold threatens our new growth.'

'Interesting,' Anise murmured.

'Something must be done and soon. Order must be restored, lest many perish and all suffer.'

I glanced at Rian. He shrugged. Neither of us knew what she was talking about.

I turned back to the Queen. 'Can you tell me exactly what it is yo—'

Music started from the chamber behind us, and the Dryad Queen raised her hand and stood up, a broad grin on her face. 'Let the feast begin!' she said, sweeping down from her oak throne towards the tables.

No, she wasn't going to tell me. I sighed. Maybe I'd get a chance to speak with her later.

We were shown to our seats at one of the tables so we could enjoy the meal with them. Sitting at the table, I eyed the carafes of golden wine. Rian screwed his nose up, and so I asked for water; neither of us were prepared to risk drinking Dryad Wine. Honey sat in wooden bowls, dripping from the honeycomb, and nuts spilt out of green leaf dishes. Rian looked at the berries on the table suspiciously, and refused to go anywhere near them, even moving one of the deep bowls further away. As the sky darkened to black, various leaves around the glade started to glow a warm greeny-yellow, and the flowers edging the clearing also began to glow various shades of blue, red, and white.

'This is amazing,' Willow said, her eyes sparkling with excitement. 'Bobbins. It's like being at a fairies' tea party.'

'Tsk, fairies are idiots,' a dryad said from the other side of the table.

My eyes widened almost as far as Willow's.

'Fairies are real?' Willow asked in amazement. 'I thought they were children's stories. Not real at all.'

'Of course they're real. Don't humans know anything about the world? They're real and they're stupid, far too vain and self-centred to be of any use to anyone, if you ask me. That's why we sent them away over the sea, so they could keep themselves to themselves and leave us alone, in peace. Their constant jabbering is so tiresome.'

'You sent them away?' I asked. Could this really be true?

'A millennia ago. And good riddance. They just spent their time getting in the way.'

I glanced at Willow. Her eyes were so wide I truly thought they might pop out of her head.

We gorged ourselves on the fruit, seeds, and nuts, and the others enjoyed the wine, gulping it down. Perhaps it wasn't as alcoholic as usual, at least that's what I hoped, otherwise they weren't going to be able to see straight for days, and the thought of that rankled me.

The music changed and a waltz started. The dryads all began laughing and shouting, pulling each other from the tables out into the vacant area in the centre, which I now realised was the dance floor. They started to twirl and spin, giggling and smiling as they went. Laughter filled the green chamber as the dance quickened.

Rian held his hand out to me. 'Care to dance?'

'I'm not really dressed for it,' I said. Dancing and I were not good friends at the best of times.

'You look lovely.'

'Liar.'

He pouted. 'You always look lovely to me, whether you're in a silk dress, a tattered suede tunic, or,' he said, leaning towards me, whispering in my ear, 'you've got nothing on at all.'

My face burnt at his words, and he grinned at me as he moved back. 'All right, you've persuaded me,' I said, unbuckling Deorwine and Glædwine, resting them against my chair. I took his hand, and as he led me to the dance floor the dryads closest to us began to giggle. Then I saw why. My black clothes had faded away, leaving me with a green gown of leaves and moss that rustled as I moved, and shone in the ethereal lights.

'How...?' I asked, looking down in awe at the beautiful dress.

'I don't know,' Rian said, his eyes glowing in the light. 'But it doesn't matter. Like I said, you're lovely.'

We started to dance, moving rhythmically to the music between the dancing dryads, spinning and twirling. I couldn't believe I wasn't treading on Rian's toes. Onyx always used to complain when we'd danced back at the Crimson Castle in Iolite. That now seemed like a world away, and so did my old best friend. I wondered if I'd ever see him again, or if he was now lost to me forever.

The music changed to a faster beat, and the melancholy thoughts faded as Rian led me through the next dance, his hand securely at my waist so he didn't lose me in the dancing throng. Even Sage and Anise had joined in, following Willow and Tarragon's example. Sage didn't look best pleased, and Tarragon initially had a slightly grumpy look on his face. Willow also had a gorgeous green gown on and looked very pleased with herself, and rightfully so. Tarragon's expression quickly changed to one of appreciation, then adoration.

After a while, we stopped for a rest, sitting back at our table, getting our breath back as we sipped at our water and ate more fruit and nuts.

'I can't believe we're in a dryad palace,' Rian said, looking around at the dryads and their wondrous home. 'It's like some sort of incredible dream.'

I nodded, gazing at the festivities. 'You're right, it's out of a storybook, not the real world at all—'

A sudden commotion out in the forest stopped me from continuing. Rabbits, deer, and badgers suddenly rushed past the hall's entrance, all terrified of something.

'What's going on?' I peered out the entrance, but could see nothing unusual, only the animals rushing through the glowing forest.

'Perhaps it's some dryad race for animals?' Rian said. 'You never know what strange rituals they may have out here.'

'Maybe,' I replied, not convinced.

'Ow! What was that?' he asked, rubbing his cheek.

I glanced down to the floor where something shone in the light, something that had just hit him in the face. I bent down and picked it up. I gasped. Dropped it onto the table like it was a hot coal.

'What's the matter?' Rian asked, picking it up. His eyes went wide. 'It can't be. Here?'

I looked around the chamber. 'Where the hell is he?' I asked, my teeth gritted, fists clenched as Rian gingerly placed the small red carnelian bead back on the table.

'What's he done to me now?' Rian looked into his glass, his face pale, then at me. 'Am I going to die this time?'

CHAPTER FIFTEEN

'Hell's teeth, not if I have anything to do with it,' I said, looking across the glade and into the trees, scanning them for any sign of the Coterie assassin. I couldn't see any trace of him anywhere. I swore.

A dryad across the table from me screamed. A scream of such pain and horror that I shot to my feet, heart immediately racing, palms clammy.

She began to smoke.

Her dress smouldered, her body burning, her hair turning to flames before she collapsed in a heap of ash.

'Our trees! They're burning!'

'Fire! Fire!'

'Murderer…'

'Flames, not the flames!'

The cries of the dryads froze my heart. I stared at the unfolding scene of chaos as dryads ran around, directionless, fear and terror everywhere. On one side of the glade, far out into the trees, an orange-red glimmer flickered. The forest was alight, fire swiftly taking hold of the trees and bracken.

'I think this time he's trying to kill us all,' I said, pointing. 'Look.'

Rian followed my gaze, his eyes filling with horror. 'Forest fire,' he hissed. 'That's barbaric. Perhaps he doesn't know about the dryads?'

'He won't care about them, one way or the other,' I said, rage and disgust tearing at my core. 'He just wants to get us, he won't care who gets caught up in it.'

More of the dryads began to smoulder and burn as others ran to them in a futile attempt to help. Anise's face was stricken with alarm and revulsion, his eyes clouded with pain.

The older dryad that had travelled with us ran over. 'The fire, it's coming this way. You must flee, Earth Spinner. Go with your friends now, before it's too late.'

'What about you?' Anise asked, his face a sickly grey. 'You must come with us.'

She shook her head. 'I cannot. I stay with my Queen, and she will not leave her tree,' she said, pointing to where the fearful looking Dryad Queen sat on her oak tree throne, quickly handing something to one of her sisters. The Queen grabbed hold of the arms of her throne, her knuckles white as her fingers clenched.

Anise looked at the Queen of the Dryads. 'Then we'll stay, too. Maybe we can help—'

'We do exactly as she says,' Sage said, taking a firm hold of Anise's hand.

'Sage, no, we have to help.'

Sage didn't let go, dragging his boyfriend along behind him despite his protestations. 'We're going. We can't do anything – we can't put out a whole forest fire.'

'Unfortunately, he's right,' Rian said, glancing around before grabbing my hand. 'You're staying with me.' A firmness, tinged with fear, filled his voice and I wasn't about to argue. As Sage said, we could do nothing but run.

We all quickly followed after Sage and Anise. I tried to avoid looking at the dryads that screamed in excruciating pain as their trees, and they themselves, burnt to death. How could such an amazing evening end in such horror? Carnelian had chalked up another heinous crime against his name. If I didn't punish him, I was pretty sure from the look on Anise's face that he would, once he found out Carnelian was behind this, and Anise had more elaborate methods with his Herb Chest than even I had with my War Fan.

As we rushed out of the glade, my dress reverted to my black suede clothes, and the crystal weapons reattached themselves to my back. We reached the horses. The forest to the south burnt, a raging inferno of flame. Ash and sparks swept past us. The smell of burning wood hung heavy in the air, thick and choking, as a menacing red-orange glow filled the forest. Dryads ran around in panic in a desperate attempt to escape the fiery maelstrom. Others stood stock still, as if awaiting their inevitable fate. My heart broke at the sight, but what could I do? Nothing. I felt totally helpless in the face of Carnelian's brutality. Again.

We mounted our horses, the whites of their eyes showing, their nostrils flaring anxiously, and headed north through the trees away from the fire. I looked for Carnelian, but once again he proved elusive. The bastard.

The wind got up. The flames began to rush towards us at ever greater speed. Outrunning them wouldn't be easy. Fire jumped from tree, to fern, to tree in a terrifying wave of gold heat. A dryad running beside me went up in flames. Her agonised, dying scream would stay with me forever. Animals ran past us. Deer, badgers, squirrels; all desperate to escape the raging inferno as tendrils of smoke drifted around us, malevolent fingers penetrating the forest.

Heat scorched the back of my neck even as we urged our horses on. The sound of wood splitting as it reached impossible temperatures raged behind me. Not far enough behind me. A dryad in front of us started to smoke. She lurched from side to side, shrieking. Burst into flames. My horse finally lost its nerve. Rian's too. They reared, unceremoniously dumping us onto the loamy forest floor. The others, oblivious to our fate, carried on as our horses bolted after them.

I gasped, the fall having knocked the wind out of me, but breathing in the sooty air only irritated my throat and made me cough.

'Up!' Rian commanded, grabbing my hand and roughly pulling me to my feet.

We plunged on, hand in hand, fear and necessity spurring us forward after the others as trees started to flame around us. Bracken and ferns lit up like candles. Trees burst with the heat of the fire, splitting, sending bark outwards as missiles. We ran on, our lungs crying out for clean air, our hearts slamming into our rib cages, our pulses almost drowning out the roar of the fire, but not quite. We jumped a fallen log, its edges beginning to smoke. We passed flaming dryads and smouldering ferns.

And still, we ran.

We broke into a clearing where short grass flared orange at the edges, the forest alight all around us except for straight ahead. We forged on. We clung to life by a thread; a thread that threatened to burn to ash at any moment. The taste of burning vegetation settled on my tongue and I tried to keep my mouth closed, but couldn't get enough air into my lungs through my nose alone. The heat intensified. As we reached the far side of the clearing, a deer shot across in front of us, taking me by surprise.

I tripped.

Lost hold of Rian's warm hand, our fingers losing touch with each other as his hand slipped from mine.

I stumbled and fell.

Rian's forward momentum took him onwards. A curtain of flames sprung up between me and him. I scrambled backwards into the centre of the clearing. The flames closed in from all sides, the inferno intent on my death. Maybe Juniper and Beryl would get what they wanted after all – me dead. I grabbed Glædwine, crouching behind it, using the crystal shield to protect me from the worst of the heat, but no weapon, cursed or not, could save me from this fiery hell. It felt like forever that I remained there as the flames surrounded me, gradually closing in as the minutes passed, intent on giving me a slow and painful death.

The heat started to burn my skin like a hot summer's sun shining on my face. The flames swam around me. I coughed on the smoke. I saw no escape, only burning to death. My last thoughts would be of Rian. At least he'd escaped this most horrific of ends. By the Stars, I hoped he'd have a long and happy life, that he'd find the Fire Opal – maybe even rescue Mal for me. Tears sprang in my eyes, quickly evaporating in the heat. My clothes started to singe. I bowed my head, preparing myself for my last, painful breaths as my hair began to scorch.

I blinked. The flames ahead of me flickered. Parted. A black silhouette appeared walking through a tunnel of flames, totally untouched by heat or fire. They walked calmly through, the tongues of red and orange moving aside to allow passage. The loud roar of flames and burning trees dimmed. The figure reached me, amber eyes bright, maroon hair glistening in the firelight, one hand securely holding my glowing Amethyst Talisman.

'Take my hand,' he said calmly, his face pale as he reached towards me. 'You'll be all right.'

I looked up at Rian. How was he doing this? Now wasn't the time. He was here. Alive. He'd come for me. I took his hand. Immediately, the intense heat around me fell away to a gentle warmth, like Rian's hand.

'I don't understand,' I said, standing up, returning my shield to my back.

'Neither do I, entirely,' he said, flames flickering in his wide amber eyes. 'But I think it's because I'm a Spinner. Come on.'

We walked quickly across the clearing and out into the flaming forest, untouched by fire as it parted in front of us like two curtains being opened at a window, leaving us in a tunnel of mere warmth. I gazed around in amazement and my heart thundered in my chest as we hurried along. Trees burnt and ferns incinerated around me. Over my head, flames licked at the leafy canopy, burning and charring. But for us, there was only warmth, and we finally escaped the fire, reaching cool, green forest. We didn't stop.

I let go of his hand. The scorching heat returned to the back of my neck, the fire still raging behind me. I grabbed Rian's hand again and mere warmth touched my skin. Rian looked at me, wild-eyed at what had happened, an element of confusion and fear on his face.

'Thank the Herbs. I thought I'd lost you again,' he murmured, pausing for a brief moment to kiss me gently on the lips. His velvet lips were warm, soft and as intoxicating as ever, even in a wildfire.

'Me too,' I said. Even my face felt cooler now, except for when he kissed me. Whatever Fire Magic he had was incredibly strong to be able to do this, to keep us safe in such a raging inferno.

'This way,' he said, and we hurried on through the green forest, sparks still flying around us as the fire hounded our footsteps, still consuming trees and vegetation with a vengeance.

'Where are the others?' I asked.

'Up ahead. They're setting up a firebreak, or at least Tarragon is.'

'How?'

'You'll see.'

I pushed leaves and ferns away as we forged on through the dark forest, still illuminated enough by the fire to see where we were going, still clasping each other's hands. Up ahead I could hear cries and screams – more dryads? – and the sound of rushing water. We burst out of the foliage onto a river bank. Ahead of us lay a wide river that moved swiftly through the trees, glistening in the moonlight and fire, a silken ribbon flowing east.

'Come on, it's only knee deep,' Rian said, leading me forwards.

I nodded. A scream on the far bank made me hesitate. A brief burst of flames lit the water. A dryad burnt. Around her stood yet more of her sisters. Beside them stood Sage, Anise and Willow, holding the horses. Tarragon stood six feet out into the river, his face one of intense concentration and apprehension. On his right wrist sat a black leather wristband with an oval rose quartz stone set in it that I hadn't seen before. Where had that come from?

'What's going on?' I asked, the shock of cold from the water making me shudder.

'Tarragon's going to stop the fire,' Rian said.

'He's what?' I asked, wading through the water, holding Rian's arm to steady myself.

The fire thundered behind us. Reinvigorated by a stiff breeze, the flames surged forwards towards the river. Smoke drifted over the water as fire licked at leaves, caressed branches and devoured whole trees. Another dryad shrieked in pain and misery as her tree burned.

'I can't put it out,' Tarragon said from ahead.

'But you can stop it,' Willow said, her voice thin and scared.

'I'll try.'

Rian and I stumbled through the water, sending spray in all directions. I slipped, almost lost my footing, but Rian held me and we toiled on, finally drawing parallel with Tarragon.

'Now!' Rian said to him as we passed.

Tarragon nodded, his eyes determined yet fearful. He placed a hand into the cool water, the other coming to rest on his Rose Quartz Wristband. He shut his eyes as we waded to the shore.

'But what's he doing?' I asked, totally confused.

'Watch,' Rian said as we reached the river bank and looked back, hands still clasped.

I did as he said.

The water around Tarragon began to swirl and bubble. Twisting and turning in little whirlpools and eddies, it interrupted the flow of the river. The whole river.

'Hell's teeth,' I swore. The river stopped. It swirled in place. The sound of the water changed from flowing to gurgling.

Then it began to rise.

In one great sheet, as far as I could see east or west along the ribbon of river, it rose in a great wall of water, leaving the riverbed dry. Rocks, once submerged, protruded from the ground. A few fish splashed around, caught in little pools that remained behind, but the rest of the water flew skyward, producing a huge barrier, one that kept the heat, the sparks, and the fire out.

CHAPTER SIXTEEN

My heart skipped a beat at the demonstration of such raw power. This was almost as impressive as Rian's recent display, although, walking through fire I did feel had an edge. A slight edge. I was biased, though.

'How long can he keep that up for?' Willow asked.

Anise shrugged. 'No idea, but hopefully long enough.'

'I think it's holding itself in place now,' Tarragon said, moving slowly backwards. 'I just need to release it.'

'I have to say I'm impressed,' Sage said as Tarragon moved back to the shore. 'I had no idea you had something like this in you.'

'Neither did I, until the dryads told me I was a Water Spinner and gave me this,' he said, gesturing to the leather wristband with the Rose Quartz stone glistening in it.

Water Spinner? I nodded sagely.

Tarragon looked at me, his eyes narrowing. 'You knew?'

'I had my suspicions after the way that wave changed course on the way into Scilla harbour,' I said. 'You know, the one you threw your arm out towards? The one that didn't drench us?'

A big grin formed on his face. 'I forgot all about that.'

'Then there was the shipwreck on the way back from Iolite,' Willow said. 'You went under. Then the sea sort of spat you out. Don't you remember?'

'And you knew about the waterfall, pool, and river in the valley after Muscari,' Rian said, giving me a wink despite his still-pale face.

Tarragon's eyes widened as he nodded slowly. 'It's been there a while then, hasn't it?'

'Ironic, really, seeing as you don't like water much.' Sage grinned.

'Thanks,' Tarragon said drily. 'It's a bit tiring, though, all this Magic Spinning.'

I hoped Tarragon had the strength to hold the water in place for long enough. Rian moved a little way down the riverbank and sat on a boulder, gazing out at the wall of water, his shoulders sagging with fatigue.

'How did you know you could walk through fire?' I asked, following him.

'It happened by accident,' he said. 'I'd stumbled free of the flames and realised you weren't with me. Tarragon and Sage tried to stop me from going back into the fire, but I managed to slip free of them, fell forwards right into the flames. I thought I was dead until I realised they weren't hot or burning me. I think your Talisman helped, too, because I took hold of it and a sort of path, tunnel, opened up in front of me, free of flames and searing heat, and it took hardly any effort at all. That's when I knew I could come back for you.'

'The Talisman enhanced your powers.' I nodded. Father's book was right. 'But apparently an Artefact's power doesn't last forever, though, so you better not use it too much.'

'How do you know that? Your father's book again?'

I nodded. 'Anyway, you rescued me in the nick of time.'

'I thought I'd already lost you,' he said, a haunted look in his eyes. 'When I lost your hand, I thought I'd killed you – that losing hold of you had left you to a horrible, painful, lonely death.'

His pale face wasn't because of using his new power; it was because he thought I'd died as a result of his carelessness.

'You didn't let go of me,' I said, sitting down. 'I tripped and lost hold of you. Not the other way around.'

'You did? I thought…'

'It wasn't your fault. If anything, it was mine.'

'Maybe it wasn't anyone's fault after all,' he said, colour beginning to return to his beautiful rose-beige skin. 'Sorry I cut it so damn fine.'

'It was getting a little close, but it doesn't matter now. You were there when I needed you,' I smiled, slipping my arms around him, giving him a squeeze. 'You saved my life. You're my hero.'

He grinned sheepishly at me. 'That's all right then, but perhaps we ought to look after each other a little better in future.'

I nodded.

We stayed by the river for several hours until dawn rolled in, the sky lightening as the fire burnt itself out. Thankfully, we only lost a couple more dryads. The remaining ones huddled together, weeping quietly at the loss of their many sisters.

Tarragon finally released the water. It fell in a great wave back into the river with a thunderous splash before flowing onwards once more on its long journey to the sea. For a few moments, the water foamed at its banks, trying to escape, but then settled into its normal, fluid motion.

'Thank you, Water Spinner,' a dryad said, turning to Tarragon, whose face now had a greyish cast to it from the energy he'd used. 'You saved many of my sisters tonight.'

He looked at the grieving dryads. 'Not enough,' he said wearily.

'You could not have done more. What we crave now is vengeance.'

'Don't worry, I've got that under control,' I said, clenching a fist without thinking about it.

'You know how it started?' Anise asked, surprised.

'Carnelian. Trying to kill Rian again. Or maybe all of us.'

Anise's eyes hardened to agates. 'If you don't get him, I will.'

'Maybe we'll do it together.'

Rian looked at me, concern clouding his eyes. 'No, Lady Merciless,' he chided.

'I didn't say I was going to kill him,' I said.

'There are ways other than killing,' Anise murmured, a steely glint in his eyes as he spoke.

I rather thought he'd say that.

Rian glanced between me and Anise and shook his head. 'No. We don't stoop to their level.'

'I'll find somewhere for us to camp and rest a while,' Anise said, moving off into the trees and muttering to himself about the differences between revenge and retribution.

Rian sighed as we all followed him.

A grassy glade provided a suitable resting place. Tarragon lay down and went straight to sleep – he needed the rest after his exertions, and so did Rian. The rest of us decided to forgo breakfast, too, none of us feeling much like eating. We snatched a few hours' sleep, although as I curled up next to Rian, my dreams filled with fire and death. When I awoke, the dryads had become ghosts again, and the others couldn't see them at all, except for Anise, of course. Whatever Magic had been in the dryad palace, it faded rapidly as day took hold.

'We will take you to the forest's edge,' a dryad said to Anise. 'Show you the northern path.'

'Thank you.' Anise nodded, his face etched with sadness.

My horse and Rian's had both followed the other horses out of the fire, so we still had our mounts and packs. We rode along, subdued, talking little as the day wore on, everyone traumatised by the night before. My stomach kept tying itself in knots. Anise looked pale and haggard. It had hit him hardest, being an Earth Spinner. I still didn't know why I could see the dryads, and they didn't seem to be in the mood to answer my questions. If only the Dryad Queen had said more. Rian and Tarragon both still looked tired, and my husband, in particular, had sagging shoulders. Sage and Willow, along with me, were the only ones relatively unscathed, although my hair had scorched a little and a burning smell followed me around. The night's tragedy had left us all deeply upset.

The oaks gave way to silver birch and poplars as we moved on. The forest was notable for its lack of wildlife today, probably still in hiding after the fire. Few sounds echoed through the trees; the odd wisp of choking smoke still drifted intermittently on the breeze, threading its way between the undergrowth from the still-smouldering trees.

We finally reached the edge of the emerald forest in the late afternoon, the trees coming to an abrupt halt, moorland stretching away into the distance where the sandy-coloured Border Mountains rose skywards, trying to touch the clouds. A chill hung in the air, not what I'd expected so close to Mere. A cold wind came down from the mountains, the growth of the trees stunted by the temperature.

'We will leave you now,' a dryad said. 'You may have a small fire at this place. Our oaks are far away now, and we know we can trust you.'

Anise nodded.

'Know you will always have our protection for what you did for us in our hour of need,' another dryad said.

'Thank you,' Tarragon said, nodding, as Anise relayed the message.

'We're so sorry for what happened,' Rian said. 'I—it was my fault, really. The assassin was trying to kill me. It was nothing to do with you or the forest.'

That's why he'd still been looking so desolate. He blamed himself?

'This was not your doing, Fire Prince. Only the assassin can take the blame for what happened last night,' said the dryad that had treated Rian with such suspicion when we'd first met – I was glad she'd survived. 'He started the inferno, not you.'

I told Rian what she'd said.

'I suppose so,' he said, bowing his head.

'There is no guilt on your part, and do not take such upon yourself,' the dryad said.

Rian nodded, looking a little happier as I repeated the dryad's words.

The dryads slowly drifted off into the trees, leaving us alone. We made camp at the edge of the forest, starting a small fire, but making sure a circle of stones contained it so it couldn't inadvertently spread into the trees.

'I didn't realise this Magic business could be so tiring,' Tarragon said with a yawn as we collected the stones. 'I feel as if I've been hit by a wagon.'

'Even with an Artefact, it can be, by all accounts, depending on what you're doing,' I said. 'So the dryads told you you were a Water Spinner?'

He nodded. 'I didn't believe it at first, but as we crossed the river they told me what to do and handed me this Rose Quartz Wristband. It's an Artefact the Queen's been looking after for centuries, after its original owner died here. Anyway, I tried doing what they said, and the water obeyed me.'

'And in the end, you didn't use it by accident or hurt anyone.'

He shook his head and smiled. 'No, I didn't.'

Anise and Sage prepared a stew. We still had little appetite but knew our strength relied on it, so we ate most of it. As I put my bowl down, the campfire reflected in the diamonds on Rian's ring sitting snugly on my finger. It gave me a kind of renewed strength, being there, and made me smile. We settled down to sleep early, extra blankets keeping us warm in the chill air despite the warmth from the fire and each other. It took a while for me to drift off to sleep. So many thoughts and feelings tumbled through my head, ranging from horror to anger, from vengeance to sympathy and grief, but eventually my tiredness took over and I fell asleep in Rian's arms.

Flaming dryads surrounded me. They smouldered, smoked, burnt, screamed, turned to ash. Whichever way I looked, they were in front of me, dying horrifically.

I couldn't escape.

I tasted ash on my tongue. Acrid smoke in my nose and throat made me choke. Heat clawed at my skin. Shrieks reverberated in my ears and skull. Agonised faces filled my vision.

I awoke with a gasp, my body covered in a cold sweat that plastered my hair to my face and neck. My heart thundered like I was running uphill. I sat up. Rian lay blissfully asleep next to me. The campfire had reduced to embers. Tarragon had insisted on taking his watch alone, but had nodded off, again, and leant against a tree, snoring gently. I shook my head, but at least we were safe from Prince Monkshood here.

I carefully got out from under my blankets so as not to disturb

Rian, placed a couple of logs on the dying fire, and left camp. I moved quietly to the edge of the trees and sat on a boulder overlooking the moonlit landscape. Silver painted the distant mountains, a river to the left a white ribbon in the light. My stomach cramped, convulsed. *Hell's teeth*. I lurched forwards, bending over a dead tree that lay on the ground in front of me, and vomited. Smoke still lingered in my nose, screams in my head. How I'd ever lay what had happened in the Dryad Forest to rest, I didn't know. Maybe that would only come when I caught up with Carnelian. Wherever the bastard was, I would find him. He would pay for the massacre he wrought.

The waves of anxiety passing through my body forced any food I'd had in my stomach out. Cold sweat covered me, making me shiver. A warm hand came to rest on my back, gently rubbing up and down in a comforting fashion.

'I'm here, you're all right,' Rian said softly. 'I hadn't realised you'd got up.'

I wiped my mouth and turned towards him. 'I'm sorry, it's…'

'Nightmares, I know. I have them most nights, too. And not just about the dryads,' he said, his moon-bleached eyes clouding, his hair shifting in the little breeze that wafted down from the mountains, making me shiver all the more.

'What else do you have nightmares about?'

'The usual things – you dying after that Moonflower Elixir, and when the Curse almost took you. Now it's the fire, too.'

'Oh.' He'd mentioned the Moonflower nightmare before, but I didn't know he still had them, and not about the Curse, too. I bowed my head. 'You never said.'

He shrugged. 'I've come so close to losing you a couple of times. I suppose it's only to be expected, really, seeing as I love you so much. I didn't say anything because I didn't want to worry you, rather like you've not mentioned yours to me since I was ill.'

My eyes widened. 'You know I've been having nightmares?'

'Yes.' He nodded. 'Of course I do. I've been sleeping next to you every night. Holding you. I've felt you tossing and turning in your sleep, talking. Once, I even thought you cried, so I held you close until you settled again.'

'You did?' My heart melted. 'I didn't realise.'

'I thought you might tell me about them when you were ready, or they'd go.'

'I didn't want to worry you, either. I keep dreaming about you, when you were ill, and I didn't want to stir things up for you again by mentioning it. They were getting better, until this happened. You being with me when I wake up, though – I can deal with them because of that, because of you.'

'I understand. When I wake up and you're here by my side, the nightmares, none of it matters,' he said, resting his forehead on mine and caressing the side of my face with his hot hand. 'I couldn't bear to lose you now,' he said simply, his face stripped bare, all his emotions of fear, angst, hope, despair, love, on display.

'N—nor I you. You're my best friend, my soulmate... my husband.'

Sobs started to wrack my body. I'd held it together until he spoke of nightmares, particularly his own. Everything Rian had been through cut me to the core. Now, everything I'd been holding back, suppressing, suddenly and unexpectedly spilt out. Being cursed, Rian's almost execution, my almost death at the hands of the Curse, almost losing Rian to Carnelian's poison, Dire Wolves and their handiwork, the Dryad Massacre, and threading through everything – Mal. Tears poured down my face unchecked. I couldn't have stopped them if I'd wanted to.

Rian held me close. He wrapped his arms around me, sandalwood in their wake, his warmth filling me. He kissed my head, stroked my hair, and whispered in my ear as he comforted me. Emotions tumbled through me like a waterfall, and for a while I wept uncontrollably. Eventually I cried myself out.

'You're all those things to me, too, and I can't bear to see you like this, know you're suffering and there's nothing I can do,' he said, kissing the tears from my cheeks, his lips soft and scorching hot against my skin. 'Jasmine said you'd suffered enough.'

'You remember that?' I frowned.

'Like I said before, I remember pretty much all of it.'

I shuddered. I truly thought he'd been too delirious a lot of the time during his poisoning to know up from down.

'Just you being with me is enough to help me through,' I said, looking into his glassy eyes. 'You're all I need.'

'I love you with all my heart, my Samphire Amethyst. You know that, don't you?'

I nodded.

He reached out and gently caressed my cheek. 'It's only you, only ever been you. What hurts you, hurts me. If you're sad, I'm sad, too. I want to feel everything you do. I want you, need you, love you. As long as you're mine, I'm whole – without you I'm nothing.'

Tears sprang in my eyes again at his heartfelt words, but not tears of pity and sadness this time.

'I feel the same. If something hurts you, it's like a knife to my chest. When I thought I'd lose you at Jasmine's…' No. He didn't need to know about my death wish. 'I need you like air, I love you so much. Without you, I'm dead inside.'

He moved a curl from my face, a wan little smile on his lips, love in his eyes. 'Then it's a good thing we're both all right and together, isn't it?'

I smiled and nodded, his words and love filling me.

'The dreams will get easier, still be there, but they'll become shades of what they are now. At least they have for me,' he said.

'Then they will for me, too, and until then we'll hold each other as we sleep and be comforted by each other.'

'Exactly what I was going to say.' He smiled, and this time the sparkle reached his eyes. 'And after the nightmares go, which they will eventually, we can still hold each other.' He looked out over the distant river. 'There's still a few hours until dawn. Shall we see if we can get a little more sleep?'

'Yes, and wake Tarragon.'

'He was asleep when you got up, too?' Rian asked.

I nodded.

'I'll damn well have a word with him tomorrow. He was the one that wanted to have a watch because of Dire Wolves and Carnelian, then insisted Willow rest and him take his watch alone, and then he sleeps right through his just like last time,' Rian said, shaking his head grimly. For a moment I was very glad I wasn't Tarragon.

We walked slowly back to camp, hand in hand. Tarragon opened an eye as we approached, then threw a branch on the fire, pretending to have been awake the whole time. Rian and I got back under our blankets, and I curled up beside him as we lay with our arms around each other, and drifted off to a dreamless sleep.

CHAPTER SEVENTEEN

A cold wind swept towards us from the north, and yet the smell of sand wove into it with the promise of heat and desert. Neither appealed to me. I preferred Iolite's more temperate climate, which wasn't dissimilar to Aerba's, maybe just a little more humid. We rode across scrubby moorland, purple and white heathers as far as the eye could see, the call of grouse in the distance as bees flew between the flowers, communicating with each other in some invisible way. The serene landscape lay in complete juxtaposition to what stretched behind us and what probably waited ahead. For that brief time I allowed myself to forget everything else and just concentrate on the jingling of my horse's harness, the buzzing of the bees, and the maroon-haired young man riding beside me.

The sandy-coloured mountains ahead, once volcanic, were now dead, or at least dormant. Clouds grazed the tops of their highest peaks, but no snow glistened in the sunlight, the arid climate too dry for that. As I gazed at the unwelcoming barrier between Flos and Mere, I hoped we had enough blankets and sufficient water to sustain us on our crossing. It would be a hard climb, without the prospect of hunting for additional food or much hope of finding water, if we ran into any difficulties.

'This is going to be miserable,' Sage said, screwing his nose up as he looked at the mountains. 'Cold and miserable. I hate the cold.' He pulled his cloak higher up around his neck.

'Are you going to complain the whole way across the mountains?' Tarragon asked from beside him as we urged our horses on through the heather.

'Quite possibly.'

Tarragon sighed. 'Then you can bugger off and ride next to someone else, if you're going to moan all the time. I don't want to hear your continuous bellyaching for the next couple of days, y'know.' He glanced back at me and winked; I smiled back.

Sage grunted, stopped speaking, and cast a quick, furtive look in Anise's direction.

'How long will it take to cross the mountains?' Willow asked.

'I'm not sure, but if we stop in the foothills tonight, start crossing tomorrow, we might be out the day after, if we're lucky,' I said, watching a bird of prey hovering to our right. It dived into the heather after some small rodent. 'At worst, it'll be the day after.'

'Then we'd better be lucky,' Sage said sourly, breaking his brief silence.

'Stop complaining,' Rian said. 'It's not going to be that bad.'

'Just you wait. Cold and miserable.' Sage flicked his eyes towards Anise, then away again.

Rian sighed and shook his head, although a grin played at the corners of his mouth.

I looked at Anise. He'd been quiet throughout the banter, his face drawn and pale. He'd been really upset by the fire and the dryad deaths – we all had – but as an Earth Spinner he'd felt it even more keenly. Perhaps Sage's moaning was actually an attempt to pull Anise out of himself and lighten the heavy atmosphere that had fallen around us since the fire, because I'd noticed him glancing at his boyfriend once or twice as he spoke. He was well aware of the pain Anise was feeling. Unfortunately, if it was an attempt to rouse Anise from his brooding, it hadn't worked, but at least he'd tried.

We made steady progress rising up from the moorland and into the foothills of the Border Mountains, stopping for the night at the boundary where moor met arid volcanic rock. We took our extra blankets out from our packs, but Rian's warmth was what soothed me through the long night as we huddled under them. Without him, I think I'd have spent the night shivering. The heat from his body as he held me tight kept me going until morning, his steady heartbeat against my back a comforting reminder of his being there with me, alive and well. The now-normal nightmares came and went as the moon travelled serenely across the sky, disappearing before the dawn light stained the morning clouds purple and pink. At least I didn't have to rush off and vomit tonight, though.

'Why didn't we get the tents out last night?' Sage asked, glancing sideways at Anise, his earring catching the early morning sunlight. 'I was freezing.'

Anise sat beside our little fire, stirring something, his eyes far away, his tongue out. I chewed on a nail as I watched him.

'You should have thought of that before we went to sleep,' Tarragon said. 'Willow and I were quite warm enough. You should've shared with Anise.'

'He didn't want to,' Sage said softly in a sullen and worried tone. He cast a quick glance towards his boyfriend and then looked away again.

'We'll get them out tonight,' Rian said, looking towards Anise who appeared to be oblivious to everything we said. He glanced back at me, a concerned expression on his face. We were all beginning to get a little anxious about Anise.

We broke camp and rode on up into the mountains. The terrain became hard and steep as our horses laboured up the rocky inclines. At times, the way became treacherous with dust and scree covering the way, everything around us a beige-yellow.

'Hell's teeth!' I said as my horse slipped, almost throwing me.

Rian frowned. 'Let's walk the next bit,' he said, dismounting. 'We don't want anyone breaking their necks out here.'

'Not a bad idea,' Willow said, dismounting, too.

I found myself walking towards the back of our group as I led my horse, only Anise behind me, as the others strode ahead chatting happily to each other as their horses laboured up the steep incline. Perhaps this was my chance to have a word with him. Slowing my pace a little, I walked beside Anise.

'Are you all right?' I asked in a low voice.

He glanced at me, pain flickering behind his eyes. Shook his head.

'Want to talk about it?'

'Not really, Phire.'

'It might help,' I said, trying to give him an encouraging little smile.

He sighed and looked at me. 'All right. You know, it's funny, but sometimes I feel I can talk to you about things, about Magic, that I find it hard to with the others. As if you understand the most.'

'And I don't have a Magic Angle,' I said, the irony not lost on me. 'I've shown no powers or special skills.'

Anise frowned. 'Be patient.'

'You sound like Rian.'

'That's because he's wise like me,' Anise said, a wan smile trying to break out on his lips. He paused, and I stopped with him, our horses glad of the rest. 'I hadn't realised how strong my bond was with nature until the fire. I mean, I always knew it was there, not that I was an Earth Spinner of course, but the connection with the flora of the land, with the herbs. Now, of course, it makes complete sense.' He bowed his head, one hand tangled in his horse's reins. 'Seeing the trees burning, the dryads in such pain, I—I don't know...'

I reached out and took his free hand. 'I understand. I mean, I'm not an Earth Spinner but I feel it keenly, too. So does Rian. We just need to work to stop Carnelian from doing anything like this again.'

'It's not just that, though.'

'Then what else?'

'Now I know about my Angle, I can see that I'm sensing other things as well. Jasmine and Hyacinth talked about droughts and floods, and the Dryad Queen spoke about the salt winds and the cold affecting the forest, and about order needing to be restored. I'm beginning to feel it now, too, to sense these things, as if nature is unbalanced in some way and needs to be saved. Whatever's causing it is starting to affect everything around us, the whole of nature. In a few places it's having a considerable effect, like the salt winds. Everywhere else, it's only small things at the moment, things you wouldn't really notice, but it's there. It needs to be stopped. Nature needs to be rebalanced, restored to its normal harmony.'

'But how?'

He shrugged. 'I don't know, and I guess that's what bothers me most. I can see it needs doing, but not how to do it, or even who could manage such a thing.'

I chewed on a nail. 'The Dryad Queen said we were "the ones". But to do what? Do you think rebalancing nature is what she was talking about?'

'Even if it was, I don't know how we'd go about doing it, Phire. We've a Fire Spinner, a Water Spinner, and an Earth Spinner. Even so, what could *we* possibly do to rebalance anything?'

I glanced at Sage. 'We may have another Magic Spinner. I mean, Sage may have a Magic Angle, too.'

'And you?' he asked, looking at me. 'You're a High Blood.'

I sighed. 'It's like I've said already – I haven't started any fires or raised any walls of water, let alone begun sensing anything.'

'But you could see the dryads when the others couldn't.'

'Only as ghosts.'

'But you still saw them. You have some sort of Magic Angle, I'm certain of it. It's just not shown itself properly yet.'

'A very weak one, perhaps. Not strong enough to do anything with. Sage is probably a better bet than me.'

'Not that even if he was a Magic Spinner, Sage's help would do anything. I mean, what would we do? How would you go about rebalancing nature, anyway?'

'I don't know, but if I could influence things somehow, I think I'd probably feel duty-bound to do it,' I said, gazing out at the mountains. 'Whatever the cost. I couldn't let the Lands, the people, suffer from storms and famine and flood if I could stop it.'

'Neither could I. I thought it was the Earth Spinner coming out in me, but perhaps not.'

'It's probably your sense of justice.'

'Like you?'

I nodded.

'Well, in the meantime I'll content myself with worrying about catching up with Carnelian,' Anise said, his eyes bright with vengeance.

'Rian's probably right, killing him isn't the answer.'

'What about maiming?' he asked, a strange look in his eyes. 'There are herbs…'

I couldn't tell if Anise was being serious or not. 'Let's wait until we've caught him, then we can decide what to do with him.'

'You think we'll catch up with him?'

'Not really, no. But I do think he'll catch up with us eventually. He'll try something else to get Rian, and I must be ready for him.'

'We.'

'What?'

'*We'll* be ready,' Anise said, looking straight at me. 'This isn't all on you, Phire. He may be your husband, but Rian is family to us. He's important. We all love him in our own ways, and we'll all help to protect him, especially as we now know Carnelian is still trying to get to him.'

For a moment, tears stung my eyes. I knew I wasn't alone in this, but having Anise actually come out and say it to me meant the world. 'Thank you,' I said, trying not to let my voice crack with the emotions I felt. 'We both appreciate that.'

Anise smiled. 'It's the truth.' He shrugged. 'We care about you both.'

'And Sage cares about you. Tell him what you've told me. He's really worried about you.'

'He is?' Anise frowned. 'How can you tell?'

'The way he keeps picking fights with Tarragon and then glancing at you, waiting for a response,' I said. 'I think he's hoping you'll intervene and talk to him.'

'Oh. I thought he was just being irritable.'

I laughed. 'Not on this occasion, no,' I said. 'It's all about you. Talk to him. He loves you, he'll understand how you feel, and he may even be able to help you.'

Anise nodded. 'I will.'

From up ahead, Rian glanced back at us, frowning as he noticed our joined hands.

'We'd better catch the others up,' I said, letting go of Anise.

He nodded and hurried after Sage. I walked up and joined Rian where he'd paused with his horse.

'Anything I should know about?' he asked as he started walking again.

'Anise is having trouble coming to terms with the fire, the loss of the dryads, and his Earth Spinning,' I said. 'And he's sensing nature's imbalance and it's got him worried.'

'Now I understand.'

'You can't have thought it was anything else?'

'I didn't, but I did wonder what was wrong with Anise. He's been unusually quiet, and I've been getting concerned about him. I guessed you were counselling him.'

'I was.'

'And?'

'He's a bit happier. He's going to talk to Sage about things.'

'Which is probably what he should have done to begin with. Like I talk to you and you talk to me. No point in bottling things up,' he said, slipping his free hand into mine.

I nodded. 'We were wondering about what the Dryad Queen said about us being "the ones". Could she have meant restoring balance to nature? Stopping the winds and the floods and drought?'

'But how could we?' He frowned. 'Where would you even begin with something like that?'

'I don't know, and neither does Anise.'

'If it was in our power, though, I guess we'd have to give it a try.' He pulled me to a halt and bent towards me, his lips brushing mine for a moment before he kissed me, sending sparks through my body, igniting my blood. He stepped back. 'What do you feel?' he asked suddenly.

'I'm sorry?'

'What do you feel?'

'Tired and a bit cold, actually. The wind coming down from the mountains can be biting at times.'

He gave me a long look. 'I mean when I kiss you?'

'Oh.' Blood rushed to my face. 'I feel all tingly and happy inside, why?'

His eyes darkened slightly as he looked at my face, his gaze flicking down to linger on my lips. 'So do I.'

I smiled.

'I also find your kisses to be very addictive and constantly want more,' he said, caressing my face. 'I'm hoping there are many, many more where that one came from.'

'Do you indeed?' I grinned. 'I think there's a fairly endless supply of them. Just as well I'm addicted to yours, too, isn't it?'

He leant towards me again, his mouth meeting mine, kissing me gently with his warm, intoxicating lips. Yes, very addictive.

'Come on, you two, stop buggering about. We haven't got all day, and Sage is getting cold,' Tarragon yelled from up ahead. By the Stars, why did Tarragon always have to interrupt us?

'I'm not getting cold, I *am* cold, I—' Sage's sour voice drifted down the path towards us, cutting off short as Anise reached him.

Rian rested his forehead against mine for a moment and sighed.

'Coming,' he shouted back.

Anise said something to Sage, and the two of them started off up the path together, without Tarragon and Willow. Tarragon narrowed his eyes and turned back, looking questioningly at me. I smiled. He nodded, and followed them at a respectful distance with Willow.

Rian smiled at me. 'Looks like your counselling has worked wonders.'

I shrugged. 'We'll see. Let's go.'

We climbed further up into the mountains, through passes, along ridges, and past great peaks that grazed the sky, some of which had shawls of white puffy clouds. And all the time the air around us grew colder until I could see my breath and my nose became damp. We camped high in the mountains, but without any firewood to scavenge, it was a cold meal for dinner.

'We should've brought some wood with us,' Tarragon noted.

'And who was going to carry it?' Willow asked. 'The horses are having enough trouble with the ground as it is. They wouldn't have wanted the extra weight. I know you wouldn't have wanted to carry it.'

Tarragon grunted.

'Let's get the tents out,' Sage said, moving towards his pack. 'They'll give us some protection from the cold.'

Tarragon kicked at the rock underfoot. 'We won't be able to get any tent pegs in this.'

'Then what do we do?' Willow asked.

'You'll have to spend a night out under the stars with me,' he said, moving a curl behind her ear as he leant and kissed her on the nose.

Willow stepped back, batting his hand away, glowering at him. 'Not in public.'

'They were kissing in public earlier,' Tarragon said, nodding towards me and Rian.

'You weren't supposed to be looking,' Rian said stiffly. 'A good friend wouldn't.'

'I am a good friend, and it's because of that I feel able to be affectionate with Willow.'

'He has a point,' Rian said to Willow. 'And we all know how we feel about each other.'

'As long as Tarragon doesn't take it too far, in public,' I said.

'You've seen it all before, Phire,' Tarragon said, buffing his fingernails on his tunic. 'And you weren't complaining.'

Sage and Anise frowned, looking between me and Tarragon.

'Really?' Sage asked.

'I haven't seen it *all* before, thankfully,' I said primly. 'Luckily you were both under a sheet. Some things are meant to stay hidden from other people's view, and that was one of them.'

Willow turned pink.

Rian smirked at Tarragon's embarrassed face.

'You can tell us later,' Anise said, leaning conspiratorially towards Rian.

'Lying on this cold rock all night isn't going to be much fun,' Sage muttered as he got the blankets out, ignoring us.

'Even if I'm with you?' Anise asked.

'I love you, but you're not going to make the rock warm or any softer, are you?'

Rian frowned. 'Hang on a minute, maybe I can do something,' he said, crouching down. He placed a hand on the bare rock and closed his eyes.

'What are you doing?' I asked.

'By the Herbs, he's finally lost his mind,' Tarragon sniffed. 'I blame the poison.'

The rock under Rian's hand started to glow a dull red.

'Hot rocks?' Willow asked. 'Clever.'

'Very clever,' I said, standing behind Rian, slipping my arms around his neck and leaning over to kiss his cheek.

He turned red. Whatever he said about public affection, he was still a little embarrassed by it.

'If I heat the rocks where we're going to sleep, they should stay warm until dawn,' Rian said, recovering his composure. 'We may not have the tents, but we'll have heat.'

'Perfect.' Willow nodded.

'Happy?' Anise asked Sage.

'Very.' Sage grinned, squeezing Anise's hand. Anise blushed.

By the time he'd finished warming the rocks, Rian had started yawning. It occurred to me he hadn't been holding my Amethyst Talisman.

'Using Magic doesn't usually make you tired like this,' I said.

'I hadn't thought about it, but you're right,' he said.

'It's because you weren't using my Talisman.'

He rubbed the back of his neck as he thought. 'You know, thinking about it, when I've used your Talisman I've been able to do bigger, more incredible things and not felt that tired afterwards, and yet when I do something without it, like light the fire when I chased off the Dire Wolves, or just now, heating the rocks, it's taken more energy out of me.' He looked down at his chest, pulling my Amethyst Talisman out. 'I hadn't thought about it, but I guess this proves that Artefacts really can enhance a Spinner's power.'

I nodded. 'I suggest saving the Talisman's power if you can. We may need it later, you never know.'

Unfortunately, the one thing Rian couldn't do was make the rock any softer, just as Sage had pointed out, but the night passed more quickly than it might have done if we'd been shivering the whole time.

As we set off the next morning, we were all a little sore and achy. After a few hours, we crested a stone ridge, and in front of us lay the great desert expanses of Mere, the yellow sun hanging high in a clear blue sky. Below us, sand dunes filled the vista as far as the eye could see. From our viewpoint we couldn't see Rill, we were still too far away from the city, but I knew it sat to the north, beyond the horizon.

Maybe there'd be news in the city about Mal.

'I don't want to worry anyone,' Anise said, 'but we're running out of water and we still have a desert to cross.'

CHAPTER EIGHTEEN

'What?' Rian asked, twisting in his saddle. 'I thought we brought enough to get us to Rill?'

'I thought so, too, Rian, but the climb through the mountains has dwindled our supplies more than I'd expected,' Anise said. 'I'd hoped to find somewhere to stock up with fresh water before we got out into the desert, but there's been nowhere along our route, not even a stagnant pond.'

I scanned the landscape – I could see no water, stream, river, lake or pool in sight, nor anything remotely green that might have signalled water. Instead, only yellow-beige terrain surrounded us, dry as old bones.

'Are we going to die?' Willow asked, her eyes looking a little wild as she gazed around and started coughing.

'Of course not,' Tarragon said. 'I'm sure we'll find an oasis or something soon if we keep travelling north towards Rill.' He urged his horse on down the side of the rocky, stone-scattered ridge.

I glanced at Rian. He had an anxious look in his eyes as he gazed back at me. 'Let's keep going for now,' he said. 'Hopefully Tarragon's right.'

I refused to be thwarted in my search for Mal by a lack of water. And I expected Rian felt similar about the Fire Opal. This wouldn't stop us. I'd drag myself out of the desert on foot, if necessary. Or on my knees. Whichever was most appropriate.

We rode slowly out of the mountains, mainly because of the shifting scree on the rocky inclines, although partly to conserve our horses' strength. Reaching the edge of the desert, the heat suddenly hit us like a wall. The way the sun reflected off the sand turned the air around us into a fiery furnace.

'You know how I said I was cold?' Sage asked, removing his tunic. 'Well, now I'm too hot.'

'No pleasing some people,' Tarragon said.

'So true,' Anise said, grinning at Sage.

I gazed out over the shifting sands, shielding my eyes with my hand as I tried to see any sign of water or life. Nothing. There was the odd brown, scrubby clump of grass, and a few dead-looking succulents, but that was it. I took my tunic off and mail shirt, just leaving my undershirt, and slipped the rest into my pack. Everyone else did the same as we paused. We had two, maybe two-and-a-half days of riding in the desert. The horses wouldn't survive that without water, and neither would we in this ferocious heat. We hadn't thought this through – *I* hadn't thought this through.

'Why don't we rest now, and carry on when it's dark?' I suggested. 'It'll be cooler and it'll spare the horses, at least a little.'

Rian nodded. 'Good idea. We'll get the tents out for some shade and shield the horses as best we can.'

We did as he said, and lay in the shade of our tents, trying to get some sleep or at least a little rest. The heat stifled everything, even thinking. Anise gave Willow something for her asthma, the hot, dry air irritating her lungs. My shirt became damp, clinging uncomfortably to my body. Rian lay on his back beside me, a hand under his head, one leg down on the sand, the other bent in the air, wide awake as the others began to doze off.

'This is my fault. I should never have led us through the desert like this,' I said miserably, covering my lower arms in case they burnt in the reflected sun. 'We should've gone by sea. I'm sorry I even suggested it now.'

'Willow and Tarragon wouldn't have thanked you for another sea voyage,' Rian said, shifting position and turning towards me. 'It's the quickest way, and time isn't on our side. Who knows what your brother is enduring at Juniper's hands? No, it was the right decision coming this way, and besides, I agreed with you.'

I chewed a fingernail. He was right about time, and it spurred me on every day, even when tiredness overwhelmed me and my body ached, wanting to give up, to be left alone to rest. But that was a luxury I didn't have. Mal didn't have. And we had the Fire Opal to consider, too.

'I just hope we all make it across,' I murmured.

'We will,' Rian said, reaching out to me and taking my hand. 'Don't worry.'

'But I do—'

'I'm an idiot!' Tarragon sat up, a broad grin on his face as everyone awoke at his loud, excited voice.

'We know that,' Sage said. 'Go back to sleep.'

'What are you talking about?' Willow asked, squinting at him in the bright light.

'Water,' Tarragon said.

'We're running out, we know, what about it?' Anise asked.

'We have plenty.'

'We do? Where?'

'I can't see any,' Sage muttered.

Tarragon pointed to himself, a smug grin on his face as he went on to buff his fingernails on his damp shirt.

'What?' Sage asked, his eyes narrowing as he sat up. 'Has the heat got to your brain and addled it already?'

'I'm a Water Spinner. If Rian can make rocks hot and start fires, surely I can conjure up some water?' He got up, moving to one of the empty waterskins.

'You think he can?' I asked Rian.

Rian shrugged and pulled himself up on one shoulder. 'It's possible. He's right about what I can do. I can make fire, so perhaps he can produce some water.'

Tarragon's face took on an expression of deep concentration.

'What are you doing?' Sage asked, tugging at his earring.

'Making water,' Tarragon said, sweat beading on his brow.

'It looks as though you're in pain.'

Tarragon paused to glare at Sage, then continued to focus on the waterskin.

'Nothing's happening,' Sage said, the sour note back in his voice as he lay down and closed his eyes. 'But do let us know if something does. Which it won't.'

'Really?' Tarragon opened the stopper on the skin and emptied the contents on Sage's stomach.

'What the—' Sage sat up, scowling at his cousin. 'What did you do that for?' He started wringing out his wet clothes.

'To make a point, and anyway, you'll dry,' Tarragon said unapologetically. 'I'll fill everything up.'

'Don't over do it,' Rian said. 'I've found using Magic without an Artefact really tiring, and I'm not sure now is the time to use your Artefact. Apparently they can run out of power eventually, and we don't know how much it's got.'

'All right,' Tarragon said, nodding. 'Raising that wall of water *with* my Artefact left me exhausted, although this ought to be easier. At least it's on a much smaller scale. I'll be sure to take it carefully.' He moved off, Willow following after him, a proud expression on her face as he started to slowly fill our waterskins.

'We'll never hear the end of this now,' Sage muttered, drying himself off before lying back down.

'He deserves a little leeway, he's probably just saved our lives,' Anise said, lying down beside Sage.

'Maybe.'

I'd never travelled at night in the desert before. For some reason, I'd expected silence, but the calls of a few solitary birds and animals that had ventured out, and the sound of the wind whistling through the sand dunes, intermittently sliced the night air. Cold air surrounded us in the darkness as we rode, our horses' hooves sinking into the sand making the going hard. We'd put our tunics and cloaks back on. I hadn't realised there would be such a huge change in temperature from day to night. Sand dunes loomed all around us out of the black sky dotted with diamond stars. The moon bathed everything in its silver light, casting deep, dark shadows between the dunes. A screechy call cut through the night as we rode across the dunes.

'Hell's teeth, what was that?' I asked, my heart thumping away at the sudden sound.

'Some sort of Sand Fox?' Anise looked out over the moonlit desert, the sand painted white in the starlight. 'They live out here, don't they? Small, light brown-coloured, with big ears?'

I shuddered. 'What else is out here at night?'

'Snakes, lizards. Some hares live out in the desert, too, I think.'

'What do they eat out in the desert, though?'

'Each other,' Sage said, gazing across the dunes.

'Don't be daft,' Rian said. 'Hares don't eat meat. Surely they'll eat foliage and that sort of thing. Maybe insects.'

'Not much of any of that out here,' Tarragon said, screwing his nose up.

'Snakes and lizards eat meat,' Sage muttered.

'Let's keep an eye out, just in case,' Tarragon said, scanning the sand around us.

'Those Death Worm things you mentioned once, Willow, they were only stories, weren't they?' Sage asked, adjusting his reins.

'The Blue Death Worms?' She shook her head. 'Bobbins, no. Grandfather's stories were about real people. What happened to them out in the deserts weren't made-up stories. They were fact.'

'You're joking, aren't you?' Tarragon asked, squinting suspiciously at the dunes.

'I'm only telling you what Grandfather said.'

'Which was?' I asked.

'They're twelve-foot-long worms that live in the desert sands,' she said. 'They come out only at night and glow blue. Oh, and they're poisonous to the touch.'

'Who'd want to touch one?' Tarragon asked, a nervous edge to his voice as he wriggled in his saddle.

'And your grandfather had seen them, Willow?' Anise asked.

'No, but he swore blind it was true and that his friends had,' Willow said.

'Let's stay alert,' Rian said. He glanced at me, his moon-bleached eyes curious, but not concerned. Perhaps they were myth, not real, after all. Even so, I decided to keep an extra-good eye out on the sands, just in case. The chill air nipped at my nose and I pulled my cloak tighter around me. We rode on, the horses less temperamental in the cool night air of the desert.

When the sun reappeared on the golden horizon we stopped, breaking out the tents, eating, then sleeping in the shade of the canvas. I awoke late in the afternoon, my right arm red and burning. The sun had moved around and my arm now lay in the full sun. I sat up, holding it gingerly. My pale skin had no chance in this sort of environment, unlike Willow's. My skin was on fire, and I bit on my bottom lip to stop from groaning in pain. I considered wafting it with my Fan to try and cool it, but concluded it probably wouldn't help much, just make me feel warmer.

'Phire, are you ok?' Anise asked as he looked through his Herb Chest in the shadow of his tent, tongue out as he sorted through his vials and herbs.

'Sunburn,' I said ruefully, waving my arm at him. 'The tent shadow moved while I was sleeping and I didn't realise my arm was in the full sun until I woke up. It must have been like that for a while.'

'Let me see.'

I got up and went over to him, walking past a sleeping Rian.

Anise gently took hold of my arm and looked at it. 'That's pretty bad, Phire,' he said. 'It'll blister and be really painful if I don't do something with it, and it could get infected, which you don't want. First we'll cool it with water, then I have some herbs that will help.'

'I can't believe it's happened. I thought I was sleeping in the shade of the tent. Ow!'

Anise poured water over my red, burning skin. Although cool, the water didn't help an awful lot. Anise dabbed my arm dry then placed a compress he'd prepared onto it.

'It's witch hazel, and a few other things,' he said. 'It should help to cool the burn.'

It didn't. My skin still felt like fire – you could have fried an egg on it.

'I don't think it's working,' I said. 'It still feels as if my arm's in a campfire.'

Anise gently pressed on it. 'You may just have to be patient, it can take a little time,' he said, his Jade Amulet hanging out from his shirt. He took hold of it to tuck it back. As he did so, a beautiful cooling sensation spread across my arm, coming to an abrupt halt as Anise let go of his Amulet.

'Wait, that was working,' I said. 'Don't put it away.'

'What?' He frowned.

'When you held your Amulet, my arm started to cool down and feel better.'

He took hold of the Jade again, his other hand still on the compress. Once more the soothing sensation spread across my arm, bringing with it the same wonderful relief.

'Were you holding your Amulet when you gave Rian those herbs when he was ill?' I asked.

'I don't know. I might have been holding it when I prepared them, and when I gave them to Rian to drink. It's kind of a habit when I'm using my herbs or when I get anxious sometimes.'

'Maybe you helped Rian get better, too,' I said. 'Maybe it was Fire and Earth Magic that saved him. That's why he survived eating several of those wretched berries.'

'What's this?' Rian asked, sitting up, looking towards us with sleepy eyes.

'I've burnt my arm in the sun. Anise is healing it for me, rather like he helped heal you – with his Earth Magic.'

'It makes sense,' Rian said after he'd heard our theory, wide awake by then. 'How's your arm feeling now?'

Anise let go of his Amulet and removed the compress. My skin still looked a little pink, but nothing more, and certainly not painful now, nowhere near blistering as it had been.

I looked at the Earth Spinner. 'Thank you. I'll try and make sure I don't do it again.'

Anise grinned. 'My pleasure.'

'Don't use your Amulet too much, though. You may only be using a little Magic at a time, but Artefacts do eventually run out of power, or so I read.'

Anise nodded slowly. 'Understood. Maybe I've been using my Magic more than I've realised. When I heal someone, I sometimes feel really tired afterwards. I certainly don't always hold my Amulet, but it is a bit of a habit, so I'll try to ration its use.'

'Might be a good idea,' I said.

Rian chewed his lip, his forehead furrowing. 'Anise, if you can use your power to speed up healing, do you think it can be used the other way too?'

'The other way?' Anise frowned. 'How do you mean?'

Rian fidgeted. 'The Mandragora Berries. Could Earth Magic have made them more potent?'

'Made their toxicity stronger and the speed of your poisoning quicker?' Anise's eyes widened, and he raised his hand to his forehead. 'Of course. That's why the poison took effect so fast, why you became so ill so quickly. Earth Magic was at work.'

'You mean the Berries had been tampered with? That's why Rian declined so quickly?' I asked.

The two young men looked at each other and nodded.

'That would explain it,' Anise said. 'Why the poison progressed so quickly, unlike what we'd been taught it would do.'

'Beryl has an Earth Spinner, too?' I asked incredulously.

'Chervil must have one, to have healed Sorrel,' Rian said. 'Why not the Coterie?'

I feared to put voice to the thoughts suddenly rushing through my head.

'What is it?' Rian asked, looking at me intently.

'Could it be the same one?' I asked. 'The same Earth Spinner.'

Rian's face blanched. 'My brother working with the Coterie?'

'We already know Chervil is making arrangements for King Narcissus' murder, and you've said yourself it's not really a Nightshade thing. It's a Coterie thing. Maybe they're in league.'

Rian chewed his lip again. 'I suppose it's possible. Damn, to think Chervil is capable of this...' He shook his head. 'My brother and Juniper working together? It beggars belief.'

'It's possible there are two Earth Spinners, I suppose,' Anise said, 'but not very likely.'

'I hope I'm wrong,' I said quietly.

'So do I,' Rian said. 'Still, I was really lucky I had Fire Magic, a Fire Artefact, and an Earth Spinner to combat my poisoning. And you.' He looked at me, totally in earnest.

'As I've said before, I'm not sure I made much difference,' I said.

Anise glanced at Rian, who raised a questioning eyebrow. 'You could've made all the difference if—'

'Time to go,' Tarragon called. 'I want to get as far as we can now it's cooler. The less time we stay in this furnace the better.'

Rian chuckled. 'Coming.'

We set off again as the sun set, the heat once more retreating and the cold returning to the desert. Odd calls from the desert animals drifted across the sands tonight, now we'd travelled further out into the desert, some setting my teeth on edge with their unpleasant noises. In the early hours of the morning, a high-pitched wail cut through the darkness, shrill and sad.

'Bugger me, what was that?' Tarragon asked, looking around.

My right hand went instinctively to Deorwine's hilt.

'I—I think it's a Blue Death Worm,' Willow said, her face strained as the noise echoed around the sand dunes again, the hairs on the back of my neck rising.

'What?' Tarragon asked, drawing a sword. 'Are you sure?'

'Grandfather said they wailed before they…'

'Before they what?' Rian asked, one of his own swords in his hand.

'Attacked,' Willow finished.

CHAPTER NINETEEN

Tarragon's face looked deathly pale in the moonlight as he scanned the sands for any sign of the Death Worms. 'I can't see anything,' he said, his voice tight. 'There's nothing out there.'

'They're under the sand,' Willow said, her voice trembling. 'You won't see them until they get close. And then it'll be too late.'

'I can't see anything, either,' Rian said, scrutinising the dunes. 'Let's keep going, and fast.' He urged his horse on as quickly as it would go across the soft sands, the rest of us following him.

I glanced around the dunes as I sped along, my heart hammering in my chest, my palms cold and sweaty. Silver sand surrounded us in the light from the stars and moon, my breath clouding in the cold air. The smell of the desert at night had an earthy, yet slightly floral, quality as we cantered across the sand. The sound of the pursuing Blue Death Worms reverberated around us as they continued to wail in their high-pitched tone. It set my teeth on edge. And it was getting closer. I turned around, but could see nothing out of the ordinary.

Suddenly, the sand next to my horse's feet undulated, shifting. The horse skidded to an abrupt halt, sending me straight over its head, reins still in hand. I landed on my back, knocking the wind out of me, Deorwine digging uncomfortably into my ribs. As I struggled to breathe, my nervous horse reared, ripping the leather reins from my hands.

A similar fate befell Anise. He landed hard. Sage hauled his horse to a stop and went back for his boyfriend.

I rolled onto my front, desperately trying to stagger to my feet as I fought for sweet air. The sand ten feet in front of me moved. Swirled, just like water. *Hell's teeth*. A large glowing blue head broke the surface – not the blue of the sea in summer, but of a sickly, ghostly hue – the skin of the creature wrinkly, like that of an old hag.

It had no eyes.

The foot-wide, twelve-foot-long Worm rose up in front of me, its mouth opening in a piercing shriek, its sharp fangs bared. The smell of rotting flesh coming from its gaping maw turned my stomach. I gasped and fell backwards, desperately trying to scramble away. It lunged.

A horse slid to a stop between me and the Worm, its rider forcing the creature back as he slashed at it with his sword. The Worm shrieked and dived back into the sand. Rian looked down at me, a relieved expression on his face as his horse frothed at the mouth. He held a hand out towards me. 'Are you al—'

Another Worm sprang from the sand. Rian's horse reared, throwing him to the ground, then bolted. The great glowing Worm dived back under the sand in Rian's direction.

'Oh, no you don't.' I sprang forwards with Glædwine, planting myself between the prince and the Worm, ducking behind the shield. The Death Worm shot out of the sand and hit diamond. It fell to the ground, knocked unconscious.

'Thank you,' Rian said, struggling to his feet.

'My pleasure,' I said. I now had both Glædwine and Deorwine in hand. I looked around. Willow was on the ground, clambering back to her feet, her horse bolting as Tarragon raced towards her.

'They spit venom!' she yelled over the wailing Worms. 'Watch out.'

'Now she tells us,' I muttered, looking around, my body tense and ready to react.

'And don't touch them.'

'Why would we want to touch them?' Sage asked from somewhere behind me.

The sand moved. A Worm broke through the sand, this time spitting venom. Rian and I both crouched behind my purple crystal shield. The venom hit the diamond. Then ran down the polished surface, hissing on the shield, evaporating and leaving it unscathed, as well as us. The Worm moved back, almost in surprise. I didn't give it any time to attack again. I lunged forward, knocking it to one side with Glædwine, Deorwine slicing the Worm's long body in two. Glowing blue gelatinous blood, or what looked like blood, stained the sand where it seeped from the creature's severed corpse.

More wailing approached.

'What do we do?' Tarragon asked, now on foot like the rest of us.

'What are they frightened of, Willow?' I asked as we all backed away from the approaching Worms. If our horses couldn't outrun them, we didn't stand a chance. There had to be another way. Surely?

'I—I don't know,' she said, her voice quavering. 'Grandfather never said. I'm sorry. I don't know what to do.'

'Water.'

I turned as a horse and rider skidded to a halt beside me. Dressed in the baggy orange trousers and yellow tunic of a Merean Low Blood, I recognised him immediately.

'Onyx?' I gasped. 'Hell's teeth, what are you doing here?'

'Looking for you, Ama,' he said, his hazel brown eyes black in the desert light, his sienna skin shining in the moonlight. 'We need to get them surrounded.'

'Then what?' Rian asked, his hand slipping around my shoulders, an annoyed edge to his voice.

'This way,' Onyx said, ignoring him. He urged his horse back the way he'd come and we ran after him, all too aware of the Worms at our heels.

My lungs wanted to burst as I ran hand-in-hand with Rian. The sand made sprinting hard work, slipping and shifting under our feet, hampering our efforts to move quickly. My muscles burnt, and my heart slammed into my ribcage, as much from fear as from my frantic run. We reached the edge of a dip in the sand where it became rather like a little bowl in the desert. We ran to the centre. Onyx slipped from his horse and sent it off up the far side of the incline.

'Now what?' Rian asked tersely. 'There's no water here. What do we do?'

I winced at the tone in his voice.

'Patience, Prince,' Onyx said, watching the sand. 'As soon as they come down here, head in different directions back up to the top. I'll do the rest.'

'You will, will you?' Rian asked with a surly expression.

The sand shifted before I could tell them to behave.

'Get ready,' Onyx said. The Worms moved directly for us. 'Now!'

We did as he'd said, speeding in different directions up the sides of the sandy bowl, although Rian ran right beside me, his hand clasping mine despite the fact I held Deorwine.

As he got to the top, Onyx dropped to one knee. He placed one hand on the sand, his rose quartz ring glistening in the starlight, his other over the top. What was he doing?

Water began surging from the sand where his hand rested, flowing quickly down into the sand bowl in a torrent.

My eyes widened as I watched him. How was he doing that? He was a Low Blood.

Tarragon grinned. 'I can help you with that,' he said, running around the bowl so he stood opposite Onyx. Water flowed from where he crouched, gushed from where his hand sat on the sand, his other on his Wristband.

'Water Spinner, eh?' Onyx nodded, a large grin spreading across his face. 'That'll make this quicker, and easier. Keep the water coming, friend.'

Tarragon nodded.

Water flooded into the bowl, encircling the Worms, guided by the hands of the Water Spinners. The creatures started screeching as the water quickly surrounded them, leaving them no escape above or below the sand as it soaked in; a spinning circle of liquid terror. Then the water, released from the circle, spiralled down, filling the bowl, touching the Worms' wrinkly skin. They started to pulsate and smoke. The water flooded over them, submerging them totally. They writhed about in the water, splashing in their futile attempt to escape. The Worms screamed as the water began to dissolve their bodies into a glowing blue soup – a soup that smelt of death and earth.

In a matter of moments, they all lay dead.

We all stood silently, looking at the glowing water, amazed and horrified in equal measure. The blue glow lit the desert, giving everything and everyone an otherworldly look. I took a deep breath. Thank the Stars for Onyx.

'Good thing you came along when you did, friend,' Tarragon said, standing up, grinning from ear to ear at the Iolitian assassin.

Onyx grinned back at him. 'It is, isn't it?'

Rian muttered something under his breath.

'We wouldn't have known what to do,' I said quietly to him. 'And even if we had, Tarragon would've found it difficult to do that on his own. You know that.'

'Hmm.'

Onyx walked around the edge of the water to where I stood with Rian.

'I've missed you, Ama,' he said, grabbing me from Rian and hugging me fiercely. I dropped my weapons as he embraced me. 'It's been so quiet in Iolite without you around.'

'I missed you, too, Onyx,' I said.

Over his shoulder I saw Rian glowering, clenching a fist, before turning away. Sage raised an eyebrow at Rian's reaction; Tarragon looked at Willow and shrugged. Anise seemed to be the only one who understood. So did I. I'd have to speak to Rian later and calm him down. Assure him Onyx was no threat to him. He never had been, and never would be.

'This is my old friend, Onyx, from Iolite,' I said as Onyx finally let me go, and the others came over to us.

'Assassin?' Sage asked, looking Onyx up and down in a slightly disapproving manner.

'One of the best,' Onyx said with a broad grin, his hazel eyes sparkling. 'Why, do you need one? My rates are very fair.'

'Not today, no. But thanks for the offer.'

'Why are you here?' Rian asked, turning back, failing miserably to hide the irritation in his voice, assuming he *was* even trying.

'I'm on a commission,' Onyx said.

'Who are you supposed to murder this time, Onyx?' Rian asked belligerently.

You could cut the tension with a knife. Onyx didn't help by slipping his arm around my shoulders, yawning as he did so. I stepped away, not wanting to upset Rian any further. I really did have to talk with him, and soon. Maybe I should have a word with Onyx, too.

Onyx grinned. 'You,' he said. 'And Ama.'

Everyone tensed, hands going to sword hilts.

Rian was no surprise, but me, too?

'Who've I upset?' I asked, looking Onyx straight in the eyes.

'You actually want me to make you a list?'

'There's a list?' I asked, raising both eyebrows in surprise. I'd actually accumulated a whole list?

'What do you think, after your performance at the Crimson Castle? There's a list as long as your arm circulating around the Coterie of people you've rubbed the wrong way.'

I flinched. 'Suppose I asked for that.'

'And are you going to try to complete your commission?' Rian asked, positively bristling. 'Or not?'

'You really think I'd have saved you from the Death Worms only to kill you now, Prince Valerian?' Onyx asked, raising an eyebrow, his black hair tied back in the low ponytail of Iolite.

'I wouldn't know,' Rian said, his knuckles white around his sword hilt. 'Maybe it's some depraved way you go about things. I don't know your particular methods, but I do know anything is possible with the Coterie.'

Onyx drew himself up to his full height, even if he was still shorter than Rian. 'I'm not Carnelian,' he said through gritted teeth. 'There are some things I'd never do.'

If I wasn't careful this was going to get out of hand.

'But you're not going to try and kill us, are you?' I asked, stepping between the two young men.

Onyx stopped glaring at Rian long enough to look at me. ''Course not, Ama. But you know that already.'

I suppose I did.

'Who sent you?' Tarragon asked, tiredness now etched into his face.

'The Coterie, of course.'

'We know that, but who in particular?' Rian asked.

'Commissions are secret,' Onyx said, sniffing and crossing his arms over his chest. He really wasn't helping his cause; I'd winkle it out of him later. 'I can't tell you, I'm afraid. You know that, too. Look, we need to go.'

'Onyx. The water... How did you do it?' I asked, curious to know how a Low Blood had saved us with Water Magic.

'Later, Ama. We'd better round up the horses. There may be other Death Worms in the area, and we don't want to hang around and find out if there are.'

I nodded, and we quickly did as he said, gathering up our spooked mounts, then heading north again, Onyx leading the way now. Rian had a permanent scowl on his face, illuminated by the moonlight, but with the speed we travelled at, I had no opportunity to talk with him.

He was jealous. No two ways about it. It had started back in Iolite when he'd first met Onyx, before we'd even admitted our feelings for each other. I thought he'd put it to one side, but it was obviously still there. Festering away. In some ways it was quite gratifying that he was that protective of me, of us, but on the other hand he may just have to live with Onyx being with us, and any animosity between the two of them would quickly become annoying. And dangerous.

As daylight seeped into the night sky, we found a sheltered spot in the shade of the first rocks we'd seen since entering the desert. We had a meal, then made ourselves as comfortable as possible in order to wait out the heat of the day.

I chose a suitably shaded spot and lay down. Rian came over and lay down beside me, quickly nodding off to sleep. Before long, Sage started snoring away happily, and the others dozed off, too. I got up quietly, venturing over to where Onyx lay, taking a waterskin with me.

'So, you were sent to kill us?' I asked, sitting down, chewing on a fingernail.

CHAPTER TWENTY

Onyx glanced at me and sniffed. 'Yes.'

'Did *she* send you?' I asked.

'Juniper? No, it was Beryl that sent me to kill you,' Onyx said, squinting in the sunlight.

'Beryl?' My dear sister was trying to kill me now, too?

'You and your princeling.'

'Don't call him that,' I said. 'Call him Rian, like everyone else.'

'Whatever. I wouldn't entirely mind killing *him*, of course, but I can see you're fond of him and he's been looking after you well. So I won't, as long as he doesn't ever hurt you. If he does, it'll be an entirely different story.'

I sighed. 'He won't treat me badly. He loves me, exactly like you said he did.'

Onyx turned towards me. 'You're completely smitten, too, aren't you, Ama? I've never seen you like this before – so happy.'

'Yes, I suppose I am. Rian and I are married now, actually – well, we've pledged ourselves to each other. No priest in Aerba would marry us, so we said our own vows. It's the best we can do.' I glanced at the gold ring on my finger that shone with the sun as the diamonds flashed in the light.

Onyx sat up and took hold of my hand, studying the ring. He nodded as he let go. 'I can see he cares for you a great deal. I couldn't have let you be with someone who didn't.'

'Couldn't let?' I asked, amazed at his boldness. 'Really?'

'I'd kill any boyfriend, or husband, of yours if I wasn't sure they were treating you properly.'

'Well, he is treating me properly. Rian loves me. Body and soul. Don't you dare lay a finger on him, Onyx, I mean that, Beryl's instructions or not,' I said, my voice steel. 'I won't let you. I'll fight you if you try.'

Onyx smiled. 'Smitten,' he said, elbowing me.

'Shut up,' I said as blood rushed to my face.

'No, I'm not going to kill him, or you for that matter. Beryl can go throw herself off the highest tower in the Crimson Castle for all I care.'

'Why's she still doing this, though? I thought she'd have given up with the two of us by now?' I asked, taking a sip from my waterskin. 'We're no threat to her, and it's not as if I'm going to march back into the Crimson Castle and demand to take over as Mistress of Iolite. She must know that.'

'I'm not sure what she thinks, other than she's not letting it rest. As you know, she's already tried to have Rian killed several times, but when Carnelian's initial attempts failed, she sent me, too, to make sure the job was done properly. Only she also said that once Rian was dead, she wanted you killed, too. Precisely in that order. Him, then you, but to leave a gap between you so you could really feel his death properly.'

'Hell's teeth. She really hates me, doesn't she?'

He nodded. 'She doesn't like that you've escaped the Coterie, I do know that much. These days she spends all her time ingratiating herself with the bitch.'

I'd only ever heard Onyx refer to my stepmother in that way, and only then when sufficiently far away from Iolite's Crimson Castle that he wouldn't be overheard and reported. He held Juniper in total contempt. He'd only ever joined the Coterie because she'd threatened his mother with death if he didn't. Juniper was good at making threats. She was also excellent at making good on them. I understood exactly how Onyx felt, even if I didn't share his use of the flowery language to refer to my stepmother.

'Beryl is doing her every bidding. She intends to take over from her as Mistress some day.' He sniffed and rubbed his nose. 'So she's doing all she can to learn about the Coterie's finer details to make sure Juniper places her in an unassailable position of trust. I think killing you and Rian is part of her plan to show her loyalty and determination.'

I grimaced. 'She almost did succeed in killing Rian, or rather Carnelian did, back in Flos,' I said, nausea rising in my throat at the memory of having almost lost my soulmate.

'Oh? I just heard he failed.'

'Rian almost died of Mandragora Berry poisoning.'

'He survived? By the Stars, how? No one ever survives that,' Onyx said, his eyes wide, a sudden look of respect on his face as he glanced in Rian's direction. Then he frowned. 'There's no way he could've survived.'

'He survived because he's a Fire Spinner; he instinctively burnt the poison out of his blood,' I said. 'With a little help from Anise, too – he's an Earth Spinner.'

'I know what those berries do, Ama, and I know what after-effects there are meant to be if a man manages to survive, even if they are temporary. How is he?' he asked, his eyes curious.

'He's… he's coming to terms with things, I think.'

Onyx nodded. 'So the rumours are true?'

'They're true, but like you say, it's a temporary thing. He'll be fine.'

'But it'll take time?'

'Some time, yes. Anise doesn't know exactly how long, though.'

'But it could be years?'

I nodded, holding back the tears stinging my eyes. 'I'm not leaving him, if that's what you're wondering. I'll learn eternal patience, if I have to.'

'He's worth it?'

'Most definitely.'

'You really do love him.' Onyx sat still for a moment, taking in the information. 'Well, if Tarragon and I can be Water Spinners, no reason why your princeli—' He glanced at me. '—why Rian can't be a Fire Spinner and Anise an Earth Spinner. What about you? I hear you're really a High Blood.'

'Is my life a completely open book in Iolite?'

'Most of it,' Onyx grinned. 'Well? Is it true?'

'Yes, I suppose I am technically a High Blood, but I can't Spin anything for Aerban Toffee. I don't think I have a Magic Angle, and if I do, it's extremely weak. How did you find out about your Water?' I asked.

'Grandfather.'

'What?' I frowned.

'He told me the old tales when I was younger and I visited Mere, although I thought them just that – old tales. I called in to see him before I came looking for you. He's not well. Running a high fever. In his delirium he said some High Bloods still have power and can use Artefacts to enhance them. I thought he was rambling, but then I remembered I'd noticed a few odd things when I'd been near water over the years. I hadn't taken any notice of them, really, but when he said that, it got me thinking. So I experimented a bit. I worked it out from there, including the fact my quartz Ring is an Artefact, and a Water one at that. I knew it had been handed down the family for generations, but hadn't realised its significance until now.'

'I don't understand. You're a Low Blood.'

'Not exactly. I guess I'm a bit like you in that respect. My mother was born a High Blood, a cousin of the Queen of Mere.' His eyes clouded. Why, I didn't know.

'You never told me that before,' I said, slightly taken aback by the revelation.

'It never seemed relevant to us as friends, and as Mother worked in the kitchens, I wasn't sure you'd believe me. And anyway, she wanted it kept secret, and I didn't want to upset her. It wasn't something she liked to talk about, so we didn't.'

'Fair enough.'

'Mother was High Blood, as was her sister, my aunt. But my mother ran off with Father, a Low Blood from Iolite, rather than enter into an arranged marriage with someone she didn't love, and my aunt fell in love with a Middle Blood. The Queen was furious with them both and Demoted them all to Low Bloods, but they're really still High and Middle, and I should be High, too.'

Onyx appeared full of surprises today. I'd had no idea.

'The Queen Demoted them? What about the King?' I asked.

Onyx gave me a long look. 'You know Mere has a matriarchy. Queen Adair's in charge. It's not as if you haven't been here before. The women are in charge in Mere. You should've remembered that.'

I screwed my nose up. 'I forgot, sorry. A lot's happened recently, you know, and anyway, when I did come here, I didn't venture much past the coast. So, you still see your grandfather?'

He nodded. 'He still lives at the palace. In fact, he's one of the Queen's advisors. Anyway, going back to Beryl, you know she's had her sights set on Elm?'

'Hmm.' I shuddered. My stepbrother wasn't what you'd call prime husband material. I'd always seen him as self-centred, egotistical and slimy. And those were his good points. He'd sometimes looked at me in a way that made me shudder, and I always did everything I could to stay out of his way. Mal used to do his best to help me avoid him, even got into a fight with Elm once, giving him a lovely scar on his face when Elm tried to be too familiar with me for my brother's liking. That's not to say I couldn't have taken care of myself that day, I just preferred to ignore it, whereas Mal had taken Elm's comments to heart. Rather like I think Rian now would. Elm had taunted Mal one too many times and ultimately paid the price for his wicked tongue. 'Poor Elm,' I said, taking a sip of water. 'Or is it poor Beryl?'

'Neither. They're married.'

I choked as I swallowed my drink the wrong way. 'What?' I spluttered.

'After you left with Rian, they became very close. *Very* close in a matter of days.'

'They always liked each other.'

'"Liked" suddenly turned to lust, for some reason.'

I raised an eyebrow.

'There were whispers that Magic was involved,' he said, waving his hands about.

'Magic? Can it do that?' I asked. 'Can it really make two people fall in love?'

Onyx shrugged. 'Lust, not love, but I suppose it's possible. Anyway, the two have been inseparable ever since. So much so that the bitch, Juniper, made them marry. They were becoming embarrassing, even to her; a couple of rabbits. Still, it suits her agenda, consolidates power within Iolite's First Family.'

Iolite's First Family, indeed. I let out a long breath. 'Rather Beryl than me. And if I was going to be enchanted into marrying anyone, Elm would be right at the bottom of my list,' I said with a shudder for effect. 'I couldn't imagine anything worse.'

Onyx grinned. 'He didn't enchant you then?' He nodded towards Rian.

I smiled. 'He did, actually, but not in some arcane or Magical way – he has other means at his disposal,' I said, gazing for a moment at Rian's maroon hair shifting in the breeze.

'Oh?' Onyx gave me a knowing look. 'I did wonder what it was. Good in bed, is he?' Onyx hesitated as he realised what he'd said. 'Sorry,' he murmured, looking towards the sand, a sad frown covering his face.

'Stop it,' I said, elbowing him in the ribs, trying to make things light-hearted. 'If Beryl's so busy with Elm, I'm surprised she's had the time and energy to send you after me,' I said, changing the subject slightly.

'There's always time for a little revenge, don't you know?'

'So if you weren't coming to kill us, why are you here?'

'I want your help. No, I need your help. Your help and probably the others', too, if things are as I think they are.'

'You need our help for what?' I asked.

'To find Mal.'

'I see,' I said, nodding slowly, things falling into place and sticking together soundly. I now knew who Onyx was in love with.

'What do you see?' Onyx asked, looking a little wild around the eyes.

'More than you realise,' I said, glancing at my old friend.

Onyx's eyes widened, his face flushed. 'You know? You know about us?'

'I've guessed,' I said. 'You and Mal are in love, aren't you?'

He nodded slowly.

'Until a few months ago, I thought you were with Aquamarine,' I said. 'You never did tell me what happened with her.'

He screwed his nose up. 'Like you say, that was over some time ago. Some of her personal habits left a little to be desired, and anyway, my heart wasn't really in it. I think I've always loved your brother, just didn't entirely realise that was what it was.'

'You can't help who you fall in love with, eh?' I glanced over at Rian.

'Ain't that the truth.' He grinned.

'Ruby, the kitchen maid, will be disappointed,' I smirked.

He elbowed me. 'I've never really been a great one for the girls. Looking back, it was always Mal.'

'I'm pleased for you both,' I said.

Onyx sighed. 'We'd just admitted our feelings to each other when that bitch imprisoned him. I was livid when it happened, but there was nothing I could do. I didn't know where he was. He just vanished one night when we were supposed to be meeting, so I knew the rumours the bitch started a couple of days later – that he'd been killed in Flos after a commission – were all lies. Everyone else just believed her. As usual. Before I could speak to you, they said you'd drowned at sea. I was at a total loss for a while. I was so relieved when I found out you were alive, Ama.'

'Juniper can't get rid of me that easily.'

'So it appears.' Onyx grinned, then sniffed. 'Was I right about Flos? Did you find anything out about Mal while you were at the palace?'

'You're well informed.'

'I'm an assassin.' He sniffed again. 'I have to be.'

'They don't have him,' I said. 'But I've been told a Flosian spy named Calder in Rill might have information that can help us.'

Onyx nodded, his eyes far away for a moment. 'I'm not going back.'

'What?'

'When we find Mal, I'm not going back to Iolite, to the bitch and her Coterie.'

'But what about your mother?' I asked, surprised. Juniper had always used his mother's life against him, threatened her if he didn't do as she wanted. 'Surely you're not going to leave her at Juniper and Serpentine's mercy?'

'Of course not.' Onyx swallowed, his eyes glistening in the sunlight as he looked out over the hot, golden sands. 'She's dead. An accident in the kitchens not long after I saw you in Quartz Town.'

'What?' I asked in disbelief. That was why he'd had that strange expression earlier when he mentioned her. His mother had always been such a caring, friendly woman; one I'd sometimes slip off to visit when I felt down, which had been more often than I liked to admit. 'What happened?' I whispered, tears standing in my eyes. She'd been quite dear to me after my own mother died, and this news came as a blow.

'There was a fire.'

'Juniper?'

He shook his head. 'No, a genuine accident. If it had been *her*, she'd be dead right now.'

I believed him. Completely.

'I'm so sorry,' I said, giving him a quick hug. 'She was very special and I'll miss her, too.'

He nodded. 'I know you will. She'll leave a big hole in my life, but...' He took a deep breath. 'So, you see, I can finally escape Iolite and the Coterie now, too.'

'But I thought you told me no one ever leaves the Coterie?' I said, giving him a little smile.

'We can now, and we will,' he said in a determined voice that sent a little shiver down my spine. 'All three of us. We'll never go back, ever again. We won't be threatened and coerced into killing for the bitch anymore. None of us. Never again.'

I nodded, a little taken aback by his forcefulness. 'Sounds good to me.'

'We three can live happily, together, away from Iolite.'

'Four.'

'I thought you might decide to leave him after all?' He glanced at me.

'Never,' I said, shaking my head.

Onyx nodded, a resigned look on his face. 'Guess I'll have to get used to him then. I suppose I can try.'

'You know, I'd appreciate it if you were less tactile with me around Rian,' I said, choosing my words carefully. I had a very fine line to walk. I didn't want to upset Onyx, or Rian either.

Onyx smirked and put his arm around my shoulders. 'Doesn't he like it?' he asked mischievously.

I glanced across the camp. Rian had woken up. He looked at us, frowned, and turned over, body tense.

'No,' I said. 'He doesn't.'

'So I noticed,' Onyx said, grinning as he looked in Rian's direction too. 'All right. I'll try not to hug you so much, but you're my surrogate sister, I can't help it sometimes. We've always been close.'

'I know. They're a bit more reserved in Aerba, and the others aren't used to it, that's all.'

'Particularly your jealous princeling.'

'Call him that again and I'll knock you into next week.'

Onyx laughed, letting go of me. 'All right, I'll stop that, too.'

Rian turned over and looked at us again. I smiled at him and he gave me a little half smile back. He got up and wandered over to Tarragon who lay in the shade of one of the tents, dozing. Rian sat beside him and nudged him awake. Tarragon sat up as his cousin started talking softly. Tarragon's eyes widened, his face fell, then a smile spread over his lips. I narrowed my eyes. What were they talking about?

Onyx paused a moment as he looked at Rian. 'You're very lucky, you know. He seems kind, and he's very handsome.' He grinned. 'Extremely good looking, actually, now that I stop to think about it.'

I slapped his arm. 'He's off limits. But I'd be glad if the two of you became friends, but that's it, understand?'

He grinned again, his eyes sparkling, and nodded. 'If you insist. But—'

'I do insist. Mal you can have, and I'd be pleased if you did, but go anywhere near Rian...'

'Understood,' he laughed. 'I'm so glad I found you, Ama. I think we stand a real chance of finding Mal now.'

'Yes, me too.'

CHAPTER TWENTY-ONE

We set off again as the sun set and the heat faded into the sand. As we rode along in the moonlight, Rian cast a few unfriendly glances in Onyx's direction. Onyx smiled back, which only irritated Rian further. I had to do something about this, and fast. The contrast with the previous night's terrain was stark as the sand gradually gave way to a rockier landscape before breaking up completely.

'Blue Death Worms don't like this area of the desert,' Onyx said. 'Now we're getting closer to Rill, we should be fine. They tend to stay further out in the wilds.'

'It's a good thing we've got you with us, Onyx,' Anise said. 'Someone who knows the region.'

Tarragon nodded. 'You got us out of a tricky spot last night, y'know. We owe you our lives.'

'My pleasure,' Onyx said with a grin. 'Anything for Ama and her friends. I'm glad I got to you all when I did.'

I gave him a warning glance as Rian's hands clenched around his reins.

Just before dawn, we reached a small oasis where shade would keep the worst of the midday sun off of us. Date palms rose over a clear pool, and verdant grasses and shrubs grew in clumps around them, sucking the heat out of the rapidly warming air. Seeing colour again, instead of league after league of yellow-beige sand, really lifted my spirits.

'We can set off for Rill late this afternoon, and be there by evening,' Onyx said as we dismounted, and the horses drank from the crystal water.

'Does that mean we get a proper bed tonight?' Willow asked with hope in her voice.

Onyx laughed. 'Yes. My grandfather has plenty of space for us all, it'll be no problem.'

'We'll be fine at an inn,' Rian said stiffly. 'We don't need to put your grandfather out, and anyway, there are six of us.'

'I wouldn't hear of it, Rian,' Onyx said. 'You're welcome in my grandfather's house, and I want you to stay with us. He's got plenty of room for all of you, and you'll be able to have a proper rest before setting off again.'

Rian nodded curtly, but didn't look at all happy about it.

'Come on, Rian, it'll be fun,' Tarragon said, gently punching his cousin on the arm. 'Some real Merean hospitality.'

Rian muttered something under his breath and Tarragon laughed.

'I'm looking forward to a soft bed,' Willow said, a dreamy look in her eyes. 'It feels like forever since I've slept in a proper bed.'

'We won't be able to stop long, we need to find Mal,' I said, worried they'd want to stay for an extended holiday.

'And the Fire Opal.' Rian nodded. 'We need to get it back as soon as we can.'

'I don't want to delay in finding Malachite, either, but a day's rest may help you in the long run,' Onyx said. 'Help restore your energy.'

Rian rolled his eyes towards the azure sky. I flinched.

We ate as the sun rose and a light breeze drifted through the palm trees, making ripples across the water of the clear pool. I smiled at the way everyone talked happily together and laughed at Onyx's jokes. Rather, all of them except for Rian. He'd vanished. Where had he gone?

I glanced around. I caught sight of him sitting over by the far side of the water, in the shade of a palm tree. He sat with his arms resting on his raised, bent knees, one hand clasping the other's wrist, his head bowed as a gentle breeze ruffled his long hair in a rather attractive manner.

Tarragon came over and sat next to me, glancing over at Rian. 'One of us needs to talk to him, y'know,' he said quietly, scratching his chin.

I nodded. 'I was thinking the same thing,' I said.

'He's got this notion in his head that Onyx is going to try and take you away from him.'

'Utter rot.'

'I know, but that's what he's telling himself.'

I sighed. 'I'll go and speak to him,' I said, getting up quietly and walking around the pool towards Rian. I sat down beside him in the shade of the palm tree.

'What's wrong?' I asked, looking out over the water.

'Nothing,' he said, his head still down, face partially covered by his hair that hung across his features like a curtain. The others still wore their hair in low ponytails, but Rian had continued to wear his loose after what I'd said about liking it that way, and now he was using it as a wall between us.

'It's obviously not nothing. Tell me, what's the matter? I'm not going until you do.'

He sighed. 'All right. I'm jealous, dammit.'

'Jealous? Of Onyx?'

'Of course, of Onyx,' he said, nodding. His voice had a bitter tinge to it.

I sighed. 'You've no need to be jealous of him. I've told you before, he's just a friend. A surrogate brother. Nothing more, and never has been.'

'It's the way he's so familiar with you all the time that rankles,' Rian said, lifting his head slightly and looking out over the pool towards our little camp and the others. 'By the Herbs, he's always hugging you or touching you.'

'We grew up together, we were best friends, of course he's familiar with me.'

'Like you say, he's your best friend,' he said, turning towards me, those beautiful amber eyes clouding.

'But you're my *very* best friend, my soulmate, not Onyx, and he never could've been. I only ever loved him as a friend, as a brother. I still do, but never in the way I love you.'

'I just don't like it, I'm sorry,' Rian said sullenly, shaking his head and looking away, his hair once more shrouding his face. 'He wants to take you away from me.'

'Rubbish, that sort of thinking will get you into trouble. Of course he doesn't want to take me away from you, and even if he did, he could want to all he liked because I'm never going to leave you. The love I have for you is the strongest, most rare, special love there could be, and it's all yours, no one else's. I love *you*, Prince Valerian.'

'I'm not a prince anymore,' Rian said grumpily, although I sensed I might be breaking down his wall. 'I'm not royalty any longer.'

'No, you're the king of my heart.'

He turned and gazed at me, a reddish tinge appearing in his cheeks as a smile slowly formed on his lips and lit his eyes. 'And you're the queen of mine,' he said, dropping the grumpy look and leaning towards me for a quick kiss. At last, I'd broken down his defences. 'Queen Samphire. Has a ring to it.'

'I think that's a little unlikely, don't you?'

'Probably, but you'll always be *my* Queen Samphire Amethyst,' he said, glancing at the ring on my finger. 'All mine.'

'Exactly, King Valerian.' I giggled and looped my arm through his. 'And don't you forget it.'

'Not sure I'd ever want to be a real king. There are a number of things I'd like to change in Aerba, but being King?' He gave a little shudder. 'I'll leave all that nonsense to someone else. All that formality and pomp. Responsibility. No. Not for me. Being third in line was fine, no pressure, but I guess no real role, either, until I became Head of the King's Warriors. That was title and responsibility enough for me.'

I rested my head on his shoulder. 'Anyway, Onyx is spoken for.'

'You mentioned something about that back in Iolite.'

'It seems it was Mal that he got together with recently.'

'Are you sure?' Rian asked, glancing at me.

I nodded. 'He told me so himself yesterday afternoon, although I'd already guessed as much. Apparently it started around the time I left for Aerba to... well, you know.'

'Yes, I know,' he said softly.

'He was eyeing you up earlier, but I warned him off.'

Rian's eyes widened. 'Really? Me?'

'I told him to stay away from you, and that goes for you, too. You're mine, and only mine, understand? If either of you get any other ideas – I'll fight you,' I said, narrowing my eyes and giving him a playful scowl. 'And if necessary, both at the same time.'

Rian grinned and kissed my hand. 'And you'd probably win. I *am* yours, Phire, don't ever doubt it. And I'm honoured you're mine.'

I wanted to melt into a puddle. 'I'm definitely all yours, don't you worry about that,' I said, moving his hair behind his ear, my fingers lingering on his cheek.

Rian's forehead furrowed in a very attractive way as I moved his hair.

'Do you think we'll eventually manage to find a new home on the archipelago?' he asked suddenly.

I shrugged. 'I hope so.'

He nodded. 'I feel kind of lost at the moment, as if I'm drifting, not having somewhere to call home.'

'I guess I've not had time to think about it, but I suppose you're right. Although, in a way, home is wherever you are,' I said, smiling at him.

He grinned back. 'Maybe you're right. As long as we're together, we're home.'

'Although a roof and four walls would be nice. You won't miss Viridi Palace?'

Rian shook his head. 'No. That will never be home again. I suppose, looking back, I was being far too optimistic thinking we'd be allowed to live there together. Father would never have let it happen. He'd have forced us apart somehow, whether it was because you died from the Curse, or he sent you away and locked you up for good while he tried to force me to marry some princess I hated. That wouldn't have worked, mind you. I'd have absconded and come to rescue you. No, I'd rather live in a wet, muddy hole in the ground *with* you, than in a lavish palace *without* you.'

'That's quite a declaration,' I said, my pulse skipping at his heartfelt words.

He shrugged. 'Not really, it's the truth. It's how I feel.'

'I love you.'

'Love you, too.' He grinned impishly. He stared over the water. 'What I'd really like is a little cottage in some hills, next to a crystal-clear pool where you can teach me to swim. Then we can bathe every day, just the two of us, and live there in peace.'

'Peace? That would be a fine thing.'

'Peace and quiet. Yes, a quiet life. I'm beginning to crave that.'

I raised an eyebrow. 'You'd really be happy? Just the two of us in a cottage in the hills? Wouldn't you get bored?'

'I don't think I would. I'd have you. I wouldn't need more than that.'

'I think you'd soon get restless.'

'Not sure I would. Maybe one day we'll get the chance to find out.'

'I think I'd like that,' I said, kissing his cheek. 'But until then, you'll stop worrying about Onyx?'

He sighed in an exaggerated fashion. 'If you say so.' A little smile played on his lips.

'I do. I've told him to be less tactile, and he says he will. I think he actually wants to be friends with you. You know, I could start getting jealous of Willow, she's been your friend forever.'

Rian looked a little sheepish. 'When you put it like that I'm being a bit daft, aren't I?'

'Yes, you are, Valerian,' I said.

He winced. 'I love you, Samphire, which is why I overreacted. I'll be nicer to Onyx. Sorry.'

'Forgiven, as long as you kiss me again. Properly this time.'

'And what do you mean by properly?' he asked, a wicked grin on his face as his eyes flicked to my lips, his pupils dilating.

'You know full well what I mean.'

'If you insist.'

'I most certainly do. Kiss me,' I said, licking my lips delicately.

He leant towards me and did exactly what I'd asked, his forehead furrowing as he sent me dizzy, setting a wildfire in my veins as he kissed me with purpose. His arms slid around me and he held me close as we lingered, an ardent intensity to our kiss.

We rode on again once the midday heat had dissipated, heading north towards Rill. I noticed Rian slowing his horse to ride beside Onyx. They spoke a few words to each other, haltingly at first, with some tension between them, but as they continued they both started to relax, and before long were talking like old friends.

I sighed with relief.

'I'm glad they're finally getting along,' Anise said from beside me. 'Having the two of them staring daggers at each other the whole time was getting a little wearing.'

'I think it was more Rian than Onyx,' Tarragon said, urging his horse past to speak to Willow. 'But at least they're putting it behind them now.'

'He might be right, actually,' Anise said, 'about it being more Rian.'

'I think it was a little bit of both, really,' I said. 'Hopefully they're over it now, and the two of them can at least be civil to each other.'

'Good,' Anise said with a smile. 'I prefer harmony to discord.'

'Don't we all?' I turned towards him. 'How are you doing?'

'Me?'

'Yes, after the fire, you know...'

'Better. It was hard at first – I couldn't think of anything else – but I'm beginning to come to terms with it, I think. At least a little, anyway. Sage is helping me.'

'Helping you what?' Sage asked, riding up beside Anise.

'Get over the dryad deaths.'

Sage's expression changed as he scrunched up his eyes. 'It'll always be one of the worst nights of my life.'

'It's something I'll never be able to forgive,' Anise said. 'Live with, maybe. Forgive? Never.'

'You'll learn to live with it, as I will,' Sage said. 'But you know you can always talk to me about it,' he said, reaching out and taking Anise's hand as they rode side by side.

I smiled. Sage couldn't be described as the most demonstrative of people. He was quite often plain aloof, in fact he'd been really unfriendly to me when we'd first met, which I couldn't blame him for at the time. Now, I could see he was beginning to mellow. Anise looked at their joined hands, surprise in his eyes melting to joy.

'Thank you, Sage,' Anise murmured.

'Anything, for you,' Sage said, letting go and riding up to join Tarragon and Willow.

'I never thought he'd do something like that in public,' Anise said, gazing after Sage.

I shrugged. 'He loves you.'

'He does, doesn't he?' Anise said, a broad grin breaking out on his face and setting his eyes alight. 'And I love him.'

Rian glanced back at us. I smiled at him; he returned my smile, then continued his conversation with Onyx. They both started laughing. I narrowed my eyes. For a moment I wondered if encouraging them to be friends was the cleverest idea I'd ever had. My past appeared to be colliding with my present, and all of a sudden an uneasiness swept through me. Perhaps I was better off with them as enemies?

The city of Rill rose out of the desert, its pink granite walls sparkling in the setting sun, making it look like a huge pink pearl in an oyster of golden sand. Inside the city, the pink gave way to white stone, little quartz specks glistening as they reflected the light and heat back out into the desert. Regimented squares stood along the way as people bustled past us.

I felt totally out of place in Rill with my pale skin. Even the Aerban men were obvious, surrounded by the Mereans with their glistening burnt sienna skin and deep black hair. Only Willow and Onyx fitted in unnoticed. Even the Mereans' bows and hunting knives were in contrast to our weapons. The other difference was our clothes. Our black suede looked out of place compared to the citizens' pastel colours. The women wore pale-coloured pantaloons and cropped tops, due to the heat, and the men wore baggy trousers and tunics. The High Bloods were in silks of pale blues and greens, the Middle Bloods in silks and linen of pale lilac and pink, whilst the Low Bloods wore cotton and linen in the pale yellows and oranges that Onyx wore.

Shops lined the streets, and market stalls, selling everything from Merean Silks and cottons to spices and oil, jostled for position. The smell of cinnamon, ginger, and cloves hung heavy in the air. Vegetables and fruit sat in shaded sections, out of the evening sun, with breads and other baked goods unique to Mere.

At the centre of the squares, black granite monuments, a stark contrast to the other buildings, sat commemorating great battles and famous leaders. At the middle of the city, the Merean Palace sat like a delicate, pale pink rose at the centre of a garden of white flowers. Its walls surrounded elaborate buildings, all on one level, that formed courtyards around gardens and water features. The scent of flowers punctuated the dry smell of the desert air.

'We're going into the palace?' Willow asked, surprised, as we headed for the main gates.

'Grandfather is a member of the extended Royal Family and has his own rooms at the palace,' Onyx said.

'Royal connections, eh?' Tarragon grinned.

'I've underestimated you,' Rian said.

Onyx laughed. 'Comes with being an assassin – always be what people least expect. Isn't that right, Ama?'

'Hmm.' I snorted.

Onyx grinned at me. 'This way,' he said, leading us into the palace, past the nodding female guards in their deep blue outfits, and to the stables. We left our horses with the yellow-and-orange-clad stable boys, and followed Onyx through a maze of passageways and courtyards to his grandfather's rooms. The thing that struck me most was that all the guards in the palace were women, men reduced to the more menial roles I'd have expected of the women in Iolite, Aerba and Flos, like cooking, cleaning, and running around after the other inhabitants. A few men wandered the passageways, bowing to us as we passed, lighting the oil lamps that were scattered throughout the palace as the light faded.

'Oil?' Sage asked, looking at the lamps.

Onyx nodded. 'There are oil pools out in the desert to the west. They pump it up and bring it to the towns and cities for heating and lighting.'

'Heating?' Tarragon asked, glancing at a male servant rushing past with two dishes in his hands.

'The desert is cold at night.'

'Of course.'

Onyx opened the door into a large set of apartments. Inside, a young Merean man, not much older than me, rushed over to Onyx.

'Onyx, sir.' He bowed. 'Your grandfather is worse. We don't think he'll see the dawn.'

CHAPTER TWENTY-TWO

Onyx tensed. 'You're sure, Ford?'

'The physician has just been, sir. He said it was unlikely he'd see the morning,' the young man said, bowing his head, his black hair shining in the light. 'I'm glad you've arrived when you have.'

'May I ask what's wrong with your grandfather, Onyx?' Anise asked, stepping forward.

'Old age, to an extent,' Onyx said, 'but he took ill just over a month ago with a sore throat, then developed a fever, malaise, aching fingers, and fatigue. No one knows what's wrong; they're putting it down to his age.'

Anise shook his head. 'Doesn't sound like age to me,' he said. 'May I see him?'

'You think you can help?'

'It's possible. I have a certain ability when it comes to herbs and medicines.'

'Anise is a wonder with herbal remedies,' I said. 'Let him see your grandfather.'

Onyx nodded, and Anise got his Herb Chest out from his pack, tongue already appearing as he thought.

'I have something from the Chamber of Earth that might help,' Anise said.

Onyx looked at me, then nodded. 'This way,' he said to Anise. 'Ford, please show our guests to some suitable rooms.'

'Yes, sir.' Ford nodded. 'Please follow me,' he said, leaving the room.

'We'll share,' Rian said as Ford opened the door to a bedroom. He nodded and continued down the corridor with the others.

The room Ford had shown us to overlooked a large courtyard garden where a little fountain chattered to itself as the water cascaded down a series of white stone bowls near our window. Inside the room, a number of cupboards sat along two walls, and a large bed rested against another, sticking out into the room, its white silken sheets shimmering in the light of an oil lamp. The walls of bare pink stone gleamed, polished to a high sheen, and handmade rugs of vibrant blues and golds covered the floor. Thin drapes hung at the windows, moving gently in the breeze that came in from the gardens, the scent of nocturnal flowers drifting with it. Rian dropped his bags and fell backwards onto the bed.

'It's like lying in a gossamer spider's web,' he said contentedly.

I raised an eyebrow. 'You aren't usually so poetic,' I said, trying to suppress a giggle. 'And when did you last lie in a spider's web?'

'I just mean this bed is so soft it's going to be a delight after camping recently. We'll sleep well tonight,' he said with a happy sigh.

I perched on the far side. He was right, it was like a soft cloud. We really were going to sleep well. We made ourselves comfortable and then got ready to join the others.

Rian sat on the edge of the bed as I headed for the door. He grabbed my hand, pulling me towards him. I lost my balance and fell onto the bed beside him in a heap.

'Hey!' I protested.

He started laughing as he lay down next to me. He reached out, his hand on my cheek, before leaning towards me and resting against me. His warm mouth met mine, his hot tongue gently parting my lips as he gave me a lingering kiss that had my pulse clamouring in my ears. I slipped my fingers through his loose hair and pulled him to me, suddenly desperate for his touch.

'This would be a wonderful bed for... never mind,' he said, rubbing the back of his neck and moving off me.

I frowned. *It* was bothering him again, and nothing I could do or say would ease his pain. Maybe Onyx had stirred things up again – just when Rian was starting to accept the situation.

Dismayed, I sat up. 'I'm sure that things will improve. Anise said that—'

'But what if he's wrong, Phire? What if we can never—' Pain filled his eyes. 'You know.'

'This isn't permanent, we just need to be patient. You were only poisoned a few weeks ago, you have to give it time. And I've told you before, I don't mind. I love you.'

'Maybe you don't mind, but I do,' he said bleakly. He stood up, face red, his eyes full of anger and despair – and tears – as he clenched a fist. 'I mind that I can't do what I want to do. What you expect of me.'

'Expect of you? I don't expect anything. It's all right, really.'

'No, it's anything but all right. It's not right at all. I literally ache for you and I can't do anything about it.'

He wasn't the only one who ached, because I ached for him, too. The side effects of his poisoning had hurt Rian more than any physical wound Carnelian could ever have inflicted. Maybe I'd kill Carnelian after all. My blood boiled as I thought of the Iolitian assassin, his pale skin, watery grey eyes, and dark, lank hair. I looked at Rian, the anguish he felt on full display. Yes, maybe I would be the person the Coterie wanted me to be all along. I'd kill Carnelian. I clenched my fist. I'd make the snide assassin suffer for what he'd done, although it would still be nothing compared to the sentence he'd given Rian.

I stood up. 'Come here,' I said, enveloping Rian in a hug of love. 'We'll face it together.'

'How can *you* face it? It's my burden,' he said, stepping back.

'Where's this all coming from? I thought you were coming to terms with things. It's not permanent.'

His eyes sparked in the lamplight. 'You really think I'll come to terms with this?' he asked with a bitter little laugh. 'It might take decades. Maybe you should find someone else.'

'So, it takes decades. There's no other man alive that would be enough for me, understand?' I needed to drive my point home. 'There's no other man out there I could ever *want*. It's you I need. More than anything. Without you, I'd be nothing. I need you like air – however long it takes. You're mine, and I'm yours, and that's an end to it.'

Rian turned and looked at me, his eyes full of tears. 'You really mean that?'

I folded my arms across my chest. 'Yes. And besides, the poison will wear off eventually.'

He frowned.

A knock at the door cut through the moment.

'Rian? Phire? You coming?' Tarragon called.

'Be with you in a minute,' I called back, and he walked off down the corridor.

'But how long will it take?' Rian asked with a sigh.

I held my hand out to him. 'It'll take however long it needs to.'

He looked at my hand, then slowly took hold of it.

'You really think we can get past this?' he asked. 'That I can?'

'With time, and love, yes.'

However, it wouldn't be easy, for either of us. All I could do was hope it wasn't decades. One thing it didn't do was diminish my feelings for him; it maybe even made them stronger. He'd put himself in harm's way for me. I'd done the same for him. We were bound together, now, by fire and love. Forever. Whatever life or the Coterie threw at us. We were together and we'd stay that way.

He sighed again and nodded. 'Any other woman would leave me.'

'Then this imaginary woman would be a total idiot, because anyone who had you would be rich beyond their wildest dreams.'

'And you were calling me poetic,' he said, a little smile playing at the corners of his mouth.

'I have my moments.' I smiled back.

He bowed his head. 'But at the moment, I'm not the man you fell in love with.'

'No, that's true, you're not.'

He looked at me, his amber eyes swimming in tears again, and full of dismay.

I let go of his hand, reached out and held his face in my hands. 'You're a better man, a wiser, stronger man than when I fell in love with you,' I said. 'You've changed in so many ways, and I love and cherish you even more than when I first fell in love with you.'

'You're happy? Truly?' he asked, hope filling his eyes.

'Happier than I've ever been in my entire life,' I said, gently brushing my lips on his before kissing him.

He hesitated for a moment, then kissed me back with such urgency, intensity and longing that he took my breath away and brought tears to my eyes. As he deepened the kiss, my heart stuttered, and I ran my fingers into his hair as I tasted his tongue. He rested one hand on my face, his other firmly wrapped around my waist, pulling me close, almost as if he didn't believe I was there, would stay with him, and he had to keep hold of me to reassure himself, to stop me from leaving. But there was no way I'd ever go, ever leave him now. We lingered in our kiss, and when we finally parted we looked into each other's glassy eyes.

'I do love you, you know,' he said, his voice hoarse. 'So much.'

'I know,' I said, my voice not much better.

'Sorry for being self-indulgent.'

'We all need to let everything out from time to time or we'd probably explode, and that wouldn't be pretty.'

He looked at me sheepishly. 'You're very patient.'

'That's because I'm very much in love,' I said, a smile finally appearing on his face, clearing any trace of tears.

'I will make love to you properly one day, wife,' he said.

'Make love?' I raised an eyebrow. 'My, you have a way with words today.'

He smiled. 'Just you wait, one day I will,' he said, leading me to the door. He paused, looking at his ring adorning my finger. 'I swear it, because if you're prepared to be patient, then so am I, however long it takes.'

I squeezed his hand and kissed his cheek. 'And it will be all the sweeter and more special when it does happen, husband.'

He paused to grin at me. 'I'll make sure it is.'

We joined the others in the living area as Ford came in with plates of salad, spiced meats, and bread. We tucked in as the young man poured us glasses of wine and, at Rian's insistence, water. Anise didn't return until quite late in the evening.

'How is he?' I asked.

Anise sat down wearily on a couch next to Sage, who immediately got up, poured him a glass of wine and fetched him a plate of food. Anise smiled at him gratefully as he sat back down next to him.

'Onyx's grandfather is bad, but not terminal,' Anise said, taking a piece of bread. 'It seems he had a throat infection a month ago, and then this came on after. This sort of thing is quite unusual at his age, probably why they thought it was to do with how old he was instead. I've been able to give him something for it, though. It'll take a few days, but he should start to feel better soon.'

'Really?' Sage asked. 'That's good news.'

'He'll need to rest for a while, that's all.'

'I knew you could do it.'

Anise smiled. 'I had a little help,' he said, holding up his Amulet. I smiled.

'Where's Onyx?' Tarragon asked, peering down the corridor Anise had entered from.

'Staying with his grandfather for now. He said he'd see us in the morning.' Anise took a sip of wine.

'He can show us to the East Quarter,' Rian said. 'Help us find this Calder.'

'Let's hope he has the information we need,' I said. Finding Mal filled me with more urgency as time went on. What was he suffering? I shuddered to think as a shard of ice stabbed at my heart.

'We'll find him,' Rian whispered in my ear.

Damn right, we would.

We woke early the next morning. Anise and Sage stayed at the palace to look after Onyx's grandfather, the rest of us going in search of Erica's contact, Calder.

'The East Quarter, you say?' Onyx said as we left the palace, heading into the city, weaving our way through the citizens.

'Yes, is that a problem?' I asked, the sounds of the city flaring around us as we walked. The smell of baking bread, spices, and smoke from fires swept along the streets with us. The heat of the day had yet to take full hold, and the stone buildings did their best to reflect the sun and keep the houses and city cool. Or, at least, cooler than the desert.

He shook his head. 'No, but they're a bit rough around there, that's all.'

'You're an assassin, won't you fit right in?' Willow asked mischievously.

'I can fit in anywhere,' Onyx said with a grin. 'And you'll fit in just fine.'

She smiled back at him.

'It's the rest of them that are the problem.' He smirked at me.

'Thanks. You don't fit in well in Flos, as I remember,' I said, smirking back. 'Didn't they run you out of Muscari once?'

Onyx's eyes widened at the memory. 'That was a complete misunderstanding, could've happened to anyone.' He grimaced.

'So you say, but that's not what I heard.'

'And what did you hear?' Tarragon asked, his eyes darting between us with interest.

'It all started when—'

'Stop!' Onyx hissed, pushing us into shadows at the end of an alleyway. 'By the Stars, what's he doing here?'

'Who?'

I peered out. Just down the street, sitting nonchalantly outside a food vendor, was Carnelian. He sat at a table, drinking from a mug. I considered my War Fan, but instead my hand went instinctively to Deorwine. I'd creep up behind him, kill him where he sat. Sword through the back. Deorwine's blade would make a more emphatic job of it than my Fan.

A hand quickly covered mine, making it impossible for me to unsheathe the blade. I turned around. Rian looked at me, his eyes staring into mine as he shook his head. I gritted my teeth. After last night, that was exactly what I wanted to do, what I needed, but he wasn't going to let me. I relaxed my hold and Rian let go of my hand. Tarragon glanced at us but said nothing.

'I imagine he's followed us here to kill me,' Rian said.

Onyx shrugged. 'Maybe. I'll go and find out.' He stepped forwards.

'You can't do that,' I said, grabbing his shoulder.

'He's not going to kill me, we're on the same mission. Anyway, if I can convince him you're not in the city, that you've already left, I can send him off on some wild goose chase and keep him out of our way. The last thing we want is him breathing down our necks all the way to Mal. I think I'll send him off to the west.'

'You have a point, I suppose.' I nodded reluctantly, wondering whether to suggest he kill him instead.

'Back in a minute.' Onyx wandered off into the street, looking as though he didn't have a care in the world. As he approached Carnelian the assassin looked up and shouted to him. Onyx went to join him, sat down, and they started talking.

'You trust him not to betray us?' Tarragon asked, watching the two assassins.

'I do,' I said. 'He'll do exactly what he said he would, I have no doubt about that.'

Tarragon nodded.

Onyx and Carnelian spoke for several minutes, then Onyx got up and continued on down the street before circling back to us via the alleyways behind the main street. I kept an eye on Carnelian while we waited. As Onyx got back, Carnelian stood up, stretched, then started walking up the street towards us.

CHAPTER TWENTY-THREE

'Back!' I ordered, pushing everyone further down the alley. We pressed against the wall as Carnelian walked past. I held my breath, my hand back on Deorwine's cool, reassuring hilt, but Carnelian kept going. I peered back out into the street, watching him until he disappeared in the throng of people.

'Told you it would be fine,' Onyx said smugly. 'I've sent him off to Aqua Magna, said you'd been seen leaving that way during the night. He knew you were in Rill.'

'But did he know you were with us?' I asked, still watching the street in case Carnelian decided to double back.

'Didn't seem to. I'm unremarkable here, just another Low Blood desert guide. You Aerbans, on the other hand, stick out like Mereans in Flos. No offence,' he said, turning to Willow and winking.

'Bobbins, none taken,' she said, smiling sweetly at him. Tarragon gave a little scowl. Maybe it was his turn to feel a little insecure?

'Even so, we'd better finish our business and get out as soon as possible,' I said, still eyeing the street.

'Tomorrow,' Onyx said. 'At the earliest. I'm not leaving Grandfather until I'm sure he's on the mend.'

I sighed internally, not wanting to upset Onyx, but at the same time eager to get going and find Mal at the first opportunity.

'You're coming, too?' Tarragon asked, glancing back at Willow, his muscles tense.

Onyx turned to Rian. 'If you'll have me. Malachite means the world to me. I want him back, and maybe I can help.'

Tarragon visibly relaxed. He obviously hadn't known about my brother's relationship with Onyx.

'I assumed you'd be coming anyway,' Rian said with a nod.

Onyx smiled. 'Thank you.'

Rian grinned back.

I let out a breath, relieved the two would now be happy as travelling companions.

'We'll head for the East Quarter by the back alleyways. Come on,' Onyx said, leading us into the maze of passageways. Unlike other cities I'd been in, the alleyways of Rill were far cleaner than I'd expected.

'I thought the alleys in Rill would stink in the heat,' Willow said, looking around. 'This really surprises me.'

'They have an underground sewerage system to stop exactly that from happening,' Onyx said. 'The alleyways were pretty much an open sewer a few hundred years ago. Then there was an outbreak of plague, hundreds died, and they narrowed it down to the alleys and open sewers being the problem. After that they basically rebuilt the city, had all the sewers deep underground, and the houses served by wells that avoided the sewers so they couldn't spread illness anymore. It's worked ever since.'

'So I see,' Willow said.

We continued on to the East Quarter. The smell of alcohol became quite oppressive the deeper we went into the buildings, even this early. Two rowdy, drunken men staggered past the end of the alley as we approached, singing badly.

'At this time of day?' Willow asked, watching them go in amazement.

'Doesn't matter what time of day it is here,' Onyx said as we emerged from the alleyway onto the street. Yelling started at an inn to our left. 'It's like that all the time. Cheap alcohol, cheap women.'

Willow scowled.

'Sorrel would love it,' Rian said drily.

A scuffle broke out further up the street. Punches were thrown, along with earthenware mugs and bowls.

'Charming,' Tarragon said.

'Does it offend your High Blood sensibilities?' Onyx asked, an amused look in his eyes.

'I like a good fight as well as the next man, but drunken brawling? It's a little uncouth, if you ask me,' Tarragon said.

Onyx laughed and led us towards another inn where things appeared a little calmer.

'You know where Calder is?' I asked.

'No, but I think I may know someone who does,' Onyx said, opening the inn door. We walked into the building where wooden tables and chairs sat in neat clusters, with just a few customers currently making use of them.

At least the temperature was cooler in here. I wiped perspiration from my brow.

'Exactly how she likes it,' Onyx said.

'Who?' I asked.

'Lynn.'

I turned to the bar. A middle-aged woman in an orange cropped top and orange pantaloons served customers, a broad grin on her face, her long hair intricately braided. She looked towards us as we entered.

'Onyx! Come over here, boy! How are you? How's your grandfather?' she asked, speaking quickly.

'I'm fine, Lynn. Grandfather's been ill, but I think he may be on the mend now, thanks to a friend,' Onyx said, walking over to the bar.

Lynn nodded. 'Good. Drink?'

'Please,' Onyx said. 'For all of us.'

'We're all drinking?' Rian asked under his breath.

'You don't have to drink it, just make it look like you are,' I said softly.

Lynn poured out the drinks – some sort of fruity red alcohol, but I wasn't sure exactly what – and smiled at us. 'Friends of Onyx's are all welcome here. Is this purely social, my boy, or is your visit for other reasons?' she asked, tapping her nose conspiratorially.

'You know me too well,' Onyx said grinning. He took a large swig of alcohol. 'We're looking for someone,' he said, lowering his voice and wiping his mouth with his sleeve. 'A man named Calder.'

'Calder?' She looked around warily. 'Not someone to be trifled with.'

'Oh?' I asked.

'He's a thief, a cut-throat. Kills without the slightest provocation.' She looked at Onyx and shifted his sleeve to reveal his Coterie Tattoo. 'At least you have a reason.'

Onyx shrugged and lowered his sleeve. 'So, where can we find him?'

Tarragon took a mouthful of the drink, swallowed, and started coughing. Willow gave him a disapproving look.

'What?' Tarragon asked, wiping his mouth.

'Nothing,' she said, tutting.

'Go left,' Lynn said. 'Take the first right, then another left. He lives in the building with the rotten wooden door. Tell him I said hello.'

'You know him, then?' Onyx asked, grinning, a mischievous look in his eyes.

'None of your business, my boy,' she said, swiping a bar cloth at him. 'But yes, we're old friends. Now go, I've got more customers to serve. Yes, what can I get you?' she said, moving along the bar to where two men stood waiting to be served, backs to us.

'We'll finish these and go,' Onyx said, moving us to a table.

I eyed the drink suspiciously. It smelt of rich berries, lemon, and cinnamon.

Rian took a sniff and turned green. 'Too much like Mandragora Berries,' he said, putting it down, his face puckered in disgust.

'I think it's nice,' Willow said, taking a gulp.

Tarragon looked at her and raised an eyebrow in surprise.

I scanned the room. In one corner, a couple of drunks talked noisily as they slurred their speech; in another corner, a young woman cosied up to a rough-looking man; and at a far table, a group sat playing a very serious-looking game of cards. The two men that had just walked in talked animatedly to Lynn. I didn't like the look of them anymore than I liked the smell of the alcohol.

'Let's go now,' I said, watching the men at the bar.

'What's wrong?' Rian asked.

'Not sure, I just don't like those two at the bar.'

Onyx narrowed his eyes, then they widened. 'Coterie,' he hissed.

'You sure? I don't think I recognise them.'

'You wouldn't, they're the bitch's latest recruits. Obsidian and Zircon. Quickly and quietly,' he said, getting up as the two men continued to chat to Lynn.

We got up, slowly making our way to the door.

'Hey, you! Stop!' one of the men yelled.

We ran.

'Right,' I said, leading the way, my heart thundering in my chest.

'But Lynn said—' Tarragon began.

'We're heading in the opposite direction,' I said, sprinting along the street, then into a side street. 'This way.' We ducked into an alley and into a stable, Rian and Onyx shutting the door behind us. 'Up,' I said, climbing the ladder into the loft space. The roof was lower here, and in the ceiling a trapdoor led to outside, but it had a closed lock. Willow pushed past me.

'This is mine,' she said, nimbly getting to work with her lock picks. In moments, she had the trapdoor open.

'You need to teach me how to do that,' Tarragon said.

'Then I'd have no special skills that you didn't have,' she said, flicking her hair.

'You'd still be special to me, though,' Tarragon said, giving her a quick kiss.

'Not now,' Rian said, moving past them and helping me up through the trapdoor.

I climbed out onto the roof as banging started at the stable door. My heart thudded painfully in my chest. If these two men were Coterie assassins they'd be awesome opponents, and no way was I risking Rian, Tarragon, and Willow's lives.

'Come out, Amethyst, we know you're in there.'

'Zircon,' Onyx said, following Rian out onto the roof.

'We won't hurt you. Juniper only wants you to come back to Iolite so she can talk to you, Amethyst,' Obsidian called.

'He's lying.'

'I guessed that much,' I said. A wall of intense heat hit us as we all got out onto the tiled roof. We shut the trapdoor, Willow redoing the lock, and crouched low. I balanced myself, one hand resting on the tiles, the other shielding my eyes from the brilliant sun. The heat from the red-hot tile burnt my skin. I quickly lifted my hand, the skin red from the heat. *Hell's teeth*. We couldn't stay here.

Onyx gestured to us as the main door below gave way, crashing into the stable. We ran across the roofs, heading back the way we'd come, staying low. At the next gap in the buildings, we dropped down onto a balcony and climbed down to the ground.

'I know the way from here,' Onyx said, indicating up the alley.

I was glad he did, because being up on the roofs had rather confused me. We sped into another alleyway, twisting and turning along it until we came out opposite a building with a rotten wooden door.

I looked up and down the narrow street. Empty. My pulse still roared in my ears, but I moved swiftly across to the door and knocked.

'What do you want?' came a sharp voice.

I winced. Not a good start. 'Erica sent us,' I said.

Silence.

Rian shrugged. 'Maybe he won't speak to us, after all.'

'In, quickly,' said the voice as the door opened just enough for us to enter. We all slipped in, the door shutting firmly but quietly behind us. Little oil lamps illuminated the room we'd entered, which had no windows. I turned to Calder – he looked to be in his early thirties with short black hair, burnt sienna skin, and the deepest brown eyes. He had quite attractive features, and his rather bent nose, probably broken long ago, gave him character. 'Why did she send you? She never does that, unless it's bad news.'

'I'm her cousin, Amethyst of Iolite,' I said. 'These are my friends. Erica said you may have some news about my brother, Malachite. Mistress Juniper has him imprisoned somewhere. I need to know where.'

'Malachite, the old Master of Iolite's son?'

I nodded. 'I'm his sister. I need to find him.'

'Are you indeed, assassin?'

I flinched. 'Ex-assassin. I'm not with the Coterie anymore.'

Calder raised an eyebrow. 'No one ever leaves the Coterie alive.'

'So I've been told, but I'm here, and I'm still alive.'

Calder rubbed his chin. 'Well, Amethyst of Iolite, you're in luck. I know where your brother is.'

Onyx let out a long breath, the relief on his face obvious, even in this dimmest of lights.

'He's imprisoned on the Tarn Archipelago, in the Malign Prison. It's on the Third Isle, furthest out into the sea. But I can't say what sort of state he's in. That place is notorious for one thing and one thing only.'

'What's that?' Tarragon asked.

'Death.'

I swallowed. 'Thank you,' I said, turning to the door. I hesitated. 'You wouldn't happen to know anything about the whereabouts of Aerba's Fire Opal, would you?'

'If you were anyone other than Erica's cousin, I'd charge an exorbitant fee for all this information.' Calder stared at me a moment, as if weighing things up. 'I can't really help you much there. I don't know where it's gone. All I know is that King Chervil would have you believe Flos took it, which they didn't.'

Rian flinched at the name of his brother.

'The King is using it as a reason to attack Flos, take over the country, but he's having a bit of trouble convincing all his ministers, Lord Wintergreen in particular,' Calder continued.

Rian and Tarragon exchanged glances.

'The Nightshade has been deployed to cause unrest and infiltrate the Flosian Palace, but war hasn't broken out yet, and I'm not sure it will. I think some sort of regicide is more likely. A covert takeover through a Flosian "puppet" ruler.'

Rian uttered a few choice oaths under his breath.

I nodded. 'When I was there, I heard Prince Monkshood talking to a Nightshade called Sorrel. They were talking about killing King Narcissus, then Monkshood taking over in name, but Chervil running things from Aerba, just like you've said.'

'You did?' Calder chewed on his lip. 'Does Erica know this?'

I shook my head. 'I never had the chance to tell her before we fled the palace.'

'Then I'll send word immediately. It also seems some sort of alliance is underway between Aerba and Iolite, but I've not been able to find out any more about that at the moment.'

Aerba and Iolite? Exactly what I'd feared.

'Thank you for the information,' I said. 'We really appreciate it.'

'It'll be appreciated even more when Erica pays me extra this month,' he said with a grin.

'I'm sure she will, and can you tell her I'm sorry about the dress?'

'The dress?' he asked, a quizzical expression on his face.

I nodded. 'She'll understand.'

'Very well, I'll tell her.'

'Thank you.'

I peered out the door into the alleyway. Things appeared quiet. We stepped out into the street and started back to the palace.

CHAPTER TWENTY-FOUR

'You think Zircon and Obsidian will find us?' Willow asked, looking around the street we'd entered.

'If they follow standard Coterie rules, they won't try and engage us again today. They know we know they're here, and they'll wait until another day when we're not so on our guard,' Onyx said.

'You hope,' I muttered.

'You know the rules, once you're seen you're compromised. You don't go back after the same mark on the same day. It's very poor form.'

'You said they were new, though. They might be wanting to impress Juniper.'

'In that case, they'll follow the rule book to the letter, won't they?'

'Suppose.'

'There's an actual Coterie rule book?' Willow asked.

'Not as such, but there's kind of an unwritten code we all follow,' Onyx said. 'You learn it right away, as soon as you join the Coterie. Flouting it usually results in an unwilling audience with Juniper and Serpentine.'

'Serpentine?'

'Juniper's executioner and torturer,' I said.

'He's not an actual torturer, Ama,' Onyx said.

'What would you call what he does to people?' I asked, sending him a sidelong glance.

He hesitated. 'All right, torture is a fairly good word to describe what he does, I guess.'

'You get tortured for not following the rules?' Willow asked, wide-eyed.

'It's been known,' I said between gritted teeth. 'Rules or instructions.'

'You remember what happened to Sapphire?' Onyx asked.

I shuddered. 'Yes, and I'd rather not, if it's all the same to you.'

'What happened to her?' Willow asked.

'You don't want to know.'

'She carried out her commission a day late,' Onyx said. 'Got confused as to the timings. When she came back to Iolite, Juniper tore her off a strip and then sent her to Serpentine who got his knife and…'

'Willow doesn't need to hear the details,' I said, feeling nauseous at the memory. 'Suffice it to say she never worked for the Coterie again.'

'Never worked for anyone again,' Onyx sniffed. 'She'd have been better off if Serpentine *had* killed her.'

'Except he didn't. Just left her permanently disfigured.'

'Did you hear she died last year?'

'No, how?'

'Morbilli Rash.'

I shivered.

'It seems to me the two of you are lucky to be alive,' Willow said. 'I think I have a new respect for you both. I thought Coterie life was all about killing other people. But it appears it was as much about survival and self-preservation as anything else.'

I shrugged. 'You're not wrong, I suppose.'

'There is, was, a certain skill in staying alive, yes,' Onyx said, nodding. 'And I'm glad I don't have to worry about that anymore.'

'What, staying alive? Because you're likely to be on Juniper's kill list once she knows you've slipped her leash,' I said. 'You'll be in even greater danger.'

'I'd rather take my chances now, with you and your friends, than go back to life at the Crimson Castle.'

'Me, too.' I glanced over my shoulder.

Rian and Tarragon walked some distance behind us. The two were in deep conversation, and whatever they talked about appeared quite intense because they both looked extremely serious. Maybe Calder's tidings from Aerba had worried them. It was the first proper news we'd had from their homeland since we'd fled, and it caused concern to all of us. The way Chervil appeared to be behaving, his scheming and conniving, unnerved Rian in particular.

We returned to the Palace, and Onyx immediately went off to check on his grandfather. Sage sat in the living area with Anise, looking at some of the perfumes he'd purchased in Flos.

'I'm surprised they've survived our adventures,' I said, looking at the little glass phials of variously-coloured liquids.

'Not all of them have,' Sage said, pulling a face and tugging at his earring.

I caught the sweet and woody scent of roses, tuberose, lavender, and something I couldn't put a name to.

'I can definitely see what you meant about the perfumes now,' Rian said, his eyes sparkling as he sniffed the heady concoction. 'Damn, it has quite an effect.' He glanced at me, something akin to lust in his eyes.

'You're impossible,' I said, although I was glad he was happier now than the previous evening.

'But you love me?'

'Yes, I love you.'

We spent the afternoon resting, although I was getting agitated about leaving to find Mal. Onyx wouldn't leave his grandfather today, though, so I'd have to be patient until tomorrow morning. Then, hopefully, we'd be able to leave for Aqua Claras.

Rian and I went for a walk in the gardens before sitting in the shade under a palm tree for a while, watching the sunlight sparkle like diamonds in the spray from a fountain, where little rainbows danced and twirled. The peace in the palace gardens made me forget our quests, and I relished being in the beautiful surroundings with Rian.

After our evening meal, we all took it in turns to take advantage of the bath house, and later I met Rian in our room. It seemed prudent to have an early night. We discarded our weapons and all our clothing before slipping under the covers.

'Have you still got your rose perfume?' Rian asked, glancing at me.

'You want me to put some on now?' I asked. 'Do I smell or something? I've only just had a bath.'

'No, but I thought it might be nice to sleep surrounded by roses, and you.'

I narrowed my eyes. 'All right, then.'

I got out of the bed, very aware that I was naked, found my little perfume bottle and dabbed a little on. I turned around. Rian was watching me, cheeks flushed and eyes dark as he looked at me.

'Hmm, that's lovely,' he said as I got back into bed with him, although I wasn't entirely convinced he was talking about the perfume.

'You're getting as bad as Sage,' I said, giving him the benefit of the doubt.

He grinned at me.

I lay down, tiredness creeping over me, my eyes heavy, when a warm hand slipped around my waist. Rian pulled me towards him, turning my face to his. His lips met mine in a tender yet ardent kiss that deepened. I raked my fingers through his long hair, sandalwood and rose in the air around us. Shocks like lightning sparked through me at his touch, and any tiredness I might have had fled. He interlaced the fingers of his left hand with my right, his other hand sliding down from my waist to my hip.

'You stole my heart when we first met,' he said, his voice like a summer breeze. 'I love you, Phire,' he murmured, leaning in to kiss me again, his mouth claiming mine, the shocks forcing their way through my body from my lips to the top of my head to my fingertips and toes. His tongue was gentle, sweet. His mouth was like fire as he let out a little moan. Finally he pulled away, gazing into my eyes. 'I know at the moment we can't…'

I held my finger to his lips. 'We've been through this last night, but things are fine for now as they are, really.'

The sweet perfume of Night Jasmine drifted in the window, mingling with the sandalwood and rose, the hypnotic sound of the fountain near our window forming a curious lullaby. Rian smiled tenderly at me. His demeanour seemed so different to yesterday evening. Suddenly a nervous anticipation filled his eyes, making me frown.

'I think I might be able to improve on "fine",' he said, his voice suddenly husky as his amber irises dilated and his eyes darkened even more. He tentatively began to slide his slightly trembling hand from my hip, moving it lower.

I raised an eyebrow. 'And how exactly do you intend to—'

My eyes widened at his touch, a silken knot tightening inside me as his hand slipped lower still.

'Something along these lines,' he said, his breath suddenly catching in his throat. 'If you'd like me to?' He paused, his hand freezing as he gazed into my eyes, waiting for my answer.

I nodded. 'I—I would.'

He leant towards me and kissed me as his hand moved again, ever so slowly, towards where I craved his touch the most. I let out a little involuntary gasp as warmth spread through my core and spiralled around me until I found myself surrounded by golden sunbursts and his endless love.

When we finally settled down to sleep, he held me in his arms, our bodies moulding together. I could sense his heartbeat in his chest, his warm breath on my neck as sandalwood enveloped me like an old treasured blanket. I'd have to get my perfume out more often if it was going to have this effect on him. I drifted off to sleep, content and happy.

The morning dawned clear, the sun streaming into our room as it rose. I turned over and opened my eyes to find Rian smiling at me.

'Good morning. Sleep well?' he asked.

'Very,' I smiled back. I moved towards him, raising myself up on one elbow. 'About last night...'

He raised an eyebrow. 'What about it?'

'Thank you.'

'You don't need to thank me, it was my pleasure.'

'Well, I'm thanking you anyway. It was... perfect.'

'Hmm.'

'Hmm, what?'

'It *was* perfect, wasn't it?' He lay languidly on the bed, running his fingers through his dishevelled hair, grinning broadly.

'You're impossible.'

'So you say,' he said with a grin. 'But I'm perfectly impossible. And you love me anyway.' He pulled me towards him and kissed me soundly on the lips. 'Better get up or Tarragon will be knocking on the door.'

I moved to the edge of the bed. The mention of Tarragon made me pause, and I turned back to my husband.

'Was what happened last night anything to do with what you and Tarragon were talking about yesterday?' I asked, suddenly connecting things together.

Rian's cheeks flushed. 'I don't know *what* you're talking about,' he said, looking away and scrambling out of the other side of the bed.

I smiled to myself. It was.

We quickly got dressed and met the others for breakfast.

'Good morning,' Willow said. 'We thought you were going to be late.'

'We overslept,' I said.

Tarragon looked at Rian, then grinned. Luckily for him he was on the other side of the table and he remained silent or I might have had my Fan at his throat before he could take another breath. On the other hand, perhaps I should thank him sometime.

'The beds are rather comfortable, aren't they?' Willow said, stretching.

I glanced at Rian. He smiled, went red, and started studying the pattern on his plate. I looked away, catching Tarragon smirking on the far side of the table.

'What's wrong with you?' Sage asked him.

'Oh, nothing,' Tarragon replied, still smirking.

I sighed.

'I hate getting up this early,' Willow said. 'Oh, good, the food's here.'

Ford arrived with plates of breads and sweet pastries. As we tucked in, Onyx arrived and sat beside me. Rian took no more notice of him than if he'd been Sage or Tarragon. Thank goodness the two of them had reached an understanding.

'Grandfather's so much better, thank you, Anise.' Onyx grinned.

'You're welcome, glad I could help,' Anise said with a smile.

'We can leave this morning. I've already made arrangements for supplies.'

'The sooner we leave, the sooner we can find Mal and the Fire Opal,' I said. I was relieved that we would indeed be leaving today, although part of me would've liked to spend another night like last night, alone with Rian, exploring our newfound pastime a little more in such a delightfully soft bed.

After our meal, we collected our packs and met in the living room with our new supplies.

'Grandfather wants to see us before we leave, Ama,' Onyx said. He was dressed in his Iolitian clothes once more, his Low Blood moss green tunic over a light mail shirt, his brown leather belt, coarse cotton shirt, black suede britches and brown boots. 'You too, Rian.'

'Why does he want to see us?' I asked. I'd never met Onyx's grandfather before, so he wasn't renewing an old acquaintance.

'Come along, would you? The longer you dither, the later it is we leave, and I don't want to run into Zircon and Obsidian if I can help it.'

Neither did I.

We left the living room and went down a corridor, all the way to the end, where Onyx knocked on a door and then opened it. We entered an opulent bedchamber. Deep blue mats covered the floor, tapestries hung on the walls, and gold leaf inlay decorated the carved coving where the wall joined the ceiling. A large four-poster bed, with a blue and green canopy, sat against the wall near the window, where a pale blue voile curtain moved gently in the early morning breeze. Sitting up in the bed, propped up by green silk pillows and covered in a deep green sheet, sat Onyx's grandfather. The elderly gentleman's warm brown eyes smiled along with his mouth as he saw us. His crinkled skin revealed laughter lines, and his white hair his age.

'Come in, come in,' he said. His voice was stronger than I'd expected as he waved us over. 'Sit, Amethyst.' He gestured at the bed as Onyx pulled out two chairs for him and Rian. 'I'm so pleased to finally meet you. My Onyx has told me so much about you over the years.'

He had? I dreaded to think what stories he'd shared about me with his grandfather. I glanced at Onyx, then Rian. Onyx's face flushed a little, but Rian looked unperturbed.

'It's wonderful to meet you,' I said, sitting on the bed and taking the old man's hand.

'Welcome, Prince Valerian, I'm pleased to meet you,' Grandfather said, nodding towards Rian.

Rian flinched but let it slide. 'I'm pleased to meet you, too, sir,' he said.

'Onyx tells me you're on the trail of the Fire Opal.'

'That's right. It was stolen from the Aerban Throne, and I intend to get it back.'

'Even though you no longer live there?'

I looked at Rian.

'I—I…' He hesitated. 'It needs to be recovered no matter where I end up. The fact I don't live there anymore doesn't matter. I have to get it back.'

Grandfather nodded. 'I hear you're a Fire Spinner.'

'I am.' Rian nodded.

'And Onyx says that he's discovered he's a Water Spinner. And you, Amethyst? What about you?'

'I don't have a Magic Angle,' I said. 'There's nothing special about me. I'm quite ordinary, I'm afraid.'

Both Rian and Onyx looked as though they were about to protest, but Grandfather raised his hand.

'It's there. You're a High Blood. You may not think you're special, but your Magic Angle is waiting to be discovered. Only High Bloods have ever been able to use Magic and Artefacts, and even then, not all have strong abilities. Yours will come, my dear. Strong or weak, it will come.'

I nodded, but unfortunately didn't believe him.

'The Fire Opal is the most powerful of all the Artefacts,' Grandfather said. 'You know that?'

Rian nodded. 'It has been mentioned to us, but we only found out recently.'

'You only found out about being Elemental Angle Spinners recently, too, so why would you have known about the Fire Opal before?'

He had a point.

'You know where it came from?' Grandfather asked.

'Even I know it was found in Iolite, Grandfather,' Onyx said, looking smug.

'No, it wasn't, you're just meant to think that.'

'What? It's one of the things you're taught in school in Iolite. The Fire Opal was mined on the island and given to Aerba as a gift of friendship.'

'It came from the Crystal Vortex in the Cave of Crystals in the land of Chroma, where all the Artefacts originated,' Grandfather said.

'The Crystal what?'

'Chroma?' I asked, surprised.

The old man nodded. 'The same time as a geode of malachite was turned into a dagger, the most vibrant green you've ever seen.'

That rang a bell. Could it be the dagger Mal was meant to have on his twenty-first birthday, the one he'd been named after? The Iolitian Malachite Dagger?

'Juniper has one like that in the Great Hall at the Crimson Castle, with a gold and silver hilt – that's an Artefact?' I asked.

'I know the one you mean,' Onyx said, turning towards me. 'But it wasn't there when I went back to the Castle after I saw you and Rian in Quartz. It was nowhere to be seen. I was rather annoyed because it's supposed to be Mal's now.'

'I wonder where it's gone?' I started chewing on a nail.

'It sounds like the dagger I'm talking about,' Grandfather said, nodding. 'The Eternal Dagger.'

'It has a name?' I asked.

Grandfather nodded again.

I blinked in surprise.

'How do you know all this, sir?' Rian asked.

'My own grandfather had Chromian blood, from before the land was lost. The old tales have been passed down through the family ever since.'

'So why haven't you told me this before, Grandfather?' Onyx asked, a confused look on his face.

'Because your Magic Angle hadn't asserted itself then. Now it has, you deserve to know the truth.'

'Are you a Magic Spinner too?' Rian asked.

The old man nodded. 'I'm an Air Spinner.'

'You should have told me,' Onyx said, frowning. 'I should've known this earlier.'

'Would it have helped you?'

'I... er... I don't know,' Onyx admitted.

'It would have put you in danger. A lone Elemental Angle Spinner in Iolite? No, it was safer for you to remain oblivious until you discovered your own power, assuming you ever did. Most High Bloods don't have a clue these days. They don't notice it's there because they're not looking for it. They spend their whole lives completely unaware of their possible potential. And it may be safer for them that way.'

'So how did the Vortex work?' I asked.

'The Crystal Vortex was a spinning vortex of golden light, rather like a stationary tornado, within the cave. Periodically, it would throw out a crystal. They were of varying sizes and different gemstones and colours. The Gemsmiths of Chroma would make them into jewellery, or in the case of the Fire Opal, just carve it. They turned one huge gem into that sword and shield you have on your back.'

I shuddered.

'The Fire Opal was smuggled out of Chroma and lost for many years until it reappeared in Iolite and the story began that it had been mined on the island, which it hadn't. Still, the story persists, as you know, and has become a kind of legend.'

'Chroma must have been an amazing place,' I said.

Grandfather nodded. 'An island with the capital, Magenta, and the Cave of Crystals surrounded by two concentric rings of land. It was lush and vibrant with wildlife and plants, but who knows what it looks like now.'

'Wet,' Onyx said. 'After all, it's been underwater for almost five centuries.'

'No.' Grandfather shook his head.

'I'm sorry?' Rian asked.

'Chroma still exists. It was never lost under the sea. That was a story put about to make sure the land was left alone. Chroma is still out there.'

CHAPTER TWENTY-FIVE

'Surely we'd know if it was?' I said.

'Why?' Grandfather asked. 'No one goes that way anymore because there's no reason to, so how would you know it's still there?'

Onyx's forehead furrowed in confusion. 'So you're saying Chroma still exists? Out in the sea somewhere?'

Grandfather nodded.

'But why would the people of Chroma want to vanish?' I asked. 'Isn't that rather extreme, for a whole land to vanish like that, deliberately?'

'They did it because they were disillusioned with the Six Lands after the Great Pestilence, caused by the overuse of Magic and Artefacts. King Cinquefoil IV of Aerba, King of All, had encouraged the use of Magic and Artefacts by the High Bloods for even the most trivial of things, rather than for great deeds, and as a result it unbalanced nature and the Great Pestilence broke out.'

'We knew something about this,' Rian said. 'Although they don't talk much about it in Aerba. Tarragon learnt it in Iolite, but then he does love his history.'

'I think the Aerbans chose to forget their part in it as much as possible. Anyway, as punishment, the Emperor of Chroma, a Quintessence Angle Spinner, placed a curse on a newly-made crystal sword and shield recently thrown out of the Crystal Vortex. He turned them into the Cursed Weapons, Aldorbana and Cwicsusl.'

'We know all about them,' I said, shifting the weapons on my back.

'At the end-of-year celebrations, Chroma gifted them to King Cinquefoil. He thought they were a lavish gift, until he found they were cursed. After his death, a few days later—'

'By the Stars, did you say days? Don't you mean weeks?' I asked, surprised.

'No, days,' Grandfather said. 'He was a strong man, but not strong enough to bear the Magical weight of the Cursed Weapons for long. Their burden was too great.'

'But I had them for weeks when I was cursed,' I said, chewing my lip, a niggling worm of unease settling in my chest. 'It wasn't days. I mean, I did feel the pressure on me, the weight, but I managed for a while before it became too much, and they started to noticeably weaken me.'

Grandfather raised an eyebrow.

'Maybe the Curse weakened over time?' Rian suggested. 'Perhaps the Magic wasn't as strong as it was when they were first Cursed?'

Grandfather didn't look so sure, but if he was right, how had I withstood them for so long? I didn't have the physical strength of a middle-aged man in his prime. I was an eighteen-year-old girl. I may have had more energy, but not brute strength.

'Maybe that's what happened.' Onyx nodded, looking at Rian.

'Well, after Cinquefoil's death, the Hexad – that's what they called the Six Lands back then – broke up. Chroma left after what became known as Cinquefoil's Folly. Weary of Magic's exploitation, they refused to let any more new Artefacts go to the Five Lands. Anyway, the Five Lands banned Magic completely. Magic Angles were forgotten, Elemental Angle Spinners slowly became myth. The Blood rules were still followed, but not to preserve Magic in the bloodlines as they had been originally.'

'It was a way of suppressing the people,' Rian said, a fist clenched.

Grandfather nodded. 'Some of the Lands turned to the earth; to Herbs and Flowers for Aerba and Flos, Trew to the Trees, Mere to freshwater Springs and Lakes. Iolite revered the Stars and Planets. They left the Elements behind. Chroma set about covertly gathering up and destroying as many Artefacts as they could find. A few were left amongst the Royal Families of the Five Lands, hidden and forgotten about, and Chroma kept a few for themselves, but most were destroyed or lost. Chroma spent twenty years looking for Artefacts, then when a tsunami wiped out eastern Trew, they used that as an excuse to "vanish", deliberately putting about the story that the whole land had been lost to the sea in a great disaster.'

'That's incredible,' Onyx said. 'To pretend to destroy a whole land like that.'

'And people believed it,' I said.

'So Chroma is still there?' Rian asked. 'It didn't disappear beneath the waves at all?'

'It's still exactly where it always was,' Grandfather said, 'but I now fear Chroma, along with the Five Lands, are in great danger.'

'Why?'

'Haven't you heard the reports of droughts and storms across the Lands, of famine and illness creeping amongst the people?'

I glanced at Rian. 'We've heard some things.'

'Reports are coming in from everywhere,' Grandfather said.

'Nature is unbalanced again, and we run the risk of a second Great Pestilence. If that happens, then thousands will die once more.'

Hell's teeth.

'Not due to the overuse of Magic, though, surely?' I asked. 'I mean, there is no Magic now.' I glanced at Rian and Onyx. 'Well, very little, not like it was last time.'

'No, not due to Magic this time,' Grandfather said, shaking his head. 'I believe it's the Crystal Vortex itself that is failing. It keeps the Elements and nature in check, but if it collapses, then the Six Lands may be destroyed, and at the very least, chaos will break out as the Elements fail.'

'So what will Chroma do to stop it from happening?' Onyx asked. 'Surely they have a plan if this were ever to happen?'

Grandfather nodded. 'They need the most powerful Artefact ever produced by the Vortex to restart it and rebalance everything, along with one of each of the Angle Spinners to actually begin the process.'

'The Fire Opal,' Rian said, his eyes widening. 'So Chroma needs to get hold of it? To restart the Vortex?'

'But we don't even know where the Fire Opal is,' I said. 'It could be lost forever, for all we know.'

'Trew's spies have been out looking for it ever since it was stolen,' Grandfather said.

'Trew?' Rian asked. 'Why Trew?'

'They know its real importance, which the Aerbans never did. Trew has always had a feel for these things, particularly the Royal Family. A race of men once lived out in the Trewan wilderness, the Senex, who lived for hundreds of years and used to have an understanding of Elemental Magic. They would advise the Royal Family on Magic, but that was long ago now. The Trewan Royal Family are trying to track the Opal down, so you must go to them, find out what they know about the Opal, and hunt it down, take it to Chroma, and restart the Crystal Vortex. I'll write you a letter of introduction to King Ash of Trew, explain to him what you're doing.'

'Now, wait a minute, Grandfather,' Onyx said, standing up. 'This isn't our business. It's not for us to get involved in, this whole restarting the Vortex thing.'

'It's everyone's business, Onyx – yours, mine, your friends', everyone's – and particularly anyone who's an Elemental Angle Spinner. If someone doesn't do something soon, we may all perish. Is that what you want?'

'No, of course not, but why does it have to be us?'

'Clean your ears out, boy. I've just said. You're Spinners. It's your responsibility.'

Onyx looked sullenly at his grandfather and sat down. 'I almost wish I hadn't found out about being a Spinner now.'

'I'm glad you did, or those Worms would have got us,' Rian said.

Onyx gave him a little smile.

I chewed on a nail then glanced at Rian. 'The Dryad Queen. She said order had to be restored, that we were the ones. Could this be what she was talking about?'

Rian nodded slowly. 'Perhaps it was. She already knew about me and Anise, and must have known about Tarragon to send that Artefact to him. Maybe she even knew about Onyx, too.'

'But we'd still need an Air Spinner and a Quintessence Spinner.'

'The Dryad Queen?' Grandfather looked at us. 'She's well?'

That was a question we couldn't answer, but I feared the answer was no.

'You've met her?' Onyx asked in surprise.

'A long time ago. Beautiful creature. If she told you this, then it's all true. The trees have a way of sensing the future, a way of knowing about all things present and those past. You'd do well to listen to her. If she's said you're the ones, then she's not wrong. It's quite a burden to take on your young shoulders, though. I only wish I was more sprightly and could come and help you.'

'You've helped us so much already,' I said, squeezing the old man's hand. 'Thank you.'

'I've done what I can. The rest is up to the three of you and your friends. I'm sure you'll find a way to fulfil your destinies.'

As long as my "destiny" included freeing my brother, that was fine with me. Rian had a determined look in his eyes, but that may well have had something to do with the Fire Opal. Onyx, on the other hand, looked less sure and certainly not overly enthusiastic as he stood up again, shoulders slightly drooping.

'We must go,' I said, aware of the rapidly climbing sun. I really didn't want to run into Zircon and Obsidian again.

Grandfather nodded. 'Say goodbye to that lovely girl for me – what was her name? Willow. She came in to see me yesterday evening. She reminds me so much of my aunt, Delta. Wonderful woman. Her son, my cousin, left Mere for Aerba years ago. He was a successful merchant, as I remember, married an Aerban girl and lived in Viridi City. They had several children, and they had children in turn, following the Aerban naming tradition, of course.

I did hear of some of his grandchildren's names – Laurel, Neem, Willowherb, and Meadowsweet.'

Willowherb? A smile slowly formed on my lips. 'Willow's his granddaughter.'

'Really?' the old man's eyes widened. 'Your Willow?'

I nodded. 'Her real name is Willowherb and her grandfather was a merchant from Mere.'

'Well, how strange,' he said with a smile. 'Do send her in to me to say goodbye.'

Onyx looked at me. 'Willow's my cousin?' His forehead creased as he thought. A big grin spread slowly across his face.

Rian smiled at me, then turned to Grandfather. 'Thank you for all your help, sir.'

'It's been a pleasure, Prince Valerian,' Grandfather said. 'And you, too, my dear,' he said, squeezing my hand. 'Now I'll write that letter for you, Onyx.'

Rian and I left the room, returning down the corridor towards the others.

'I guess that seals it, then,' Rian said, pausing. 'I *have* to find the Fire Opal. It's my responsibility, after all. I must recover it for Aerba and for the safety of the Six Lands.' He could protest that he'd left his former life behind all he wanted, but deep down, he was still a loyal Prince of Aerba.

'*We* will recover it,' I said, stopping and taking hold of his hand. 'We all need to go with you to find the Opal and restart the Vortex. You can't fix the Vortex on your own, and anyway, I'd never let you go alone. We do things together now, remember? I'd go with you into hell if I had to.'

'You would? Really?' he asked, turning towards me.

'Of course. We make a good team, you and me.'

He smiled. 'We do, don't we?'

I cupped his face in my hands, drawing him into a little kiss. 'Yes, we do.'

'I'm still getting used to that, I suppose, having someone with me all the time. I rather like it.'

'Good, because you're stuck with me.'

'I wouldn't have it any other way now, wife,' he said, kissing my nose. 'Come on.' We carried on along the corridor and joined the others. 'Willow, Onyx's grandfather wants to say goodbye to you,' Rian said. 'You know where to go?'

'He does? Why?' Willow asked.

'He just wants a quick word before we go,' I said, not wanting to give away the surprise. She frowned, nodded, and hurried off to see the old man.

'What are you two grinning at?' Tarragon asked us.

'Onyx and Willow are cousins,' I said with a smile.

Tarragon's eyes widened. 'No.'

'Yes,' Rian said. 'And there's a lot more. We'll fill you all in as we travel.'

We left the palace via a side gate, moving quickly out into the throng of citizens, leading our horses so as not to attract too much attention. I glanced back to the main palace entrance as we took a side street. Zircon and Obsidian sat drinking outside an inn down the street from the entrance. I smiled as we headed away from the palace. They'd not know we'd escaped them for a while. That should give us the chance to get a decent distance between us and the Coterie. Hopefully, Carnelian was halfway across Mere by now, heading west, while we headed in the opposite direction, to the east coast.

As soon as we left the city gates, we mounted our horses and set off on the main road to Aqua Claras. We told the others everything Grandfather had said. Willow filled us in on her family history. Onyx beamed from ear to ear.

'So you think that's what the Dryad Queen meant, that we're supposed to rebalance nature by restarting the Crystal Vortex?' Anise asked.

'Sounds a little far-fetched, if you ask me,' Sage muttered, fiddling with his reins.

'Maybe your Magic Angle will be able to help us.'

'I'm like Phire, I don't have one.'

'Yet.'

Sage grunted. 'We'll see.'

'How far to the coast, Onyx?' Tarragon asked.

'Four days, all going well,' Onyx said. 'We camp tonight, but after that there are small villages and inns along the way.'

'Good. I take it there are no Blue Death Worms this way? Or Dire Wolves?' Tarragon asked as he looked around at the dry, dusty landscape, and gave a little shudder.

'No, nothing like that,' Onyx laughed, then frowned. 'Dire Wolves?'

'It's a long story,' I said.

'I think we have time,' Onyx said, so we recounted our adventures to him.

We'd reached the edge of the desert, now, where scrubby bushes tried to gain purchase in the less-sandy soil. Bright red little birds flitted from bush to bush, collecting seeds and insects, chirping happily to each other in the sunlight. Perspiration had quickly broken out on my brow. I wiped it away before shielding my eyes to get a better look at the rolling landscape surrounding us. In places, the breeze picked up the sand and dust, making little dust-devils, rotating for a short distance before collapsing in on themselves.

Onyx laughed after we'd finished speaking. 'There are no Worms or Wolves here. Well, not the sort you're talking about. You don't need to worry, you'll sleep well tonight, Tarragon.'

Tarragon scratched his chin. 'It's probably wise to set a watch, though, y'know.'

'You and your watches,' Sage muttered. 'Are you going to stay awake this time?'

'I've already apologised for that, profusely.' Tarragon glanced at Rian, then bowed his head.

'We don't need a watch because of any Blue Death Worms or Dire Wolves,' I said, looking back down the road to make sure we weren't being followed. Although the road was clear, I knew the Coterie wouldn't let us go that easily. Once Obsidian and Zircon realised their mistake – and Carnelian, too, for that matter – they'd be after us again. We couldn't let down our guard until we were out at sea, on our way to the Third Isle and the Malign Prison.

'So, are there many ships in Aqua Claras, cousin?' Willow asked with a grin.

Onyx smiled back. 'It's a main port, so, yes, but I'm getting us passage on a particular vessel.'

'Oh?'

'My aunt, Pol, is in port. She's a ship's captain, has her own merchant vessel. I sent a messenger to ask her to wait for us. She's due to take a shipment of silks and oil to Trew, so I'm sure she'll be happy to stop in at the Third Isle on her way.'

'That would be very kind of her,' Rian said. 'You're sure she won't mind?'

'The Malign Prison is hardly a salubrious place to stop,' Sage said, a sour expression on his face.

'She's very fond of me, both her and her First Mate, Holm. They're like second parents to me.' His voice caught for a moment. I glanced towards him. Tears stood in his eyes. He cleared his throat. 'They'll be happy to help us.' He lowered his voice so only I could hear. 'Besides, Aunt Pol doesn't know about Mother yet, so I need to tell her.'

'It'll be good for you to be the one to tell her about her sister,' I said softly. 'You'll both get comfort from that.'

'I hope so,' Onyx said, looking straight ahead before raising his voice again. 'My aunt's quite a character, being a ship's captain. Only Mere has women captains, and I'm really proud of her.'

'And to think she's really royalty,' Rian said. 'I couldn't imagine a High Blood in the Aerban Court, even a Demoted one, becoming a ship's captain.'

'Captain Valerian,' Tarragon smirked.

'I don't think so,' Rian said, giving Tarragon a long look. 'Do you?'

Tarragon made a face. 'Probably not, no.'

'I think my aunt always loved the sea, at least that's what Mother said,' Onyx said. 'In truth, she's probably happier roaming the waves than sitting at Court.'

I glanced behind us again. The road was empty for as far as I could see. It should have reassured me, but for some reason it didn't. There were too many assassins in Mere for my liking, and they were all after me and Rian.

CHAPTER TWENTY-SIX

The night passed uneventfully, much to Tarragon's relief. We set out early the next day, making our way to a small village by early evening, and a little inn. It was nice enough, a few rowdy patrons in the bar as the evening drew on, but overall they had good food, decent beds, and we wanted for nothing.

Rian and I snuggled into our bed, not removing our underclothing – I didn't trust the bedding quite enough for that – and quickly nodded off to sleep after the hours we'd spent in the saddle. My nightmares had been a lot better, but tonight they were back. I dreamt of Rian once more lying on a bed of straw in the barn, writhing and crying out in pain. Dryads burst into flames in front of me as their trees caught light, combusting in the great green forest as Carnelian laughed. Glowing Blue Worms rose from the sand in front of me, spitting venom; I ducked behind Glædwine just before they sprang towards me, smashing into the purple crystal shield. A Dire Wolf appeared, and leapt at me. I turned, fearing my time had run out and the jaws of death were about to close around me and I'd never see Rian again.

I awoke covered in sweat, my shirt clinging to me, my heart racing, Rian snoring gently beside me. I took a deep breath, trying to calm myself, but even after several minutes my heart still pounded in my ears and rattled in my chest. The dreams were so vivid, so real, they made me nauseous. There was no way I was getting back to sleep like this. I sat up.

The little oil lamp that burnt in the corner of the room was down to its last dregs of oil. It was maybe an hour before dawn? I wouldn't get back to sleep now, and I saw no point in trying.

I carefully slipped out of the bed so as not to disturb Rian, and pulled on my tunic. Although a lot stronger now, he still needed his sleep, and I had no intention of waking him because of my nightmares. I grabbed my britches and boots, dressed, and quietly left the room, locking the door behind me. What I needed was a little air. Those dreams had really disturbed me, and I wanted to get the afterimages out of my head, confine them to memories. Deorwine and Glædwine joined me as I made my way down the stairs and out the back of the inn where the stable yard sat below our window, the only window looking this way.

I'd been a little upset when I'd discovered this last night – smelling horse all day was one thing, but all night, too? Not pleasant. I'd tried to swap with Sage, but he was having none of it and neither was Onyx, even when I'd pleaded with him.

I stepped out into the yard area, moving to one side as I looked around for any company, but all appeared still and quiet. I screwed my nose up at the smell that greeted me. I sighed, rolling my neck to try and release the tense muscles, taking a deep breath of cool air, trying to force the nightmares away as I ignored the smell of the stables and their occupants. The hairs on the back of my neck suddenly rose.

A cold blade rested at my throat. An arm around my collarbone kept me from moving.

Hell's teeth.

Obsidian chuckled. 'You've made this all too easy, Amethyst,' he said. 'I was told you were a great assassin, Lady Merciless, but you're easier to get to than a sweet in a shop. And now you'll pay for your carelessness.'

I swallowed, clenching a fist at being taken by surprise, wondering how to get hold of Deorwine sitting happily on my back.

'Lady Juniper will reward me greatly for your death, Lady Merciless,' Obsidian continued as Zircon appeared out of the shadows and entered the back of the inn. 'She'll likely make me wealthy, and I'll rise quickly in the ranks of the Coterie. And Zircon, too, for succeeding in killing the boy where others have failed.'

Rian.

A shard of ice slammed into my heart. He lay upstairs, asleep. At least the bedroom door was locked. Zircon would have trouble getting in there. I hoped. The thought of the assassin getting in and killing Rian as he slept made me feel nauseous. My husband would have no idea what happened, or if he did, it would be a few seconds of terror and then pain and then nothing. I had to warn him. I had to help Rian.

'Any last words, Lady Merciless?' Obsidian asked, a note of triumph in his voice.

'Yes,' I said, attempting to keep my heart rate under control and my hands from shaking. I knew what to do. I knew how to handle this – by the Stars, I'd been trained long enough. All I had to do was not freeze, even though fear for Rian threatened to block out everything else. 'You can tell her to go to hell!'

I slammed backwards into Obsidian. After three steps, where the assassin, taken by surprise, stumbled, we hit a wall and fell to the ground. Obsidian dropped his knife as I rammed my elbow into his gut as hard as I could. I scrambled up, moving back across the yard towards the inn door, drawing Deorwine as I went, but Obsidian lunged forward, blocking my way, pulling his sword free.

'Rian!' I screamed as loudly as I could, hoping it would be enough to wake him and save him from death. 'Rian!'

'He can't save you, you know. You're out here alone. No help is coming.' Obsidian snarled like some rabid animal.

'I wasn't expecting it to,' I said. 'Rian!'

The assassin's eyes narrowed. 'You think you can warn him? Too late. He's probably dead already.'

He better not be, or Zircon would pay.

Obsidian moved towards me, brandishing his sword in a menacing manner, a vicious grin spreading across his face.

I grabbed Glædwine from my back, and before Obsidian had a chance to react, I swung at him with Deorwine, forcing him to parry my blow in a clumsy fashion. With him off-balance, I struck at him again, slamming Glædwine into his face, the shield knocking him further off-balance as blood ran from his nose. My crystal sword smashed once more into his metal blade and he finally lost his footing, falling backwards into the empty stable beside the inn door, hitting the floor. He screamed and stopped moving, his sword clattering to the ground.

I frowned. I hadn't hit him hard enough to knock him out. I moved towards him tentatively, sword at the ready in case of a surprise attack. Stopped. The prongs of an upturned pitchfork stuck out the front of his chest, blood trickling from his mouth, eyes wide in surprise. Someone in the stable yard had been careless, leaving the fork lying on the ground. Good for them.

I turned and sprinted back into the inn. The ice in my chest rested around my heart like a hand, squeezing it tightly and painfully. My breaths came in ragged gasps as I ran up the stairs two at a time.

As I reached the top of the staircase, Tarragon appeared at his bedroom door, bleary-eyed.

'What's happening?' he asked.

Onyx appeared from the end of the passageway, knife in hand, as Sage peered out of his room, eyes wide and alert.

'Not now,' I said tersely.

The lock on our room door was broken. I kicked the door open. Froze.

A body lay on the floor in the shadows at the end of the bed, dark blood seeping onto the wooden floor like a pool of darkness. My heart crashed into my rib cage as a sob started to work its way up my throat. I was too late?

'Thanks. If you hadn't woken me...'

Startled, I almost lost hold of my weapons. I turned sharply to see Rian on the far side of the bed, slightly dishevelled, sword in hand, blood dripping from its tip.

The sob worked its way out of my mouth. I dropped my weapons and scrambled over the bed to him, flinging my arms around his neck. He dropped his sword and wrapped his arms tightly around me, pulling me against his warm body as if he could make me one with him.

'Damn, are you all right? Are you hurt?' he asked, stroking my hair. 'Shh, it's okay.'

'I'm okay, but for a moment there I thought I'd lost you,' I sobbed. 'I shouldn't have left the room.' I shook, tears falling as I clung to him, filled with guilt and relief. 'I'm so sorry.'

'Calm down,' he said, sitting me on the side of the bed as he crouched in front of me. 'I'm fine. What happened?'

'Is everything all— Oh,' Tarragon said as he saw the body on the floor.

Onyx swept in. 'Zircon.' He looked over at me. 'Where's Obsidian?'

'In the stables. Dead,' I said, turning towards him.

'Best I go and check,' Onyx said, heading for the door.

'Onyx,' Rian said.

Onyx paused. 'Yes?'

'Do that, but then we're leaving. Immediately.'

Onyx nodded and left.

Rian glanced up at Tarragon as Sage appeared in the doorway.

'Five minutes, then we go,' the prince said.

'We'll get ready,' Tarragon said.

Sage's eyes widened as he caught sight of the dead assassin. The two cousins left the room, pulling the door closed behind them.

'I'm so sorry. I—I had a nightmare,' I said, wiping my eyes. 'Well, several, actually. I got up and went out for some fresh air.'

'Me again?'

'You, dryads, Worms, Wolves, you name it, it was all there in one great jumble. So I went for a breath of fresh air, only to find Obsidian and Zircon waiting for me in the stable yard.'

'Then what happened?' he asked gently, looking into my eyes.

'I managed to get away from Obsidian, but Zircon was already on his way up to you, which is when I yelled at you, hoping I'd wake you.'

He nodded. 'Good thing you did. I came to immediately when I heard your voice.'

'I fought Obsidian. He's dead.'

'You…?'

I shook my head. 'No, he fell on an upturned pitchfork.'

Rian flinched. 'Nasty.'

'Then I came straight up to you, and when I saw…' I glanced at Zircon's body. 'For a moment I thought it was you. What happened here?'

'Your yell woke me. I realised you were outside, and I grabbed a sword as the door broke open. I knew it couldn't be you, so I was ready when Zircon came in. I took him off guard,' Rian said, looking at the man's lifeless body at the end of the bed. 'I didn't have a choice, really. It was him or me.'

'I know,' I said, kissing his forehead. 'And neither would I, if Obsidian hadn't fallen. Neither of them would have stopped until they'd killed us.' I hesitated. 'I'm so sorry I left you.'

'Don't worry about it,' Rian said. 'Next time, wake me and we'll go together.'

I nodded.

He smiled. 'Now, let's get ready to leave. Hopefully we haven't woken the whole inn.' He paused and looked at me. 'Thank you for yelling,' he said, kissing my hand. 'My shield,' he murmured, looking deep into my eyes.

It was only as he kissed me that I realised how much I was shaking. I got up off the bed and we quickly finished dressing and collected our packs.

'Let's go,' I said. We left our room, and Zircon at the end of the bed, before quietly joining the others.

'Bugger, I was really looking forward to a good cooked breakfast,' Tarragon said as we left the village far behind.

'You'd never have got it once the questions started,' Onyx said, adjusting his horse's reins. 'They probably wouldn't have let us leave until the militia got here.'

Tarragon huffed.

'You should be glad they didn't try and kill all of us in our beds,' Onyx said. 'I would've.'

'Then it was lucky Phire had a nightmare,' Anise said, 'and lucky you weren't after us, Onyx.'

Onyx shrugged and grinned.

'We all owe her our lives,' Sage said, nodding.

They owed me nothing. Onyx was being kind; no assassin would have gone after the whole company once his two marks were dead.

I glanced at Rian, still feeling a little guilty about leaving him, but the look he gave me said he was having none of it. It wasn't my fault. I'd saved them, saved *him*. I sighed and stared at the road ahead, trying to put Zircon and Obsidian from my mind.

The further we went, the busier the road got. We passed carts and wagons as they rumbled along, throwing up clouds of dust behind them. They were laden with heaps of fabric, and jars of spices and oil, heading to and from the coastal port of Aqua Claras. The merchants wiped dust from their sweaty faces, urging their reluctant horses on as they headed to the port with their wares.

I hardly slept the next night, spent at another well-kept inn. Although the immediate threat posed by Obsidian and Zircon had now passed, I still couldn't relax, even with the door locked and bolted. Rian drifted off to sleep happily, but I remained awake, staring at the ceiling of our room. The inn was larger than the previous night's, but the food was not as good, and Tarragon had spent the evening with indigestion, complaining about it at length until Anise went to find his Herb Chest, and Sage got so fed up he went to bed early.

I turned things over in my mind in a never-ending loop of Mal, Fire Opals, Magic Spinners, Crystal Vortices, and assassins. Then there was Beryl and Juniper. I just couldn't settle. Couldn't put these things from my mind long enough to fall asleep. And this time, I wasn't going to try and take a nighttime walk to clear my head. Instead, I kept an ear out for any creaks on the stairs, any unexplained footsteps, and that didn't help me sleep, either.

'You worry too much.'

I turned over. Rian lay looking at me, his amber eyes glowing in the light from the little oil nightlight.

'I've always been a worrier,' I said. 'Whether about Mal, missions I was sent on, Beryl – or you. Now I have Malign Prisons and Fire Opals to add to the list.'

He reached out and took my hand, absently spinning the diamond wedding ring around my finger. 'Everything will be fine, you'll see,' he said, smiling. He moved his hand and shifted a curl from my face.

'But there's so much at stake, how can it be?'

'Because we'll face these things, and conquer them all, together. You and me, but also Tarragon, Willow, Sage, Anise, and Onyx.

And your brother, too, when we rescue him. We'll be alright, Phire. We'll do it together.'

I desperately hoped he was right. 'You really think we can?'

'We can,' he said with a nod.

I looked back at my wedding ring twinkling in the dim light. 'Where did this come from? Your ring?'

He gave me a sad little smile. 'It was my mother's. She gave it to me just before she died. She told me to give it to the girl who made my heart sing, the one who was my best friend, my soulmate. The one I wanted to spend my life with, grow old with. The one I was going to marry.'

'Oh,' I said, my heart twisting and swelling both at once. I was all those things to him, as he was those things to me. 'You're sure you don't still want to wear it, if it was your mother's?'

He shook his head. 'Like I said, she told me to give it to you – well, not you directly, but you know what I mean, and that's what I've done. I've honoured her wish, and it's made me very happy that you now wear it.' He smiled.

I smiled back, humbled and touched by his words. 'Thank you,' I said, my voice catching. 'I wish I'd known her.'

'So do I. She'd have loved you – and I think you'd have loved her, too. We were very alike.'

'Then there's no question she would have been very special to me.'

He kissed my forehead. 'Now, you need to get back to sleep.'

'I haven't been to sleep at all yet,' I said ruefully.

'Then you definitely better get some sleep. I don't want you falling out of your saddle tomorrow because you decided to take a nap then, instead. Now, come here.' He reached out and I dutifully moved towards him until I was resting in his warm arms. 'You're cold,' he said.

'I hadn't realised.' I'd been too busy worrying.

'I'll soon have you warmed up, then you'll sleep,' he said, holding me tighter.

His warmth and steady heartbeat finally lulled me into a relaxed state, but sleep still came intermittently. I kept waking, not with nightmares, but with sensations of hot and cold sweeping through me, my heart pounding, and such an uneasiness that I shuddered. Each time, his heartbeat, his love, would lull me back to sleep, only for me to awaken a short time later in exactly the same way. By morning, I was exhausted, and the worrying continued. And I could add another thing to my list – the worry I'd nod off during the day and fall out of my saddle.

CHAPTER TWENTY-SEVEN

I yawned. My eyes ached. All I wanted to do was sleep, but that wasn't an option on horseback, so I grasped my horse's reins tightly and concentrated on keeping my eyes open. Rian glanced at me, a worried look in his eyes, but he said nothing. Despite sleeping well himself, I knew he'd worked out I hadn't slept much, even when he had been holding me. Still, one night of little sleep wasn't so bad, as long as I slept better tonight, which should be aboard Onyx's aunt's ship, so everything should be fine. It would be safer aboard, and I wouldn't need my keen assassin senses at night. I hoped.

As we got closer to the coast, the land started to turn even more fertile. Scrubby bushes were replaced with trees, grasses waved gently in the onshore breeze, and a few fields of crops encroached on the road. Wildflowers grew in amongst the weeds on the roadside verges, and wagons rumbled along on their way to and from Aqua Claras, laden with goods.

'How far to Aqua Claras from here, Onyx?' Sage asked.

Onyx shielded his eyes from the sun and sniffed. 'Three, maybe four hours at the most. We should be there by late afternoon and able to catch the evening tide.'

Sage nodded. 'Then perhaps we ought to stop for something to eat?'

'Sounds a good idea,' Willow said. 'Tarragon's stomach has been rumbling for a good hour now. Despite his large breakfast.'

'I can't help it if I'm hungry,' Tarragon pouted at her. 'All this travelling is tiring and it increases my appetite.'

'Bobbins.'

'What about those buildings up ahead, Rian?' Anise asked, pointing. 'They don't look like they've been used for a while. They'd be the perfect place to stop.'

Rian nodded. 'Good idea. We'll rest for a bit, eat, then continue on to Aqua Claras.'

We guided our horses off the road and up a little lane to where a small cluster of farm buildings sat. A barn, pigsty, and a couple of stables sat around a little courtyard. A decent-sized farmhouse had once stood guard here, but its blackened shell spoke of a fire some time ago, and now looked a forlorn sight.

We tethered our horses, and Sage and Anise set about making our lunch. I stood an old barrel upright and sat on it, gazing past the courtyard to a little group of trees. The sea couldn't be too far away now, but I couldn't smell any salt on the air yet.

We sat in the warm sun, enjoying the fine weather; who knew what it would be like out at sea, but I hoped for Tarragon and Willow's sakes the weather would be calm, although Anise was probably prepared if not.

Willow and Onyx sat huddled together in deep conversation. Since his grandfather's revelations, the two of them had spent quite some time together chatting, getting to know each other and their families better. I smiled, pleased for them both. Tarragon caught my smile and grinned at me, giving me a little nod – he was pleased for them, too.

Rian got up and stretched. 'Back in a minute,' he said, wandering along towards the old barn and disappearing behind it.

I watched him go, conflicted. On the one hand, I should give him his privacy. On the other, maybe I shouldn't. I got up and walked quietly past the pigsty, approaching the back of the barn from the other direction, careful not to make any noise. I just wanted to keep an eye out for trouble – otherwise, I'd leave him in peace.

The ring of swords set the hairs on the back of my neck prickling. I broke into a run, my heart in my mouth. I reached the back of the barn and for a second did the one thing an assassin should never, ever do.

I froze.

Rian parried a blow from Carnelian as the determined assassin tried to beat the prince back. Their blades flashed in the sunlight as Rian grimly held his ground, his skill matching that of Carnelian.

'Onyx!' I yelled back towards the courtyard before grabbing Deorwine and Glædwine.

Carnelian saw me approaching, shoved hard into Rian, making him stumble, and met my sword stroke with his blade. He swung his other arm at me. In his hand he held a small axe. Not standard Coterie issue, but very effective. The other thing that wasn't standard Coterie issue was the slingshot hanging from his belt. Perhaps he was trying something new? I swiftly moved my arm and Glædwine blocked the axe's blow.

'Stay out of this, Amethyst-sweetie.' Carnelian glowered at me, taking a step back, swinging his axe menacingly. 'You can take your turn in a minute when I've finished with your princeling.'

'But I want my turn now,' I said, lunging at him, sidestepping and slashing at his back with my crystal sword.

Carnelian parried with his sword. Rian swung at him, his blades catching the sunlight, dazzling the assassin for a moment, but he still deflected Rian's blows with his axe.

'Surely the two of you can do better than that?' Carnelian jeered, a cruel grin on his face. He swung at me with his blade, hitting Glædwine, jarring my hand, a sudden pain spiralling up my arm, then twisted and swiped at Rian, who sidestepped out of the way. Carnelian swore. He lunged at me again. I blocked. He turned and threw his axe at Rian, just as Onyx and the others rounded the corner of the barn.

My heart lurched.

Rian ducked and the axe, mercifully, went flying just over his head and into a tree with a sickening thud.

I swung my sword at Carnelian. He parried. I feinted to the left then lunged to the right, catching the cocky assassin off-balance. He tripped. Stumbled backwards. Fell. I took my chance. I dropped the crystal weapons and jumped on him, grabbing my malachite War Fan, opening it and holding it towards his throat, breathing hard, my pulse thundering in my ears. I'd dreamt of this moment, of having him like this, at my absolute mercy.

Carnelian raised his head, took one look at my Fan and laughed. 'What are you going to do, waft me to death with it, Amethyst-sweetie?'

I gritted my teeth and pressed the amethyst button. The thirteen razor-sharp blades popped out, glinting in the sunlight.

'Oh, it's *that* fan.' He looked at the blades, then at me, his right eye twitching.

A smug little grin spread across my face. 'You're going to answer my questions,' I said, my voice as determined as I could make it.

Carnelian sighed. 'The Coterie doesn't divulge information, you know that.'

'But you're not the Coterie and you're amongst colleagues – me and Onyx – and I will use this if I have to,' I said.

Carnelian wrinkled his nose. 'Go on then, ask, Amethyst-sweetie. We'll see if I answer or not.'

'You're here to kill Valerian? Yes?'

He scrunched his nose up for a moment as he considered his answer. 'Yes and no.'

I moved the Fan towards his neck. 'Explain, and make it good.'

'Yes, I'm here to kill Prince Valerian, but not just him – you, too.'

'Who sent you, the bitch or Beryl?' Onyx asked as he moved towards us.

'The bitch?' Carnelian frowned, turning slightly to look at Onyx. 'Which one's the bitch?'

I suppose he had a point. I could name at least two candidates –
more, actually – in Iolite when I stopped to think about it.

'Juniper, of course,' Onyx said.

'You've acquired some colourful language since I last saw you,
Onyx. I'm disappointed in you,' Carnelian said.

Onyx shrugged. 'Not really. I don't tend to see you outside the
Crimson Castle – after all, it's not as if we're friends.'

'True.'

'Just answer the damn question,' Rian said, standing beside
Carnelian, his swords in his hands.

Carnelian glared at him for a moment. 'Both, I suppose. Beryl
wants *you* dead, Your Highness, but it's Juniper that wants
Amethyst dead. Didn't she send you, Onyx?'

'No, Beryl sent me to kill them both,' Onyx said with a shake of
his head.

Carnelian tried to nod, then thought better of it. 'Interesting.
They both want you dead, Amethyst-sweetie. You've really upset
them, haven't you?'

'Why? I'm no threat to them now I'm not in Iolite.'

Carnelian laughed. 'Beryl hates you, pure and simple, that's why
she wants you dead. Pure, unadulterated hatred. But Juniper? Oh,
you're a bigger threat to Juniper than ever, now. Don't you know
that?'

I pulled back slightly, shaking my head in confusion. Beryl I
understood, but Juniper? Why try and kill me now? Unless it was
because I'd left the Coterie.

'You're looking well, Prince Valerian, considering everything.
Tell me, are the rumours about the side effects true?' Carnelian
asked slyly. 'I've always wanted to know, but anyone I've ever given
Mandragora Berries to has died, so I've never been able to ask
before.'

Rian tensed, his knuckles going white around his sword hilts. I
grabbed Carnelian's tunic and held my Fan at his throat, nicking
his skin. A little trickle of warm blood ran down his neck. I wasn't
sorry.

'Careful, Amethyst-sweetie, you might hurt someone,' Carnelian
said, amusement in his eyes.

'I intend to,' I said. 'You.'

He glanced at Rian's angry face. 'I take it the rumours are true,
then. That's interesting. I'll have to make a note of that.'

I pressed the Fan into his neck a little more.

'If he's not good enough for you at the moment, I'm happy to take you on, Amethyst-sweetie,' Carnelian whispered so only I could hear, a wicked glint in his eyes. 'On a temporary basis, if you want – damaged goods and all that.'

'You bastard,' was all I could spit out.

'If you wanted something more permanent, you'd probably make quite a good wife, actually, once I'd broken you in.'

'Do you have a death wish or something?' I asked. 'One more word and I'll—'

'Do what you should've been doing these past few years? Actually kill someone?'

Hell's teeth.

I gasped. 'You know?'

'Of course I do.'

He had me flummoxed. How could he know about Mal doing my killings for me? I swallowed.

'Maybe I will. I've been planning your death long enough,' I said.

Carnelian raised an eyebrow. 'I don't think you've got it in you. I don't think you've ever really had it in you.'

'Shall we see?' I pressed the Fan's points into his neck a little more, my hands clammy. Another rivulet of blood ran down his neck.

'Phire, no,' Rian said, stepping forward, placing his hand on my shoulder. 'As much as I'd like you to, don't.'

'But this is exactly what they trained me for,' I said through gritted teeth, bitterness in my voice and hot tears standing in my eyes. 'To kill. That's all I'm good for, isn't it?' I hissed at Carnelian.

His eyes widened and he suddenly looked unsure. 'Maybe I misjudged you. Given the chance and the right motivation, you'd have been an excellent assassin.'

'Given the chance? What do you mean, given the chance?'

'The reason I know about you is because I was doing all your killing for you.'

I shook my head. 'No, Mal was doing my killing, not you.'

'What?' Onyx's forehead furrowed as he took a step forward. 'Mal was killing for you?'

Sage's eyes narrowed. 'What's this?'

Up until now, Rian and I had kept this little detail secret from the others. Sage, in particular, had been upset by Crown Princess Angelica's death and this news was something I'd been keen to keep from him.

Carnelian laughed. 'Didn't you know, Onyx? Our Lady Merciless has never killed anyone, not one single person.'

Onyx's face turned ashen, the muscles in his neck taught. I'd have to explain to him later. But Carnelian killing for me, not Mal? I couldn't understand this. Although, thinking about it, it would explain some things, such as how Angelica was killed in Aerba, Mal captured in Flos, and how Flint knew everything that had happened, so quickly.

Mal had never been in Aerba. He'd been abducted in Flos before the princess' assassination. That's how Flint knew he was out of the picture. Carnelian had killed Angelica and already reported her death to Flint before I'd got anywhere close to Tansy.

'It was all me.' Carnelian grinned, his eye twitching again. 'Malachite was always sent in the opposite direction to you, when you were sent on a mission, Amethyst-sweetie. Juniper wanted to keep him away from you so he couldn't interfere. I was sent to make your kills before you got there. I was the one that gained you a reputation for deftness, efficiency, and ruthlessness. It was all me, not Malachite.'

'Damn,' Rian murmured, grabbing Sage's arm as he took a menacing step forward. 'Leave it, Sage,' he hissed.

I stared at Carnelian. For a moment, I was speechless. Not Mal after all?

I readjusted my grip on my Fan. 'But Moonstone said Mal was doing my killing, that Juniper didn't know anything about it.'

'You were told wrong. Juniper orchestrated it all. Every last detail.'

'Then what I want to know is why? Why did *you* do it? Didn't Juniper trust me to do it myself?'

'No, not really. I don't think she trusted you at all. She was more interested in it being done properly, than who actually did it. What she wanted was a Master Assassin, one she could promote, who would earn such an imposing reputation that their services would be in huge demand and available only to the highest bidder – and she chose you to be it. She asked me to give you that reputation. I've always had a soft spot for you, so I was happy to oblige her.'

I raised my eyebrows, astonished. I sat up a little.

'You worked hard, trained hard,' Carnelian said. 'Your skill wasn't in question and I respected that. Your resolve was, though. I was happy to help you, and anyway, I've always enjoyed it. Killing is definitely my forte. Sorry about your sister, Prince Valerian. She was dead easy to kill, if you excuse the pun. Your father, too, for that matter.'

Rian didn't grace Carnelian's words with a reply, although he was as taut as a bowstring ready to release its arrow. Sage positively bristled with anger to the point that Anise came and stood beside him and took hold of his other arm, just in case he needed to restrain him.

'Then why did she send Flint to kill me after Aerba?' I asked.

'Because your usefulness was at an end, and as I said, you're now a threat to her.'

'But why? You said that before, but I've left the Coterie, I'm no threat to any of them now.'

'No one ever leaves the Coterie alive, Amethyst-sweetie, you must know that by now. No one is ever free of it, and you certainly never will be.' He paused a moment. 'No, it's what you're capable of that's spooked her. That's why you're a threat to her. There's only the two of you, and with you out of the way, she'll be free to fulfil her new mission to take the Five Lands.'

'Capable of? What two of us? And how could I stop her taking the Five Lands on my own?'

Carnelian frowned, a genuine look of surprise in his eyes. 'You really don't know, do you?' He laughed. 'Oh this is priceless, you don't have a clue.'

I shook my head, my blood pounding in my ears.

'You're special,' he said with a grin.

'You're not the first to say that, and I still don't know why.'

He laughed again at my confusion. 'I'd love to tell you, but that would really spoil you working it out on your own. I tell you what, let me give you a clue. Birthmark.'

'What?'

'That's all I'm saying. Birthmark.'

'Ignore him,' Onyx said. 'He's toying with us.'

'I'd never do a thing like that,' Carnelian said in mocked offence. 'I don't need to toy when I can take action. And the Coterie is taking action.'

'How?' Onyx asked.

Carnelian looked at him, a cruel smile forming on his thin lips. 'There are Coterie assassins in all the capitals of the Five Lands with orders to kill the Royal Families if they don't comply with Juniper and Chervil. Even your grandfather, Onyx.'

Onyx's hand went to his sword hilt, but Rian reached out and shook his head.

'The families don't know who the assassins are in their midst – but they've all been embedded for some time,' Carnelian continued. 'Where the Coterie hasn't been able to get much purchase, the Nightshade is there with the same orders.'

'It can't be true,' Tarragon said, his eyes wide in disbelief. 'Even the Nightshade wouldn't—'

'Oh, it's true, all right,' Carnelian sneered. 'You Aerbans may be interested to know Lord Wormwood and his wife have met with an unfortunate "accident".'

'Accident?' I asked, not sure whether to believe him or not.

'All right, they were assassinated. Sorrel's now in charge of the Nightshade.'

'The Herbs help us,' Sage said, his face blanching.

'What?' Rian looked stunned. He glanced at Tarragon – the blood had drained from his face.

'You know, while we're answering questions, Amethyst-sweetie, I'm going to ask you one,' Carnelian said. 'I'd love to know what happened to my sister. She's not been heard of for some time. Citrine came after you when you travelled south from Cotula, but she seems to have vanished. We've had no word from her since, which is a little odd. Do you know anything about her whereabouts?' He stared into my eyes.

CHAPTER TWENTY-EIGHT

I didn't know how to respond. To tell him she'd been killed by creatures in the Cilantro Forest may give him an answer, but who knew what sort of rage he'd fly into once he'd been told.

'She caught up with us in Cilantro Forest,' Anise said. 'But we gave her the slip in the trees. Haven't seen her since.'

I was relieved Anise was a better liar than me.

'I think we lost her at Cilantro port,' Rian said. 'She's probably back in Iolite by now.'

'Is that true?' Carnelian's eyes bore into me as he pulled himself up a little onto his elbows.

'Every word,' I said, keeping my voice steady and my Fan near his throat.

'Perhaps you're right and she's back home. I haven't had word from the Crimson Castle for a while, too busy running around Flos and Mere after you,' he said, glancing back at Rian. 'I should've finished you a while ago. I've been careless. Shame about the Mandragora Berries, really. I was hoping I might take both of you out, actually, but the result is still worth celebrating,' he said with a wicked grin which he directed at Rian. 'Same with the fire, but never mind.'

'I'll never forgive you for everything you've done,' I said, my voice a low growl.

Carnelian shrugged as best he could from his position on the ground. 'Doesn't bother me, but what I can't fathom is why you'd want to stay with this ex-Prince of Aerba,' he said, sneering at the Rian. 'No position, no home, nothing. He's lost everything.'

Rian took a step forward.

I lunged at Carnelian, knocking him backwards, my War Fan raised, the blades poised above his neck. I wanted to kill him. *So* much. Kill him for what he'd done to Rian. To the dryads. To all the others he'd murdered or maimed. Somewhere in the red maelstrom of my mind a little voice, clear as a bell, told me to stop. I hesitated. Surely I'd be doing the world a favour?

Don't be Lady Merciless – please – even for me.

I glanced up at Rian as blood ran down Carnelian's neck.

Rian's face was strained, his eyes pleading with me to stop. I swallowed. No, I wouldn't be Lady Merciless. I was better than that. I moved back.

'Get the hell out of here,' I said to Carnelian. 'And if I ever see you again, I *will* kill you.'

'Or I will,' Onyx said.

'Is there a queue and can anyone join?' Anise asked, his eyes hard as agates as he looked at the assassin.

'Really? You're letting him go?' Sage asked.

'We're just giving him a head start – then we'll go after him and kill him – it's only fair to give him a chance, even if it's only a small one.'

Sage looked at Anise in surprise. Anise hadn't forgiven Carnelian for the forest fire, and I wasn't sure he ever would.

'I'll be right behind you,' Sage said.

'Go back to Iolite and tell Juniper and Beryl to leave us all alone,' I said.

Carnelian got up and dusted himself off, his hand then going to his throat, smearing the blood onto his fingers. 'Well, I'd like to say this has been fun, but it hasn't. I'll also send your regards to your stepmother and sister, shall I?'

'You can tell them to go to hell.'

Carnelian nodded, a little smile playing on his lips as he looked at the wet, scarlet blood on his hand. 'You could have been good, Amethyst, a real expert. Lady Merciless in the flesh.'

'This way she's better than that,' Rian said, staring at Carnelian.

The assassin chuckled. 'Says the homeless ex-Prince.' He turned and ran off.

Rian slipped his hand into mine, but I wasn't in the mood. I walked away from the barn and through the trees that nestled near the farm, returning my War Fan to its clip as my heart slammed into my ribcage. I swore under my breath. I didn't want to speak to anyone, not even my soulmate. Mainly because I was filled with shame at my conduct. Anise or Onyx may well have taken my place if I hadn't got in there first, but the fact that I'd so nearly killed Carnelian really upset me.

It was as if a red mist had descended on me. All I wanted to do was kill, and that was so against my nature it made me nauseous. This whole charade of Lady Merciless made me sick, all so Juniper could claim to have the greatest assassin alive, available for the right price? That's all I was to her – goods to be bought and sold. And if I'd been caught? Collateral damage, I suppose, and at least she wouldn't have lost the real expert assassin. Having the myth of Lady Merciless made the Coterie more enigmatic and sought-after. Lie after lie. But now she wanted me dead for a reason I didn't understand. Beryl, I did, but not Juniper. And what the hell did birthmarks have to do with anything?

I sighed as I cleared the trees and sat on a large rock overlooking the grassland. I wanted to curl up and be left alone to weep forever.

'Why didn't you tell me?'

I flinched.

'Go away, Onyx,' I said without turning around. I couldn't do this now.

'Why didn't you tell me you hadn't been killing anyone? That someone got there before you every time?' he asked as he sat down beside me, unperturbed.

I sighed. 'Because it was too difficult, and too dangerous. When I got back to the Crimson Castle I was always congratulated for my kills. Contradicting that would only have put my head in a noose, and when it kept happening, it became even harder to admit to, so I stayed quiet.'

Onyx nodded slowly. 'I can understand that.'

'I had no idea who was doing it, but I could hardly ask around, so I didn't say anything to anyone.'

'Not even Mal?'

'Not even Mal. I didn't want him worrying. Then all this started. When I saw Moonstone, he told me Mal had been doing my killing for me, to keep me safe. Everything seemed to fall into place when he said that, but it appears he was misinformed. It was Carnelian, and Juniper was behind it all along.'

'I'm amazed they kept up the deception for so long.'

'Two years. Two years Carnelian was killing for me, and I didn't know and couldn't tell anyone. It was torture at times, keeping it to myself.'

Onyx nodded. 'You still should have said – either to me or Mal.'

'I didn't want either of you in any more danger than we were in already.'

'That's your problem, Ama, always worrying about everyone else.'

I shrugged. 'Can't help it.'

Onyx rubbed his forehead. 'I have to say I was impressed with you just now.'

'Leave it.'

'No, truly,' Onyx said. 'Your self-restraint is most remarkable. I couldn't have done it. I'd have killed Carnelian where he lay.'

'You're not weak like me,' I said. 'You have the guts and resolve to see these things through. I don't think I have. I don't think I could kill. Carnelian's right about that, I don't have it in me. You're stronger than me.'

'You really think so?' he scoffed. 'Turns out you're the one with the principles, the morals none of the rest of us have – but should. I never wanted this life, but it was the only way out to keep my parents safe. After Father died, I did try to get Mother away from the Crimson Castle, out of Iolite, but she wouldn't go, refused to come back to Mere, mainly due to pride, I think, but it left me with no option but to continue. I've just become numb to it all. The first kill was the worst, but each time I told myself I was keeping others safe, and now it's just another fish to skewer. You're not weak, Ama,' he said, reaching out, turning my face towards him. 'And with that poison maiming Rian in the way it has, you're the strongest of us here to not kill Carnelian in revenge.'

I looked at Onyx, at his sincere brown eyes. 'Then why do I feel so wretched? I almost killed him. I was this close,' I said, emphasising the point by holding up a thumb and index finger. 'I'm so ashamed.'

A twig snapped. My hand went to Deorwine's hilt, until I realised it was Rian, and I relaxed.

'Don't be, you've nothing to be ashamed of,' Rian said.

He must have walked over with Onyx and in my misery I hadn't noticed. He sat on my other side.

'Like Onyx says, you showed great self-restraint,' Rian continued. 'I think any one of us would have been excused for killing him where he lay, but you didn't. You're better than that. We all are.'

'It doesn't take away the fact I've been planning it for a while,' I said, bowing my head.

'So have I,' Rian said gazing over the grasses that swayed in the wind. 'But as long as we don't follow through, they're only thoughts in the end, wisps of passing fancies.'

'Passing fancies?' Onyx laughed.

'Well, what would you call them?'

'Ruminations.'

'By the Herbs, you sound like a cow.'

'Rude – but true.'

I sighed, shaking my head at them. 'So if we put my murderous thoughts, and near-actions, to one side, I can't believe Juniper was just using me to project this myth of Lady Merciless until she was ready to kill me for some reason I don't understand.'

'She's been using all of us for years,' Onyx said, his voice like granite. 'Gaining the Coterie a fearsome reputation. She's never cared about us as individuals.'

'But why would she do this?'

'Guess it was the first step in her plan to take over the Five Lands.'

I turned to Onyx. 'First step?'

Onyx nodded. 'She forms the Coterie, makes it a source of fear, takes control of Iolite, then starts to work her way around the Five Lands, starting with Aerba. You do know she's been cosying up to Chervil?'

'Cosying up?' Rian asked, an eyebrow raised. 'We know they're in league.'

'I think she plans to marry him.'

My mind baulked at the suggestion.

'But he's almost young enough to be her son,' Rian said, aghast.

'He *is* young enough, but what's that to gaining control over Aerba and Flos?' Onyx shrugged. 'A minor detail.'

'Surely Chervil won't do it willingly?' I asked.

Rian bowed his head. 'Chervil will agree to anything to get Flos under his control,' he said bitterly. 'He always wanted to be King of Aerba, and I don't believe he cared how it happened. And Flos? I'm quite sure that to rule Flos and the other Lands he'd happily align himself with Juniper, he's that driven to get his hands on power. You know, I don't think the Nightshade are going to kill King Narcissus after all. It will be the Coterie.'

Onyx chuckled. 'The Nightshade aren't well-renowned in that area, are they? Whatever Carnelian says. They're more of a sledgehammer cracking a proverbial nut. The Coterie would do it with little noise and an element of finesse.'

'Hmm.'

'If what Carnelian says is true, there's Coterie or Nightshade at all the Royal Courts poised to kill,' I said.

'I need to get word to Grandfather,' Onyx said, his eyes glistening.

'We need to get word to Trew and Flos, too,' Rian said.

'We'll do it as soon as we reach Aqua Claras,' Onyx said, nodding. 'And we'll just have to hope we're quick enough.' He paused and looked at Rian. 'You know you, or someone, is going to have to do something about your brother. And when they do...'

Rian tensed. 'We're nowhere close to that yet.'

I glanced at Onyx, then Rian. Onyx meant the succession.

'Anyway, it has nothing to do with me anymore,' Rian continued. 'Chervil made sure of that.'

For a moment, silence fell.

I chewed on a nail. 'Hell's teeth. We should have asked Carnelian about the Fire Opal. Erica said the assassin that killed Angelica took it. Maybe Juniper's behind the theft after all.'

Rian swept my hand from my mouth. 'Stop it.'

'I've been trying to get her to stop chewing her nails for years, never had any luck,' Onyx said.

'Guess I'll have to try harder.'

'Would you two stop? I'm saying, what if Juniper had the Fire Opal stolen because she knew what it could do and didn't want Chroma getting hold of it and restarting the Vortex?'

'But you said she never lies, and when you asked her back at the Crimson Castle if it was in Iolite, she said no,' Rian reminded me.

'True. I've never known her to lie before,' I said.

Onyx rubbed his chin. 'Lie? No. Not answer a question straight or conceal information? Yes. She could've had it taken and then hidden it somewhere not on the island.'

'Then when she told us it wasn't in Iolite, maybe she was being truthful,' Rian said.

'Or Carnelian could have passed it on elsewhere and it could be anywhere in the Lands by now.' I sighed. 'I'm second-guessing everything.'

'We all are, and we'll continue to until we know the truth.'

'So, I'm assuming a trip to Trew is on once we've got Mal back?' Onyx asked. 'See what they know about the Fire Opal?'

I glanced at Rian. He nodded.

'Are you intending to go through with the whole Chroma thing and the Crystal Vortex?' Onyx asked, rubbing his chin again.

'I think we have to, don't we?' I asked.

'I guess it's about who else will do it,' Rian said. 'Who else *can* do it. There is no one. It has to be us. Even the dryads knew that.'

'And the missing Spinners?' I asked.

'We'll have to find them – maybe they'll be in Trew.'

Onyx squinted. 'I want to come, too,' he said. 'I'm a Water Spinner. I know you've got Tarragon, but I might be able to be of some help.'

'You're sure?' I asked him.

'Unless you intend to leave Mal behind when we find him, which I assume you don't, then I'll be coming, too. Anyway, he'll want to stay with you, and I'm not leaving him once we've got him back. And, as I say, I want to help. Grandfather made me realise I want to do all I can, help heal the land.'

'It's what the others said, too,' I murmured, remembering their reactions when we'd told them everything.

There was no going back for any of us now, not that there was actually anywhere for us to go back to. We could only move forwards. The distant Archipelago, where the Blood Rules were no longer followed, had to be our ultimate destination, but until then, we had to do what we could to help the Five Lands – or Six Lands.

'I still don't see how I'm a threat to Juniper,' I said. 'I never intend to go anywhere near Iolite again. Surely she realises that?'

Onyx shrugged.

'Maybe it's your Magic Angle,' Rian said, running his fingers through his hair, distracting me for a moment.

'B–but I don't have a Magic Angle,' I said, chewing a nail. Onyx slapped my hand away from my mouth. I glowered at him.

Rian made a face. 'That we've noticed. It doesn't mean you aren't affecting things somehow, though, and we haven't realised it.'

'Never thought I'd say this, but he's right,' Onyx said, nodding.

'Thanks,' Rian said drily.

'My pleasure.'

'I wish we could work it out,' I said. 'I wish I knew what it was.'

'Then why don't we?'

'What?'

'Why don't we work it out?' Onyx said.

'How?' I asked.

Onyx turned to me. 'Like I did. We'll try each Element until something happens.'

'What, you think it's as simple as that?'

'Worked for me. I tried fire, then air, and when I tried water, I very nearly caused a flood in my room.'

'And that's how you worked it out? By trying each one in turn?' Rian asked, raising an eyebrow.

Onyx nodded. 'I had a hunch it was water all along, but that's how I found out for sure. It's as good a way as any, but we can do it later. If we don't get down to the coast soon we'll miss the tide, and we need to send those messages as soon as possible.'

CHAPTER TWENTY-NINE

The fishing town of Aqua Claras sprawled out before us. We rode into a maelstrom of people, mainly pink and lilac-wearing Middle Bloods, all jostling for position. Wagons moved up from the harbour, bringing cotton, sugar cane, and maize from Trew, potatoes and tea from Iolite, perfumes from Flos, and herbs from Aerba. Other wagons headed towards the merchant ships nestling in the port with silks, spices, precious metals and oil.

The heady smell of spices mixed with salt air and fish, and, I thought, a little Saliivia. By the look on Rian's face, I was right. He'd been tricked into taking the drug by his brother once, and had been extremely ill. To many others, taking much smaller doses, it was a pleasurable experience. Not to me. I liked to be in control – probably my assassin training. I'd only ever had a sprinkling that Anise had used in the Moonflower Elixir. I had no intention of getting addicted to anything, especially when the withdrawal was reputed to be fairly hideous. No. I'd never go anywhere near Saliivia.

'We'll stop just ahead, there's a messenger I know,' Onyx said, indicating a building at the corner of the street. 'He can send couriers to Grandfather and the Royal Families, warn them of the threat from the Coterie and the Nightshade.'

'Good.' Rian nodded. 'The sooner they know, the better.'

We waited with the horses until Onyx had sent the messages, then headed down towards the harbour. A plethora of ships, mainly merchant, but a few passenger and a couple of naval ships, were moored to the stone walls of the docks, their sails of white and yellow neatly furled over the masts' yardarms. The water shone in the sunlight, the sky a clear azure blue but, out towards the horizon, dark clouds gathered and the sea churned with white foaming tips.

'You got your Herb Chest at the ready, Anise?' I asked as we dismounted and collected our packs.

He looked out over the water. 'I have,' he said. 'I hope I won't need it too much, but you never know with Willow – and Tarragon, too.'

'That's the problem.'

'We need to sell the horses,' Onyx said. 'My aunt can't take them on her ship.'

'We'll do it,' Tarragon said, nodding at Sage, and the two led our horses away to the farriers overlooking the harbour.

I hefted my pack onto my shoulder and waited for them to return, looking out over the waves. Somewhere, across the sea, lay the Third Isle and hopefully my brother. I hadn't seen him for so long. By the Stars, I was desperate to see his cheerful, smiling, porcelain oval face, his strawberry-blond hair in its low Iolitian pony-tail, and his silky, laughing, blue-green eyes the colour of the deep sea.

Rian's hand slipped into mine. 'We'll find him soon,' he said, also looking out over the water. 'It won't be long now. We'll know if he's there in a couple of days' time, and if he is, we'll get him out.'

'I hope so, or I might be inclined to go to Iolite and have it out with Juniper in person – with these,' I said, indicating the Crystal Weapons sitting on my back.

He turned towards me. 'You'd really take her on directly?'

'I'm beginning to think I might, if Mal isn't there. I have to find him, Rian, I have to rescue my brother from whatever hellhole Juniper has him trapped in.'

'Let's hope it doesn't come to that,' he said, squeezing my hand.

'So do I, really, but if I'm forced to…'

'I know. Although, it's not her, as much as who you'd have to get through to get to her, that would be the problem.'

The whole Coterie. That's who I'd have to get through. He wasn't wrong. But I wielded the Cursed Weapons. Anything was possible with them in my hands.

Tarragon and Sage returned and we all headed down to the harbour wall with our packs.

'Aunt Pol's ship is over there,' Onyx said, pointing at a mid-sized merchant vessel with white sails. It had an ensign at the stern of the ship – the flag of Mere with its distinctive black diagonal lines signifying oil, on a bright blue background. The ship had a dark wooden figurehead of a young woman, her painted black hair flaring behind her as if in a great wind, one arm holding tight to the ship so she didn't fall, the other stretched forwards as if to part the waves, her white dress billowing in the wind.

We walked along the docks, dodging lobster pots, discarded fishing nets, and crates of evil-smelling fish. The wooden merchant ship, *The Spirit of the Seas*, had several gangplanks lowered onto the docks, all being used to bring goods up onto the ship to be stowed in the hold, ready for the voyage to Trew. Men loaded barrels of oil, spices, and silks in an array of colours that peeked out their packaging as they were taken aboard.

Onyx paused a moment.

'What is it?' I asked.

His face looked grim. 'I'm not looking forward to telling Aunt Pol about Mother, Ama. She won't know. This isn't going to be easy.'

'I'll be there if you want,' I said, patting his arm. 'I don't mind coming with you.'

He hesitated. 'No, I need to do this myself. It's my responsibility to tell her.' He walked along the dock and looked up to the side of the ship where a late-middle-aged man stood directing operations. Dressed in the lilac and pink of a Middle Blood, he issued orders and shouted at the men to move faster.

'That's Holm, my aunt's First Mate – in more ways than one,' Onyx said as the sailor glanced down at us, a frown on his face, until he spotted Onyx.

Onyx waved. 'Holm!'

'Onyx, my boy, get up here!' Holm called, a big grin crinkling the burnt sienna skin of his face. He was darker than Onyx, a true Merean, like Onyx's mother had been.

Onyx scrambled up the gangplank with us following behind.

'Holm, it's so good to see you,' he said, hugging him.

'It's been too long, my boy,' Holm said, his black hair shining in the sun. 'When we got your message, Pol was overjoyed to help you in your search. It may delay us a bit, but we're not due to put in at Spindle for a while. We have time in hand and Trew can wait.'

'Thank you,' Onyx said. 'These are my friends, Ama, Rian, Anise, Sage, Tarragon and Willow – my cousin.'

'Cousin?' Holm raised an eyebrow. 'You're Merean, my girl?'

'My grandfather was,' Willow smiled. 'Onyx and I have only just found out we're related.'

'Pol will be interested to hear this.'

'Where is she? There's something I need to tell her,' Onyx said, a cloud passing behind his eyes.

Holm raised an eyebrow. 'Bad news, my boy?'

Onyx nodded.

'Your grandfather?' he asked softly, leaning forward.

'No. M—mother.'

Holm's eyes sparkled in the sunlight, a sadness settling there. 'Come with me. Kelby, show our passengers to their cabins,' he said to an orange-clad young Merean man as he led Onyx away. Onyx glanced back at me, his eyes shining, then disappeared into the ship. I hoped he'd be all right.

'This way,' Kelby said, leading us below deck. 'How many cabins do you need?'

Rian glanced at everyone. 'Three for us, and one for Onyx.'

Kelby looked at us, his eyes narrowing a moment, then nodded, showing us to suitable quarters.

Rian and I shared a small cabin, its bed not much bigger than a single, with a porthole looking out the side of the ship away from the dock where all the loading was currently taking place. The sunlight sparkled on the water as it reflected the light like a mirror. Foaming white horses crested waves outside the harbour walls. Although it didn't look too rough out there, Willow might have something to say about it.

Rian glanced at the bed. 'This is going to be cosy,' he said, grinning.

'You better not fidget too much, or one of us will end up on the floor,' I said. 'Although, if it's rough, one of us might fall out anyway.'

'I'll be sure to hold tight to you, that way neither of us will fall.'

I laughed. 'You hope.'

'Don't worry, I'll keep you safe.'

I smiled at him.

We all met on deck as the sun slipped below the horizon, just as the sailors raised the gangplanks and Holm gave the orders to cast off. Onyx came out on deck with a woman I could only describe as being the spitting image of his mother, of a similar age, only slightly taller. Burnt sienna skin, dark hair and eyes, a beautiful round face, and a strength that belied her sex, something I'd noticed in many Merean women since I'd been in the country, probably a result of Mere being a matriarchy.

'Amethyst, how lovely to meet you at last,' she said, taking my hand. Her smile tried to reach her red-rimmed, glassy eyes, but failed. The news of her sister's death had hit her hard, just as it had Onyx.

'I'm pleased to meet you, too,' I said. 'I've heard about you from Onyx.'

'For an assassin, he talks a lot.'

'Do not,' Onyx said, pouting.

'Yes, you do, nephew.'

'Only to family, and close friends, no one else.'

'So you say.'

'We've caught the tide,' Holm said, coming over as the ship glided out of the harbour into the open sea. 'Where is it you said you wanted us to put in?'

'The Third Isle of the Tarn Archipelago,' I said.

'The Malign Prison?' He shuddered. 'Are you sure about that? You really want to go there?'

I nodded.

'You truly think your brother's there?' Pol asked, a worried look in her eyes.

'That's the information we've got from Rill,' I said.

'You know what that place's reputation is like, don't you?' Holm asked, his forehead furrowed. 'Few have ever left the prison alive.'

Onyx nodded. 'Which is why we've got to get Malachite out as soon as possible.'

Pol gave him a questioning look.

'I need him back by my side, Aunt,' Onyx said. 'And sooner rather than later.'

Holm looked at Pol and nodded.

'Very well. I'm not sure if you've told me everything, Onyx, but we'll do as you and Amethyst want. Holm and I, of all people, understand. I wouldn't like anyone special to me holed up in that place.'

'Thank you,' I said.

Kelby came out on deck, a broad smile on his face. 'The evening meal is ready – I hope you all like fish?'

Willow ran to the rail and threw up.

'Herb Chest, Anise,' Tarragon said, watching her.

Anise nodded. 'I'll get it,' he said, moving off.

'Is there any alternative to fish?' Sage asked hopefully.

'Crab or lobster?' Kelby suggested.

'Anything else? Bread will do. I'm allergic to seafood, you see.'

Kelby scratched his ear. 'I think we might have some cheese and Trewan Wheat Crackers, and we certainly have oranges and pears.'

'Sounds wonderful,' Sage said with a grin.

We had a pleasant evening with good food, although Willow declined to join us and stayed in her cabin with a bucket. The next afternoon the wind was with us, and I went out on deck with Rian, Anise, and Sage to watch the water skimming past and the dolphins playing off our port bow.

'Sea voyages can be so freeing,' Rian said. 'The feel of the wind on your face and the salty tang in the air.'

I glanced at him. He'd tied his hair back again. I think it'd whipped into his eyes one too many times, and he'd got fed up with it.

'The last thing we need is you getting all poetic on us,' Sage said, staring out at the water.

'It is quite refreshing,' Anise said, taking a deep breath. 'But I still prefer land.'

I smiled and gazed out over the water. We were making good time. It wouldn't take long to get to the Third Isle at this rate. The thought made butterflies start fluttering unpleasantly in my stomach. Would Mal be there? Could we rescue him? I feared what sort of state he would be in by now. If Juniper had indeed decided to keep him for something important, then hopefully he'd have been looked after reasonably well, but that was no guarantee. What she might have done to my brother made me feel physically sick.

'So, shall we try then, Ama?' Onyx asked, coming over and looking at me.

'Try what?' I asked, frowning.

'To find your Magic Angle, of course.'

'And you really think aboard ship is the safest place to do it?'

He shrugged. 'It's as good a place as any.'

'What if I'm a Fire Spinner and set light to the ship, or a Water Spinner and we start taking on huge amounts of water, or an Earth Spinner and we get stuck in seaweed? Have you truly thought this through?' Although this was all true, the real reason was far more banal. I was scared. Scared to find out I didn't have a Magic Angle like most of the others.

'If that happens, I can control the fire – or Onyx and Tarragon can put it out, and get rid of any excess water,' Rian said, leaning with his back to the rail. 'Anise can sort any seaweed, I'm sure.'

I shook my head in disbelief. He wasn't helping. In truth, I didn't want to do it, but having a solid answer about whether I did have an Angle or not was probably not a bad idea in the long run. I sighed and, reluctantly, nodded. 'All right, but on your heads be it. I don't think it's a good idea. So, what first?'

'Water, of course,' Onyx said. 'Here.' He emptied the contents of a bucket that lay on the deck overboard. 'Try and fill it up.'

'Just like that?'

'Concentrate on it, and imagine it filling.'

'Worked for me, y'know,' Tarragon said, sauntering over.

I looked at Tarragon, then at the empty bucket and imagined water slowly seeping into it, filling it to the brim. Nothing. I tried again, willing water to fill the bucket.

'Are we trying to find out Phire's Magic Angle?' Tarragon asked.

Rian nodded.

'Go on then, try and fill it,' Onyx said, nodding towards the bucket.

'I am,' I said. 'Nothing's happening.'

'Try harder.'

'She *was* trying fairly hard – or she was in pain,' Tarragon smirked.

I glowered at him for effect. 'Perhaps I'm not a Water Spinner,' I said, shrugging.

'Try fire then,' Rian said. 'Here, see if you can set light to this rope.' He leant over and retrieved an old frayed rope from the deck.

'You better get ready to put it out, just in case,' I said to Onyx and Tarragon. They nodded. I took hold of the rope and imagined it bursting into flame. Nothing. My shoulders slumped. I concentrated. Willed it to burn. Still nothing. I tried again, screwing my face up in the process.

'Full marks for effort, but no, you're not a Fire Spinner,' Sage said with a grin.

'This is pointless,' I said.

I didn't know why I was doing this. The further we went, the more apparent it became I had no Angle. Totally pointless.

'You must be an Earth Spinner, then,' Tarragon said. 'Anise, have you got something we can use to prove Phire's an Earth Spinner?'

'Let's see.' Anise rummaged around in his pocket and pulled out a dried blue flower of some sort. 'Here. Try and bring it back to life.'

'You can do that?' I asked, my eyes wide in amazement.

'It's fairly simple, really. The flower's only been dried.'

'Bringing something back to life is simple?'

'It's only a flower. I don't think I could do it with anything much bigger. Go on. Try.'

I took hold of the flower and looked at it. The pale blue petals lay flat and dried in my hand, so I concentrated on them, willing them back to life.

'This is ridiculous. I told you I didn't have a Magic Angle,' I said, passing the flower back to Anise, tears stinging my eyes at my failure.

Anise gazed at the flower with an almost loving look, and the little petals sprang back to life.

'That's amazing,' I said in a hushed tone, totally in awe of his Earth Magic.

'Not sure what use it is, bringing a flower back to life,' he said. 'Here – for you.'

'Thanks,' I said, taking it from him and inspecting the beautiful live flower in my hand. 'I'm obviously not really a High Blood after all. I'm Middle, like Willow. I'll never be any sort of Elemental Angle Spinner, and no use to us on our mission to restart the Crystal Vortex.'

'Of course you'll be of use,' Onyx said, slipping an arm around my shoulder. He glanced at Rian and let go. 'You'll be able to watch our backs with those Cursed Weapons of yours.'

'They're not cursed anymore,' I said primly, not that Deorwine or Glædwine would actually take offence.

'There's still two we haven't tried,' Rian said in a steady voice, rubbing the back of his neck as he glanced at Anise, his eyes grave.

Anise nodded, returning Rian's look. 'I was wondering that myself, Rian. Do you think it's possible?'

'Would explain a few things,' Rian said, chewing his lip, glancing anxiously at me.

I scowled. 'What are you two—'

Suddenly the heavens opened. Rain fell in heavy droplets. Then ceased just as abruptly. None of us had even had the chance to move inside.

The wind dropped. The ship gradually slowed to a stop.

Hell's teeth, not again.

I moved over to the side, Sage following me, and peered over the rail as a shiver ran down my spine, searching for—

The melancholy, yet ethereal, song started. My blood froze as an unworldly green glow coloured the water around us.

CHAPTER THIRTY

'Get the men below deck and tie them up. Now!' Pol ordered, and the sailors started shouting to each other and running across the deck – this was no panic, though, but rather a well-rehearsed, even well-used, drill.

'Morgens?' Rian asked, his eyes wide. He glanced at me, then grabbed hold of my shoulders. 'Hit me.'

'What?' I asked.

'I don't want them taking me from you, Phire. Hit me. Tie me up like last time. I don't want to die.'

'They won't take you, because I won't let them,' I said, gritting my teeth and clenching a fist as I looked up at the limp sails. We needed the wind. Now.

Beside me, Sage glanced up, too. 'If only the blasted wind would get up, we could get away,' he said, scrunching his eyebrows together, nostrils flaring.

It began like a whisper, then a call, then a roar. Wind slammed into the sails. The fabric billowed under the sudden assault, gradually forcing the ship forward through the calm water, picking up speed until we cut through it like a hot knife. The vibrant song around us changed to shrieks of anger as we left the morgens behind. The wind took us away from the sea creatures, leaving them screaming with rage far behind as we sped across the waves.

'What happened?' Rian asked, looking back at the vanishing morgens then up at the sails.

Anise looked at me and Sage. 'I'd say one of you two did that.'

Sage looked at me. 'It wasn't me,' he said.

I shook my head. 'I didn't do it.'

'Neither of us would even know how to.'

'Well, one of you did it,' Anise said; his eyes narrowing as he looked at us.

The day had arrived. I went out on deck for some fresh air and to watch for the island. Captain Pol had indicated it would be in sight very soon. Not only did I feel nauseous, but the butterflies had returned, shifting in my stomach, which didn't help.

Nerves weren't something I tended to suffer from too much when on a mission; I was too well-trained, and things were always well planned out in advance. But this was unpredictable. We had no plan. No escape route, nothing. The overriding thing though? This was the biggest mission of my life. This was for my brother, and probably the reason it felt different to all the others. Rian and Onyx came out on deck and joined me at the rail looking out over the water.

'Land ahoy!' yelled a sailor from the crow's nest.

'Mal.' I peered across the water in an attempt to bring the island to us faster. Sure enough, land emerged from the haze on the horizon, looming out of the murky air.

The Third Isle, the home of the Malign Prison, rose in front of us. The place looked more like a large black granite rock than an island. There appeared to be no greenery, nothing but dead stone. A little shiver crept down my spine. Was he still there? Was he alive? All my hopes and fears collided within me at once, and I gasped for air as the butterflies moved in a frenzy. If Mal was inside, I'd free him. I clenched my fists and swore it to myself: I wouldn't leave without him.

'Bugger, I'm not sure I like the look of that place,' Tarragon said as the others joined us. 'It's a bit grim, foreboding. You think we can get in?'

Onyx gritted his teeth. 'We'll get in, whatever they throw at us. And if he's there, we'll free him.'

'Damn right,' I said, staring at the black prison. For a split second I wondered who was more determined to free Mal – me or Onyx?

'We'd better get ready,' Rian said. 'This may be tough. We'll need all our wits about us, and our weapons.'

'Not to mention our Magic Angles,' Tarragon said. 'You ready to set light to things, Rian?'

'If you're ready to flood them?'

'Absolutely.'

Fire or flood may not be what we needed – or air or earth. Rather, what we needed was stealth, our fighting skills, and a healthy dose of luck. I didn't know what lay ahead of us, but I'd take the island apart a piece at a time to find Mal if I had to. If he was there, I had to have him back, rescue him from Juniper's clutches. The nerves I'd been consumed by vanished, replaced by a grim resolve to free Malachite at any cost. I glanced towards Rian who gazed intently at the black isle; well, almost any cost. I feared losing Rian to free Mal. Something I couldn't countenance. I'd have to find a way to keep Rian safe and free Mal at the same time.

I only hoped my training would allow me to do what I needed to do. A long time ago, I'd said to Rian that killing in self-defence was something I could probably do, if pushed. I hoped I wasn't pushed, but now the question was, would I only do it in self-defence? Would I do it to save Rian, or to save Mal? Could I? Their lives were the most important things to me, now, even more so than my own.

'Let's get ready,' Rian said, moving toward the cabins with the others.

I stared for a moment longer at the Third Isle as it loomed large in front of us. The ominous island and the prison structure at its crest seemed to sneer at me, as if daring me to challenge its authority, its might. But challenge it I would, for I would have my brother back.

I followed Rian down to our cabin to collect our weapons.

'You're to be careful. I know you want him free, but don't be reckless about it,' Rian said as he sheathed his swords.

'I won't,' I said. 'As long as you're careful, too. You're very precious to me.'

He smiled his lopsided smile, moving a curl over my ear. 'I'll protect you until my last breath.'

'I'll defend you and be your shield.'

He leant towards me, tilting his head a little and kissing me gently.

'We'll both be careful.'

CHAPTER THIRTY-ONE

The Malign Prison lived up to its name. The black granite building rose up from the basalt rock of the Third Isle like a natural part of the island. Carved into the rock, steps led from the small harbour, winding their way up to the menacing structure looming above us. Water lapped at the steps where our little rowing boat was moored, *The Spirit of the Seas* anchored off shore, the figurehead looking anxiously after us. A gull cried plaintively overhead, but no other sound greeted us.

The eerie quiet made my heart skip in my chest, my muscles tense, my hands taking a firmer hold of my crystal weapons. I scanned the area. The empty harbour extended to the rest of the island. There was no sign of a living soul, just broken barrels and old rotting crates. No one in sight. The hairs on the back of my neck rose, and I took a deep breath to steady myself.

'Doesn't look like anyone's been here for a while,' Onyx said, a note of despair in his voice.

'Maybe they're all inside,' Tarragon said, looking around.

'Or maybe Onyx's right and there's no one here at all,' Rian said, echoing my fearful thoughts.

But Mal had to be around somewhere, didn't he? Because if not here, then where? I glanced at Onyx. His expression was one of fear and doubt, now, something I hadn't seen from him before, and it shook me to the core.

I took another deep breath. 'We won't find out down here. Come on,' I said, leading the way up the steps, across a clifftop and up a winding staircase towards the prison entrance.

Broken weapons lay scattered around the steps with more rotten barrels and other rubbish. I swallowed. A chill washed through me. I hadn't wanted to buy every step up to the prison in blood, but the lack of any guards made me seriously doubt if anyone had been on the island in years – anyone alive, at any rate. Mal should have been imprisoned for four, maybe five months at most. Enough to drive him mad in this austere, oppressive atmosphere. My pulse hammered in my ears, my vision narrowing as I focused on what was to come.

'Who does this place belong to?' Willow asked, looking around warily.

'Supposedly Mere,' Onyx said.

'So how would Juniper be able to use it?' Sage asked.

'She has unscrupulous friends in high places,' I said, my knuckles white on Deorwine's hilt.

'Several unscrupulous friends,' Onyx agreed. 'She can access all sorts of places most people can't. This would be easy for her.'

The sun shone on the granite walls of the prison, little quartz crystals embedded in the rock twinkling like a seam of diamonds. There were no windows as such, but a multitude of small holes, not much more than a foot square, with rusty iron grilles barring the openings. The cells would be small and severe, with little light, and would no doubt be as uncomfortable as possible.

We reached the entrance. A large, thick wooden door hung off its hinges, creaking in the breeze coming up off the sea. It set my teeth on edge, and a cold sweat broke out over my body. I wiped my palms on my britches.

'I really don't like this,' Tarragon said, his muscles tense.

Neither did I.

'Now what?' Sage asked, looking around, his swords in hand.

'We go in,' I said, taking a step forward.

Rian grabbed my arm. 'Be careful, all right? No heroics?'

'Me?'

'Yes, you.'

'As long as you promise to be careful, too.'

He nodded, leaning forwards and giving me a quick peck on the lips.

'Not now,' Onyx said, moving past us.

If not now, when?

Rian gave me a little smile, and we followed after Onyx, weapons ready, stepping into the gloomy interior.

'We need light,' Tarragon said, picking up some discarded torches that lay scattered on the dirty floor. 'Rian, can you…?'

Rian nodded. The torches sparked into life, flaming brilliantly and illuminating the guard-room-cum-entrance-hall of the Malign Prison. *Austere* didn't do it justice. The whole place had an aura of foreboding despair. I shivered.

A rat scampered past Sage's foot. He swore.

'Let's split up, tackle the floors in twos. It'll make things quicker,' I said, moving into the corridor where a great shadowy staircase rose up to the floors above. A musty, dank smell filled the prison, somehow making the darkness darker. It weighed on us like a heavy blanket. Willow coughed. I really wanted to cover my nose, breathe through my sleeve, but with Deorwine in one hand and Glædwine in the other, I'd have to put up with it, even though it made breathing harder.

'Onyx, you come with us,' Rian said, moving past me. Only then did I notice that although he carried a flame, it wasn't because of a torch. He held it in his hand.

'How the hell are you doing that?' I asked, amazed.

He gave a little smile and shrugged. 'Not entirely sure, but I've been practising a bit. It happened the first time by accident out in the desert while you were asleep and scared me sh—'

'Quiet!' Willow hissed, her eyes wide as she looked up the stairs. 'Someone's up there.'

'Are you sure?' Onyx asked, raising his torch, his sword glinting in the firelight.

She nodded. 'I'm sure I heard something.'

'Then we take this slow and carefully,' Rian said. 'Tarragon, Willow, check down here before you come up. The last thing we want is someone coming at us from behind. Rest of you, with me. Let's go.'

Despite his protestations to the contrary, Rian was still a prince at heart, still the one to give orders and direct us when things got tough, and I loved him for it. Right now we needed a leader, and he was the steadying force that kept us on track. If my brother truly did languish here, he was in hell, and we had to get him out.

Tarragon and Willow moved through a doorway on the ground floor, Willow brandishing her lock picks in case she needed them, while the rest of us climbed up to the first floor. Sage nodded, and he and Anise started searching while Rian, Onyx, and I went up to the second floor.

'You check this level, I'll go up to the next one,' Onyx said, looking up to the final floor.

'We stay together,' I said, shaking my head.

He smiled. 'I'm a trained assassin, Ama, just like you. I can handle anything that comes my way, and if I can't, I'll yell.'

'You better.'

'Don't worry, I will.'

'I always worry. You know that, and so does Rian.'

Rian nodded as he peered down a dark corridor. 'She does. Constantly.'

'I'll be fine,' Onyx said, climbing the stairs two at a time. 'See you in a few minutes.' He moved on up the stairs, his torch casting strange, hideous-looking shadows around the walls before the light faded and darkness encroached on us.

The flame in Rian's hand flared.

'Ready?' he asked, the flickering flame reflecting in his amber eyes, making them appear alive with fire. He was much more comfortable with his Magic now.

I nodded.

We walked down the dusty passageway, cold air wafting past us, making me shiver as its icy fingers slipped down my neck. Cobwebs filled almost every corner. The smell of unwashed bodies lingered in the small cells around us. Many had open doors, the wood rotten, although some still appeared in good condition. Every now and then the silence split as the scuttling sound of a rat, or the creak of a rotten door in the wind that swept into the small cell windows from the onshore breeze, echoed down the empty corridors.

We peered into each one, looking for any sign of life, but found only emptiness. No sign of Mal anywhere. No trace whatsoever. My shoulders slumped as we returned to the landing where Onyx had left us.

'If he's not in this prison, where is he?' I asked, desperation beginning to take hold. 'Where can the bitch be hiding him?'

Rian glanced at me. 'Onyx's language is rubbing off on you.'

I frowned. 'Sorry, slip of the tongue.'

'Doesn't matter, because that's a fairly good description of her, and I was only acquainted with her for a very short space of time.'

'But long enough to see what she's like?'

He nodded. 'By the Herbs, how you survived – you and Mal – I don't know. With a woman like that as a stepmother, I think I'd have gone completely mad.'

'If it hadn't been for Mal, I would have done.' I glanced up to the next floor. 'Where has Onyx got to?'

'I'll take a look,' Rian said.

'And leave me in the dark? No, thank you. I'll come, too.'

Rian bent over and retrieved something from under a pile of rags. 'Here,' he said, passing me a battered torch. It immediately burst into flame. I sheathed Deorwine and took it from him. 'You need to stay here in case they find Mal down there,' he said, nodding towards the lower floors.

'All right,' I said, rather begrudgingly. 'But be careful.'

He smiled and climbed the stairs before beginning his search for Onyx.

I stood, shield in one hand, flaming torch in the other. Waiting. Pondering. Ruminating, as Onyx called it. Maybe Juniper didn't have Mal at all. Maybe he really had been killed in Flos when I'd gone to Aerba on my mission to kill Angelica after all? Maybe he really was dead and had been for some time? I shook my head. I couldn't think like that. He had to be alive; I had to believe it. I sighed and looked down the stairs. No sign of any torchlight. *They must all still be searching.*

A metal clang behind me made me jump out of my skin.

'Hell's teeth!' I turned around.

A large, closed wooden door stood behind me. A door we hadn't yet opened. How had we missed it? And who, or what, might be inside? Only one way to find out. I looked up the stairs, considering going to get Rian and Onyx first. Another clang echoed around the chamber beyond the door.

Suddenly, a yell sounded from above. Was that Onyx? The ring of steel as swords connected echoed down the stairs. At the same time, cries scurried up the steps from below, the sound of fighting breaking out there, too.

What should I do? I couldn't stay here, and as I could see no light from anywhere, I was on my own. No, not alone. The Cursed Weapons were with me, and whoever, or whatever, lay beyond that door. I'd rather face this new danger head-on than be taken by surprise. I turned back to the door, wiggled my hand enough that I could grasp the torch with my shield hand and reached out to the rusty door handle.

The door opened with a creak, making me shudder as the sound echoed around the prison. Inside, a large chamber reached up to the roof where the odd shaft of sunlight entered from the dilapidated beams. I raised my torch, noticing another in a holder by the door which I lit. Then wished I hadn't.

Two torture racks sat on the far wall, and metal chains attached to rusty rings in the stonework sat on another. I recognised a pillory and stocks. Chains and harnesses hung down from beams in the roof. This had to be some sort of torture chamber. I swallowed. A gust of wind forced its way into the room from above, setting a rusty chain swinging, clanging against another, crying out as if in pain and torment.

My torchlight caught something in the centre of the chamber floor, sending a golden flare across the room. I moved over to it and crouched down.

Recoiled.

It couldn't be, could it? I swallowed and reached down to pick it up. It felt cold and smooth in my hand. I stared at it. The gold ring was inlaid with malachite. My heart thundered in my chest. My breath caught in my throat. Then it was all I could do to take little shallow breaths for a moment as I looked in horror at the ring I'd given Mal for his nineteenth birthday.

He'd been here.

A noise behind me made me twist, coming to my feet in one smooth movement.

A black shadow stood in the doorway, barring my escape. It stepped forwards into the room. The tall man, clad in black, chain mail covering his chest, looked strong from the way he carried himself, but not overly muscular. He held a huge sword in both hands, his face hidden behind a metal face mask and hood. His menacing stance had the hairs springing up on the back of my neck. I slipped Mal's ring on my index finger and threw the torch to one side, grabbing Deorwine from my back.

'Where's Malachite of Iolite? Where's my brother?' I demanded, changing my stance, preparing to fight.

The man dropped his head to one side as if confused, then raised it again.

'Where is he?' I asked between gritted teeth.

The response he gave me wasn't verbal, but more of a guttural growl.

He lunged towards me, the great sword swinging at my head. I raised Glædwine, the sword connecting with the purple diamond shield. It glanced off, but sent a massive shock through my arm with the impact, very nearly numbing my whole arm.

'Hell's teeth.' I stumbled backwards, desperate to stay on my feet.

The man swung at me again. Again, I raised my shield, parrying the swordstroke, as once more the force of the blow spiralled up my arm, making me flinch.

I couldn't withstand such brute force. He reminded me a bit of Mal; my brother could be elegant, refined in his fighting style when he wanted to be – but he could also apply brute strength and tended to floor me every time, unless I quickly danced out of the way. This man had the strength to floor me very quickly, and then I'd have no chance.

As he struck at me again I twisted around, sidestepping the blow. I sent Deorwine at his mailed back, but missed as the momentum of his stroke took him past me. He grunted and turned back to me.

I didn't give him a chance to strike again.

Instead I lunged at him, Deorwine slicing through the air, meeting the man's sword in response. As the two weapons met, a great ring echoed around the torture chamber. I swept forward again, dodging his sword, swinging mine at his side, but the chain mail caught it at such an angle that other than a nice bruise, the man remained unhurt.

Where were Rian and Onyx? Were they all right? I could really do with their help.

The man lunged at me. I blocked with Glædwine, but the blow sent me backwards into the stocks and I hit the floor, dazed for a moment.

I looked up. The man chuckled, a deep, guttural, animal sound that sent shivers down my spine. I narrowed my eyes, jumped to my feet, and swung Deorwine at him with everything I had. The crystal blade forced the great sword to one side. I smashed Glædwine into the man's face, dislodging his mask and sending him tumbling to the floor, his sword skittering across the stone slabs. Finally, I had the upper hand.

'Where's my brother?' I demanded.

The young man rolled to his feet and stood up. He turned to face me.

Unmasked and unhooded.

I gasped as ice took my heart, which threatened to stop at any moment.

The man's strawberry-blond hair clung to his twisted, pale, sweaty face. His silky, blue-green eyes looked blankly at me with no emotion in them whatsoever. He stared right through me.

He had no idea he was trying to kill his younger sister.

CHAPTER THIRTY-TWO

By the Stars.

Malachite.

I froze in place, wanting to throw up at the look of anguish on my brother's face, the blank look in his eyes. The scarily blank look. Was Mal even in there? This had to be some sort of Magical enchantment. Another attempt by Juniper to kill me? To get me to kill Mal? Nausea rose in my throat. What had she done to him? And how? My knuckles turned white around Deorwine's hilt as my breathing came in shallow, fast breaths.

He snarled like an animal, grabbing a dagger with a gold and silver hilt from his belt.

'Mal, please stop,' I said, tears forming in my eyes. 'It's me, your sister. Don't you recognise me? It's Amethyst!'

'Amethyst must die,' he said in a rasping, menacing voice not his own, sending a shudder down my spine.

The stone dagger in his hand flashed green, more vibrant even than my own weapons. He lunged at me. I sidestepped out of his way, my hands cold and clammy. My vision had become like looking down a tunnel, and even then it seemed as if everything was behind a clear pane of glass. Waves of ice and fire rolled through me as I tried to contain the sweeping fear and the shaking of my body.

Again, Mal snarled and lurched in my direction. I twisted, my shield connecting with his dagger arm, sending him sideways. He stood between me and the door.

I looked at the dagger in his hand and my blood ran cold. The Malachite Dagger. I'd never noticed how vividly green it really was back in Iolite. Perhaps it had been the lighting in the chamber at the Crimson Castle? Nor had I realised how sharp its edge was that now glinted wickedly at me in the half light. I shivered as I looked at the Malachite Dagger Father had promised Mal on his twenty-first birthday, the one Onyx's grandfather said was an Artefact. And if it was, what would happen if I allowed it to hit my Crystal Weapons?

Malachite against diamond.

Artefact against Artefact.

My Amethyst Talisman had destroyed the Curse when Aldorbana and Cwicsusl had held me in their grasp, but usually, according to Anise, Artefact against Artefact would destroy both if they were the right ones, and diamond and amethyst were two such Artefacts that didn't mix. I'd been lucky, probably because of the Curse, but what would happen this time? Malachite against diamond? I didn't know. Would the dagger and my Crystal Weapons be destroyed – would their coming together destroy me and Mal, as well? I didn't want to find out.

I backed away as Mal made little rushes at me like a dog trying to intimidate its quarry. I watched him, kept my eyes locked onto his face for any glimpse of a change in his blank expression.

Footsteps approached. Rian and Onyx flew into the doorway, their swords bloody. Rian took one look, his eyes widening, fear clouding them, his swords held at the ready.

'Stay back!' I commanded, still looking at Mal.

'But—' Rian began.

Onyx started to step forward, his sword raised.

'Don't kill him; it's Mal,' I said, not taking my eyes off my brother as he took another step towards me.

Onyx hesitated and Rian grabbed his shoulder, pulling him back.

'Mal?' The anguish in Onyx's voice broke my heart.

Mal paused. Turned to the door and looked at Rian and Onyx. He turned back to me, disinterested in them.

'Kill Amethyst,' he rasped. He lunged at me once more, thrusting the dagger at my face.

I ducked and rolled to one side, coming back to my feet, sword still ready to strike, shield poised. My training hadn't prepared me for this. I didn't know what to do as I stared at my brother. I couldn't kill him. I had to stop him. I had to knock him out, somehow, without our weapons connecting. I couldn't risk that happening. But how?

Onyx stepped towards Mal, who immediately realised and lashed out, his dagger missing Onyx by inches. He growled at the assassin, eyes blank, face twisted into pain and menace.

Onyx stumbled backwards, Rian grabbing him before he could fall.

'By the Stars, Mal, stop this,' Onyx said, his voice almost breaking. 'Please – don't you recognise me? It's Onyx. Put the dagger down. You don't want to kill your sister!'

Mal stared at him for a moment before looking away, his eyes still blank and uncomprehending as he turned back to me. 'Amethyst must die.'

'Please, Mal, no,' I said, but he took no notice. He slashed at me with the dagger. I twisted away, Glædwine missing the malachite blade by a fraction of an inch. I took a breath, poised for him to strike again.

We'd reached a kind of stalemate.

I daren't attack him for fear of killing him. Every time he came for me I had to dive out of the way in case his Artefact connected with mine, because I didn't know what would happen if they met. If Rian or Onyx got too close, Mal would swipe at them, forcing them backwards with a fury I'd never seen from him before – but then, this wasn't Mal, not truly my brother.

Before I could think further, Mal lunged at me, stabbing with the malachite blade. I tried once more to twist out of the way, but a discarded metal chain on the floor, unseen in the shadowy light, caught my foot. I stumbled.

'No!' I screamed, willing Mal's blade to miss me.

It did, but instead, the Malachite Dagger smashed into the purple Diamond Shield of Glædwine.

A blinding white light filled the chamber as the dagger shattered in a roar that echoed throughout the whole prison, shaking the granite walls. I lurched to one side, falling hard to the cold stone floor as bits of dust and grit scattered around me, the chains in the ceiling creaking and jangling in protest. Mal tumbled backwards across the room, slamming into the stone block wall, knocking him unconscious. He slumped to the floor, head lolling to one side. I heard Rian swear as he and Onyx ducked in the doorway, sheltering from the falling debris.

The prison settled. The shuddering stopped.

I sat up, shaking my head. The Crystal Weapons were still whole, but the Malachite Dagger lay in a thousand shattered pieces on the ground. I dropped my weapons and scrambled over to Mal. He lay against the wall, his face finally at peace. I gingerly touched his neck, feeling for a pulse as Onyx and Rian rushed over to us. I sighed. Mal's pulse beat strongly, his breathing steady.

I looked up at Rian and Onyx, tears welling in my eyes. 'What has she done to him?' I asked, my voice shaking as I bit back the impulse to scream and swear.

'I don't know,' Rian said, shaking his head, his eyes slightly wild as if he'd seen something and had only just started to comprehend what it truly meant. 'But thank the Herbs you're both still alive.'

'At least we've found him,' Onyx said, sniffing as he held Mal's head in his hands. He leant forward and kissed his forehead, moving his strawberry-blond hair from his cheek. 'That bitch won't get him back now. He's ours again, Ama.'

'Let's get him out of this hell hole,' I said.

Rian nodded and, with Onyx's help, they took an arm each and carried Mal out of the torture chamber.

'We need Anise,' I said. I ran ahead, Deorwine and Glædwine materialising on my back as I sped down the stairs. 'Anise!'

'Well, that was fun,' Tarragon was saying as he climbed the stairs, wiping one of his blood-covered swords clean on a rag he'd found lying around somewhere.

'Fun?' Willow snorted.

'There were only a couple of them.'

'We were all outnumbered three-to-one by those Iolitian soldiers.'

'That's only slightly more than a couple. It wasn't something we couldn't handle, even if they did ambush us.'

Willow groaned and sheathed her swords. 'You need to learn to count.'

'Where's Anise?' I asked, cutting through their banter.

'I'm here, Phire, what's going on?' Anise asked as he came running down a passageway.

'We've found Mal,' I said. 'But he's enchanted in some way.'

'It's all right, Phire,' Anise said, patting my shoulder. 'I'll take a look at him.'

I nodded, the stress of the fight suddenly draining my muscles of energy – my mind too, a little. I started to tremble at the enormity of it all.

Tarragon looked up the stairs where Rian and Onyx were bringing Mal down. My brother's head nodded forwards as he sagged between them, still unconscious.

Tarragon gasped as he saw him. 'Bugger me, what happened?'

'He tried to kill Phire,' Rian said.

'He's not himself,' I said. 'I couldn't get through to him.'

Anise's eyes narrowed. 'Interesting. Let's get him outside, then I can take a proper look at him,' he said, leading the rest of the way down the stairs and towards the entrance as Sage and Willow followed after us, checking we were alone.

I shielded my eyes from the bright sunlight as we exited the prison. It took a moment for my eyes to adjust. *The Spirit of the Seas* still sat offshore, bobbing up and down peacefully on the waves. Outside, the warm sun helped the chill in my bones, the fresh air welcome in my lungs.

I glanced at Mal. His face looked paler than normal, if that was possible. His hair was matted and scruffy, and he hadn't shaved in a while. I glanced at Onyx. His eyes had a haunted look to them. He'd got Mal back, but had he lost him, too? Had we both lost him? A chill swept down my spine.

We carried my unconscious brother down the steps, and just as we made it to the docks he started to come around. He groaned, tried to escape Onyx and Rian's grasp, twisting. They lost hold of him and he fell to the ground. He shook his head. Looked up at me. Expression blank.

There was no recognition at all. Nothing.

'Who are you?' he rasped – still not quite his normal voice, but at least it was a little closer to the Mal I knew. 'Where am I?'

The enchantment appeared to have been broken by the Artefacts, but Mal still wasn't there, still not back with us.

'Mal, it's me, Amethyst,' I said, crouching in front of him. 'Your sister.'

Nothing. My eyes grew blurry with tears.

'You remember me, don't you? I'm your sister.'

Mal stared blankly at me. No look of recognition. No understanding. Nothing at all.

I glanced at Onyx. He knelt beside me.

'Mal? Don't you remember us?' Onyx asked, tears welling in his eyes.

Mal looked at him. Shook his head. 'I don't know any of you.'

'He's been drugged in some way, it's affected his mind,' Anise said, his voice strained. 'This is dark Earth Magic.'

'Can herbs do that?' Sage asked, raising an eyebrow. 'Enchant and wipe memories?'

'If they're strong enough and in the right proportions, yes,' Anise said, nodding sadly. 'But you have to be pretty mad to do it.'

'We can bring him back, though?' Onyx asked. 'Can't we? Make him better again?'

'I can try. Let's get him back to the ship. My Herb Chest is there. I'll see what I can make up for him.'

I nodded and held my hand out to Mal to help him up. He looked at my hand. Looked at me. I sighed and took his hand, pulling him up with Rian's help. With Onyx on one side and Anise on the other, they got Mal to the rowing boat with help from Sage and Willow.

Rian rested his forehead against mine, his hand caressing the side of my face. 'Dammit, for a moment I thought I was going to lose you – again – wife,' he said, then slipped his arm around me.

'To be honest, so did I,' I said.

'I'm so lucky to have met you, Samphire Amethyst, so lucky you're mine,' he said, leaning towards me, his velvet lips meeting mine, turning my blood to fire. 'I love you.'

'I love you, too,' I said, hugging him as best I could with the Crystal Weapons on my back. I looked at the rowing boat where Onyx fussed over Mal like a mother hen. 'I—I can't believe what she's done to him.'

Rian followed my gaze and shook his head sadly. 'Anise will be able to help him,' he said, kissing my forehead. 'Don't worry. If anyone can help him, it'll be Anise.'

'I know, but even so, whatever enchantment or Magic has been used on him, it's pretty strong. Even Anise will have trouble with that.'

'We'll see.'

I rested my head against his shoulder. 'You know, I didn't know what to do back there. Obviously I couldn't kill Mal, but I was scared of letting the Malachite Dagger and the Crystal Weapons touch.'

'Because of some Artefacts not mixing, you mean?'

I nodded. 'I didn't know what would happen if they hit each other. Father's book said nothing about malachite and diamond. Luckily they didn't completely destroy each other, or us, only the Malachite Dagger shattered. I guess it wasn't that eternal after all.'

'Did you see that flash of light?' Rian asked, glancing at me. 'When they met? Do you know what that was?'

'No,' I said, shaking my head. 'I don't know why that happened, or what it means. It was rather like the one when we broke the Curse, though, and struck Cwicsusl with the Amethyst Talisman. Maybe it's to do with Artefacts touching each other?'

He nodded. 'That's what I wondered, and it's got me thinking. Have you ever seen anything like that on any other occasion? A bright white flash?'

I swallowed, my mind going back to Jasmine's barn. 'Maybe.'

'Go on.'

'It was when I—I thought you'd died,' I said quietly, glancing at him. 'I thought I'd lost you, and then I wondered if I saw a flash – but I'm not sure, my eyes were shut at the time so I could've imagined it. It probably wasn't real at all, just me freaking out.'

'You mean when I was holding your Amethyst Talisman and you were holding your hand around mine?' he asked, his eyes clouding in thought. 'That's when you saw the flash?'

I nodded, frowning. 'You remember? You saw it too?'

He nodded. 'You didn't imagine it, Phire, it really did happen, whether your eyes were open or closed. There was definitely a bright light, only for a split second, but it was there.'

'You really do remember everything from that hideous day, don't you?' I asked, looking at him.

He bowed his head. 'Pretty much, yes,' he said. 'And I wish I didn't. I don't think I'll ever forget the excruciating pain, your tears, or you being there and your love sustaining me, giving me the will to carry on.'

I looked at him, gazing into his eyes, emotions building inside me, one on top of the other. He truly remembered. I stifled a little sob, my heart aching at his words, at the fact he remembered such a traumatic day. I'd hoped he wouldn't. But then I recalled the violent hallucinations after I'd taken the Moonflower Elixir when we'd attempted to rid me of the Curse in Cilantro. It was no different, really. I even remembered a few of the stomach cramps, but I hadn't had to endure the extreme pain Rian had.

'I think your Fire Magic had something to do with it, too,' I said. 'Quite a lot to do with it, actually.'

He took hold of my upper arms and turned me towards him. 'It was you who saved me, Phire. You who kept me going when I could've given up and let nature take its course. You made me fight it. You helped me to endure that pain, and because of your love for me I survived. Because of your love and, I think – I think also because of your—'

'Stop buggering about, you two, and get a move on,' Tarragon yelled from the little boat. 'Anise wants to get back to the ship and his Herb Chest as soon as possible, y'know.'

Rian nodded and waved. 'All right, coming.'

'My what?' I asked, gazing into his serious amber eyes. 'Because of my what?'

He hesitated. 'Your... nothing. We can talk about it later. They're waiting for us, come on,' he said, leading me down towards the rowing boat.

I frowned. Talk about what later? I didn't have time to worry about that now.

We joined the others in the boat and rowed back to the ship where Pol and Holm helped us aboard. We took Mal straight down to Onyx's cabin while Anise went to get his herbs.

'You think Anise can do something?' Onyx asked, looking worriedly at my brother who we'd laid on his bed in the cabin. A shaft of sunlight reached in from the porthole on the wall, illuminating the room.

'If anyone can, Anise can,' Sage said as Anise returned. 'We'll go up on deck, give you some room,' he said, and left with Tarragon and Willow.

Mal lay on the bed, his face strained, his muscles tense. Onyx sat on the bed beside him as Anise rummaged around in his Chest, tongue out, and started decanting various herbs and phials of liquid into a mortar before crushing everything with a pestle.

'Saliivia?' Rian asked, squinting at what Anise was doing.

Anise shook his head. 'Not for this, Rian, no.'

'Mal, can you hear me?' Onyx asked, moving Mal's hair from his pale face and stroking his head.

My brother remained silent, staring blindly up at the ceiling of the cabin.

'Mal, please,' Onyx said brokenly, tears standing in his eyes.

Mal didn't move. Didn't even blink.

'By the Stars, I'm sorry,' the assassin said, shaking his head. 'I need to get some air.' He sniffed and rubbed his nose before getting up and leaving the cabin, shoulders sagging, shutting the door behind him.

'Should I go after him?' Rian asked, looking to the door.

I shook my head and took Onyx's place on the bed. 'No, give him a little time alone. This is hard for him.'

'And you, too,' Rian said, stepping forward and resting his hand on my shoulder.

I nodded, taking hold of him, not trusting myself to speak.

'Let's try this,' Anise said, pouring his concoction into a mug. 'Help him to sit up.'

I moved and propped Mal up. 'You need to drink this,' I said to my brother. 'It'll help you to feel better.'

He didn't respond. Still didn't blink.

I chewed on a nail and looked towards Anise. He gave me a reassuring smile and nodded as Rian stepped back. Anise brought the mug to Mal's lips.

'Drink. This will help you, Malachite,' Anise said.

For a moment, Mal sat there. As Anise held the remedy to Mal's lips, he started to sip. I noticed Anise's hand go almost imperceptibly to his Jade Amulet. His Earth Magic coursed into the liquid as Mal took a small mouthful, but even after he'd swallowed, his eyes were just as blank as before.

'Have some more, Mal,' I said.

He did as I said. Still nothing.

I glanced at Anise. 'Why isn't something happening? Why isn't he remembering?'

'I don't know,' Anise said, frowning. 'Maybe the Magic is just too strong.'

Desperation gripped me. If Anise couldn't help Mal's memory, who could?

Come back to me, Mal, come back – that one thought spiralled around in my mind as I willed my brother better, my hand on his shoulder.

Mal started to drink again. The ship hit a wave, making us all lurch. Anise caught his hand in his Amulet's chain, the force breaking it. I made a grab for it as it fell, just as Anise did the same thing. I still had one hand on Mal's shoulder as my hand closed over the Amulet, Anise's closed over mine, his other hand still holding the mug from which Mal was drinking.

A bright white flash filled the room, just like the one there had been the day I'd thought Rian was dying, just like there had been back in the Malign Prison when Mal had hit the Crystal Weapons with the Malachite Dagger. An intense white light.

'Damn,' Rian gasped from the far side of the cabin as the light faded.

Anise looked wide-eyed at me, then Mal.

Mal took a deep, shuddering breath. His face contorted for a moment as he swallowed the last of the remedy. He coughed. Then turned towards me, his silky blue-green eyes no longer blank. They focused. Somewhere deep inside his soul, I saw something stir as his body relaxed.

'Amethyst?' Mal said, his voice back to normal, if slightly croaky. He looked at me, his forehead furrowing deeply. 'Is that you?'

'I'm here, Mal, you're all right,' I said, tears falling down my cheeks as an intense wave of fatigue washed over me. 'You're safe, free.'

'I—I don't remember… I… Where's Father and Mother?'

I swallowed, a shiver sweeping through me as exhaustion set in. 'They're not here, Mal,' I said quietly. 'It's just you and me.'

He looked around, his eyes focussing and unfocussing. 'Where are we?'

'We're on a ship headed for Trew.'

'What's Trew?' he asked, his body tense again.

'It's the Land east of Iolite – you remember, don't you?' I asked gently, holding his hand in mine. 'You went there with Onyx a while ago.'

Mal looked at me. Frowned. His eyes darting about as he thought. He shook his head.

'I–I don't remember any Trew, or Onyx, or Iolite. I only remember you and Mother and Father.'

I glanced at Rian. He looked back at me, something wild in his eyes I didn't understand, his face pale and strained. Anise's face wasn't much better.

'It'll take a while to bring him back, Phire,' Anise said, composing himself, 'but we've made a start. He will remember in time, we just need to look after him until then.'

My brother's eyes were full of confusion as I pulled him into a hug. I had my brother back with me, away from Juniper's clutches at last. She'd not succeeded either in her attempt to kill me, or indeed to get Mal and me to kill each other.

As I pulled back and looked into my brother's eyes, I knew he was a long way from the Mal I'd last seen at the Crimson Castle some five months ago. My brother may have been there in body, but that was about it. His mind still hid in him somewhere, I could sense it, see it deep in his eyes, but it would take time to help him find his way back to us, as Anise had said.

I feared the quest for Malachite had only just begun, but as I looked wearily at Rian, I knew he would be with me. We could do this. We could, would, bring Mal home.

Together.

EPILOGUE

I sat on a barrel on the deck of *The Spirit of the Seas*, Deorwine and Glædwine propped up beside me, watching a freshly-shaved Mal as he sat talking quietly to Onyx. His face still had a greyish tinge, his eyes haunted, sometimes darting about the deck as he and Onyx spoke, almost as if he didn't know where he was, or couldn't quite believe what he was seeing. He had at least remembered Onyx, now, although not what they'd so recently had together. And that broke Onyx's heart.

Thankfully, I hadn't had to explain Mother and Father's deaths in the end, but I had had to tell him about Beryl's treachery. Mal didn't seem as surprised as I'd expected him to be, and although her actions hurt him, he took it well enough. As he sat with Onyx, I hoped he'd somehow remember his love for the assassin who was so clearly besotted with him. And the sooner the better. Onyx could probably help him heal quicker than even I could.

'It's going to take him a while to get over this,' Anise said, coming to sit beside me. 'I'm so sorry.'

'Juniper has a lot to answer for,' I said, gritting my teeth as my fists clenched. 'But at least we've got him back and he's free of her.'

'I don't believe he was just drugged, I definitely think she used Magic, too, somehow. We already know there's an Earth Spinner out there. I think she used them to make an elixir that she gave to Mal to, in effect, brainwash him. This enchantment was too powerful to be natural.'

Nausea filled my chest as I shook my head. 'You mean like they tampered with the Mandragora Berries that Carnelian gave to Rian?'

Anise nodded.

'Why? Why would she do that to him?' I asked, incredulous at Juniper's heartlessness and brutality.

'So she could control him,' Rian said. 'So she could use him to kill you, make you pay for what you'd done in the worst possible way.' He walked over to us, coming to stand behind me, leaning over and draping his arms over my shoulders, resting his head on mine. 'And because she sees you as a threat. Back before we met, you only really had Mal and Beryl as family. She probably thought if she could get your brother to kill you without realising what he was doing, that would be the worst possible death for you, and when he realised what he'd done, the worst possible thing for him, too.'

'I can believe that now,' I said. 'I think it's fair to say she hates me enough to do that to me, and him. Although I think he's a bigger threat to her than me. He's the rightful Master of Iolite, and now he's escaped her, she's on dodgy ground. I'm no threat compared to him.'

'She failed in her plan, though. You thwarted her.'

'But will he ever be Malachite again?' I asked, my eyes tearing as I looked across the deck. I'd returned his ring to him, and although it had jogged a few memories, it hadn't had the effect on him I'd hoped it would.

'With enough rest and peace, yes, I think so,' Anise said. 'Together, you and Onyx will be able to help him get back to his former self.'

'I'm not sure there's going to be much rest or peace in the near future, especially if we're going to go on to Chroma to restart the Crystal Vortex,' I said.

'I think we have to,' Rian said, chewing his lip. 'Balance has to be restored, and we're the only ones who know how – or, roughly how. No one else has a clue.'

'Only because Onyx's grandfather was able to tell us,' I said. 'But we still need the other two Spinners.'

Rian glanced at Anise. 'Well...'

'I hope Mal recovers,' I said, glancing back at my big brother. 'I hope he remembers about him and Onyx. I hope he remembers everything.'

'It'll take him time, but the two of you know enough about patience already, don't you?' Anise said, glancing at me and Rian before bowing his head.

Rian turned towards his friend. 'You still think everything will be all right?'

Anise smiled. 'Yes, it's not permanent, the poison just needs time to work its way out of your system, that's all. And poison like that will probably take some time before it leaves you completely, and until it does, you just need to relax and stop worrying about it.'

'Easy for you to say,' Rian said, a note of bitterness in his voice, although it wasn't directed at Anise.

'I know, but don't give up hope. Either of you. Just be patient. And give Mal time to recover – he's still in there, somewhere. I'm sure he'll find his way back to us.'

'I'll find him again, don't worry,' I said, watching my brother closely.

'We'll all find him, together,' Rian said.

I rested my hands on his arms. 'Together. And we'll keep caring for him until we do, as well as find those elusive Spinners,' I said, resolve to complete both tasks filling my soul, not to mention the determination I had to retrieve the Fire Opal. I'd find a way to complete all three tasks, and I wouldn't rest until they were done.

'About the missing Quintessence Spinner,' Rian said, rubbing the back of his neck as he glanced at Anise again. 'Carnelian spoke about a birthmark. Do you know anyone with one? Perhaps an unusual one? Didn't you read something about it from your father's book to me once, back in Iolite?'

My mind drifted back to our flight from the Crimson Castle, when I was falling in love with him. I nodded. 'The book did say something about there being only two Quintessence Spinners at any one time, and about identifying them by a birthmark on one wrist, but there were no drawings to show what it looked like – hell's teeth.'

'What is it?' Rian asked, as if prompting me.

'Juniper. She has a cluster of freckles on one wrist. At least, that's what I always thought they were, but could they actually be a birthmark rather than freckles? Could she be one of the Quintessence Spinners?'

'I admit I hadn't seen that coming,' Anise said, his eyes clouding. 'That makes things more problematic. Perhaps her aim is to destroy the Crystal Vortex, unbalance nature and step in. That's why she's doing what she's doing?'

Rian frowned. 'Damn. If she knows about the Spinners and the Vortex, you could be right. If you need the Fire Opal and the Spinners to save the Vortex, maybe the same combination could be used to destroy it, permanently. She could then take over what's left of the Lands and rule.'

'With your brother at her side,' Anise said with a shudder.

'I wouldn't put that past her,' I said. 'Saving the Vortex wouldn't be on her list of things to do. Quite the opposite, in fact – she'd be much more interested in domination.'

'But she'd have to know about Chroma still existing.'

'If Onyx's grandfather knows, he can't be the only one,' Rian said. 'There must be others who know, too, and if she already knows about the Magic Spinners, there's a high probability she's aware Chroma is still out there, and not submerged like the stories would have it.'

'And if she knows all that, and she's a Quintessence Spinner, she's in a perfect position to potentially destroy the Vortex, Rian.'

'Assuming she has one each of all the other Spinners,' I said. 'She'd have to have them, too. But there aren't any High Bloods in Iolite.'

Anise shrugged. 'So she's found them elsewhere, in the other Lands. We know she has connections high up all over the place.'

Hell's teeth. Anise was right. Juniper was probably working towards the exact opposite of what we were; and her aim? Destruction and oppression. We couldn't let that happen. Mal certainly wouldn't, once he recovered and he understood what was happening.

'Anything else?' Rian asked, letting go of me and walking around in front of me.

I shook my head. 'I'd never made the connection before, between her cluster of freckles, or birthmark, and what was in Father's book,' I said, frowning. What an idiot I'd been not to see it all along. 'You know, it's funny, but I've always thought her birthmark was actually rather like…'

I froze. My eyes widened. For a moment I struggled to breathe.

'Rather like what?' Rian asked, his rich voice unwavering as he crouched in front of me taking my hands, looking into my eyes, deep into my soul, as if he already knew the answer.

I started to tremble.

His leather wrist strap that I still wore had slipped, exposing my Coterie tattoo. The one that covered the little group of…

I glanced down at it, my heart slamming against my ribcage, my mouth suddenly dry as I looked up at him wild-eyed.

'Mine.'

DRAMATIS PERSONAE AND GLOSSARY OF TERMS

LAND OF IOLITE

Agate – Librarian at the Iolite University.

Amethyst/Samphire (Phire) – Wife of valerian. Ex-assassin. Daughter of the late Master of Iolite. Younger sister of Malachite and twin of Beryl. Legendary member of the Iolite Coterie of Assassins and known as Lady Merciless.

Beryl – Twin sister to Amethyst, and sister of Malachite.

Carnelian – A notorious assassin. Member of the Iolite Coterie of Assassins.

Citrine – Dead assassin. Sister to Carnelian. Member of the Iolite Coterie of Assassins.

Elm – Son of Juniper. Member of the Iolite Coterie of Assassins and involved in Coterie business.

Emerald – Dead Mistress of Iolite. First wife of Lord Peridot. Mother to Malachite, Amethyst and Beryl.

Feldspar – An assassin and member of the Iolite Coterie.

Flint – Chief Assassin of the Iolite Coterie of Assassins.

Juniper – Mistress of Iolite and Leader of the Iolite Coterie of Assassins. Mother of Elm. Widowed second wife of Lord Peridot and stepmother to Malachite, Amethyst and Beryl. Originally from the land of Trew.

Malachite (Mal) – An assassin. Older brother of Amethyst and Beryl. True Master of Iolite. Member of the Iolite Coterie of Assassins.

Moonstone – Librarian at the Iolite University.

Obsidian – An assassin and member of the Iolite Coterie.

Onyx – An assassin and member of the Iolite Coterie. Best friend to Amethyst and Malachite.

Peridot – Dead Master of Iolite. Father to Malachite, Amethyst and Beryl.

Topaz – An assassin. Carnelian's girlfriend and member of the Coterie.

Zircon – An assassin and member of the Iolite Coterie.

LAND OF AERBA

Angelica – Dead Crown Princess of Aerba. Eldest child of King Finule and Queen Myrtle. Older sister of Chervil and Valerian.

Anise – Herbalist and ex-King's Warrior.

Bergamot – King Finule's cousin and Chief of the Military. Father of Sage and Sorrel.

Chervil – King of the Land of Aerba. Second child of King Finule and Queen Myrtle. Younger brother to Crown Princess Angelica, older brother to Valerian.

Finule – Dead King of Aerba. Husband of Queen Myrtle. Father of Angelica, Chervil and Valerian.

Hyssop – Captain of the ship *The Sea Urchin*.

Myrtle – Dead Queen of Aerba. Wife of King Finule. Mother of Angelica, Chervil and Valerian.

Sage – Cousin to Valerian and ex-King's Warrior. Younger brother to Sorrel.

Sorrel – Older brother of Sage, cousin to Valerian and King's Warrior.

Tarragon – Cousin and best friend to Valerian. Ex-King's Warrior.

Valerian (Rian) – Husband of Amethyst/Phire. Exiled Prince of Aerba. Third and youngest child of King Finule and Queen Myrtle. Ex-Head of the King's Warriors.

Willowherb (Willow) – Ex-King's Warrior-Attendant.

Wintergreen – King Finule's cousin and Chamberlain. Father of Tarragon.

Wormwood – Head of the Nightshade.

LAND OF FLOS

Erica – Cousin of Amethyst/Phire and Malachite. Wife of Gladiolus.

Gladiolus – Husband of Erica.

Hyacinth – Husband of Jasmine.

Jasmine – Cousin of Amethyst/Phire and Malachite. Wife of Hyacinth.

Narcissus – King of Flos.

Monkshood – Prince of Flos.

LAND OF MERE

Calder – Flosian spy working with Erica.

Holm – First Mate on *The Spirit of the Seas*.

Lynn – Inn owner and friend of Onyx.

Onyx's Grandfather – member of extended Merean Royal Family.

Pol – Captain of the ship *The Spirit of the Seas*. Aunt to Onyx.

CAPITAL CITIES

Adamas – Capital city of Iolite.

Muscari – Capital city of Flos.

Rill – Capital city of Mere.

Viridi – Capital city of Aerba.

CREATURES

Dryads – Creatures from the forests of Flos.

Powlers – Lake dwelling creatures, now seldom seen in Aerba.

Merean Blue Death Worms – Great worms that live out in the deserts of Mere.

Morgens – Creatures of the sea and lakes that take their victims down into the depths and drown them. Their beautiful song is as enchanting as it is dangerous.

Mynogres – Legendary creatures that once roamed the forests of Aerba.

TERMS

Artefacts – Crystals that could enhance the power of an Elemental Magic Spinner.

Blood Class System – Hierarchical system you are born into. Your Blood Class cannot be changed. Each Blood Class has particular rules and a dress code they must adhere to.

Blood Rule Decree – Laws governing the Blood Classes, including rules on relationships and naming of children.

Elemental Angle Spinners/Elemental Magic Spinners – Ancient High Bloods who could wield Elemental Magic.

High Bloods – The Royal Family and extended relations.

Iolite Coterie of Assassins – Order of Assassins led by Mistress Juniper and run from Iolite.

King's Warriors – King Finule's best Warriors.

Low Bloods – All citizens that do not fit into the High and Middle Blood Classes.

Magic Angle – The Element a Magic Spinner could wield: Air, Earth, Fire, Quintessence or Water.

Middle Bloods – Lesser nobles, high status citizens and priests.

The Nightshade – Aerba's spy network.

Thyme – Aerba's sacred herb.

ACKNOWLEDGEMENTS

Firstly, I want to thank Peter and Alison, aka Elsewhen Press, for rescuing Phire and Rian, and giving them a fantastic new home. You have my eternal gratitude, and I'm so glad you've loved their story as much as you have.

My biggest thanks go to my husband and daughter for their never-ending love, support, and supply of chocolate! To my sister who inspired me with the idea of Magic Angles and Spinning, I couldn't have done it without you.

To my original editor, Lauren Dooley, thank you for believing in me, Phire, and Rian – this amazing journey wouldn't have started without you. Editor Nicole Lindsay has travelled the entirety of the Six Lands with me, and my thanks go to you, too.

Two of my writer friends, Emma Bradley and Estelle Tudor, continue to offer great inspiration, and are amazing sounding boards when it comes to ideas and writing in general. Thank you both!

To everyone who has read and enjoyed Phire and Rian's story – THANK YOU! I hope you've had fun on their adventures, and with the various twists and turns along the way. If you want to know more about my writing and books, then please visit my website www.aerinapeltun.com and sign up to my newsletter!

Happy reading!

Aerin

Elsewhen Press

delivering outstanding new talents in speculative fiction

Visit the Elsewhen Press website at elsewhen.press for the latest information on all of our titles, authors and events; to read our blog; find out where to buy our books and ebooks; or to place an order.

Sign up for the Elsewhen Press InFlight Newsletter at elsewhen.press/newsletter

CURSED WEAPONS TRILOGY BY AERIN APELTUN

BOOK 1: THE AMETHYST TALISMAN

ISBN: 9781917507332 (epub, kindle) / 9781917507233 (304pp paperback)

BOOK 2: THE MALACHITE QUEST

ISBN: 9781917507349 (epub, kindle) / 9781917507240 (288pp paperback)

BOOK 3: THE OPAL KING

With Malachite rescued, Samphire and Valerian's attention turns to the rapidly failing Crystal Vortex. With their friends at their side, they must forge on across treacherous seas and foreign lands in search of Valerian's stolen Fire Opal, even as they come to terms with their new Elemental Spinning powers.

Samphire fears that she may be confronted with her greatest nightmare, and it becomes apparent to Valerian that he may yet have to take on his biggest, and most unwanted, challenge. As they reach the end of their desperate quest, they must face their families and confront their fears.

Can they save the Crystal Vortex, and the Six Lands? Through their love for each other, can they both find the strength to accept their fates? And will the assassins sent to destroy them succeed, or can their love save them one last time?

ISBN: 9781917507356 (epub, kindle) / 9781917507257 (308pp paperback)

Visit bit.ly/TheCursedWeapons

ALSO BY AERIN APELTUN

CRYSTAL BLOODS

AERIN APELTUN

CRYSTALS MEAN POWER
CRYSTAL BLOOD MEANS DEATH

"Stop toying with me. We can never be together, and this, whatever this is, is too painful. It has to stop before we hurt each other anymore."

Within the island kingdom of the Starlight Order, Princess Sorsha must protect her life's blood at all costs, for when shed, her blood produces magical Blood Crystals. If knowledge of her existence escapes, there are those that would covet her blood and even kill her for the Crystals she would shed, including the Emperor Taliesin of Merribor.

Sorsha is about to be Pledged to an unknown Prince of the Celestial Isles, when she is sent with Prince Etienne of the Sun Order to find out why the isle of the neighbouring Moon Order has fallen silent. Etienne is also to be Pledged, to one of the Seven Starlight Princesses of Sorsha's home island, but despite this, the two grow close.

Discovering Taliesin is raiding the Celestial Isles for their artworks, and consequently their Blood Crystals, Sorsha and Etienne set out to stop him. Even as Sorsha struggles to keep her secret safe, their forbidden love grows, and when Etienne reveals his own secrets, he changes their relationship forever. They attempt to outwit Taliesin, but can they thwart his plans before he can use their blood, and their Blood Crystals, to conquer the world? Or will they die trying?

ISBN: 9781915304742 (epub, kindle) / 9781915304643 (352pp paperback)

Visit bit.ly/CrystalBloods

Children of the Tithe

TRACEY M CARVILL

Book 1 of the Changeling Trilogy

*"Second Star to the right and straight on 'till morning'",
she had muttered, and the figure had laughed as its slender
fingers enclosed her small hand and pulled her gently to her
feet. "Yes," it agreed. "Come, little Wendy-Bird"…*

Heidi was always told that she had an old soul for her age,
so when she awakes and finds herself and other children
thrown into a world of enchantment and fear, she knows
she needs to get home, no matter the consequences.

Leading a group of young survivors through an
unknown world of savage beauty, Heidi has to keep her
head and figure out which of the strange creatures they
encounter are friendly … and which are dangerous.

Some, she is going to learn, can be both.

"One of the most frightening things I've ever read"
— Shelby Novak, 'Scare You to Sleep' podcast

"Carvill is a master of darkness"
— Sam Pegg, 'The Edge' magazine

ISBN: 9781917507301 (epub, kindle) / 9781917507202 (296pp paperback)

Visit bit.ly/ChildrenOfTheTithe

Bookworm series by Christopher G. Nuttall

Bookworm

Elaine, an inexperienced witch in Golden City, has her life turned upside down when she triggers a magical trap to end up with all the knowledge in the Great Library stuffed inside her head. Avoiding the Inquisition she tries to understand what has happened to her. But she is a pawn in the dark plans of one who wants the Grand Sorcerer's power.

Bookworm won the Gold Award in the Adult Fiction category of the 2013 Wishing Shelf Independent Book Awards.

ISBN: 9781908168320 (epub, kindle) / 9781908168221 (368pp, paperback)

Visit bit.ly/Bookworm-Nuttall

Bookworm II – The Very Ugly Duckling

Not every ugly duckling becomes a swan ...

In the wake of the disastrous attack on the Golden City, Lady Light Spinner has become Grand Sorceress and Elaine, the Bookworm, has been settling into her positions as Head Librarian and Privy Councillor. But any hope of vanishing into her books is negated when a new magician of staggering power appears in the city, one whose abilities seem to defy the known laws of magic.

ISBN: 9781908168382 (epub, kindle) / 9781908168283 (432pp, paperback)

Visit bit.ly/Bookworm2-Nuttall

Bookworm III – The Best Laid Plans

Elaine and Johan prepare to leave Golden City, with Daria and Cass, to search for the Witch-King. But Elaine is arrested on the orders of a new Emperor, puppet of the Witch-King. She must escape and destroy him. Privy Councillors and Heads of the Great Houses have bowed to the Emperor. Only Elaine and her friends can prevent an all-out war.

ISBN: 9781908168764 (epub, kindle) / 9781908168665 (400pp, paperback)

Visit bit.ly/Bookworm3

Bookworm IV – Full Circle

Until now the Witch-King had remained hidden as a lich. But Elaine was intent on his destruction. Bonded to the unknowingly powerful Johan, she was the only other magician who understood the deeper layers of magic. As they slowly made their way towards the catacombs in Ida where his lich was hiding, he had to rely on the new Emperor to stop them.

ISBN: 9781908168948 (epub, kindle) / 9781908168849 (416pp, paperback)

Visit bit.ly/Bookworm4

All now available as audiobooks from Tantor

ABOUT AERIN APELTUN

Aerin Apeltun is an English writer based in the East of England. She started writing stories as a child, and has always loved reading about fantasy worlds. Aerin now loves to develop and write about her own worlds and mythologies.

Having been listed in a number of writing competitions, Aerin's Upper YA Romantasy, *Crystal Bloods,* was published by Elsewhen Press in February 2025, with a sequel to follow in 2026. Upper YA Fantasy Romance trilogy, *The Cursed Weapons*, out now, will be followed by a New Adult Historical Romantasy duology scheduled for 2026/7; she is always busy working on something!

A Second Class Archer, Aerin has had various careers in school/university administration and insurance, as well as a stint at the local library, but writing is her passion. She also loves to draw, and is a keen fantasy cartographer, designing maps for her worlds. Aerin enjoys travelling, taking inspiration from nature and landscapes for settings and characters in her books.

www.ingramcontent.com/pod-product-compliance
Lightning Source LLC
Chambersburg PA
CBHW030615170726
48283CB00002B/617